WHAT READERS ARE SAYING ABOUT
I LOOKED AWAY

★★★★★ 'WOW, just WOW! I was absolutely blown away by this book' Goodreads

★★★★★ 'Riveting' NetGalley

★★★★★ 'The twist almost made me drop my Kindle in shock' Goodreads

★★★★★ 'This book completely stunned me' Goodreads

★★★★★ 'I couldn't stop thinking about it' Goodreads

★★★★★ 'Oh my – this book was an absolute DELIGHT' NetGalley

★★★★★ 'I couldn't put it down. It seemed so real, I was in pieces by the end' NetGalley

★★★★★ 'OUTSTANDING' Goodreads

★★★★★ 'Highly recommend . . . be prepared for surprises!' NetGalley

★★★★★ 'Kept you guessing right until the end . . . I couldn't put it down' NetGalley

★★★★★ 'Jane Corry gets better and better' Goodreads

★★★★★ 'I loved it from beginning to end' NetGalley

★★★★★ 'A must-read' Goodreads

★★★★★ 'This had me frantically turning the pages to find out what happened next' Goodreads

her

★★ NetGalley

ABOUT THE AUTHOR

Jane Corry is a former magazine journalist who spent three years working as the writer-in-residence of a high security prison for men. This often hair-raising experience helped inspire her previous *Sunday Times*-bestselling psychological thrillers, *My Husband's Wife*, *Blood Sisters* and *The Dead Ex*. Jane was a tutor in creative writing at Oxford University and is a regular contributor to the *Daily Telegraph* and *My Weekly magazine*. She is an award-winning short story writer and also lectures all over the world on creative writing as well as speaking at literary festivals. *My Husband's Wife* has recently been optioned as a television series. Jane's books are published in more than 35 countries.

I Looked Away

JANE CORRY

PENGUIN BOOKS

PENGUIN BOOKS

Published by the Penguin Random House group of companies
whose addresses can be found at global.penguinrandomhouse.com.

Penguin
Random House
UK

First published 2019
001

Copyright © Jane Corry, 2019

The moral right of the author has been asserted

The publisher is grateful to quote from *Poems from a Runaway* by Ben Westwood
© Ben Westwood, 2017. Reproduced by kind permission of the author.

Set in 12.5/14.75 pt Garamond MT Std
Typeset by Jouve (UK), Milton Keynes
Printed and bound in Great Britain by Clays Ltd, Elcograf S.p.A.

A CIP catalogue record for this book is available from the British Library

ISBN: 978-0-241-98463-5

JANE CORRY

THE OTHER WOMAN

You made one mistake . . .

But the only way out is murder

Coming Summer 2020

www.penguin.co.uk

JANE CORRY

My Husband's Wife

FIRST COMES LOVE
THEN COMES MARRIAGE

THEN COMES MURDER

When lawyer Lily marries Ed, she's determined to make a fresh start.
To leave the secrets of the past behind.

But when she takes on her first criminal case, she starts to find herself
strangely drawn to her client. A man who's accused of murder. A man
she will soon be willing to risk everything for.

But is he really innocent?

And who is she to judge?

www.penguin.co.uk

In memory of my mother: the warmest,
kindest grandmother of all.

Also to my husband,
children and grandchildren — as well as my funny,
naughty network of new granny friends.

Finally, a big hug to Doris, our
much-loved grandmother, who lived with
us for all those years. My sister and
I had to call her by her first name as
she thought 'granny' made her seem old!

I shouldn't walk too fast.

But if I go too slow, I will be a moving target.

Every bone in my body is scared in case I feel a hand on
my shoulder. A tugging at my arm.

Cars drive past. Some kerb-crawl, as if checking road
signs. I'm frozen with terror. What if they want
something else?

I move on. Squat on a damp pavement.

'Please help me,' I plead. 'Give me something to eat.'

My belly might be full for a time. But what happens
after that?

Will you get me on the street?

Ben Westwood, poet and author of
Poems from a Runaway

DAILY TELEGRAPH
CHILD DIES IN 'TRAGIC ACCIDENT'

A young boy has died in what police are describing as a 'tragic accident'. No further details have been released.

Prologue

Saturday 17 August 2019. A date that will forever be engraved on my heart, although I don't know that at this precise minute in time. Right now, it's simply a scorching summer day, just as the forecasters predicted. Roger and I have the rest of our lives before us. It's what the marriage counsellor said when she signed us off. You've agreed to give him a new start. It's a clean slate. Don't look back.

But although I'm trying to take her advice, I can't quite ignore the invisible scar that I carry around with me. A constant nagging pain inside.

'Doing something' helps. That's why I'm walking into town in my new turquoise sandals with gold trimming – which I'm rather pleased with – to replace my favourite 'miracle' moisturizer. I'd never win a Glamorous Granny competition but I do get a real kick when people say, 'What? You've got a grandson of four? You don't look old enough.' At forty-nine, I've finally settled into my skin in a way I never did as a gauche teenager. I have my family and my own interests now, as well as my voluntary work at the prison. It keeps me busy. Helps to distract me from the past.

'*Big Issue*,' pipes up the woman squatting on the pavement

outside Boots. She speaks in the same hopeful voice, but without the accent of some of the other homeless people I've seen around here. I've regularly bought magazines from her and she can seem rather abrupt, though she's pleasant enough.

She arrived on our high street around eighteen months ago in her purple 'hippy trousers' (the type that balloon at the sides and then taper to the ankles), along with those silver and gold tattoo stars down her neck, a baggy navy-blue windcheater, plug earrings, shaved head and a weather-worn face that could make her age anything from forty upwards. After seeing her a few times, I started to give her a little extra for something to eat, which she promptly stuffed into one of her voluminous pockets. 'Ta,' she always said. Then she'd brush her hands together as if washing off some unseen dirt from the money. Another of her habits, I noticed, was to hum quietly, although it was hard to make out a proper tune.

One day, I found myself asking how long she'd been homeless for. 'On and off,' she said vaguely. It was the beginning of a series of short conversations each time I bought a magazine. She even told me her name was Jo (although the way she said it made me suspect it wasn't the one she was born with), and how she 'couldn't be bothered with school' as a child. ('Mind you, I used to read a lot in prison,' she declared.) I wondered what she'd been in for but didn't like to ask. One time we had a fascinating discussion about whether the new government homeless-ness guidelines were actually going to help people on the streets.

When the weather got bitter, I was so worried about

her that I even tried to find her accommodation – although that didn't work out. Maybe I got too involved, but it's my nature to help. It seems so wrong that in this day and age we still have people without homes and food. But a few months ago, when the old suspicions about Roger began to loom again, I saw Jo staggering out of the pub, blind drunk. It wasn't exactly the waste of my money and everyone else's that upset me. It was more the thought that I had been taken for a ride. Of course, I don't care for alcohol myself. Not with my history.

Since then, I confess I've tried to avoid her, sometimes crossing the street and pretending I haven't seen her. But on this particular scorching August morning, for some reason I feel the need to stop.

'Thanks,' she says, looking down at the palm of her grimy hand. It's the correct change for the magazine. Her disappointment makes me feel bad. There's something about this square-jawed, skinny, shaven-headed woman that gives her both a vulnerable and tough air at the same time. I find myself reaching into my bag for some extra money.

And then I see her. Carole.

For a minute, I stand riveted to the spot as I take in the sight of this woman who so nearly destroyed my family. I'm not the kind of person who swears much, but I could happily curse to hell those shapely twenty-denier sun-kissed legs, flaunted shamelessly in those strappy creamy stilettos. Her nipped-in dress (so much more stylish than my summer jeans) show off that slim waist in such a way that I wonder if the woman ever eats. I can put on four pounds just by looking at a chocolate bar.

Carole's arms are bare, I notice – she's younger than me and has no need of sleeves to hide the loose flab that sneaked up on me a few years ago, in my mid-forties. My rival has long brunette hair (not dead straight and mousy like mine), which pretends to nestle naturally below her shoulders, but I know for a fact is blow-dried every Thursday. I'm aware of this because one of my friends goes to the same hairdresser. This is the sort of medium-sized, honey-stoned Oxfordshire town – just twenty minutes from the city itself – where everyone knows everyone else's business.

I wish to God that we'd never set eyes on this place. Or her.

Carole is now walking along the high street straight towards me with that confident stride, navy handbag swinging from her shoulder. Her tinted sunglasses are artfully perched on top of her head as if to show off the designer brand rather than be of practical use. She is wearing bright coral-orange lipstick. The same shade that I'd found on Roger's shirt just after Christmas. 'Mine!' it had screamed out at me.

I choose safe shades myself. Either translucent lip gloss or – for special occasions – Pale Peach. But where has 'safe' ever got me?

The very sight of the woman makes my knees judder. I put out my hands to steady myself but in so doing drop my purse. Coins clatter on the pavement. What is she doing here? The last time I'd driven past Carole's pretty brick-and-flint cottage with honeysuckle around the door, it had a SOLD sign outside. Roger had sworn she'd moved back to London. Yet here she is, heading straight for me.

'It's Carole's,' my husband finally admitted at Christmas when I confronted him about the lipstick. 'I'm sorry, Ellie. This is the real thing. We've put down a deposit on a place in Clapham.' Then he groaned as if he was in pain. 'The thing is, I love her.'

No. He couldn't. I wouldn't allow it. Of course, Roger had had his liaisons before but he'd never mentioned the word 'love'. That belonged to us. His family.

I had tugged his lapels, pulling him towards me. My husband still wore brown tweed jackets indoors, just as he had during his lecturing days.

'How can you throw away twenty-eight years of marriage?' I had sobbed. 'I thought we'd grow old together. And what about the children?'

'For pity's sake, Ellie,' he said, pushing me away as if he couldn't bear my touch. 'The kids are grown up.'

But children need their parents, however old they are. Don't I know that all too well?

Fear then turned to anger. 'What about Josh, then?' I spat. 'Do you really want us to tell him that his granddad has left us for another woman? What will he think of you when he grows up?'

Roger shrugged. 'I'll be there for him. Carole likes kids. She's always wanted them. She won't mind if he comes to stay at weekends.'

'You can't do this! I won't let you!'

He took another step away, eyeing me as though I was a stranger. 'Let's face it, Ellie. Ever since I found out what you did, I just can't see you in the same light. We're not too old to start again. So . . .' He seemed to hesitate. 'I want a divorce.'

There was only one thing to do. Years ago, I'd promised to give it up. But old habits die hard. Luckily, kitchen scissors were at hand.

'For God's sake, Ellie!' he screamed, grabbing a tea towel to press to my bleeding wrist. 'What's wrong with you?'

I have a sudden flashback of my stepmother's voice. 'What's wrong with you, Ellie?'

It chills my bones to think of it.

After they had sewed me up at the Radcliffe, Roger told me (with a sad look on his face), that maybe, on reflection, I was right. He couldn't break up the family. He was going to stay. And yes, he would finally agree to counselling if I absolutely promised not to hurt myself again. He said that he'd told Carole and she'd 'accepted it'.

'Here you are, love.'

The *Big Issue* seller's voice breaks into my thoughts, bringing me back to the present. At my feet, she is scooping up my scattered coins on the pavement. 'They're all here. Honest.'

Embarrassed, I reach down to accept them. As I do so, I glimpse the cream stilettos. Smell an overpowering sickly scent. Then I hear Carole above me. Loud enough so only I can hear. She has one of those little-girl voices that are so irritating in women of a certain age – yet which some men fall for, every time. 'I thought you should know, we're still seeing each other,' she hisses.

I peer up at her, my heart thumping.

'Roger wants me to be part of the family. Is your grandson enjoying his new playhouse, by the way?'

How did she know about that? Roger had bought it for

our garden as a present for Josh. He must have seen Carole without telling me and mentioned it in conversation. My mouth goes dry. Or was it even possible that she had been there when Roger chose it?

I feel sick at the thought. Maybe the shop staff assumed that she was his real flesh-and-blood grandmother . . .

'Leave me alone! You're a liar,' I say shakily.

She puts her head on one side, as if questioning me. 'Really? From what I've heard, you're the one who's been doing that all your life. Some might say that you're not fit to look after children . . .'

Had Roger betrayed me? Or had she found out from someone else? Maybe she'd looked up my name. There would be a record somewhere. What would I do if it came out?

'How dare you,' I try to say, but the words are strangled in my mouth. Before I can get them out, Carole has disappeared, swallowed up by high-street shoppers with their smart carrier bags.

'I'm back,' I call out. I lock the door behind me, hands still shaking, then put my keys carefully in the blue-and-white Wedgwood bowl on the hall table, next to Roger's set with the 'Granddad' fob that our daughter had given to him last Christmas. Over the past year, we've become increasingly conscious about security after a spate of burglaries in the area, including a physical assault on a neighbour. But right now, I feel more upset by the shock of seeing Carole.

Somehow I force my voice to sound normal. But my mouth is dry with fear. I head for the fridge to pour myself a glass of elderflower cordial. I make my own every summer from the bushes in the garden. Its rich herbaceous borders and extensive lawns are partly why we bought this house, a lovely Queen Anne on the outskirts of town with a pale-lemon exterior, sash windows and gracious chimneys. There's also a little copse where I've seeded poppies and forget-me-nots in memory of Mummy.

You're never too old to need a mother.

Even after all these years, I still get flashes of her lovely, caring, kind face, and her soft skin that smelled of roses. I can still feel her cheek against mine. In my distant memory, I kneel next to her in her beloved garden, side by side as she weeds until she is too tired and needs to rest. I walk with her in my head along the country lanes. It was she who had taught me the names of all the wildflowers and hedgerow plants. We would pick and press them between the pages of the *Children's Encyclopaedia Britannica* before taking them out, flat, and labelling them with the help of my well-thumbed wildflower book.

She loved forget-me-nots best. My own favourite was cow parsley, also known as Queen Anne's lace. I used to finger the delicate white flowers and cried when they fell apart in my hands. 'It's all right,' said my mother. 'There are others you can pick.' It's one of the few memories I have of my childhood, so I hang on to it tightly, scared of breaking it. How she would have loved her grandchildren. And how she would have adored Josh . . .

'I'll be with you in a few minutes,' Roger now calls out from his study.

Radio 4 is blaring out from the kitchen with advice on making the perfect cheese soufflé. I always leave the radio

on even when I am out. I find its measured tones soothing, apart from the news, which I turn down. There's
enough to worry about as it is.

I wash my hands with my favourite Neal's Yard laven-
der soap at the ceramic double sink and put the kettle
onto the Aga. But inside, my head is still whirling. Should
I tell Roger I saw Carole in the high street – even though
he'd told me she'd moved? I desperately want to. But the
counsellor said there should be no accusations. I'm meant
to act like I trust him. I even pretended to be pleased
when he gave me a silver bracelet last month out of the
blue. Did he really think that a guilt present could make
everything better again?

'Dad behaved very badly but he's sorry,' my daughter
told me when it all came out. 'Can't you forgive him? I
don't want to be one of those families where the grandparents don't talk. My friends are constantly saying how
lucky we are. Josh loves you both so much.'

Josh! My real reason for carrying on. At times I can't
believe my only grandson has been with us for four
years – nearly five. It's impossible to imagine life without
him. 'Ganny!' he calls out excitedly when he comes round
to visit, using his baby name for me, which has stuck.

Officially, Monday is my 'Josh day', when I look after
him while my daughter works. Unofficially, I see my precious grandson every day. Try keeping me away! From the
minute they put him in my arms, I felt a melting in my
solar plexus and an intense rush of love that took me totally by surprise. It was – dare I say it – even stronger than
the love I'd felt for my own children when they'd been
born. How could that be?

As Josh has grown older, I've become even more besotted. Nothing else in the world is as treasured as his slobbery baby kiss on my cheek: those soft, chubby, warm toddler arms around my neck; the joyous amazement on his face when we blow dandelion clocks and make footprints in the snow; his look of intense concentration as he spells out flashcard words (M . . . U . . . M), or bakes chocolate crispy cakes while standing on his special little stool in our kitchen.

But Josh's 'best' treat is the Swiss music box my mother gave me which now sits on my dressing table. After she died, it was such a comfort, making me feel she was still close. It's a wooden box with a flower carved into the top. You have to turn the key twice and then lift the lid. 'Close your eyes,' I often say to him. Instantly he will squeeze them tight with that total trust that only children have. The sound of 'Edelweiss' fills the air. Then 'Open!' I say, and his eyes will be full of wonder.

'Magic, Ganny!'

My grandson has made life worth living again. I won't allow Roger or some prowling divorcee like Carole to ruin his life in the way my stepmother destroyed mine.

'You're always welcome to come out here, Mum, if you need time to think,' offered my son on Skype after I'd told him about Roger's latest affair. 'Here' was Australia – the furthest away he could get from his father, whose 'philandering', as he put it, 'makes me sick'. But the thought of not seeing my only grandchild for weeks, maybe months, was unbearable.

So too is the idea of sharing him with another woman. How can I allow Josh to grow up calling Carole 'Granny'?

She would be the glamorous gran and I would be the small, mousy, dowdy one. She would shower him with gifts to win his affection. I could just see her taking him to the zoo or a show. He might – the very thought made me wince with agony – grow up to love her more than me.

'Hi.' My husband emerges from his study, brushing his mouth against mine. I try not to think that this same mouth was on Carole's not so long ago. Those hands caressed the most secret parts of her body. His voice told her he loved her. Maybe still does. But it doesn't matter, I decide, providing he stays.

'Hi.' I step back, feeling like a minor character in a play. Actually, Roger would make a rather fine lead actor, and not just because his lines are so convincing. He is a good-looking man, my husband. Plenty of hair still, even for his age (sixty-five). The sort of bonhomie that comes from charming flocks of students for years. A need for an audience coupled with a natural gift for making people laugh, though he generally saves it for a crowd rather than wasting it on me. A prepossessing figure of six foot three, which he carries off well in his Home Counties uniform of beige chinos and open-necked shirts. It's too hot today for the tweed jacket.

'Did you have a good time in town?' he asks.

I almost break my self-imposed promise not to mention Carole but stop just in time.

'Yes, thanks.' Our clipped politeness feels unnatural, but at least it's better than the old rows.

'What have you been doing?' I ask.

In an ordinary relationship, this might have been a perfectly acceptable question, but after an affair, as I've learned all too well, everything you say, watch on television or read about in the papers is stacked with new meaning. So my 'What have you been doing?' could easily be translated as 'Who have you been sleeping with today?'

'Just some DIY,' he replies. 'I'm not happy with that wiring for my stereo in the study so I've bought some thinner cabling that won't look so intrusive.'

Roger has always been a practical man. It was one of the things that appealed to me when we met all those years ago. If he could fix things, my naive eighteen-year-old self had thought, then maybe he could fix me too.

'And the new neighbours came round to tell us they're re-landscaping the garden,' he adds. 'They wanted to check we weren't being disturbed. We got chatting and they asked me round for a coffee but then Amy called. There's some crisis with a deadline and she wondered if we could have Josh for a couple of hours.'

Yes! Suddenly the day has got a whole lot better. When our daughter announced that she and her husband had decided to move out of London to be near us, I'd felt an intense rush of love and gratitude. Apparently, I am part of a growing trend. I do have my own 'work', although I see it as more of a hobby, to be honest. Making the odd mosaic table for craft fairs in aid of charity is hardly a full-time occupation. So when the children need an extra pair of hands – like now, during the summer break, just before Josh goes to 'big school' – I make sure I am always there.

There's something about a child who has come from your own child. It feels like a miracle that the daughter I gave birth to has now had a baby of her own, formed partly from my own genes. It has created an invisible umbilical cord between us.

My grandson, Josh, doesn't just love me. He trusts me. He idolizes me – rather than telling me what I should or shouldn't be doing in that patronizing manner that adult children are so fond of. He will never betray me like his grandfather did (and might still be doing). But, just as important, he really is a clean start. My chance to get family right this time. I won't repeat the terrible mistakes I have made before.

Forcing myself to put Carole out of my mind, I begin to plan the day ahead. The three of us will have a jolly lunch together instead of Roger and me attempting to make polite conversation. I'll get out the sugar-free, everything-free bottle of juice for Josh that my daughter insists on, while my husband will have a glass of dry white. I will stick to my usual sparkling water with a slice of lemon. Afterwards, we'll play in the garden. Perfect.

Then Roger spoils it.

'I don't feel like lunch, if you don't mind. I'd rather get on with that rewiring job.'

'OK,' I say slowly, thinking of the counsellor's advice. Keep busy. Retirement brings its own stresses if you don't do enough.

He reaches for my hand and squeezes it as though seeking reassurance. I get a flash of that long hair, those long legs. I squeeze my husband's hand back, but inside, that invisible wound begins to burn all over again.

There's the sound of a door slamming outside. Little feet running up the path. Hammering on the door knocker. My daughter's voice calling out. 'Josh! Wait for Mum.'

My grandson, in the little red T-shirt I bought him last week, is leaping into my arms. Wow! He's almost getting too heavy to hold now but I breathe him in. Josh is proof, as if any were needed, that I've done the right thing in keeping my little family together.

'Throw, Ganny! Throw!'

My grandson is going to play cricket for England one day. I just know it! He has the most amazing eye for the ball.

'Too high!'

I try again.

Smash! Josh whacks it with the plastic cricket bat we brought back from our springtime 'let's-make-it-work-again' mini-break in the Scilly Isles.

'Brilliant!'

'Again. Again!'

I glance up at the sky. The sun has gone in. It's getting muggy now. The air has become close, as if a thunderstorm is imminent.

'Just one more!'

The ball soars into the air. Over my head and towards the house. 'Race you, Ganny!'

I hang back, letting him win. And as I do so, I glimpse Roger through the French windows of his study. There is something about him that, even at this distance, doesn't seem right. He is walking up and down the room, phone to his ear, waving his arms as if arguing. Didn't he say he needed to fix that cable?

A nasty cold feeling snakes through me. *We're still seeing each other.'*

'I've got the ball, Ganny!'

I don't want to row with my husband in front of my grandson.

'See how far you can hit it, darling. I'll be back in a minute.' I draw closer to the house. Roger's back is now to me. Then he turns sideways. Tears are streaming down his face. And in that instant, even though I can't hear the words, I know. My husband is talking to Carole. He still misses her. He's going to leave us. All my resolutions to turn a blind eye disappear.

Furiously, I rattle the handle. It's locked. The noise makes him start. Guilt springs to his face. Instantly he tries to cover it but it's too late.

He mouths something while making signs that this is an urgent call. I bet it is. 'Open up, you bastard!' I yell. (I should add here that this is not a word I use frequently.)

He turns his back on me!

I rattle the handle again. This time so hard that it threatens to come off the door. Reluctantly, or so it seems, he puts the phone in his jacket pocket and opens up.

'It was her, wasn't it?' I demand, storming in.

'What are you talking about?'

'You know damn well. Give me your mobile.'

His hand covers his pocket protectively.

'No. Please.'

Too late. I've swooped and got it. Feverishly I try to check the last number but he pulls the handset from me. I grab it back. He snatches it again. His face is red, his eyes scared.

'Carole was with you when you chose the bloody play-house, wasn't she?' I yell. 'Come on. Admit it!'

He hesitates. Only for a second. But it's enough. 'It wasn't like that . . .' he says haltingly.

'You bastard!' I scream. 'You're not worth it anyway. You've blown it, Roger. This is it. Keep your tart. She's welcome to you. But don't think you're having the family too. I'd rather die than let her play granny.'

And then I remember. Josh. Where is he? Oh my God. How could I have taken my eye off him? Damn Roger. But I am also horribly aware with an itchy crawling sensation that sends my arm hairs standing upright that this is my fault too.

The lawn is empty. Panic rises in my throat, blocking my windpipe. I try to reason myself out of it as I race down the garden. It's child-proof, isn't it? After Josh's birth, we reinforced the existing fence between us and the neighbours. He can't get over the padlocked side gate that leads to the road. It's too high. He isn't on the wooden slide set we bought for his fourth birthday. The playhouse, perhaps? I rush over, peering inside. A table and chair with his colouring book, half scribbled in. Nothing else. Nor is he in the summer house.

The church clock chimes.

And then my heart stops. When people say that, they mean it as a turn of phrase. But mine really does feel as though it's stopped beating at precisely the moment that I look behind the playhouse and see a broken panel in the fence. How did that happen? We checked it only last week. There's a gap. Big enough for a child to get through . . .

I tear at the splintered wood, cutting my hands, oblivious of the pain, fighting my way into next door's garden.

That's when Roger's words come back to me. 'The

new neighbours came round to tell us they're re-landscaping the garden . . .'

There's a pond. A large pond with a fancy water feature in the centre.

And there, floating on the surface, is a small red T-shirt.

PART ONE

Before the Accident

Forget-me-not (*Myosotis sylvatica*)

A blue wildflower.

The story goes that, once upon a time, a pair of lovers were having a picnic on a cliff. The girl spotted a beautiful blue flower growing on the edge. 'How lovely!' she exclaimed.

The young man immediately jumped up to pick it for her, but he lost his footing and fell. 'Forget me not!' he cried as he plunged to his death.

A reminder — as if we need it — that love can be lethal.

I

Ellie
HMP Longwaite, Oxfordshire
Four months later

I look round my cell. It's bare apart from a Formica-covered table, a stiff upright chair, a cardboard box to store my clothes in, a bowl to do my business in after lock-up and two narrow beds. Mine has a pillow that's as hard as a rock because it's new. They're always like that when you start a sentence. 'Reckon they make them tough so you can't get a bloody wink of sleep,' my cellmate told me.

She's not here at the moment. So I lie on my back and let my mind drift. I've spent all my life trying to forget the past. But perhaps now it's finally time to face facts.

My freedom might depend on it.

When I look back at my childhood – the part before the accident – it is the small things that stand out. Silly, almost trivial incidents. Only later did I realize they were the harbingers of the horrors to come.

Take boiled eggs. When I first showed my grandson, Josh, how to crack one open, I heard my mother's voice as clearly in my head as if she was standing next to me in our kitchen in our leafy north London suburb. 'You gently tap its head with a spoon,' she'd said. 'Then take your knife and carefully slice it across the top.'

'But doesn't it hurt the egg?' I'd asked.

My mother gave me a lovely warm hug. I can still feel it now. 'You silly sausage! It's not a person. You're so sensitive, Ellie. What am I going to do with you?'

But she'd spoken in a kindly way. I don't have many memories of my mother but I rarely recall her being cross, apart from one occasion.

My parents had bought me a doll. It must have been a birthday or Christmas because in those days, children only got presents on special occasions. She was very beautiful, with a china face and yellow curly hair. When I turned her over, she said 'Mama' in such a heart-rending fashion that I wanted to hold and keep her safe for ever. 'I wish she was real,' I said. 'Can't you have a baby, like my friends' mummies?'

'No,' my mother said. She glared at me as if I had said something very rude. 'I can't.'

Then she picked up a pretty blue bowl which she had always loved, and threw it against the wall. For a second she stood there staring at the pieces on the floor. Then, without saying another word, she left the room.

As I knelt down to gather the pieces of china I began to cry.

'It's all right,' my father reassured me, helping gather up the bits. 'Your mother just needs to lie down for a bit. She'll feel better when she's had a rest. Now let me finish this off or you might cut yourself.'

The lines on my father's forehead reminded me of

something called 'corrugated cardboard', which he used to wrap things up.

'I'm sorry, Ellie,' my mother said when she finally came out of her room. 'I was tired. Sometimes it makes me snap.'

Even now I can hear my childish reasoning in my head. 'Snap' meant broken. Twigs snapped when you walked on them. Did that mean she was going to be broken too? Just like the pretty blue bowl? Maybe that's why pavements had lines across them, I thought: because someone had tried to smash them up. My mother had once told me that if you walked on a pavement crack, it could be bad luck. Instead, we had to step over each one in order to stay safe. But we mustn't tell anyone that or they'd think we were silly.

I began to have nightmares. 'Shhh,' my father said when he came in to comfort me because my mother wasn't feeling well again. 'It's all right.'

But I knew he was lying because his forehead had turned into corrugated cardboard again. Before long, my mother couldn't walk me to school because of the tiredness. So my father took me instead. His legs were too fast for mine but we had to rush because he needed to get back and open the stationery shop. The shop had been in my mother's family for years, and Dad had taken it on after my grandfather had died. Once, however, we stopped by a tree, which was hollow in the middle. 'Look down there,' my father said with a note of wonder in his voice. 'Can you see the mushrooms growing at the bottom? Don't touch. They might be poisonous.'

Yet I wanted to. Supposing they were actually magic and could stop Mum being tired?

Sometimes our neighbour Miss Greenway would collect me if my father needed to look after Mummy. She smelled of talcum powder and had pretty yellow hair like the girl on my shampoo bottle. She also asked if I needed the 'toilet' instead of the 'lavatory', and when she took me home for some tea once, I noticed that she held her knife and fork in a way that my mother called 'common', whatever that meant.

'It's no trouble at all,' she would always say to my father when she took me back home. Then I would run up into my mother's darkened bedroom with the blue striped curtains and tell her about my day. Occasionally she would listen to me talk about my new best friend at school – they always seemed to change. But often she would turn over, moving her pillow to a different position as if it was annoying her, and tell me, 'Come back later.'

When it was my sixth birthday, I wasn't allowed a birthday party because 'your mother isn't well enough'.

'Couldn't you do one for me?' I asked my father.

He gave a strange little smile. 'It wouldn't be right. Not under the circumstances.'

What did that mean?

Later, when new friends asked how long my mother had been ill for, I found it hard to say. Sometimes it felt like it had been months. Sometimes years. I know that one more Christmas came and went because I remember not getting a stocking for the first time in my life. 'You're a big girl now,' my father said.

What did that have to do with it?

One day when Miss Greenway met me from school instead of Daddy, I noticed her eyes were all red, as if someone had coloured in the white bits. She didn't smell of talcum powder this time, either. 'Your father said you're to come to our house for a bit,' she told me.

'Why?' I kept asking as her soft, squashy hand held mine all the way back.

But instead of answering, she just squeezed my hand harder.

I didn't like Miss Greenway's house. It was the same size as ours but darker because 'electricity is expensive'. She lived with her mother, Mrs Greenway, who always shouted, 'Speak up!' whenever I said something. In the bathroom, there was a bottle on the window shelf that said 'Air Freshener' with a picture of pink-and-white flowers on it. Out of curiosity, I pressed the lid down and this smelly stuff came out that made me sneeze. I rushed out and shut the door behind me in case I got into trouble.

Tea was shepherd's pie. 'Your father said it was your favourite,' said our neighbour when she put the plate in front of me.

The potato on top was lumpy but I ate it because I didn't like to be rude. 'Does it taste all right, dear?' she asked. She had a high-pitched voice that squeaked. It reminded me of the kittens our teacher had brought into school last term in case any of us wanted one. (I wasn't allowed because we 'had enough to cope with already'.)

'Are you sure you wouldn't like any more? Look – I've made you a jelly for afters, although it is a little on the runny side.' Her face went sad. 'I'm afraid I'm not used to cooking for children.'

It wasn't like the jellies with mandarin slices inside that my mother used to make but, like the shepherd's pie, I ate it all up politely.

Afterwards, we sat in what she called the 'lounge'. I wondered where the sitting room was. 'My mother and I usually read after tea,' I told her.

'We don't have any children's books in the house but you can look at this if you like.' She handed me a magazine. 'It's the latest *Woman's Realm*. Look – there's a picture of Prince Charles on the front. About time he got married, don't you think?'

Luckily, she didn't seem to expect me to answer that particular question. Instead, she sat down on the sofa with her feet tucked underneath her while I flicked through the magazine. I'd never seen my mother read one. My father always said she had her 'nose in a book'.

There was a gold clock on the mantelpiece. It had a steady loud tick. Miss Greenway's mother, who was knitting on a chair by the fire, kept looking at it. 'When is the child going home?' she asked loudly, as if I wasn't there.

I'd been wondering the same myself.

'*Mother!* We have to wait for her father.' Miss Greenway patted the seat next to her on the sofa. 'Nearly time to put the telly on now. Would you like to watch the news with us?'

She said the word 'news' as though it rhymed with 'moos' rather than 'mews'. In our house, we listened to the radio instead.

A very serious man appeared on the screen, talking about a war which had happened in a place called Vee Et Nam. There were horrible pictures of children who were still hurt.

'Speak up, will you,' said old Mrs Greenway, shaking her stick at the television. 'I can't understand you.'

'I keep telling you, Mother.' Miss Greenway's voice was different. Sharper. 'You need to get your hearing checked.'

At last the door knocker sounded. Our neighbour leapt up as if she'd been waiting for this rather than watching the television. I noticed that her mother gave me a look as if she felt sorry for me. My father's voice was at the door.

It was hushed. Low. Then it came closer.

'Ellie?'

He was talking to the maroon swirls on the carpet instead of me. 'Your mother wants to see you.'

I couldn't put on my coat fast enough. 'Is she better?' I asked.

Miss Greenway gave a cough.

'What did he say?' roared the old lady. 'Is she dead yet?'

'Mother!' Miss Greenway turned to my father. 'I'm so sorry.'

'Dead?' I repeated. The word tasted nasty in my mouth. 'I don't understand.'

'Your mother wants to say goodbye,' said my father, as if he had a frog in his throat (I knew this meant that something was stuck in it). His leather-gloved hand held mine tightly as we walked down the drive and then to our house next door.

None of this made sense. 'Where is she going? Why can't we go with her? And why did Miss Greenway's mother ask if she was dead yet?'

His hand only gripped mine harder. It hurt, but I didn't like to complain.

All the lights in our house were on. It was as though we

were going to have a party, except that no one else was there apart from a woman I'd never seen before. She was wearing a nurse's uniform just like the one in my dressing-up box.

'Your wife's been asking for her,' she said, grabbing my hand and pulling me up the stairs. 'Quick. Before it's too late.'

She pushed me into my parents' bedroom. The furniture was the same. The dressing table in the window overlooking the ash tree outside. The tall wooden wardrobe with faces in the lines of wood (one looked like a lion). My mother's pink fluffy slippers by the bed.

But this yellow face that was staring up at the ceiling wasn't my mother's. Nor was the thin chest that made a strange sound as it went up and down. Whose black eyes were those staring at me? And that thin arm that reached out before falling on the sheet?

'Come,' she whispered. 'Lie next to me.'

When I'd been small, it had been such a treat to climb into bed with my parents on a Sunday morning. The three of us would play counting games and tell stories. But then my father had said I'd got too big and it didn't happen any more.

For a time I'd missed it. But now, I was terrified by the thought of sliding inside the sheets with this thin yellow shape that was pretending to be my mother. 'What have you done to Mummy?' I whimpered.

'It's all right, Ellie,' whispered my father. 'Your mother looks different but she's the same inside. Lie down next to her like she says. She only wants to cuddle you.'

Forcing myself, I obeyed. The sheets felt wet. My

mother's hand began to stroke mine. It was hard and bony.

'Kiss me, Ellie,' she murmured.

My father nodded at me from the side of the bed. I leaned over the yellow figure and placed my lips on her right cheek. It felt so cold.

'Again,' she whispered.

No! Throwing back the sheets, I ran. She let out a cry as if I'd hurt her.

'Come back,' called my father.

Running down the stairs, three at a time, I flew past the nurse and out into the garden towards the bent apple tree with the rough skin where I used to read. I was shaking so much that the branch I was sitting on began to shake too. I took great gulps of breath.

'Ellie?'

My father was coming out of the back door towards me. He walked up to my tree, standing underneath and holding out his arms. I thought he was going to be cross. Instead, his face was smooth now under the moonlight as if he had ironed out the lines in the corrugated cardboard. 'You can come down. It's over now.'

He's standing over me with a belt. 'You're a bad girl.
What are you?'
   'A bad girl,' I repeat.
   'Just like your mother.'
I press my lips together.
   'Go on!' yells my dad. 'Say it!'
But I won't.
When the belt hits my skin it feels like it's on fire.

2

Jo
Bristol

'Can you hear me?'

I wake with a start. It takes a second or two to shake off my dream. He was lunging towards me, a black look on his face. Hands on my throat. Nails digging into my skin . . .

'It's not real,' I tell myself. The bloke staring down at me isn't the man from my nightmare. Though this one doesn't look too friendly either.

'I said it's time to get off. We're here.'

I rub my eyes, confused with exhaustion and the shock of being woken. Where am I? For a minute, I think this man is a cop but then I realize his uniform belongs to the bus company. Even so, I am scared. And I don't know why.

'OK, OK.' I pull myself up and stumble down the aisle. I still can't stop shaking.

Outside I can see a sign. WELCOME TO BRISTOL BUS AND COACH STATION. I breathe a sigh of relief. I've never been to Bristol but I know it's bigger than the last place. There'll be more people, more places to sleep, more places to hide. More police too, but they don't care about people like me, unless we cause trouble. They've got enough on their hands. So with any luck I can go unnoticed.

I ease myself up to standing, picking up my pile of *Big Issues* as I do so. The bus driver puts his hands to his nose. OK. I know I stink. Maybe he ought to try being homeless himself sometime. He's probably the type that thinks we want to live like this. Mind you, there is some truth in that.

'Get a move on, will yer,' says the driver. 'Some of us have got homes to go to.'

That must be nice. I wish there was someone waiting for me somewhere. Somewhere I could close my eyes and sleep for days.

A big bloke with a beard grabs my arm as I jump off the bus. I freeze. 'Get your hands off me,' I snap.

'Only trying to help you down the step, love. Look out. You've dropped some of your magazines.'

Oh no. Someone's already trampled on the top one. And the one below. I can't sell them now.

'Let me give you a hand.' I look down at the ground as the bearded man starts to gather them up.

'*Big Issue* seller, are you, then?' he asks nosily.

I start to shake. *Leave them*, I tell myself. *Get a move on before there are more questions.*

I dive through the crowds and over a busy road in front of a bus. A horn blasts but I've made it. My chest hurting, I race down a road and then another, almost tripping over a jagged glass bottle on the pavement. A siren screams from somewhere, scaring me witless. I glance behind to see if anyone's following me. There's a woman glaring; she has a pale face and sunken eyes. My heart is pounding. Then I realize she's only a mannequin in a shop window.

34

The bracelet on my arm has dropped down so you can spot it below my sleeve. I push it up so it's hidden again. I think of the *Big Issue* magazines I had to leave on the ground. What a waste. I paid good money for that lot. Not everyone realizes you have to pay for them up front.

I'm in another road now with graffiti on the walls and a row of dingy shops, many boarded up. 'Jewellery bought and sold' reads one sign. There's a light on inside.

A youth with a big earring like a giant Polo mint is on his iPad at the counter.

'How much for this?' I ask nervously.

He gives me the once-over. 'I need to see it properly, love.'

I'd pushed the bracelet so high up my arm that it takes ages to get it off.

I feel like I've stopped breathing as I watch him turn it round, examining the markings on the inside and then holding it in the palm of his hand as if weighing it.

'Thirty quid,' he says finally.

'Think I was born yesterday?' I scoff, trying to sound tougher than I feel inside. 'It's silver. Worth much more than that.'

His eyes narrow. 'Where did you get it from?'

'It was a present.'

'Sure it was.'

My mouth goes dry. 'It's mine to sell. Honest.'

Too late, I wish I hadn't come here. What if he calls the cops?

'And you don't want to keep it for old times' sake?' His voice is heavy with sarcasm. His face comes close to mine. There are pockmarks in his rough skin and his breath

35

stinks like a dog's. 'Look, love. I get a lot of people coming here all the time with stories like this. I have to be careful. So I'll give you fifty tops and that's it. Got it?'

I've no choice.

'Cash,' I say weakly.

The money is in my hands so quick that I know I should have pushed for more. Then I find myself being bundled out of the door. I turn back to say that I've changed my mind. But he's put up the 'Closed' sign and turned off the light. That bastard knew a bargain when he saw one.

I finger the notes in my right-hand pocket as I pass a crowd of kids on the pavement. I walk for some time, not knowing where I am. A wicked wind bites into my bones. Some roads are much posher than others. One is full of boarded-up windows and dustbins. The next has huge houses with flash cars parked outside.

There's a neon sign for a twenty-four-hour supermarket. Perfect. I buy a packet of Rizlas and some baccy and a couple of other things before going back outside, constantly looking behind me just in case.

It's getting cold now. Summer seems to have disappeared overnight. I try not to think about winter and how I'll survive it. I walk past a big Boots store. Reminds me of Oxfordshire and some of those too-good-to-be-true ladies who helped me. There's one in particular who stands out in my mind. Wonder what she's doing right now? I can just imagine her having something to eat with her husband. She'll have cooked something fancy or maybe he's taken her to some posh restaurant. Later they might watch a bit of telly. Then she'll have a long bath with smelly stuff and lay her head on a soft pillow. I want to be like that woman. But her and me? We've got nothing in common. Never will have.

I go past a newsagent with a placard outside.

HUNT ON FOR OXFORDSHIRE MURDERER

My skin breaks out in goosebumps. For a second the face seems familiar but I can't quite pinpoint it.

I shake my head and walk on, still wondering about that picture.

Then I see a sign for a hostel. Maybe I'm in luck after all. I push the door open. Looks like a right dump, with dirty white paint peeling off the walls. 'We're full,' says the young kid at the chipped desk. She's got one of those silver studs on her tongue. 'Sorry.'

'How much for a room?'

'Twenty quid, but like I said, we're full.'

I put on my old-lady face. 'Please, love. I'm cold and it's scary out there. Someone's just tried to mug me.'

It's not true but it could be.

The girl hesitates.

I grab my chance. 'There must be somewhere,' I plead. 'A broom cupboard. Anywhere.' My eyes fill with tears.

'All right,' she says grudgingly. 'You can have our emergency room. There's a communal toilet at the end of the corridor. Breakfast isn't included.'

She takes me to a place that's as small as a prison cell. The bed is narrow and hard and there's no window but I'm inside.

I should be knackered, but I toss and turn all night, going over everything in my head, trying to decide what to do.

When I finally nod off, I have a nightmare about the man again. 'Stop!' I try to scream, but the words won't come out. His hands are squeezing my throat so hard that blood is gushing up through my mouth. My body is rigid with terror.

I wake up to the sound of banging on my door. 'Shut up,' says a voice. 'You're waking everyone.'

After that I can't get back to sleep, so I stuff my things in my bag and set off. The busier the place, the better. So I follow a 'City' sign, shoving my way through the crowds going to work and keeping my eyes peeled. I'm not alone. It's not until you're like me that you realize how many folk spend their lives in hiding.

Just look at that figure under a grey blanket with a dog lying guard on the pavement. What's his story? The figure sits up. Stretches. Yawns. Then I realize it's a woman.

I sit myself next to her. She stares at my shaved head. Bloody cheek. It's not like she's an oil painting herself with all that spiky hair.

'Fuck off,' she snarls. 'This is my patch.'

Her dog, with its yellow spotted neck scarf, gives a low throaty growl. OK. I get the message.

I walk on quickly, putting my hand in my pocket to check the money from the bracelet is still there.

I pass a market stall. Five pounds for a beanie! It's a lot, but I need something to cover my head – I feel too exposed, like people are staring. I peel out a note, making sure the bloke on the stall doesn't see the rest. Then I pull the hat right down over my forehead and glance behind me. Still nothing.

Somehow I've got to fill the hours ahead. That's the

weird thing about being on the streets. It's a mixture of boring and terrifying.

Still, it gives you a chance to see things you'd miss if you were rushing round with the rest of the world. Take that girl over there, sitting next to an older woman at the street café. She's got to be seventeen or eighteen yet she's stroking her mother's hair like she's a young kid. The other day, I saw a couple sitting on the grass in a park having a picnic but looking really hacked off with each other. Then this little bird landed on the rug. The bloke gave it a crumb and the girl clapped like he'd done some magic trick. They seemed OK after that.

I stop for a minute by a park with a statue. There's a couple taking a selfie, giggling, cheek to cheek. Young love! Makes me feel all soft and angry at the same time. I want to march up and tell them that they'll never find this again and to keep it safe. Because if they don't, someone or something will smash it into a thousand pieces.

I walk past, down a subway into this sort of concrete circle where kids are hanging out on bikes, smoking butt ends. One tells another he'll see him in 'Crack Alley' later on. I don't have a good feeling about this place. So I keep my eyes down and walk through another subway where there's a pillow on one side like it's waiting for its owner to return.

When I come up into a different street, it starts pissing down with rain but – stroke of luck here – I'm right outside a church with a stone cross on the top.

I used to believe in this kind of stuff but not any more. So I just sit on one of the side pews, watching tourists forking out a quid for each candle. Every now and then they drop one without noticing and I scoop it up quick. I have a sense of calm, the first in days. I feel my eyelids slowly drooping.

I'm woken by my belly making 'empty' noises. That's another thing about being on the road. You can tell the difference between needing to eat and eating because you're bored. Ever seen a fat homeless person? Thought not.

There's a bloke selling doughnuts on the street. I quite fancy something sweet. I reach down into my right-hand pocket and go all hot and cold. Where's my money? Someone in the church must've taken it while I was asleep. What a bloody idiot I've been!

I belt back, shoving my way through the late-afternoon stream of crowds. But the place is empty.

What am I going to do now? I haven't got any money for a hostel and I can't go to a crisis centre. So I just keep going until my feet hurt. My stomach is aching with hunger. I walk and walk because I don't know what else to do. A seagull swoops above me. Lorries screech round giant roundabouts. Posters outside a posh theatre invite me to buy a ticket, though it's not for the likes of me. A man sits by the side of the road, his hat upturned for coins. Next to him is a mouldy loaf of bread. Past a shop with a notice that says 'It's Pie Time!' *In your dreams*, I think to myself.

I'm down by a river now. Must be some kind of harbour. There's this drop below me with boats bobbing around. I gaze at the water. What would it be like to jump in and never come up?

'Don't,' says a soft Irish voice behind me. 'It's not worth it.'

I turn round fast. It's a young man holding a cardboard sign that says 'Homeless and Hungry'.

Usually I keep myself to myself. But the shock of everything makes me come straight out with it. 'I don't have anywhere to go,' I sniff. 'I got robbed.'

He looks all sympathetic, like he knows what that's like. 'That's tough.' He puts out his hand to shake mine. 'The name's Paul, by the way.'

A real gentleman! His teeth are surprisingly white and even. Not a smoker or druggie, then. I see that his shirt-sleeve is torn.

'Where are you heading?' he asks.

'I don't know,' I say.

'Not got anywhere to sleep?'

I shake my head.

'It's getting dark. You don't want to be out here on your own. Why don't you come along with me?'

'Ha! I'm not that daft.'

'C'mon!' He laughs like I've said something funny but in a nice way. 'You're old enough to be my mum. I'll help you find a place for the night.'

I hesitate. I'm cold and my stomach's rolling on empty. This bloke doesn't seem like the type to be dangerous. So I find myself walking by the river with him and then along more pavements and back alleys. 'Where are we going to?'

'A place called Stokes Croft. You'll be OK there. It's where we all hang out.'

There are loads of arty shops here with music blaring out and walls covered with graffiti. Neat pictures as well as faded messages like 'Bugger Brexit' in red, blue and white. Then we get to this big factory building that's all boarded up like it's empty, with loads of 'Keep Out' notices. 'Round the back,' he says. There's a smashed window. 'Just crawl through,' he tells me. 'Watch out for the broken glass.'

It's a bit of a struggle but I make it.

I stand up. He's next to me. Then he flings his arms out wide like this is some kind of palace.

'Welcome to our place.'

3

Ellie

Death is part of our life here in prison. I'm not just talking about the murderers or, at least, the ones who've confessed. It's the death inside you that comes from not having fresh air or being able to smell the flowers in the garden or feel the arms of someone you love around your neck.

Then again, it's no more than I deserve.

My father and I had an appointment to see Mummy in a place called a 'funeral parlour'. That's where she'd been taken to after 'passing away'. I wasn't entirely sure what that meant but I felt as though I should do, so I didn't like to ask. 'Why couldn't you have kept her at home in bed?' I said instead.

I had to repeat the question twice before my father answered. Maybe he couldn't talk much because he hadn't had any dinner for ages, even though people kept ringing the bell with lamb casseroles and apple pies and something called a 'fon doo'. You have to eat enough to think properly. Mummy always used to say that.

'The undertaker needed to make her look nice,' he eventually replied.

'What's an undertaker?'

'Someone who . . . who looks after people like your mother.'

'But she looks nice as she is,' I protested. 'You're always telling her that.' It was true. Mummy had soft dark hair and her skin smelled like roses. Then I remembered the colour of her face the last time I'd seen her and my chest began to get so tight that it was like someone had wrapped a giant elastic band round it and was squeezing hard. 'I don't care about the yellow bits. I just want to see her.'

'Poor lamb,' murmured Miss Greenway, who had come round to 'help tidy up a bit'.

But my father was looking out of the window with an expression on his face as if he expected my mother to come walking up the path and open the front door.

Looking back, I wish my father had never taken me to see my mother's body. Didn't he realize how much it was going to affect me? In those days, I don't believe it was as common as it is now for young children to go to funerals, even when it was a parent's. But despite everything that happened afterwards, I believe my father was a good man. He must have thought it would help me come to terms with her death.

Whatever the reason, the details of that terrible day are still indelibly imprinted on my memory. And I can't stop my mind playing it over and over, all these years later, as I sit in my cell.

From the outside, the funeral parlour looked like a shop that was closed up. In the books I'd read, a 'parlour' was like a sitting room. This one was a whole house with white curtains across the window and a vase of white

44

plastic flowers on a table next to a big gold cross. A man in black took us into the back. It was so quiet that I could hear myself breathing.

My mother's eyes were closed. Her face was no longer yellow. She was all white and shiny instead.

'What's happened to her chin? I cried out. It was a different shape: long and pointed like my face in a mirror at the fairground where my parents had taken me once.

'It's the muscles, love,' said the man in black. 'They sag when people die.'

'But she can't have died!' I screamed out. 'She's just passed away. You told me that, Daddy. Didn't you?'

I clung to his arm, pulling at his sleeve desperately. 'Make her wake up, Daddy. MAKE her!'

His voice sounded as if it was being squeezed out like toothpaste from an empty tube. 'I can't, Ellie. Her body is broken now.'

'Then mend it,' I wept. Hadn't he fixed the boiler when it had 'gone on the blink' by lighting it again? He was 'good like that'. My mother was always saying so. He'd even fixed the lid of my music box after it came off its hinges.

'Sometimes, love, people can't be mended.' My father had tears running down his face. They scared me. Adults weren't allowed to cry. My mother used to say that too. 'Maybe this wasn't a good idea.' He took my arm and made towards the door.

'Did she die because of me?' My voice sounded small, as if it was someone else's. We were in the street now, heading towards the car. I couldn't stop shivering. It was like some monster was in charge of my body, shaking me

45

around like the jellies Mummy and I used to make together. Even my teeth rattled.

'No! Of course she didn't die because of you. Why would you think that, Ellie?' A motorbike roared towards us and Daddy picked me up quickly to get to the other side safely.

'I upset her,' I said in a small voice.

'How?'

'That time when I asked why she couldn't have a baby and then she smashed the blue bowl.'

He shook his head. 'It had nothing to do with that, Ellie. She was ill. The doctors couldn't make her better.'

'But she wanted to have a baby, didn't she?'

'Yes.' He'd nodded his head. 'We both hoped to give you a brother or sister. It just didn't happen.'

I said nothing, because I didn't want to upset him any more. But inside, I knew the truth. I'd hurt my mother by talking about it. And that's when she'd started to be poorly. Then she had died. So it had to be my fault.

Years later I was visiting an exhibition of black-and-white photographs at the National Gallery when I was struck by a portrait of a girl from Edwardian times in mourning dress. Her hair was scraped back from a high forehead with a black velvet Alice band. Her eyes were soft and gentle. Her mouth turned down. She bore an air of sad acceptance. Instantly I knew how she felt.

As I stood there, jostling with other art-lovers around me, the photograph took me back to my mother's funeral. There I was, standing by the open grave next to my father in his long grey coat. In my hand I held an early daffodil from our garden. At his instruction, I threw it into the earth on top of the box.

'Why has she got to be in there?' I asked.

'What did she say?' hollered Miss Greenway's mother.

'Shhh,' said someone else.

Afterwards, people came back to our home, including the mother of a boy called Peter Gordon, who had been friends with Mummy. We used to be playmates when we'd been small and then we went to the same schools, though we didn't talk much now. My head was patted. Someone I'd never met before gave me a hug. Would they still be nice to me if they knew I had upset Mummy so much that she eventually died?

Everything changed after my mother's funeral. Daddy went back to work, so Miss Greenway started walking me to school. 'It's no trouble, Nigel,' I heard her tell my father. 'I've told you that before and I mean it. It's not as though I have anything else to do.'

I'd never heard her call my father 'Nigel' before.

Miss Greenway always seemed very nervous when she was with me and would hold my hand so tightly when we crossed the road that she almost hurt me. 'You're in my care,' she kept saying. 'I need to get you back in one piece or your father would never forgive me.'

She talked a lot (my mother used to say that our neighbour 'prattled'). She'd also ask questions like who my favourite film star was and what my father's 'best' meal was. I didn't have an answer for the first but I did know that my mother often used to make a dish called 'toad in the hole'. It made my eyes water to think about it. I missed her so much.

One day I found myself having to jump over the

pavement cracks. My mother's voice told me that if I didn't, my father might die – just like she had.

'Do be careful,' Miss Greenway would keep saying. 'You might fall and injure yourself.'

But I couldn't stop.

Miss Greenway would take me back to her house after school until my father returned from work.

At first, I didn't like this, because her old wrinkly mother smelled of a sickly perfume that tickled my nose. She would also stick out her tongue at me when no one was looking and laugh. Her deafness seemed to come and go. Sometimes she spoke softly and sometimes really loud. 'I tell you,' she'd shout at Miss Greenway right in front of me so that my ears rang. 'No good will come of this.'

I didn't know what she meant but I'd stopped asking questions because no one answered them.

My nightmares got so bad that my eyes grew black underneath. 'Your daughter needs more fresh air,' declared the doctor when my father took me to the surgery one Saturday morning.

Summer was coming by then. The grass smelled different and the birds began to sing. They reminded me of the way my mother used to whistle songs.

'We're going on holiday,' my father announced.

My parents had taken me to the sea once in a place called Devon. We had built a castle with real paper flags. But this time, we weren't going to a beach. We were going on an 'educational trip'. Part of this involved visiting a Roman villa near a place called Newcastle.

'Look, Ellie,' my father said. 'The Romans were so clever that they had underground heating.'

But it was the mosaics I was drawn to. 'They made pictures out of broken glass and pottery,' said my father, noticing my interest.

Again I thought of the blue bowl my mother had smashed.

'I'd like to do that.'

He smiled as if I'd said something silly. 'It's not easy.'

'But putting broken things together could be a way of making them better again, couldn't it?' My heart began to feel light, as if a ray of hope had pierced its way in.

My father stopped smiling. 'I suppose it might.' Then he gave me a quick hug. 'You are a funny little thing.'

When we got back after our week away, it was nearly night time. But there was a light on and, when we opened the front door, a delicious smell was coming out from the kitchen. There was a note on the table. *Supper in the oven.*

'How very kind of Miss Greenway,' said my father. 'Toad in the hole. My favourite!'

Later, when we'd finished eating, he went round to thank her. He was gone so long that I began to get worried. What if something happened to him like it had to my mother?

When he got back he gave me an extra-long hug. I thought I saw tears in his eyes. 'What's wrong, Daddy?' I asked.

He smiled in the way adults do when they pretend everything's fine when it's not. 'Nothing, Ellie. I promise.'

Even though we missed Mummy terribly, my father and I were content with each other's company. Or so I thought.

49

I used to love sitting at his feet in the evening by the fire while we each read our books from the library. Sometimes he would quote me poetry. His favourite was John Masefield. How I loved those descriptions of the sea! I could have listened to my father's voice for ever.

We would play Ludo together and card games too, although once, when I got out the Happy Families pack and put Mrs Baker on the carpet, he shook his head. 'I don't think so, do you, Ellie?'

Quietly I put the game away. Then I tried to make it up to him by suggesting draughts and letting him win.

Daddy always made sure I did my homework and that it was put in my satchel for the following day. My lunch money was always laid out too. I'd help him make his sandwiches for the shop, just as Mummy had done. 'We're a good team, you and I, aren't we?' he said. 'Your mother would have been proud of you.'

Then he turned away but not before I saw that his eyes were wet. So I tried to cheer him up with a joke that I'd heard at school. 'Why did the tomato blush?'

He was trying to sound as though he wasn't crying but his voice came out cracked. 'I don't know, Ellie.'

'Because it saw the salad dressing.'

And even though I didn't understand why the joke was so funny (something I couldn't tell the others at school or they'd say I was stupid), he smiled. Then it was all right again.

In the autumn we'd gather conkers in the park and I showed him how Mummy had taught me to make little people out of them by sticking in pins for arms and legs. I even asked him to do some cooking with me – something else I'd always done with my mother. We found her old cookery book with one of her favourite recipes. *Mum's special macaroons*, she'd written down the side. But when Dad and I whipped up the egg whites, they went all flat. 'Never mind,' he said brightly. 'We can just buy them.' But it wasn't the same.

'What shall we do for Christmas, Ellie?' he asked when the shops began to have their decorations up. It seemed impossible that Christmas could take place without Mummy. 'We could go to your aunt's in Scotland if you like. She's invited us.'

I didn't care for my father's sister. When she'd visited us here, she kept telling my mother that I was 'too grown up for my own good', whatever that meant.

'I'd rather stay in our house with just you and me,' I said.

He nodded. 'Good. I'm glad you said that.'

So when Miss Greenway invited us to spend the day with her and her old mother, I expected my father to turn down her invitation. But instead, he said that was very nice and that we'd been wondering what to do with ourselves. 'It wouldn't have been polite to say no,' he told me later.

We had to dress up, Daddy said. So I wore my navy-blue velvet dress that was getting too small for me, with a matching Alice band, and my father put on his best grey trousers and what he called his 'turtleneck jumper' (though it didn't look like the turtles' necks in my encyclopaedia). Miss Greenway was at the door to meet us before we even had a chance to knock. She was wearing a short red squirly patterned dress that showed her knees. 'Oooh! Milk Tray,' she gushed when I handed them over as instructed earlier. 'You shouldn't have. And presents too! You've spoiled us.'

'Not at all,' replied my father. 'I'm very grateful to you for the care you've shown Ellie.'

He gave me a little nudge. 'Yes,' I said, remembering my manners. 'Thank you.'

When we went into the lounge, the old lady was sitting in her chair, knitting. 'He's brought the child, I see,' she announced to her daughter as if we weren't there. 'Playing happy families, are we?'

Miss Greenway blushed. 'Don't worry about Mother,' she whispered. 'She rambles a bit, especially after a nap.'

But after lunch, when Daddy had nodded off in a chair in front of the Queen's speech and Miss Greenway had gone upstairs to 'freshen up', I went into the kitchen. The old lady was washing up. Her neck was all wrinkled, I noticed, like a tortoise's. 'May I help?' I asked politely.

She stuck her tongue out at me.

'That's very rude,' I said.

'Don't be daft, love. I'm just trying to cheer you up, that's all – make you laugh.'

I repeated something I'd heard my mother say once to my father. 'Well, it's a funny way of showing it.'

She shrugged. 'Maybe you're right.' Then she handed me a cloth with *Greetings From Lyme Regis* on it. 'Let's just get on with this, shall we? Now tell me, what do you young things like to do nowadays?' Her eyes went misty. 'When I was your age, we'd go ice-skating on the village pond . . .'

After that, I quite liked it whenever Miss Greenway took me back to her house because I'd sit with her mother and she'd tell me stories. She always had a big jar of toffees by her chair. 'Never had one before?' she gasped when I told her that Mummy hadn't allowed me to have sweets because they were bad for your teeth. 'You haven't lived, love. Go on – try one.'

They were soft and sweet and comforting. When one stuck to the top of my mouth, Miss Greenway's mum showed me how to pick it off with my finger.

It was the following summer, when I was eight and a half years old, that my father came into my room. 'How would you like a new mother?' he asked.

The younger me might have thought they had put my real mother back together again. But I knew now that was impossible. 'What do you mean?'

He was red in the face, like he'd got sunburn.

'I've asked Miss Greenway to marry me. She'll love you as much as I do. Do you think you could love her too?'

I thought of the way our neighbour held my hand when we walked to school and back. How she made butterfly cakes with me and helped do my homework. And how my father seemed much happier when she was around. I wanted to please him. And besides, if I upset him like I had done with my mother, he might die as well.

'Yes,' I said. 'Of course.'

My father gave me a lovely warm cuddle. 'Everything's going to be fine now, Ellie.'

I believed him.

More fool me.

Bluebell (*Hyacinthoides non-scripta*)
Said by herbalists to help prevent nightmares.
However, the bulbs are extremely toxic. Some swear that
if you wear a wreath made of bluebells, you will be compelled
to speak the truth.

4

Jo

I follow this bloke Paul. We go through one big empty room and then another. I'm beginning to get nervous. It's enough to freeze the brass balls off a monkey. 'Our place', he had said. But I can't see anyone else. And then we stop. There's a woman – maybe a bit younger than me – sitting next to a shopping trolley stuffed to the top with clothes and blankets, like she's carrying all her worldly goods around with her. Her head is slumped forward. She seems to be asleep, although her right hand is still on a dirty trolley wheel, as if she's scared someone's going to walk off with it. A couple of men are squatting next to her, knocking back booze. There are loads of empty bottles next to them. One looks like he's shooting up. He stares up at me with a 'So fucking what?' glare.

There's a bark from the corner, and that's when I spot the narrow-eyed, spiky-haired woman I'd met this morning.

'You,' she snarls. She has blue and red heart tattoos all down her arm and up her neck.

'No fighting, ladies,' says my rescuer. 'This is Jo, everyone. Someone get her something to eat, will you?'

No one moves.

'For crying out loud, show a bit of hospitality.' Paul grabs a bread roll out of Spiky Hair's hand.

'Piss off! That's mine,' she howls.

Paul rips it in two. 'It's nice to share. You know that.'

He hands one half to me. I tear off chunks, stuffing them in my mouth.

'We haven't got enough ourselves,' hisses Spiky Hair.

'Where are your manners? Give the lady a chance.'

It's a long time since someone called me a lady!

Then he gives me another look. 'Fresh on the streets, are you?'

'No, but it's my first time in Bristol.'

'Ugh,' says this posh voice. 'I do wish people wouldn't talk and eat at the same time.'

'Sorry.' Reluctantly, I swallow the last piece of bread. 'I was sleeping in some stables before. There was this homeless committee that got it for me. They were talking to the council about finding me a proper home. But it didn't happen.'

'What about before that?'

I'd hoped he wouldn't ask. I give a watered-down version of the truth. 'I was inside for a while,' I admit. 'Nothing serious. Just dealing and a bit of theft. But I got used to the bed and regular food. It's hard being out again, if you know what I mean.'

'Sure I do. Not right, is it? They should help you more when you get out. Pam will tell you that.'

He points to the posh cow who had told me off for eating while talking just now. 'Used to be a barrister until she got nicked. Fraud, wasn't it?'

'Fuck off, Paul.'

But she says it like she doesn't care.

'When she got released, she didn't have anywhere to

56

go, pinched stuff to get gear and got done again. Now she's out – until she gets caught again. What do you call it, Pam?'

She makes a snorting noise through her nostrils. 'It's a continuous spiral of descent.'

He splutters with amusement. 'Never uses one word when she can use two. That's our Pam. A real lawyer for you. It's her way of saying you've hit shit bottom.' Then he hands me cardboard for a mattress and some sheets of newspaper. 'Here. Stuff some up your jumper and keep another to put over your face at night. You'll be surprised how that keeps you warm.'

'Thanks,' I say. But I can't help looking at all those blankets in the shopping trolley.

'Don't even think about nicking one of those,' says Paul. 'She'll scratch your eyes out. Take a swig of this instead.' He hands me a bottle of vodka. 'It'll put fire in your belly.'

Before long, I feel the warmth spreading through my veins. 'Pass it on,' orders the man next to me. He's wearing a pinstriped suit like he works in an office, but the trouser hems have come undone.

Then a woman with a load of silver hooped rings in her eyebrows comes back, carrying cardboard boxes. 'Look what the pizza place left out for us!'

There's a mad rush as the others hurl themselves towards her, stuffing their mouths. Even the trolley woman wakes up and dives in.

'Leave enough for the rest of us!' shouts another man, elbowing me out of the way.

It's gone before I even get there.

My mouth is drooling with saliva. I almost tasted that pizza with its melted cheese and tomatoes drizzled in oil.

'Oi,' yells the same man. 'That bitch has nicked an extra slice for herself. Look, she's hidden it in her cardigan.'

'No, I ain't,' spits the trolley woman.

There's a flash of metal.

'Leave it out!' Paul's voice is like thunder. With one hand he snatches the penknife from the bloke and then swiftly puts his other hand into the trolley woman's cardi pocket and comes out with the pizza slice. Then he grinds it into the ground with his heel. NO! I'm tempted to dash forward and scrape it up but I don't like to seem pushy.

'If you're going to act like kids, you'll get treated like them,' he says.

The place goes quiet for a bit. Then the woman with the spiky hair starts singing 'It's a Long Way to Tipperary.'

Everyone else joins in but I just clap and sway from side to side. I knock into the man with the suit but he doesn't seem to mind. For the first time in ages I feel myself relax. I find myself giggling like a teenager. We get louder and louder, forming a circle and linking arms.

'Shut up, you lot!' roars my Irish friend. 'Do you want the cops to come and move us on?'

But they don't listen. Instead, someone's started up again. It's our song.

I drop my neighbour's arms and stick my fingers in my ears. 'Stop!' I yell. 'STOP!'

I can feel my breath getting shorter.

'What the hell's got into you?' asks the spiky-haired woman.

'Didn't you hear what he said?' I say. 'We'll get moved on if you don't stop this racket.'

'Who do you think you are?' slurs the trolley woman. 'And why do you keep rubbing your hands together like that and humming? Drives me bleeding mad, it does.'

I don't know what to say.

'Leave her be!' hollers Paul. This bloke's got a voice on him. Everyone slinks back to their old spots. I lie down on the cardboard with my legs curled up. Some of the others have huddled together to keep warm. I'm on my own. But that's OK. I'm used to that.

There's no other way.

5

Ellie

I was a flower girl at my father's wedding. I wore a pretty pale-pink dress which Miss Greenway made from something called a 'Simplicity' pattern, and carried creamy white roses. Everyone looked at me. It made me feel quite grown-up. Not long now until I was nine! It would be the second birthday I'd had since I'd lost my mother. Sometimes I still wondered if she wasn't dead at all but had gone away for a bit. Now I realize it was just my mind trying to protect me from the truth.

As an adult, I can understand why my father decided to get married again within two years of my mother's death. A good part of it, I am sure, came from his desire to provide a stable home for me. And I suppose he was lonely. He was, after all, only in his mid-forties. But at the time, I felt confused. Miss Greenway was so different from my mother. It wasn't simply her fair hair and that tinkly voice or the way she hung on to my father's hand as if she was in continual danger of falling over a cliff. Or even the way she'd started to change her voice so that she said 'Ay dooo' instead of 'I do' during the ceremony. It was simply that she wasn't Mummy.

One day, we were all going to go to heaven. We'd been taught that at school. So what, I wondered, as I watched my father kiss Miss Greenway on the lips at the altar, would my mother say when we got there too? It was all so confusing . . .

When we left the church, I took care to avoid the pavement cracks outside. 'See,' I said to Mummy in my head, 'I haven't forgotten.'

Afterwards, there was a reception at a big hotel, where the waiters held the doors open for me like I was a grown-up! There was an uncle and aunt from my father's side but no one from my mother's. We sat at a table at the end of the room, and ate something called 'cocko van' followed by a yummy chocolate pudding.

'You'll have to call me "Mum" now,' said my father's new wife, giving me a hug. Her cheek was next to mine. It was soft and flabby and didn't smell like my mother's had.

Really? I looked at my father questioningly. 'Sheila's right,' he said, though his voice sounded uncertain.

I still found it hard to think of Miss Greenway as 'Sheila', let alone 'Mum'. But I didn't want to cause any trouble. I had to be a good girl and not do or say anything that might upset anyone.

'Hah,' cackled the old lady, who was there too. 'Mum indeed!'

'Mother,' said Miss Greenway. Two little red spots appeared on her cheeks. 'Please try to contain yourself. And haven't you had enough champagne already?'

'Stuff and nonsense. I'm only pouring some for the child. Here, Ellie. Drink up. It's not every day you get a new mother.'

'Actually, Eileen,' said my father, 'I'd rather my daughter didn't have anything. She's too young.'

'Better make the most of it, then, hadn't she?' The old lady shook her head. 'Or she'll be old before she knows it, like my daughter here. I can tell you, I never thought she'd get a husband. Still, I've got to hand it to her. Couldn't get her feet under the table fast enough. Could you, Sheila?'

What was wrong with having your feet under the table? It was only polite when you were eating, wasn't it?

'I think we all ought to calm down a bit,' said my father. His face was what my mother used to call 'set'. It usually meant he wasn't pleased about something. 'Ah, good, the food has arrived.'

'About time! I'm starving. Calls itself a five-star? I always thought this place gave itself airs and graces. A bit like my daughter pretending to be posh so she doesn't show up her new husband.'

'Mother! That's quite enough.'

'Still, I won't say no to a bit more wedding cake.' Then the old lady began to shovel a second slice into her mouth as if someone was going to take it away from her.

'I'm sorry,' whispered Miss Greenway – Sheila – as she smoothed down her long white dress beside me. 'My mother's just a bit overexcited. It makes her say silly things.'

'It's OK,' I said, embarrassed.

'I meant what I said, dear. I really do want you to call me "Mum". I've always wanted a daughter like you.' Her eyes grew moist. 'I thought I'd left it too late to have a family.' She squeezed my hand hard. It hurt, although I didn't like to pull it away. 'I'm so lucky.'

*

63

Sheila moved in with us, and brought Mrs Greenway too. 'Why can't she stay in her house?' I asked.

'Because she's not well enough for your mother to live on her own.'

It was a few seconds before I realized that he was referring to Sheila.

'Your mother treats her duties seriously,' he added. 'It's one of the things I like about her.'

He spoke as if my own mother hadn't done the same. This made me feel upset on her behalf. 'What kind of duties?' I asked.

My father shifted from one foot to another. 'Like . . . well, like looking after people who depend on her.'

Like Mrs Greenway? But she didn't seem to depend on anyone to me. She had her own sitting room on the first floor, where the television was always on very loud. She watched programmes that made you laugh like *The David Nixon Show* (which made me believe that magic was real after all!) instead of serious ones like *Tomorrow's World* or the news, which my father liked. Sometimes I would squat outside on the floor, listening to her TV set. It was nicer than sitting with my father and Sheila, all snuggled up together and whispering before telling me it was time to go up to bed.

I was doing that one evening when the old lady suddenly opened her door, catching me by surprise. 'Might as well come in,' she told me. 'What are you waiting for?'

It became a nightly routine. I'd perch next to her on a small sofa with cushions that had pictures of bullfighters on them. She'd bought them in Spain, she told me proudly, when she'd been on something called a 'package holiday'. She also told me things I didn't understand. 'You watch that daughter of mine. She can be all sweetness and light. But if you don't do what she wants, she can turn on you just like that and then . . .'

She stopped for a bit as if she was going to say something else but had changed her mind.

'What?' I said.

'Nothing, child.' She patted my hand. 'Just forget I said that.'

At the time, I didn't set much store by our conversation. Her mind 'rambled', as my father said. Besides, Mum, as I was trying my best to remember to call her (I couldn't bear to say 'Mummy'), was really nice to me. She bought me new clothes – my favourite was a pretty red dress with white spots. And she often shared treats like fruit-and-nut chocolate bars and gave me hugs.

Sometimes at night, when I said my prayers, I felt guilty. 'Dear God, please tell Mummy that I'll always love her best.'

I only hoped that she got the message safely.

(The other day we were allowed to go into the prison chapel. And once again I found myself saying the same prayer.)

At weekends, when my father was around more, we would go out for family drives. This meant that Mrs Greenway and I would sit in the back of the car sucking toffees, which she'd hand me secretly from her pocket while my new mother sat in the front next to my father, who was at the steering wheel.

Every now and then we'd go to a wood for a walk and to pick flowers. Later I would press these between pages of the *Children's Encyclopaedia* as my real mother had taught me. Then, just as before, I would stick these into an album and look up their names in my book of wildflowers. In late summer and autumn, my real mother and I used to pick blackberries and I would help her boil them up in a big saucepan and watch, fascinated, as she sieved them through a large muslin sheet, tied to the legs of an upturned stool in the kitchen. But when I asked my new mother if we could do the same, she laughed as if I had said something very stupid. 'I'm not the jam-making type.' Strangely, she'd stopped baking now we lived with her. Gone were those butterfly cakes and shepherd's pies and toads in the hole. Instead, we ate a lot of Captain Birdseye Fish Fingers and a new food called Arctic Roll, because they were 'easier'.

Sometimes, if the sun was out, we would go to a pub, where my father and new mother would go inside for a drink while Mrs Greenway and I would sit in the garden with a lemonade each and a packet of crisps.

'She won't be able to do that for much longer,' said my companion one weekend, jerking her finger at my new mother as she disappeared into the pub, hanging on to my father's arm.

'Why not?' I was busy munching my last crisp, at the same time as Mrs Greenway. We both agreed that we could do with a couple more but neither of us had any money.

'Because she's expecting, that's why.'

'Expecting what?'

'Oh dear. Never mind. You'll find out soon enough.'

That night at tea, before my father got home, my new mother made fish fingers for the fifth night in a row. 'I'm sorry,' I said, pushing one around with my fork. 'I've gone off them.'

I thought she'd tell me not to worry and that she'd find something else instead. But she fixed me with a disapproving look. 'In that case, you can go without, young lady. We didn't have nice things like this during the war. You should consider yourself lucky.'

That night, when the winter wind was howling outside, Daddy came in to tuck me up in bed, as he always did. 'There's something I want to tell you.'

'Is it to do with the fish fingers?' I asked anxiously.

'No. Why? What about them?'

'It doesn't matter,' I said quickly.

I tried again. Daddy and I used to play lots of guessing games when we'd been alone. He used to say how quick I was and that I was a 'clever girl'.

'Is it because she's expecting, then?'

His face registered surprise. 'You knew?'

'Mrs Greenway said. But she didn't tell me what she's expecting. Is it a present?'

He smiled. 'In a way, it's exactly that! She's going to have a baby, Ellie. A brother or sister for you. Isn't that wonderful?'

I leapt out of bed and flung my arms around him. At last I'd have someone else to play with. Someone to talk to in this house who wasn't older than me. I'd be like all the other girls at school.

'Thank you, Daddy! Thank you.'

But it was only later, when I was saying my prayers, that I felt sad. My real mother had wanted a baby so much. 'I hope you don't mind,' I whispered out into the dark. 'I still love you best. Cross my heart and hope to die.'

My nose is still bleeding today when I get to school. A few weeks ago, I came in with bruises on my arm and when the teacher asked how I got them, I said I fell over in the park. Today I tell them our cat scratched me, even though we're not allowed pets in our flat.

They say they've got to ring someone called a social worker.

She's a nice lady called Jill. I get called out of class to talk to her. I tell her about the other stuff my dad does to me and how my mother doesn't stop him 'cos she's scared.

She says I'm safe now. I don't have to worry any more because no one's going to hurt me again.

Maybe that means I'll get some tea. I can't sleep at night when I'm hungry.

6

Jo

'Jo?'

I can't see the face but I know the voice from somewhere.

I open my mouth to yell 'Help' but the word won't come out. Strong hands are wrapping something long and wiry round my neck and pulling it taut. There's no breath left in my body. *So this is it*, I tell myself. I feel almost calm. This is what death feels like.

Then I feel a sharp stab in my ribs. 'Shut up, lady. Some of us are trying to get some shut-eye.'

Relief washes through me as I open my eyes. It was only the same old nightmare again. 'It's not real,' I repeat over and over to myself. 'It's not real.'

But my body isn't convinced. It continues to shake even though I don't know why. It's almost like my mind knows something that the rest of me doesn't.

It's bloody impossible to go back to sleep because my newspaper blanket is soggy with dew. I make my way towards the broken factory windows, stretch my arms and legs and stare up at the sky. It's streaked with pink. It might be the centre of a big city but right now I can only hear the odd car or bike go by.

Then I hear a siren scream. I scuttle back to the safety

of my cardboard mattress and curl up, trying to control my shivers, till the others begin to stir.

'You kept us up with your nightmares all night,' grumbles a kid with green hair.

My skin prickles. 'What did I say?'

'Dunno. Load of rubbish it was.'

'Stop arguing,' says a small bird-like woman I hadn't noticed before. She's running her fingers through her long hair like a comb. 'Can't wait to be out of this place. Won't be long now. I'm on a list. They'll find me somewhere soon.'

'You've been saying that for months,' snorts the man in a suit.

Paul is standing over me. He seems different today. 'Come on, Jo,' he says sharply. 'Time to get going.'

'Where?'

'Start with the toilets at the coach station. They're 20p. You can have a bit of a wash-up there before you begin working.'

'But I haven't got a job right now. I used to sell the *Big Issue* –'

'Forget it,' cuts in a pretty girl with light-brown skin. 'There are too many of them as it is.'

Paul puts his arm around her. 'Faduma prefers to use her looks, don't you, love? Go and put your slap on, there's a good girl. Maybe you could train Jo here.'

She gives me a look like I'm something the cat brought in. 'You must be crazy. Men don't want some old hag with saggy breasts.'

I start up. 'Bloody cheek . . .'

My Irish friend comes between us. 'Don't take Faduma the wrong way. It's just how she is.'

'I'm no prostitute,' I say.

Paul's eyes narrow. 'And I'm not a pimp. You've got a cheek saying that after everything I've done for you.' He waggles his finger at me. 'Faduma wouldn't sell herself, would you?'

'No bloody way,' she hisses. 'But you can still make people pay without touching.'

I don't get it.

'She might be like a little cat with us but Faduma's got charm, believe it or not. She uses her looks to soften people's hearts.' Paul speaks like he's her master. 'She asks passers-by to give her a couple of quid so she can "get the bus to work". A few of those every day and you're home and dry.'

Clever.

He looks at me like he's sizing me up. 'But you'd be better off with straight old-fashioned begging. People will give you money because you'll remind them of their mum like you reminded me of mine. You just need to find yourself a spot near the buses and put up this sign. Here. I've done one for you.'

There's no way I can do that. All those people . . . .

He gives me a sheet of cardboard. On it in thick black capital letters are the words OAP. HUNGRY AND HOMELESS. PLEASE HELP.

Paul grins like he's pleased with himself. 'I took a guess with the age. Did I get it right?'

'No you bloody didn't! I'm not that old.'

'Oh, sorry. Better change that, then. I don't like to lie.'

The woman with the spiky hair and dog gives a snort. 'Is that right, Paul?'

'Enough of that. I've got faith in this one.' He touches my arm like we're friends again. 'We haven't had a mature lady for a bit. They always melt a few wallets.'

He gives me another look. 'Now, these are the rules, Jo. Keep that beanie of yours on. The shaved head seems a bit threatening. When someone gives you food, you can eat a bit yourself but you've got to bring most of it back for the rest of us. Any cash donations have to come straight back here too. It's how we work. Don't try to get away with anything. We'll be checking up on you.'

He pats my back. 'Off you go. And remember to wash first. No one will want to come near you if you stink.'

Stiff with cold and hunger, I make my way towards the bus station, looking over my shoulder all the time. I don't know what to do. I feel safer with someone like Paul to look out for me, but I don't want to do this. My heart starts to pound when a tall man seems to be following me, but then he turns off in another direction. It's only just morning and the sky's still that dark-pinky colour. Loads of people are getting off the buses or walking past, dressed up for work. What I'd give for a nice cosy office job in the warm. Then I'm back where I got off the bus last night.

There's a woman trying to push her pram with a screaming kid inside up a ramp.

'Want some help, love?' I ask, but she ignores me like I'm not here.

I scurry through the main area, keeping my head down. Past a stall selling coffee and croissants. My mouth waters. There's a sign on the wall saying NO MODERN

SLAVERY OR HUMAN TRAFFICKING DEAL-
ING IS ALLOWED TO TAKE PART ON THESE
PREMISES.

At last I find the toilets. I'm desperate for a pee. This morning, I couldn't bring myself to squat in the corner like the others. A snotty-looking woman in a business suit is coming in at the same time. She gives me a sideways look as if to say, 'What are you doing here?'

It's a relief to sit down on a proper seat in privacy. Then I go to one of the basins. Hot water! That feels good. I splash my face and squeeze out some soap, running it over my scalp and rinsing it again. Heaven.

'Excuse me,' says Snotty Face. 'I don't believe you're meant to do that here.'

Too late. I just have. Then I take off my anorak and the T-shirt I'm wearing underneath and rub another squirt of soap under my armpits.

A navy-suited girl with high heels at the sink next to me moves away. I put my head under the dryer – I might not have any hair but it still feels good – and then get dressed and go into one of the cubicles. Perhaps I can hide in here for a few hours and figure out what to do. There's no way I can beg like Paul told me to. I've already dumped the sign he gave me in a bin.

After a bit, I hear people outside starting to moan. 'That one's been occupied for ages.'

Someone hammers on the door. 'Hurry up!'

I keep quiet. An hour passes, maybe two, as I sit and doze in the warmth.

Then it happens.

I see the shiny black shoes under the door. More hammering. I begin to shake.

'Are you all right in there?'

There's a sound like someone is getting down on the ground.

A black-uniformed arm.

It's the police!

'Better break the door down, then, and see if she's OK.'

There's nothing else for it. I'm going to have to open up.

'I'm OK,' I say, pulling down my beanie and unlocking the door. 'Just got the squits, that's all.'

The policewoman's eyes narrow. 'Really? Looks to me like you're hiding from someone or something.'

'Why do you think that?'

'There's no need to be aggressive.'

'I'm not,' I say, feeling my fists clench into balls.

'What's your name?'

'What's it to you? I haven't done anything wrong.'

She stares like she might have seen me somewhere before. 'I think we ought to pay a visit to the police station and check out your identity. Come with me, please.'

There's a queue of people staring at us. My throat is tightening with panic. I've got to get out of here.

'Let the lady go,' says a woman in the crowd. She's one of Paul's gang, I realize. 'Stop bullying her,' she continues. 'Like she says, she hasn't done nothing wrong.'

Some of the others are now agreeing with her. There's confusion. The policewoman seems to be doubting herself. I use the opportunity to dash past, racing out of the bus station as fast as I can. Over a main road. Past a café

74

and office blocks. There's a park ahead. Just what I need. Maybe I can hide there.

Don't ask me why, but I'm pretty sure my life depends on this.

Hawthorn (Crataegus monogyna)
Long associated with fertility. On the first day of
May, young women would take a sprig of blossom and keep
it close to attract a husband. It is also known as a tree of
protection, offering shelter from storms.

7

Ellie

Time passes really slowly here. Every minute counts, ticking its way towards freedom – or not. It's like that for many adults, not just those in prison. But when you're a child, time goes by in a different way. As I look back, there appear to be periods when my life was concentrated into small intense patches, such as when my mother died. At other times, it seemed to rush past, like my new mother's pregnancy. A baby takes nine months to grow, yet it seemed to me, back then, that it happened in a few weeks. It wasn't until I was older that I realized Sheila must have been pregnant when they'd married.

To my excitement, I was allowed to help my new mother get ready for the baby. It was the first time I'd been invited into their bedroom since the marriage. The old wooden wardrobe had gone and in its place was a line of white sliding doors with mirrors on them. My mother's pretty Victorian dressing table had been taken away too, with all her little trinkets and pictures. In its place was a matching white table with a mirror that went up and down when you moved it. (We're not allowed mirrors inside prison in case we crack the glass and use it to stab someone or self-harm.)

But the thing that really drew my eye was the new big

bed with a maroon bedspread on top that Daddy said was called 'candle wick'. How strange to think that my father got into this every night with a woman who wasn't Mummy. There was also a chest of drawers and shopping bags with little white baby clothes inside. My task was to put them in the drawers.

'Thank you, Ellie,' Sheila had said. 'You've done a lovely job.' Then she picked them up and did them all over again. They looked just the same to me afterwards but she seemed happier.

'Don't you mind about the baby?' asked one of my friends at school.

'Why should I?'

'It shows they've done it,' she sniggered.

'What do you mean?'

Another of the girls laughed. 'Don't you know?'

I didn't want to look stupid, so I made out that I'd suddenly got it. 'Oh, *that*,' I said airily. 'I see what you mean now.'

But I didn't.

Then one day in biology, our teacher announced that we were going to be studying 'reproduction'. There was a wave of laughter round the class. 'Your dad and new mum will know all about that,' whispered my friend, whom I was beginning not to like any more.

We all sat in front of a big screen, which was lit up almost as if we were in the cinema. My father used to take me every Saturday afternoon to the matinee at the local Odeon but we hadn't been for ages. Now, in the classroom, there was a large drawing of something that looked a bit like a bulb. When she was well, my mother and I would plant bulbs in the autumn and then green shoots would come through in the spring. 'This is a womb,' said the teacher. 'It's in a lady's tummy.'

Then there was a picture of a little fish, which was called a sperm.

'Men produce these. Lots of them swim into the womb but only one will fertilize the egg. That means it gives it life. Then a baby starts to be made.'

The class began to giggle again. It was no good. I had to ask. 'How do the fish get into the womb?'

Some of the other girls looked as though they didn't understand either. But my friend dug me in the ribs. 'It's because a man and woman have sex, stupid,' she hissed. 'Just like your dad. My mum says it's disgusting, so soon after your poor mother.'

Was it? Why?

That evening, I went upstairs to Mrs Greenway and repeated the conversation. I'd hoped she would tell me that the friend was silly. Instead, she was silent for a few minutes, even though the television continued to blare with her favourite programme, *Coronation Street* (which I'd never seen before. She was always watching either that or *Crossroads*. I couldn't make up my mind which one I liked best.) 'Some people might say your father found someone else too fast,' she said eventually. 'But it was nearly two years and, besides, he was lonely. Men don't always do well on their own. He needed a woman to look after you. My daughter needed a husband too. Time was running out for her. She was always desperate for a child.'

Never before had I heard the old lady talk so much in such a serious voice without her usual cackles of laughter.

Then she sighed. 'She thought it was getting too late to have one of her own. So she wasn't careful enough.'

'What do you mean?'

'Nothing.' She gave herself a shake. 'Don't listen to me. Your father's right. I should learn to keep my opinions to myself. Now, how about something to eat?'

Getting up, she made her way to the gleaming golden trolley where she kept her tea cups, a teapot and a pretty biscuit tin with a picture of a kitten on it. Her fingers struggled to open the lid. 'Flipping arthritis,' she grumbled.

'Shall I help?'

'Thank you. You're a good girl.' Then her hand patted mine as we tucked into chocolate digestives together. 'We're in this together, you and I. Let's just hope everything's all right when the baby arrives.'

'Why shouldn't it be?' I asked as we settled down on the sofa to watch TV.

'Things will change, mark me.'

'I don't understand.'

Her hand patted mine again. 'Even if you did, there's nothing you or I could do about it. Don't go mentioning it to your father or we'll both end up in trouble. Now shh. The adverts are over. We don't want to miss the next bit. Do we?'

I found myself snuggling up to her. It felt comforting, especially with everything changing all over again because of the baby who would be here soon. 'Do you mind if I call you Grandma?' I said suddenly. 'I've always wanted a grandmother like the other girls at school. My grandmas and grandpas all died before I was born.'

Her face went all red. For a minute, I thought I'd offended

her. Then she beamed and put her arm around me. 'I don't mind at all,' she said. Tears were glistening in her eyes at the same time. 'In fact, I'd rather like it. We'd better tell those two.' She chuckled. 'Wonder what my daughter will make of that! She'll probably think we're ganging up on her.'

It was nearly Christmas. This was always an exciting time, because my birthday was the day after. Before everything had changed, I'd loved all the sparkly lights and the way that everyone was happy as though they were celebrating my special day too. Mummy used to say that I had been the best Christmas present anyone could ever have given her.

Since she'd died, my father and I hadn't had a tree. But this time, we had a huge one in the hall with lots of parcels underneath.

'Not as big as the package in my daughter's stomach,' wheezed Grandma Greenway as we prodded and felt the presents to guess what was inside. 'They reckon she'll have it in a couple of weeks or so.'

'How will they unwrap it?' I asked.

She gave me a sharp look. 'I wouldn't ask if I were you. It will only scare you half to death.' She shuddered. 'If someone had told me what it was really like, I might never have let a man near me.'

'What do you mean?'

She waved a hand in the air. 'It doesn't matter. Now why don't you play me the tune on that precious music box of yours?'

On Christmas Eve, in the old days, we used to go to

the carol service for children at church in town. We'd each get a little present. Once, I'd received a small angel made of silk to hang on the tree. I didn't know where it had gone. Lots of things from those days seemed to have disappeared after my new mother had had 'a bit of a clear-up'.

'Do we have to go?' she moaned when my father suggested we went to the service. 'My back is aching.'

'Not if you don't want to, dear.'

'But we always do,' I burst out. 'Please.'

My father hesitated. 'I could take her on my own if you don't mind.'

He spoke to my new mother as if I wasn't in the room.

She shrugged. 'Go ahead.'

It was a lovely service. We sat next to Peter Gordon and his parents and sang my real mother's favourite carol, 'Away in a Manger'. Mrs Gordon gave me a big hug afterwards and Peter wished me a 'Happy Christmas' rather awkwardly, as if he knew this was a particularly difficult time for me. Lots of people patted my head afterwards. Someone told my father that they 'wished him well'. He held my hand tightly as we went home. 'I know life has been hard, Ellie. But it will be all right now.'

Yet as we got to the house, he began to run. 'What is it, Daddy?' I called out. 'Wait!'

There was an ambulance outside. My new mother was being carried into it on a stretcher.

'It's started,' she whimpered. 'I told you not to leave me.'

That wasn't true! She'd said we could go.

'My darling. I'm so sorry. Don't worry. I'm here now. I'll come with you.'

'May I come too?' I pleaded. Daddy was upset. Surely he'd need me?

'No.' To my dismay, he steered me towards the house as though he didn't want anything to do with me. 'Go inside, Ellie. Mrs Greenway will look after you.'

'You've made me tread on a pavement crack,' I howled.

'What are you talking about? Just go inside, will you?'

On Christmas Day, Grandma Greenway and I didn't know how to cook the turkey, so we ate the sliced ham in the fridge instead. We both looked longingly at the presents under the tree. 'Better not open them until they come back,' she said. I agreed, although I was itching to know what was inside. Then we stayed up really late and watched a film called *It's a Wonderful Life*. I was so tired that I fell asleep on her shoulder. When I woke up, she had her arm around me. I felt warm and cosy. *Please don't let my new mother come back too soon*, I found myself wishing. Then I immediately felt guilty for such an uncharitable thought.

The next day, I woke up with a start. I was nine now. Not eight like yesterday! 'It's my birthday,' I said to Mrs Greenway.

'So it is, love,' she said. But I couldn't see any presents. Maybe Daddy was going to bring them when he got back from the hospital.

'I hope everything's all right,' Mrs Greenway kept muttering.

Then I felt selfish for thinking about my birthday when my new mother was in hospital. Mrs Greenway and I had boiled eggs for breakfast. The yellow bits were all hard, although I ate them to be polite. Finally, my father returned. He seemed tired but he was smiling. 'You've got a baby brother!' he said.

Never have I seen my father look so happy. Not even when my real mother had been alive.

I jumped up and down with excitement. A brother! I'd look after him and play with him. I'd love him for ever and he would love me too.

'When can I see him?' I asked, hugging my father tight.

'We'll visit just after lunch if you want.'

I counted the hours down on the clock. Grandma Greenway and I sat in the back of the car, holding hands. Every now and then she squeezed mine tight as if to say, 'Don't worry.'

Why should I? What was there to be nervous about?

My new mother was in a room all of her own. She was sitting on a bed with a white blanket in her arms. 'Go and say hello to your baby brother,' said my father.

I tiptoed up. He was so tiny! What a funny face! So red and crinkly.

My new mother was looking down at him, ignoring me.

'Would you like to hold him, Ellie?' said my father.

Really? But I'd never held a baby before. 'Sit down on this chair by the bed and make your arms into a round circle like this,' said my father, demonstrating. Gingerly, I did as I was told. 'That's right.'

My new mother hesitated. 'Go on, darling,' said my father. 'It's important for Ellie to bond.'

She placed the little bundle into my lap. I could hardly breathe with the weight of love and responsibility. 'Hello,'

I whispered. 'I'm your big sister and I'm going to love you for ever and ever.'

Then he suddenly moved and my arms wobbled.

There was a scream. 'Catch him, Nigel!'

My father steadied me just as my new mother snatched the white bundle away from me. 'You could have dropped him, you silly girl.'

I burst into tears. 'I'm sorry. I didn't mean to.'

'It's all right,' soothed my father. But my new mother's furious face made me shiver with fear. Then my little brother burst into tears as if he was cross with me too. 'Come on,' said Grandma Greenway, putting her arm around me. 'Let's leave them to it. I've never been particularly fond of babies anyway. Not at all interesting in my opinion. Get us a taxi home, will you?'

This last remark was directed at my father.

'It's all right, Ellie,' he said. 'Mum's just tired. She'll be fine when she comes home.'

'Thank you for the baby,' I said. 'He's the best birthday present I could have had.'

His face changed. 'Of course,' he said quietly. Then he patted me on the head. 'Nine years old today. How could I have forgotten? I'm sorry, Ellie. I'll make it up to you soon.'

8

Jo

I hang out in a park for a few hours but it's started to rain.
I go under some trees but I still get wet. You have to be
careful on the streets. Pneumonia can be a killer in winter. So I head back into town, keeping my eyes peeled, and
slink into a smart shopping centre. The first place I see is
a mobile-phone shop. Great. I go right in, pretending to
look at the display cabinets.

'Can I help you?' says a young bloke.

'Yeah. I need a pay-as-you-go.'

Of course I can't afford one but I pretend to be interested while the kid talks me through the different models.
I have my back to the door, expecting that any minute
someone will come in and tap me on the shoulder.

But no one does.

'Ta,' I say eventually. 'I'll think about it.'

'Timewaster,' I hear him muttering as I leave. But I
don't care. The coast seems clear. With any luck, that
policewoman will have found someone else to bother by
now. Even so, I can't take any chances. A bus is coming. I
jump on through the exit doors even though I haven't got
a card or cash to pay the fare. No one seems to notice. I
wait a few stops and then I get off again.

There's a crowd of schoolkids coming towards me,

jabbering away in a foreign language, with teachers trying to keep them in order. Shoving myself into the middle of them, I elbow my way through. When I come out the other side, I glance behind. I can't see anyone. I keep on running, down a side street, across a road, and then onto another main road again. I stop, panting for breath.

Reckon I'm safe now. But I'm bloody starving. Then I see a bloke in a suit eating chips out of a paper bag and then chucking half of them away in a rubbish bin. I make a dash for it but someone else beats me to it. From the back, she looks like she's posh with that smart red coat. Then she turns round and I see her face – it's all scrawny and she has a desperate look in her eyes. 'Go on,' she says, holding out the paper. 'Take a few.'

'Thanks,' I say.

'Not that many,' she snaps before walking on, hugging the chips close to her. I want to cry with disappointment. Once more, I walk on, riffling through every bin I pass. I get lucky with a squashed banana and half a Yorkie bar with teeth marks on it.

Then I go past this big building with huge pillars and a sign saying BRISTOL CITY MUSEUM AND ART GALLERY. FREE ENTRANCE.

Ignoring the stand asking for donations, I go through a couple of the rooms and find the quietest one. I sit down on a bench opposite a picture of a river with some children playing on the edge. The artist has done it by drawing lots of dots instead of proper lines. Not bad. Then I realize someone's standing over me. My heart carries on beating madly even when I see from her uniform that she's just one of the attendants. 'Sorry to bother you, madam, but we're about to close.'

Madam? I would laugh out loud if I wasn't so freaked out.

I'm back outside again. It's already getting colder. Where now? Daft question. I've got no choice unless I want to sleep on the streets. Slowly I make my way back to the dark empty factory at Stokes Croft.

Paul is there.

'What you got for me, then?'

'Sorry,' I say. 'No one gave me anything.'

Paul shakes his head. He's smiling but I can tell it's false. 'Sure you didn't keep something back for yourself?'

I put on my 'What you talking about?' look.

'Course not.'

He tuts like I'm a kid who's done something wrong. 'You've got to earn your keep, Mother, otherwise you can find somewhere else to sleep.'

My chest starts to race again like I'm having a panic attack. I've had a few of those before and they're not nice. 'I'll try harder,' I promise.

Pam and the man in the suit come back. They're lugging bags of biscuits, sandwiches, fizzy drinks and a bottle of wine. 'What about the money?' says Paul sharply. 'It's your signing-on day, isn't it?'

Suit Man grumbles something about 'bleeding me bloody dry' and then hands over some cash.

The shopping-trolley lady has a ring. There's a heated argument about whether it's a real diamond or paste.

The kid with green hair has a Swiss Army knife which he found in a skip. He's also brought back a big box of

Kit-Kats. 'They were being loaded off a van and no one was looking,' he says proudly.

Posh Pam snorts. 'I loathe chocolate.'

'Beggars can't be choosers,' says the man in the suit, laughing like he thinks he's cracked the best joke ever.

They all go into the 'pot'.

'What about her?' demands the spiky-haired dog woman, pointing at me. 'What did she get?'

'Nothing yet,' says my Irish friend. 'Give her time.'

'But she's got to do her bit,' whines the bloke who was shooting up when I got here. 'No point in having her here if she can't earn her keep.'

'I've told her the same.' Paul's voice is low and threatening. 'She will.'

We plonk ourselves down around a fire someone's made out of planks of wood. ('Got them from an allotment,' says the bloke, looking pleased with himself.) I try to get nearer but the others push in front. Wind is whistling through the broken windows. I can't stop shivering with cold.

'Why are you here, then?' asks Faduma. She seems friendlier than before.

'What?'

'Come on. We're all on the street for a reason. See Hugo over there in the business suit? He used to be an estate agent but lost everything when his wife took him to the cleaners in the divorce. He didn't have any family to stay with so he ended up here. So what did you do?'

I think of the bracelet. I'm glad it's gone now. 'Nothing.'

'So maybe someone's done something to you.' Her eyes narrow. 'You seem scared of something, Jo.'

'Dunno what you're talking about.'

'Yeah. Right. I've been that way myself, you know. I get it.'

'What happened to you, then?' I say, trying to change the subject.

A dark look crosses her face. 'I overheard my dad making plans to sell me to some local sex traffickers.' She says it like it's no big deal.

'Didn't your mum try and stop him?'

'Nah. They needed the cash or the landlord was going to chuck us out.'

'Which country were you living in?'

'Here, of course. In Birmingham, where I was brought up. I jumped out of my bedroom window. Managed to get down to London and ended up here.'

Paul comes back and she stops.

'Californian red, anyone?' he asks. 'It's a good year,' he says, laughing and pretending to examine the label. 'You did well here, Pam. Go on, pass it round.'

This time I don't need any persuading. I'm already freezing. Then one of the blokes starts strumming his guitar. The green-haired young man and Pam begin to dance, their faces close. His hands are on her bum. I start to relax. The drink has made me feel loads better.

'Pipe down, will you?' says Paul. 'Or we'll get done for being drunk and disorderly, not to mention squatting.'

'Spoilsport,' grumbles the young man, who's still got his hands all over Pam.

We settle down for the night. It's quite early but Paul says the earlier we go to sleep, the earlier we can get up to catch the best pitches. He lies next to me. His breath is sweet and sickly. I don't do drugs but I saw him rolling

something earlier next to the bloke who'd been shooting up.

The next thing I know, there's a body over mine. I can't
breathe with terror. I try to yell out but a hand covers my
mouth. 'Shut up. Then you won't be hurt.'

It's Paul. My Irish 'friend'.

'Fuck off,' I hiss.

He laughs. 'I like a woman who fights back. But no
one's going to help you, even if you scream. It's part of
our initiation rite, you see. Everyone who joins our little
band has the pleasure of my company.'

Pleasure? I have a flash of a man on top of me, pump-
ing away. I'd hated it and done nothing about it. I'd let him
do what he liked just to keep the peace. But now something inside me breaks.

'Ow!'

I can taste his disgusting skin where I bit him on the
wrist, but it doesn't stop him.

'Feisty, I like that. I've always had a thing for older
women.'

His hands are pinning mine down. His weight is almost
crushing me. I can't breathe. He bites my left nipple
through my top.

I get a leg free and knee him in the groin.

'That's enough.'

He's angry now, like that other man. I'm fucking terrified but I know that if I'm going to survive, I can't show
it. The others must be able to hear us unless they're all
drunk. Then I remember what Faduma had told me. If
anyone's going to help me, she's the one.

'Rape!' I yell out. 'Faduma. Help!'

He clamps a hand on my mouth again. I'm going to suffocate. His hand works down underneath my trousers.

Then I feel another weight on top of us. I'm going to be broken. My body will snap. 'You little cow!' roars Paul. He's off me now, wrestling with Faduma, who has leapt on top of him. Then they've stopped, and my new friend is panting, holding a knife. Paul watches her warily.

'I warned you last time,' she hisses. 'If you try this kind of stuff again, I'll hand you in.'

Paul laughs. 'Even if you get murder for it?' He raises his voice. 'That's right. Our little Faduma stabbed her dad. Did you know that?'

She'd left out that bit in the story she gave me.

'The bastard deserved it,' she said. 'And yes, I mean it. Leave Jo alone or I will hand you in. Fuck the consequences.'

For a minute they just stare at each other, and then Paul starts laughing. 'Stupid bitches, you're not worth it anyway.' He swaggers off to his corner and lies down.

Faduma leads me by the hand to the other side of the building. We're both shaking. We watch as Paul turns over and goes to sleep.

Then Faduma's fingers press something into mine.

'It's a train ticket', she whispers. 'Found it yesterday outside the station. Thought it might come in useful but I reckon you need it more than me.'

I strain to read the small writing in the dim light. My eyesight's not what it was.

'It's for some place called Penzance,' she says.

The name seems to stir something inside me even though I've never heard of it before. Still, I need to get out of this place. Penzance sounds good. The name feels safe.

'Ta. But what about you?'

'Don't you worry. I can look after myself. Reckon it's time for me to beat it too.'

Then she gives me a shove.

'Just go.'

I don't need her to say it twice.

9

Ellie

My father and I spent ages getting the house ready for my little brother. It was lovely doing things together without anyone else. We were a team again. Just Daddy and me.

I helped put up the little crib with its blue bows in the bedroom that used to belong to my real mother but was now Daddy's and his new wife's. Then I tucked in the blanket with a Peter Rabbit picture embroidered onto it by Grandma Greenway. She'd been sewing it as we'd sat side by side on the sofa in front of *Coronation Street*. Every now and then she'd cluck loudly if she didn't approve of something that one of the characters was doing. (The girls enjoy audience participation here in prison too. There's always a lot of shouting and 'You silly bitch' or 'Don't trust him!' when we watch 'Corrie' in the communal lounge after tea.)

My father had also brought the pram out of the garage. He said it was a 'silver cross' (even though it didn't look like a cross at all). It hadn't been allowed in the house before now because that might have been unlucky.

'Why?' I'd asked.

'Just a silly old wives' tale,' he told me.

The silver cross took up half the hallway. I practised holding the handle and pretending that I was pushing my new brother along. It made me feel grown-up but also scared. My new mother had looked so angry with me when I'd almost dropped him. I had to be more careful in future.

I could tell that my father was worried too. 'You must make allowances for Mum when she comes home,' he kept telling me. 'Giving birth is very tiring. It can make people overanxious.'

He spoke as if he was talking to himself.

Even Grandma Greenway seemed unsettled. 'Mark my words,' she kept muttering, 'nothing will be the same now.'

Such remarks were always made when my father wasn't around, and I was too frightened to repeat them to him in case they were true.

On another day, however, she seemed a bit brighter. 'Tell you what,' she announced. 'You can help me perm my hair.'

I'd seen her do this at the kitchen table. It involved several bits of paper and a horrible-smelling white lotion along with hair rollers that looked like small hairy sausages. I was always discouraged from entering when this complicated procedure was going on. So now the responsibility of being invited to join this sacred rite was almost overwhelming. 'You can pass me each paper and roller when I say,' she declared imperiously.

My father left us to it, apart from when he tried to come in to put on the kettle. 'Away with you,' scolded Grandma Greenway. 'Can't you see that your daughter is doing an extremely important job here?' Her words made my chest puff out with pride.

'I apologize for disturbing you, ladies,' said my father with a wink. She winked back, although I wasn't sure why.

I felt warm inside: it was like being part of a happy family again.

At last the day arrived when my new mother and little brother were coming home. They would have been back sooner, said my father, but there had been 'complications'. He said it in the kind of voice that discouraged further questions.

My father went off to collect them and, after a bit, Grandma Greenway and I stood by the window in the sitting room, watching for the car. 'I remember coming back from the nursing home with her,' she murmured. 'Barely eighteen, I was. No one could have guessed the troubles ahead. A bit like now.' Then she squeezed my hand.

My father's blue Ford Cortina was coming into our road. It pulled up outside our house. Then Daddy jumped out and ran round to the back to open the door. Grandma Greenway and I pressed our faces to the window. Our breath made the glass mist up and we had to rub it to see more clearly.

My father was helping my new mother out. She had a little bundle wrapped in a white blanket in her arms and she was carrying it very carefully, as if it was breakable. I had a flash of my real mother's precious blue bowl that she had smashed into tiny pieces. I shivered.

'It will be all right,' said Grandma Greenway, giving me a squeeze round the waist. But I knew she was only trying to make me feel better.

The door opened. 'Hello,' called my father. His voice had a wobble in it, although I could tell it was pretending to be jolly at the same time. 'We're back.'

I was so excited! I wanted to see my new little brother again. Rushing out into the hall, I almost bumped into them.

'Careful,' said my new mother sharply.

My father nodded. 'Your mother's right. Babies are like china, Ellie. Very fragile.'

That nasty coldness ran through me again.

'Now let me help you sit on the sofa, Sheila,' he continued. 'Then Ellie can go next to you to get a better look.'

'Just as long as she doesn't breathe on him or he might get germs.'

'Stop fussing, for pity's sake.' This was Grandma Greenway. 'The child hasn't got anything wrong with her and, anyway, babies have to build up their immunity.'

'How about congratulations, Mother?'

'I've already said that in my card. Let's take a look, then, shall we, Ellie?'

Together we sat on either side of the white bundle. I could see him much clearer than I'd done in the hospital. My brother had such bright-blue eyes and the sweetest little rosebud mouth I had ever seen. 'Oh,' I breathed. 'He's absolutely perfect.'

Instinctively, I stroked his tiny fingers. His skin was so soft!

'Have you washed your hands?' demanded my new mother.

'Yes,' I lied. I usually told the truth but I didn't want to let go. He loved me! Those funny little noises surely showed that he was happy to see me. We were going to be friends for ever!

'Has he got a name yet?' said Grandma Greenway. I could tell from the quiver in her voice that she was moved too.

'Michael,' said my new mother.

'Really, dear?' said my father. 'I thought we'd decided on –'

'No. Michael suits him better than anything else.'

The old lady made a strange sound. My new mother gave her a look that made me uneasy. It was as though they were having a silent angry conversation.

'Michael,' I breathed, continuing to stroke the little fingers. 'I like that.'

'It's absolutely freezing in here, Nigel.'

'I've just banked up the fire, dear.'

'I told you we needed central heating. It's much colder here than in the hospital. There's actually mist on the window. Do you want your son to get a chill?'

Central heating was very expensive, I knew. Only one other house had it in our road. We had the coalman, like nearly everyone else. I loved the smell when he delivered it in his lorry and tipped it into the shed.

'Of course. I'll sort it out immediately.'

'In my day –'

'I don't want to know about your day, Mum.' My new mother stood up. 'This is mine. And my priority is this baby's health. Now I'm going to have a lie-down with him. Nigel, help me up the stairs, will you?'

I jumped up. 'May I give him a little kiss on the cheek?'

'I don't think that's a good idea. Like I said earlier, you might have germs.'

'Sheila. Don't you think that . . .' My father was whispering something into her ear.

She frowned. 'All right, then. But just a little one.'

I pressed my lips against his cheek. It felt so soft. Just

like the velvet coat my mother had made me before she got sick. 'I love you, Michael,' I whispered.

He looked back at me with those bright-blue eyes. 'I love you too,' he seemed to say.

'There's something else, isn't there, Sheila?' said my father.

'Is there?'

'You remember.' My father put his hand in his pocket. 'There's been so much going on, Ellie, that I'm afraid we let your birthday come and go. This is a late present for you.' He held out a box.

'Thank you,' I gasped, opening it expectantly. Inside was an alarm clock. I bit back my disappointment. I'd been hoping for a locket – all the other girls at school had one.

Even so, I flung my arms around my father's waist. As I did so, I could see my new mother glaring at me. I should have thanked her first.

'Thank you,' I said.

She nodded. 'It's to make sure you get yourself up in time for school. You're a big girl now and you'll need to show us how grown-up you can be. Now I'm going to bed, so go and play quietly. I don't want you bothering Michael.'

Why had she changed? It was like my new mother had gone into hospital and a different one had come out. That afternoon I went into town for some errands with Grandma Greenway. 'My daughter's just being overprotective,' she assured me. 'Lots of new mothers are like that. It will be all right soon.'

But I made sure not to tread on any pavement cracks. Just in case.

It's my tenth birthday today but I didn't get any presents or a cake. Instead, we have cold rice pudding. 'I don't like it,' I tell them. 'It makes me sick.' But they force me to eat it and then I throw it up. 'Told you,' I said, but then I get into more trouble for being 'cheeky'.

It's cold in the children's home, especially at night. I sleep in a bunk bed. I'm on the top and I'm scared of falling off. There are three other bunk beds in the room too.

I keep thinking about Mum. I haven't seen her for nearly two years. The people here say they don't know where she is but I don't believe them. What if Dad's hurting her again? So I open the window and climb out. It's a bit of a drop to the ground but I'm OK. I walk along this road and a car stops. The driver tells me to get in. He takes me to a police station and they give me a chocolate biscuit when I tell them it's my birthday. Then the people from the children's home arrive and bring me back. It's not the first time.

'We've told you before,' they tell me. 'This is your last warning. If you do that again, we're sending you somewhere else.'

I cry myself to sleep.

The next day, this nice smiley couple comes to take away the girl in the bottom bunk. They are going to adopt her.

'No one will want to adopt you,' says one of the care workers. 'You're too difficult.'

10

Jo

My heart thumps as I slide the ticket into the machine at Bristol Temple Meads station.

I wait for an alarm to go off or someone to come up and ask what the hell I am doing. But the ticket shoots out the other side and I nip through the barrier before it closes again. Penzance, here I come!

Keeping my head down, I make for the last carriage. Every seat is full apart from one. I plonk myself on that but a young woman comes up. 'This one's reserved,' she says, pointing to a slip of paper sticking out at the top. Groaning, I ease myself up and she takes my place. Snotty cow.

My legs are killing me after all that walking. I need to sit down.

'Can I help?' says a voice behind me.

My heart stops. It sounds just like ... I slowly turn round. 'May I see your ticket?'

It's the train inspector! Nervously, I hand it over. His eyebrows raise. He looks at me, taking in my old jacket and muddy trainers, and then back at the ticket. 'First class,' he says like he doesn't believe it himself. 'At the front of the train.'

'How long's the journey?' I ask.

'This one's four and a half hours.'

He doesn't call me 'madam', I notice.

The train has already pulled away. I stumble as I walk, clutching the sides of the seats. I pass a young child sitting on her mother's knee. 'Mum,' it's saying, 'why hasn't that lady got any hair?'

'Shhh.' The woman clasps her child protectively. 'Don't upset her. She's drunk.'

I want to tell her it's not true. It's hard to stay upright when the train is moving like this, especially when you're no spring chicken. But the smell of last night's wine is still on my breath.

The door ahead opens slowly, like it's reluctant to let me in. I stare around. Just look at those big posh plush seats! I take the seat nearest me at a table. An old bloke with grey hair is sitting there, reading a book. He lifts his head and stares. 'I haven't got two heads, you know,' I want to tell him.

He sniffs. The expression on his face suggests that he doesn't care for my company. I know I smell, but I can't help it. 'It's not like I can have a shower,' I want to say. He gets up and moves to another seat opposite.

He's left a cup of coffee behind and an open packet of sarnies. There's one half left. 'Excuse me,' I say, putting my hand out and touching his shoulder. He jumps as if I'm about to sock him one. 'Don't you want this?'

He shakes his head. Probably thinks it's dirty now I've breathed on it.

I wolf it down quickly. Ham and egg. My favourite. Quickly, before he changes his mind, I swig back the coffee even though it's too sweet. That's better. For the first time in days I feel almost stuffed.

My eyes begin to close with the comforting rhythm of the train. It's so warm and cosy here. I try to keep them open – I need my wits about me – but it's no good. I can't help drifting off again.

Even though I know it's dangerous.

Bramble or blackberry (*Rubus fruticosus*)
Believed to invoke evil spirits and also cure whooping cough. Beware of picking after Michaelmas Day or it's said that the Devil will get you.

II

Ellie

You're allowed to keep a certain number of personal possessions in prison (provided they're not a safety risk), but after a bit I handed in my watch for safe-keeping because I kept looking at it, which made the waiting worse. I hadn't realized it could take so long for a case to be tried.

The strange thing is that, when you're a child, you don't remember the separate weeks or the months so much as the seasons. By the time our central heating was installed, the daffodils were out and my little brother, Michael, had started to smile and giggle at me. When he learned to roll over, it was summer and, if I was a good girl, I was sometimes allowed to push him round the garden in the pram just as long as my new mother was next to me.

I always took care to avoid the crazy-paving bit on the patio because of the cracks. I couldn't get rid of the anxiety that something might happen to my little brother. I felt the same about my father and Grandma Greenway and even, I suppose, my new mother. After all, my real mother had died. What if death took away everyone else I loved? And Michael was particularly vulnerable because he was so small.

Even worse, I couldn't get rid of the fear that I might accidentally be responsible for something bad happening to one of them. Look how I had upset Mummy by asking why she didn't have another baby. It wasn't long after that when she got sick. I didn't dare mention any of these fears to my father or Grandma Greenway. Instead, I tried to be the best sister and daughter possible.

My new mother, to my excitement, sometimes allowed me to help out a bit. My best treat was helping to bathe little Michael after I came home from school. 'Careful not to get water in his eyes,' she would say as I dabbed rather enthusiastically with the sponge. Afterwards I would go upstairs and spend the evening with Grandma. 'Isn't Michael sweet?' I kept saying.

She sniffed. 'He's all right as far as babies go. It's not my favourite age. Mind you, they don't get much better when they're grown up.'

Then her lips would tighten and she'd stare at the television. 'Hah!' she'd snort. 'There's that group called Abba. Swedish they are.' She sniffed. 'Music doesn't sound like it did in my day.'

It was when the leaves on the trees turned gold that it happened. Michael had started to crawl. He was so quick! 'Just look how fast he can get from one side of the room to the other,' I would say to Grandma Greenway.

Sometimes, now, the two of us were allowed to be in charge of him while my new mother got dinner ready. 'Don't take your eye off him for a second, mind,' she'd tell us. And we didn't.

But then, one day when I was trying to do my long-division homework, I heard a cry from the kitchen. 'Help me, someone!'

I rushed in. Michael was making a strange noise. His

face was red. 'I don't know what's wrong!' screamed my new mother. Her face was all pale and she was holding him in front of her. 'What shall I do?'

Quickly, I snatched him, placed him over my knee and tapped his little back. Nothing happened.

'He's dying, he's dying!'

'No, he's not!' I yelled back. I wouldn't let that happen. I tapped again, using four fingers this time instead of three. He coughed and immediately a small black object shot out.

A raisin.

She'd been baking. That's where the raisin must have come from.

Instantly Michael looked the right colour again. 'You're all right, you're all right,' cried my new mother, snatching him from me and holding him against her.

Her eyes were still wide with terror. 'How did you know what to do?'

I was beginning to shake now, even though my little brother was safe. 'My first-aid badge at Brownies,' I stammered.

She began to cry. 'Thank you.' Then she blew her nose. 'The raisin must have fallen on the floor. That wasn't my fault, you know.' She glared at me as if daring me to argue back. I stayed silent. It was easier that way.

That night, when my father came home, he gave me a big, warm cuddle. 'You saved your brother's life today,' he said. 'We're very proud of you.'

When I went up to Grandma Greenway's sitting room after tea, I expected her to congratulate me too. Instead, she didn't even mention it until just before I went down to bed. 'You did well today, love. But there will be more occasions like this. Mark my words.'

I didn't like to ask my father what the old lady meant. Usually, he didn't have much time for me in the evenings anyway. Instead, he would always kiss my new mother on the cheek when he got in and ask if she was 'all right'. Then he would cradle Michael in his arms, looking down on him as if he couldn't believe he was actually there.

'My son,' he kept saying. 'My son.'

Eventually, he might ruffle my hair and ask me about my day and whether I'd been a 'good girl'.

'Yes, Daddy,' I'd reply, thinking about the homework I'd finished before tea and how I'd helped my new mother at Michael's bath time, making sure he was properly dry before we put him in his soft blue pyjamas that smelled of Dreft washing powder. Then we'd sit down together and I'd wind the key of my music box. He loved clapping his little chubby dimpled hands to the tune.

Later, after the accident, the people looking after me asked if I'd been jealous. The truth was that I wasn't. I loved Michael so much that it actually hurt inside. I'd have done anything for him. In fact, I followed him around constantly to make sure he didn't pick up any more raisins or small things on which he might choke. Brown Owl had given me a special badge for my uniform when she'd heard that I had saved my baby brother. I wore it with pride.

'That one deserves to be the mother – not you,' said Grandma Greenway to my father's wife when I was giving Michael his breakfast in the high chair and my stepmother was filing her nails at the kitchen table. 'The kid could have died if it hadn't been for Ellie. I've told you before. You've got to see the doctor about –'

'Stop your silly ramblings, right now.' Those two pink spots appeared on her face again just as they always did when she was angry. 'You don't know what you're talking about, Mother.'

Then she carried on filing her nails. My new mother hadn't wanted anyone else to touch my little brother in the early days. But since he'd almost choked, she was more than happy for me to look after him. 'She's lost her confidence,' said Grandma Greenway darkly. 'Now if something goes wrong, she can blame someone else.'

My tenth birthday came and went without much fuss. 'I'm far too busy to give her a party,' I overheard my new mother telling my father one evening. That wasn't fair! I'd be the only one in the class not to have one. Why hadn't Daddy stuck up for me and insisted? But at least I had Michael. He was the best gift ever.

By the time the daffodils came out again, my little brother had started to walk. This meant I couldn't take my eyes off him for a minute. He'd lurch from one piece of furniture to another, often falling over and bruising his knee. Then he'd burst into loud tears and my father's wife, who was usually 'trying to have a bit of a rest', would come running in.

'What have you done to him?'

'Nothing.'

'Don't be ridiculous, Sheila,' Grandma Greenway would say. 'Kids are always bumping themselves at that age. If you did your share of watching instead of always sleeping, you'd see that.'

'Shut up, Mother. Stop criticizing me all the time, otherwise you can go and live somewhere else.'

No! I couldn't lose Grandma as well. But as she and I agreed, there was no point in arguing. We just had to sit tight and let her rages blow over.

Yet – and I know this sounds dreadful – I sometimes wondered how much easier life would be if my new mother wasn't here and it was only me and Daddy and Michael and Grandma Greenway . . .

That woman back in the children's home was right.

No one wanted to adopt me. When I tried to run away again, I got sent to a stricter place. It had bars on the windows. We had lessons there too but I didn't pay much attention. All I wanted to do was grow up so I could get out.

And now, at last, I'm eighteen! I can live in a hostel. Do what I like without someone telling me what to do. I get a job in a supermarket, which is great 'cos it means I get a discount on my food bill. But the best thing is that the girls I work with are really friendly.

'Want to come clubbing with us this Friday?' they ask.

I don't tell them I've never been into a club before. They might ask questions and I don't want to tell them about being in care for most of my life. So I splash out my earnings on a sparkly dress and high wedges. 'Look at you!' says one of them and then I feel all embarrassed 'cos they're just wearing jeans.

When we get there, the music is so noisy that I can't hear what my friends are saying. Then they disappear into the crowd of dancers and I'm left feeling stupid. Maybe I ought to go home. Then this bloke comes up to me. He seems older than most of the boys here but maybe that's because he's got a beard and is big without being fat. He has a gold chain round his neck and he's dressed smartly too, with shoes that gleam in the lights. 'Can I buy you a drink?' he asks.

I don't tell him that I'm not much of a drinker because you'd really get it if you were caught in the children's home. So I ask for a gin and tonic as we sell a lot of that in the supermarket. He gets me what he calls a 'double'. When the last song begins, he pulls me towards him and kisses me. My first time! Some of the boys in the home used to try it on with me but I didn't fancy them. This one is different. Something inside me knows he's a man rather than a boy. It scares and excites me.

'My name's Barry,' he says when he finally pulls away.

Barry. I run the name round in my mouth. It sounds friendly.

'Want to come back to my place?' he asks, all casual.

'OK,' I say, trying to sound cool. The gin and tonic has given me a nice spaced-out feeling.

He has a flat of his own. I wonder how he can afford the rent but then he tells me that he's an electrician and earns 'good money'. My heart beats really fast when he starts to undress me. I feel so flattered that he wants someone like me, who's no one. 'How did you get these scars?' he asks when he undoes my bra and sees the marks on my back.

'My dad,' I say, like it doesn't matter. 'It was a long time ago when I was a child.'

His eyes narrow. I get a scared feeling running down me. 'Does he still hurt you?'

I shake my head. 'Haven't seen him for years.'

'Well, if I ever meet him, I'll give him what for.'

Then he runs his hands over my breasts. They're big hands. Capable, like they can do anything. 'You're beautiful,' he says. 'Stay with me. I promise I'll never let anyone hurt you again.'

The next week, I move out of the hostel and into Barry's place.

If only I'd known then what I do now.

12

Jo

'GET OFF ME!' I yell

I'm thumping my fists against the man's face. Scratching his cheeks with my fingernails. But he's wrapping the belt round and round my throat. I splutter. Choke. Gasp. I feel my face going hot and red. I can't breathe. I smash my head against his chest but it makes a metallic sound as if he isn't human . . .

'Are you all right?' asks a voice.

It's a girl with a trolley loaded with drinks and snacks.

My head is resting on the table. It aches. Had I been banging it again? 'Just having a bad dream,' I say, feeling silly.

She gives me a nervous smile and moves on. I try to pull myself together. The bloke who'd let me have his sandwich has gone. But there's a squashed Mars bar underneath his seat which I pocket for later.

Outside there are rows and rows of fields. No shops. There are cows too. Then a terrace of pretty cottages flashes by. What I'd give to live somewhere like that. It must be nice to have a place to call home, with your own front-door key.

I'm bursting for a pee so I walk down the carriage to the toilet, again clutching at the seats to stay upright.

Again, folk look away but I smile at them anyway, feeling really smug. I'm in first class. For once in my life, I'm as good as this lot.

There's a puddle on the floor. Hope the next person won't think it's me. I've still got my pride.

I wash my hands at one of those clever machines on the wall where you put your hands in and the soap and water come out automatically, followed by the dryer.

Then I stumble my way back to the seat just as the announcement comes: 'We are now approaching Penzance, where this service will terminate.' My heart flutters. I'd started to feel safe on the train. But now what?

I walk outside and the wind hits me. I thought it was cold in Bristol, but this is bloody parky. Even though it's only September, it feels like winter.

I walk up a little slope and then round a corner, past a supermarket. That's when I see it. The sea. It looks dark and scary. I shiver and force myself to look away.

There's a bus parked over the road. It says 'The Lizard' on the front. What kind of name is that? Still, who cares. I've got to get out of here.

I put on my 'help me' look for the driver. 'I've gone and lost my bus pass in town. I haven't got any money for a ticket back home and I don't know what to do.'

Tears trickle down my cheeks. It's not hard to make them come.

'Hop on, love. I shouldn't do this but I can tell when someone's in trouble. Just make sure you fill in one of these.'

I don't like forms. They scare me. 'What's this for?'

'To apply for a new bus pass, love.'

'Right. Thanks.'

The bus moves. I settle back in my seat. I've got enough food for a bit. Now all I have to do is find some shelter for the night.

But then what? I try to ignore that thought and settle down in my seat as the bus speeds up.

Buttercup (Ranunculus)
A flowering plant found in grass and meadowland.
Can be poisonous to both humans and animals.
    Just because something is pretty, doesn't mean it's safe.

13

Ellie

It was two weeks after my eleventh birthday. I'd been
allowed to look after my little brother on my own for a bit.
It was snowing, so we couldn't play outside like he wanted.
Instead, we were cuddling up together on the window
seat in the playroom, which had become our special reading place.

On that day, we were looking at the pictures from a
Peter Rabbit book that my father had bought him when
Michael suddenly leapt up and ran out of the room.

This wasn't unusual. He was a lively child and would
only sit for a short time. I followed him into the kitchen.

Earlier that day, I'd been helping my new mother to cut
up vegetables for lunch. 'Pass the cruet so we can flavour
them,' instructed my new mother.

'The what?' I asked.

Grandma Greenway let out a cackle. 'Come off it,
Sheila. You're getting too posh for yourself. Just say salt
and pepper like the rest of us.'

'Shut your mouth, Mother.'

I gasped. Once, before Mummy had died, we'd heard
someone say that on the street and she'd walked me on
briskly, saying that wasn't the way that nice people spoke.

Now there was no one in the kitchen. A sharp potato

knife lay on the table. My brother went straight for it as if he knew it was the one thing he shouldn't do.

'Put that down!' I shouted.

I tried to take it off him but his stubborn little fingers hung on. 'Michael!' I shouted. 'Give it to me.' I twisted it towards me.

Then he let out a terrible scream.

'Cut!' he howled.

'No you're not,' I said, even though I could see it was true. Blood began to drip onto the floor, but he was still hanging on to the knife.

'Hand it over,' I snapped and I tried to yank it backwards. It would serve him right if he got hurt now.

Then I heard footsteps running down the stairs. 'What is going on?' It was Sheila. 'Oh my God.' Her voice rose. 'Michael, are you all right? What happened?'

'Ellie.' Then he pointed at me accusingly.

'It wasn't my fault,' I protested. 'I was trying to get the knife off him before he got seriously injured. Ouch!'

I gasped as Sheila's hand lashed my cheek. 'You wicked, wicked girl.'

She was hysterical, which made my brother scream even more. Someone needed to do something. I went into a sort of remote-control calmness that didn't reflect the panic inside and rang 999. By the time we got to hospital, blood was everywhere. Michael needed three stitches.

'How did this happen?' asked the doctor.

'My stepdaughter,' hissed my new mother, pointing at me, 'stabbed my son.'

I butted in quickly. 'Nonsense. I was trying to get the

potato knife off him. It should never have been left out in the first place.'

'And whose fault was that?' Sheila said.

'Yours,' I spat back.

'Stop lying, Ellie.'

'I'm not!'

But as I spoke, I was aware that my cheeks were burning red with the horror of it all. It made me look guilty, however much I protested.

The doctor gave me a disapproving look. 'You're very lucky that your brother wasn't injured more seriously.' Then he turned to my new mother. 'Just make sure you keep an eye on him.'

She was furious all the way home. Strangely, she seemed more upset by the doctor's words than the cut on Michael's thumb. 'He implied it was my fault for not watching my own son. I ought to call the police.'

'Then why don't you?' I retorted.

'Maybe I will. Let's see what your father says, shall we?'

I was almost sick with fear, waiting for him to come home. I'd only been trying to stop Michael from hurting himself. Surely my father would believe me.

But when he got in, he didn't seem convinced. He looked both stern and sad at the same time. 'I want to believe you, Ellie, but this is serious. Are you jealous of your brother?'

'No. Of course not. I love him.'

My father sighed. 'Sheila thinks you cut him on purpose.'

My eyes filled with genuine tears. 'How could I do something like that?'

I tried to forget how, just for one moment, I'd thought it might serve him right. 'Just because Michael pointed at me doesn't mean I did something. He's a baby, for goodness' sake.'

I could see I'd hit home there.

Sheila was furious when my father declared that it seemed to have been a 'bit of a misunderstanding'.

'Our son needed stitches. Aren't you going to punish her?'

My father began to stride around the room, hands in his pockets. The corrugated-cardboard lines had sprung up on his forehead again. 'Very well, then. I'm afraid you can't have any pocket money for a month, Ellie.'

'What?'

'And you can't go on the school outing either,' chipped in my new mother.

'That's a bit harsh, don't you think, Sheila? It's educational.'

'Then she can't be allowed to go to that party instead.'

But I'd been looking forward to it for ages! Christine, one of my schoolfriends, had asked everyone in the class. Her mother had known my real mother and was always kind to me.

'And you can confiscate that music box of hers for a week too, Nigel.'

'I think that's unfair, Sheila.'

'Whose side are you on?'

'You're not having my music box and that's the end of it!' I yelled.

Then I ran up to my room in floods of tears and hid it carefully in the bottom of my chest of drawers. On the way,

I passed Grandma Greenway's room with the television blaring out. The door was ajar. I ran in, hoping for some sympathy. 'It's not fair,' I sobbed, throwing myself on her lap. 'I didn't mean to hurt Michael.'

'Shhh.' She put her arm round my shoulders. 'I know you didn't. But the thing is that my daughter was scared by the doctor.'

'Why?'

She sighed. 'It's complicated. The truth is that my Sheila has always been scared of anyone in authority. You see, the welfare people took her away from me once when she was a toddler, because I couldn't afford decent lodgings for us both. I had a devil of a job to get her back. After that I was terrified that someone might try to separate us again. And I think I've passed on my anxieties to her.'

Then tears started rolling down her plump red-powdered cheek. I'd never seen her cry before.

'Don't think too badly of Sheila. She means well.'

No she doesn't, I told myself. I hated her. If only she'd never married my father! Then everything would be all right. As for calling her 'Mum', there was no way I was going to do that any more. She'd only wanted me as a daughter until she had a child of her own. Michael could do no wrong. It wasn't fair. Inside, a slow angry resentment began to burn . . .

Not long after that, my brother fell out of his high chair when I was giving him his tea and had forgotten to strap him in. I'd only turned my back for a second but it was enough. He knocked his head on the corner of the table. I waited for him to cry but it was as though he had sucked in his breath and was holding it. Then his eyes seemed to go up to the ceiling and he went all floppy.

I kept shaking him, shouting out his name. Then a big bump sprang up on his head. Sheila came in and began to scream.

Forcing myself to stay calm like the last time, I dialled 999 for an ambulance but when we got to the hospital, Michael started running round like nothing had happened. The doctor said it was mild concussion but he wanted to know who had been looking after him.

Michael was too young to explain what had happened, of course. And – guess what – I got blamed again.

This time my stepmother did take away my music box. Not just for one week but for two.

'I hate you!' I shouted at her.

'Ellie, go to your room.' I'd never heard my father so angry.

'Don't you think you've overstepped the mark there, Sheila?' I heard Grandma Greenway saying as I went miserably up the stairs. 'The poor kid's mother gave that music box to her. It's downright cruel, taking it away. Besides, we don't really know what happened. Your Michael might be young but he likes to get his own way.'

'How dare you speak about your own grandson like that,' hissed my stepmother. 'Anyway, you're a fine one to dish out advice. It's amazing I'm still normal with the childhood you gave me.'

'But that's just it, love. Your head is all over the place. You can't pin your troubles solely on me. Maybe you should get some proper help from the doctor –'

'Get out of my sight.'

'Sheila!'

This was my father.

Then someone shut the sitting-room door. But I could still hear furious voices rising up from below.

That night, I cried myself to sleep. How could Daddy have let my stepmother take the music box away? He knew what it meant to me. It felt like it wasn't me and him any more. But him and her.

When I was finally allowed to have it back, there was a scratch on the side that hadn't been there before. I didn't say anything. What was the point?

Barry and I are going out to dinner. It's to celebrate our three-month anniversary. 'Do you like Chinese?' he asks me.

I'm too ashamed to tell him that when I was in the children's home, we used to go into the bins for the leftover Chinese cartons that the staff had for themselves and then lick them clean.

'Love it,' I say.

Living with Barry is brilliant! He says I don't need to work any more 'cos he earns enough. I miss the girls from the supermarket but I like keeping house for him. I'd always wanted a place of my own and I take real pride in keeping it clean. Sometimes, if I miss a bit of dirt, he gets funny with me, but that hasn't happened since last Wednesday.

Now we're going out for a special date! I feel so grown-up when the waiter sees us to our seats and actually puts a serviette on my lap. How fab is this?

Then Barry puts his hand across the table. I think he's going to hold mine but then I see he's holding a little blue velvet box. He opens it. Inside is a ring. 'It's a real diamond,' he says proudly. 'Will you marry me?'

I put my hands over my mouth and give a little shriek. Some of the people at the next table look across and begin clapping when they see the ring. It's like I'm a film star.

'Yes,' I say, my heart bursting with happiness. 'Yes, please.'

14

Jo

Bloody hell. This Cornwall's a big place! The bus goes through one village after another. Some of the houses are huge, with smart cars in the drives. There's council houses too, but much nicer than any I've seen before, with proper gardens in front instead of dumped sofas with foam spilling out and fridges with the doors off.

Brrr. I shiver, pulling my jacket around me. It's not warm like it was on the train. My stomach is rumbling too. I was going to save the Mars bar until later but I wolf it down. Then I begin to worry. What am I going to eat tonight? What am I going to do when the bus stops? Where am I going to sleep?

I close my eyes and imagine what my life might be like if I wasn't here right now. Then I jump with a start when the driver calls out. 'You're home now, love. Good luck. And don't forget to fill out that missing bus-pass form.'

'I won't,' I say. 'Ta.'

All the other passengers are walking ahead of me, carrying their shopping and nattering. It's like they all know where they're going. Apart from me.

There's a wooden signpost. It says LIZARD POINT. Not knowing what else to do, I follow the arrow down a lane and then along a narrow path. I can taste salt on my tongue. The sea again. It's really far below and even though there's a barbed-wire fence between me and the cliff edge, my knees start to quiver. The waves are even angrier than when I saw them in Penzance, as though they're trying to throw themselves against the rocks. The wind is so strong that I'm almost blown sideways.

'Go back!' screams a voice in my head. But I can see a café at the bottom of the footpath and I'm starving. That chocolate seems a long time ago.

I can hardly open the door in the wind. In my state, they'll probably throw me out before I can get in, I tell myself. But a pretty waitress with a big bust gives me a hand. 'Take a seat over there, love. We're about to close but you're in luck. We've got some soup left on special offer.'

I want to cry at her kindness. I have no money to pay for it, but I say yes anyway. Cream of mushroom! I gobble it down along with three thick slices of bread. It doesn't get any better than this.

'Anything else?' she asks when she takes my plate away.

I think of my empty pockets and shake my head.

'Why don't you take a look at the menu?' she urges.

I can't resist. My stomach is still gnawing. When you're thin like me, the cold makes you even hungrier. So I order a baked potato with beans and cheese. As I wait for it to arrive, I look outside. Rain has started. It's dribbling down the window like it's weeping.

The potato fills me to bursting but my chest feels heavy at the thought of finding somewhere out there to sleep.

'Bet it gets rough in these parts,' I overhear a man saying to the waitress.

'You can say that again. We had a couple that died here last year. They were trying to take pictures and a wave just came in and got them. Here one minute and gone the next.'

I shiver.

'Have you got a toilet?' I ask.

'I'm afraid you have to go out into the car park.

It couldn't be easier.

I make my way to the Portakabin marked 'Ladies'. As I come out I can see the waitress through the window. Her back is turned. It's now or never. I feel a twinge of regret, but I can't risk her calling the police because I can't pay. I start to run along one footpath and then another, bowing my head against the driving rain and feeling like shit. That girl was so nice to me. Now she'll be told off by her boss for losing money. Maybe she'll even get sacked.

I walk until it's too dark to see anything. Again and again, my feet almost slip in the mud. Anyone could fall off the cliffs here. I push through some prickly bushes with yellow flowers. Ouch.

There's a building at the top of the path. It looks like a garden shed with a rough metal roof, but there's a cross on the side. I head for the door. Please, be open. I turn the big round iron handle. Yes!

Inside, it is damp and quiet. Spooky. There is a single flickering candle in a glass jar. My eyes go straight to the wooden box on the left with a notice. 'Donations like yours mean we can keep our church going. Thank you.'

I could break it open. I can't pretend I'm not tempted.

I walk over and lift the box up. Coins slide around inside. But I can't do it. It doesn't feel right.

Instead, I settle myself down on one of the wooden pews. It's hard as nails but I pick up one of the cushions that people kneel on when they say their prayers and use it as a pillow. As long as I don't roll over and fall off, I'll be all right.

The wind is howling outside like a baby bawling. Rain beating on the roof. But I drift into sleep. I must have done because the next thing I know, sunlight is streaming in, forcing my eyes open.

A man in black is standing over me.

15

Ellie

Things weren't quite the same after that last awful row between Sheila and her mother. The two barely spoke, although Grandma Greenway tried. 'I've upset her by saying she should see the head doctor,' the old lady confided in me. 'Like I said, she's scared they might take away Michael like they did to her as a kid. Now she can't bear the sight of me.'

I tried to reassure her, but it was true. My stepmother acted as though her mother didn't exist. 'I think she's planning to send me away so I don't say anything else that might embarrass her,' whispered Grandma Greenway a few weeks later. 'I overheard her on the phone to someone.'

Surely not. When I told my father, he said I mustn't worry myself. 'Old people often get things wrong,' he said.

Soon came the day of my school trip to the British Museum in London, the one my stepmother had tried to stop me going on as a punishment. We all went on a coach, although I felt really out of it as the others were still chatting about Christine's party, which I hadn't been allowed to go to.

Then we went into a room with beautiful green-and-blue

pictures on the wall, made up of little stones. 'I've seen these before,' I exclaimed. 'They're mosaics.'

'That's right,' said our teacher. 'Well done, Ellie.'

Her praise – the first I'd received for some time – made me feel better inside. I spent ages looking at how the different stones had been put next to each other to make a picture. So clever! Then I thought of my mother's blue bowl. I could see the broken china in my head. Just like the cracks on the pavement, which must be avoided at all costs. And suddenly I had an overwhelming feeling that I needed to get home quickly to make sure everything was all right.

'I feel sick,' I told the teacher. It wasn't exactly a lie. My stomach was churning with nerves.

'I'm afraid we can't leave until the coach comes to collect us. Go and sit down for a while.'

It seemed ages before the day was over and we could make the return journey. Then we got stuck in traffic. I sat on the edge of my seat all the time, willing the driver to go faster. In my head, I kept seeing my mother's waxy figure in the undertaker's. But this time my father was lying next to her. What if he'd died, as my mother had done? I shouldn't have been such a bad daughter.

'Miss,' called out one of the girls. 'Ellie's throwing up.'

Too late, a bag was shoved in front of me. I was sick all down my brown pinafore dress.

'Poor you,' said the teacher kindly. 'Travel sickness, I expect.'

By the time the coach finally turned into the school playground, I'd been sick several times more. 'I'll need to find your father to explain,' said the teacher, looking at her list. 'I've got him down here as saying that he will be picking you up.'

But he wasn't there. My heart plummeted as if fear was sucking it out of my body.

Then Christine's mother arrived to meet me. 'Your father asked me to collect you. There's been a bit of trouble.'

I was so terrified that I could hardly get the words out. 'Is Daddy all right?'

'Yes, dear.'

Relief washed through me. That was all right, then. Nothing else mattered unless – oh no. 'Please don't say it's Michael . . .'

Her eyes were moist.

'Actually, it's . . .'

My stepmother, then? I know this was awful but for one moment, I imagined her not being there any more. We could go back to our old life, Daddy and me. We'd have Michael, of course, and his grandmother. The four of us could lead a happy life together without arguments or –

'I'm afraid Sheila's mother has been taken ill . . .'

No! I had a vision of the old lady sitting on the sofa next to me, as we cuddled up in front of *Coronation Street*. I'd grown to love her as the grandmother I'd never had.

'What's happened?' I cry.

'It's a bit complicated, dear. You might just see her if you're quick but –'

I broke off into a run, ignoring the cries of 'come back' behind me.

As I reached the house, I could see a white van outside. Grandma Greenway was being led in by a pair of nurses, one on either side of her.

'Where is she going?'

'To a special home for the elderly,' snapped my step-mother, who was standing on the doorstep, her arm firmly linked through my father's. 'About time too. Look what she did to me.' She pointed to her eye, which was red and bruised.

'Help me, Ellie!' came a feeble cry.

I ran back to her. 'Sheila's telling lies,' she said, clutching at my hands. 'She's sick in the head. I didn't touch her. They're sending me away. I'm telling you, Ellie. And if you're not careful, they'll do the same to you.'

16

Jo

The man staring down at me is wearing a black dress with a dog collar. But there's something different about him from other vicars I've met. He's wearing orange running shoes with bright-blue laces. And he's young with a nice face. I feel my heart start to slow down.

'Are you all right?' he asks.

I nod, wrapping my arms around me.

'You look cold,' he says. 'Spent the night here, did you? It's not that warm when there isn't a service on, I'm afraid.'

I nod again dumbly.

'Still,' he adds. 'It's better than outside. Pretty chilly for September, isn't it?' He rubs his hands. 'Now, what can I get you?'

Is this some kind of trick? Perhaps he's trying to buy time until he can call the cops. Maybe he thinks I'm dangerous. Perhaps he's right. Mind you, he doesn't look scared. This bloke's got guts. I'll give him that.

'Coffee perhaps?' He gestures towards a door I hadn't noticed before. 'We've got a new kitchen. Took us years to get the money but now it's up and running. Only instant, I'm afraid. Will that do?'

'Ta.'

My voice comes out as a croak. The freezing winds yesterday have got to my chest.

'Won't be a minute.'

I think about doing a runner but if the vicar is going to turn me in, I might as well have a hot drink first.

'Sugar?' he calls out.

This is getting even weirder.

'No thanks.'

He's back with a mug that has JESUS LOVES YOU written on one side. I turn it round so I can't see it.

'Not a Christian, then,' he says, noticing.

'Never done anything for me,' I mutter.

'I don't know.' He grins, nodding at my mug. 'You've got a drink out of Him, haven't you?'

I shrug. 'Suppose so.'

He produces a half-empty packet of biscuits. 'These are all I can find, I'm afraid. Plain, unfortunately. The jam ones always go first.'

I gobble them down.

'When did you last eat?' he asks.

I think of the meal I didn't pay for last night and feel a rush of guilt.

'Dunno,' I mumble, my mouth still full.

'Why don't I go to the bakery and get you something hot? You can stay here if you like.'

He's not offering me money to buy it myself, I notice. It's the way it works.

'OK,' I say, polishing off the last biscuit.

'When I get back,' he says, 'you can tell me a bit more about yourself.' His forehead goes all wrinkly like he's worried. 'You will wait here for me, won't you?'

Then he leaves. My body needs hot food. But what if I'm right and he's gone to get the cops after all? I feel a bit dizzy. Perhaps it's because I'm still stiff from the pew. I've slept in worse places, though.

I try the door where the vicar had got the biscuits. Maybe there are some more there. But he's locked it. That's when I notice the little plastic tree below a red-and-blue stained-glass window. It's got messages hanging down from each branch.

Please make my dad better, says one.

I feel a pang in my chest. The writing looks like a kid's.

There's a bowl next to it with little bits of paper and string tags tied to each one with a notice:

Feel free to write a prayer for anyone you know in need.

I've never been one for this kind of thing – although I've got a dim memory of lighting a candle for someone I once loved. Yet curiosity makes me read some of the other messages too.

Please make Sammie better.

I take a piece of paper, scribble some half-remembered lines and hang it up.

There's another message on the branch below. *Forgive me,* it says simply.

For what, I wonder. Suddenly, I don't feel comfortable in this place. I need to get out.

Then I hear voices. The vicar's back with the police! I should have gone when I had the chance.

The heavy door swings open, crashing into the wall and echoing into the rafters above. It's a crowd of young lads, hoodies over their faces. I hide in a corner between the prayer tree and the organ. I can't see them but I can hear all right.

'Where did you say they kept it?' demanded one of the voices. It was rough. Scary.

I shrink back even more.

'Here.'

This is another voice. It's gentler. 'But like I said, I don't think you ought to . . .'

There's a loud sound like someone has raised a stick or maybe an iron bar and bashed into something. A bit of wood flies towards me and lands by my feet.

'Look at that! There's got to be at least fifty quid if not more.'

'Quick, before someone comes.'

'I don't think –'

'Shut up.'

I feel a sneeze coming on. Pinching my nose, I manage to stop it although I can't help making a bit of a noise.

'What's that?'

There's a silence. I keep holding my nose, my heart thudding.

'Come on. Let's get out of here.'

The door slams. I wait for a few minutes to make sure they've gone. Then I stand up, my joints creaking.

Shit. They've broken open the collection box and nicked all the money. And now the vicar will think it's me.

I could stay here and explain what happened but will he believe me? Why should he? And even if I haven't got the money on me, he might suspect me of hiding it somewhere or perhaps having an accomplice who's run off with it.

He'll be here any minute. I've got to go.

I struggle for a moment with the latch on the door. The boys slammed it so hard that it seems to have stuck. Then I manage to move it.

The church clock strikes as I run out under a wooden arch. It feels like a bad omen. I belt it down a side lane – and come face to face with the boys. I nearly leap out of my skin. One is at least six foot three. He swaggers towards me and twists my right arm behind so that I yelp with pain.

'So there was someone in there after all.' His face is close to mine. He stinks of fags and booze. 'What are we going to do with you, then?'

17

Ellie

More months passed. The house was so lonely without Grandma Greenway. Even little Michael seemed to feel it. 'Gone,' he would say, holding his arms out on either side in the cute way he did when he'd finished everything on his plate.

Sheila had converted her mother's old bedroom into an extra playroom for Michael but in my head I could still see the red-and-black Spanish-bullfighter cushions on the sofa and hear the strains of *Coronation Street* and *Crossroads*.

I say 'Sheila' because after the knife and then Grandma Greenway being taken away I couldn't bring myself to think of her as my new mother any more.

'Why not?' asked my father. His voice had an edge of fear to it, as if I had just done something dangerous. He was looking older too, I noticed, with baggy skin under his eyes and even more corrugated worry lines on his forehead.

'Because she's not nice or kind like a mother should be. She's not . . .' I tried to search for the right word but there was only one that would do. 'She's not normal.'

We were out walking Michael at the time. He was swinging on our arms between us on the way to the playground. It was a Sunday morning and the church bells were pealing. Recently, Sheila had started going to church every week and if anything prevented her, like when Michael got a bad cold, she would snap at me for the smallest thing. Even when she did go, she'd be nice to me for a bit afterwards and then be unkind again.

Father and I took a while to get to the playground because I had to stop at each crack and slowly step over. I used to do this quickly to avoid being spotted and questioned. But now something told me I had to be particularly cautious.

'Why do you need to do that?' he asked.

Then I told him something I'd never told anyone before. 'Mum said we had to do that in order to stay safe.'

He gave a small sigh. 'I know she used to think that. But it's not exactly true, Ellie. Let me tell you something about your mother . . . She was . . . well, she wasn't very well.'

'I know that.'

'No. Before she got cancer, she was what we call "depressed".'

'What does that mean?'

'Your poor mother used to get very sad because, as you know, she wanted to give you a brother or sister.'

'Brother or sister. Brother or sister,' chanted Michael. He had started to repeat words like a parrot. One had to be careful.

Tears pricked my eyes. 'I miss her so much.'

A look of sorrow flitted across my father's face. 'I miss her too, you know,' he said softly. 'But if it wasn't for your new mother –'

'Sheila,' I corrected firmly.

Another sigh. 'If it wasn't for Sheila, I don't know what I'd have done. She's given us all a new lease of life, hasn't she?'

'How?'

He looked down at Michael, who was skipping along. 'You wouldn't have had your little brother if it hadn't been for her, would you?'

That was true. I stroked the soft flesh of his chubby hand.

'Let me tell you something about your . . . about Sheila.' He seemed to draw in a sharp breath. 'She was born in London during the Blitz. The East End, where she and her parents lived, was bombed heavily.'

I'd learned about this in history, one of my favourite subjects.

'Even though she was so young, during the war, it made her into an anxious child and she never grew out of it.'

'You grew up during that time too,' I pointed out.

'I was older – a teenager actually. Yes, it was frightening for us too but in my day boys weren't meant to show they were scared. Sheila had it worse than I did. She and her mother lost their home – in fact, they were lucky to have got to the air-raid shelter at the time. Her father was killed in action so she was brought up alone by Grandma Greenway.' He shook his head. 'Poor woman. I admire her.'

I thought of the story Grandma Greenway had told me about the welfare taking Sheila. Maybe it was best not to mention that.

'Then why did you send her away?' I protested. 'She was an old lady. She wanted to stay here, with us.'

'We had to, Ellie. The doctors said it was for the best.'

'Sheila wanted to get rid of her.'

'That's not true. She was simply worried about her.'

He spoke as if he was talking to himself. I thought back to when Michael had swallowed a raisin and Sheila had done nothing. It was as if she'd been frozen with shock. Then I remembered that Grandma Greenway had said something recently about her needing the help of a 'head doctor'.

'So you see,' my father continued, 'you've got to be nice to her. Please, can't you call her "Mum"?'

'No,' I said stubbornly. 'I can't. Not until she starts being kind to me.'

My father let out an exasperated sigh. 'She loves you, you know. It's just that she feels insecure because we have a past that she wasn't part of.'

'Then she should be grown up enough to understand,' I retorted.

'You've changed, Ellie,' my father said. 'You used to be kinder.'

He was right. Since they'd sent away Grandma Greenway, I'd felt angry and cross with everyone, even Michael. It seemed that he was the only one in our family who was happy. Yet everything had changed for the worse since he'd been born.

'Swing!' he now called out joyously, breaking off from our hands and running towards it.

I chased after him. Gently I helped him onto the special one for toddlers with a bar across the front. Then I pushed him.

'Not so hard,' said my father.

I hadn't meant to. The swing flew much higher than it usually did. Michael squealed with delight. 'More! More!'

I caught the swing as it came back and gave it a softer push.

'That's better,' said my father. He put his arm around me. 'I know this is a difficult time for you. You're probably nervous about starting your new school next month.'

'Not really,' I said, walking away and leaving my father to push Michael. Actually I couldn't wait to go to secondary school. The hours were longer and I also intended to sign up for as many after-school clubs as I could. Anything to get more freedom, away from Sheila.

When I came downstairs for breakfast the next morning, I saw my mother's special china tea cup and saucer on the kitchen table. It was a pretty design with a blue-and-yellow floral pattern. No one had used it since she had died, but now it had tea in it. I picked it up.

'What are you doing?' demanded Sheila.

'This belonged to my mother,' I said tightly.

'Well, everything here is mine now,' she said. 'And frankly, after what you did, I don't think you have any right to complain about anything. So don't go running to your father about this.' She raised the cup to her lips. 'Or you'll be sorry.'

I ran up to my bedroom, burning with hate. One day, I'd get my revenge on that woman, I told myself. Then I remembered one of the TV shows I'd watched with Grandma Greenway before they'd sent her away. It was really an adult programme but, as we both agreed, I was almost a grown-up now. It was about a stepdaughter who had hated her stepmother so much that she'd stabbed her in the bath. She'd been caught but, as we decided, cuddled up on the sofa together, she'd been too obvious.

If I were going to do it, I told myself now, I'd have to be much cleverer about it.

I start feeling sick in the morning soon after that. At first, I think it's the stomach bug doing the rounds but then my breasts get sore.

'You're up the spout,' says Barry.

I know what that means. One of the girls in the last children's home had got up the spout 'cos she'd had a thing with one of the boys. There was real trouble over that.

'How can you be sure?' I ask him.

'I know about this kind of thing.'

I'm worried he might be annoyed but instead he's pleased. 'Clever girl.' He gives me a hug. 'We might be able to get a council place now to save on the rent.'

'But I thought you said we had a lot of money.'

He won't look me in the eye. 'They've had to let me go at work because of cutbacks. It's OK. I'll get another job. Until then, we might have to sell that ring of yours to tide us over, but don't you worry. I'll get you an even better one before long.'

I don't mind. I'm having a baby! Now, at last, I'll have a real family of my own.

18

Jo

The youth towering over me has eyes like black bullets. Mean-looking with a crew cut. Blue-and-red skull tattoo on his neck with the words 'No Fear' underneath. Jumping from one foot to the other. Wired. He looks like he's high on something. That's when I notice the red penknife swinging from the belt round his low-slung jeans.

'You saw us just now, didn't you?' he snarled. His hooked nose is so close to mine that I can see the hairs inside.

Someone once told me that if you're threatened – like now – you've got to work out which one is the leader and go for him. Then the others will get scared and run. But he's bigger than me. I don't stand a chance.

'I won't say anything,' I plead.

Those cold eyes narrow. 'So you did see us, then?'

Too late, I realize I should have pretended I hadn't.

I begin to shake so that my teeth rattle. 'I'll tell the vicar that I smashed open the box if you want.'

'What vicar?' scowls the boy.

'The one who was here a few minutes ago,' I stutter. 'He's coming back with something for me to eat.'

'Better get out of here, then,' says one of the others. He's smaller with a long jagged white scar on his cheek.

His face is narrow and sharp like a little mouse. He looks too young to be doing this sort of stuff. He reminds me of someone. But I can't think who.

'What about her?' demands another, pointing at me. 'I don't trust her not to talk.'

I'd say anything – do anything – right now to get out of this in one piece. 'No, I won't,' I say. 'Promise.'

The skull-tattoo kid reaches down to his belt. 'Maybe we should show her what will happen if she does.'

My body won't move. I'm shit-scared.

'Leave her alone.'

This is the mouse boy.

'Why?' The older boy's eyes narrow. 'Fancy her, do you?' He hands him the knife. It's open and has a sharp gleaming blade. 'I said you had to prove yourself if you wanted to join us. Go on.'

'Please, no!' I howl. My legs give way and I slump to the ground.

Then I hear a scream. 'My knee! You fucking little bastard. Get him, boys.'

I look up. The kid who looks like a mouse has stabbed the ringleader. He's lying on the ground, blood oozing.

'Run!' yells my defender. 'Let's get out of here. Quick!'

I try to keep up, running behind him until my chest hurts so much that I have to stop. Down lanes, over fields and past a herd of cows. 'Keep going,' says Mouse Boy every now and then. At last I get to a wooden gate. I lean against it, catching my breath. The sea is in front of me. Waves are crashing against the rocks. I am sick with fear.

'Why did you help me?' I blurt out when I can finally speak.

"'Cos I don't like to see a woman getting hurt.' He glances down at the ground for a second. 'It reminds me of my mum. She had this boyfriend who'd beat her up sometimes. Didn't like me either. See this?' He points to the scar on his creamy brown cheek. 'He stubbed his cigarette end here when he was drunk, saying I was a "bloody Paki".'

I'm surprised he's telling me so much so soon. But maybe it's the shock. He could have been stabbed too for attacking the leader. We're both lucky to be OK.

'Didn't your mum stick up for you?'

'She said we needed him to pay the rent. We had a big row. I said I was going out to see friends and didn't bother coming back.'

'Your mum will have worried herself sick.'

He shrugs like it doesn't matter, though I can tell it does. 'Then she shouldn't have put him first, should she?' His voice is hard but it doesn't hide the pain. 'It's why I ran away from home. Been on the streets ever since.'

If I had a quid for every time I'd heard a story like this, I'd be rolling in it. 'I'm homeless too,' I find myself admitting. It's never wise to give too much of yourself away but something makes me need to show this kid he's not alone.

'Not that bad, is it?' he says. 'Just as long as you keep safe.'

I shiver, like someone's just trodden on my grave.

'How old are you?' I ask as we climb over the gate.

We're walking along together now. There's no fence along the edge of the cliff. The sea is far below. It would be so easy for one of us to fall over, or be pushed . . .

'None of your business.'

153

But – don't ask me why – I'd like to know more about this boy. 'Want to tell me your name, then?' I ask.

'Tim. What about you?'

I could make one up but what the hell. 'Jo.'

'That's my sister's name.'

'Where is she now?'

'Don't matter.'

He goes silent.

The path is even narrower now. I daren't look down.

'Where do you sleep at night?' I ask when we get onto more even ground.

'Ask a lot of questions, don't you? Anywhere. The best places have got a roof. Darren was good at finding them.'

'Was that the boy who told you to stab me?'

He nods. 'I met him a few months ago in Falmouth when I was looking for a place to sleep. He said I could come along with him and his mates. Then they wanted me to take all the risks. One time they got me to break into this news kiosk and nick the takings. The police came and I had to leg it. It was a close-run thing. After that, we went further south and started going to villages and breaking into church collection boxes. I was planning on leaving them anyway before you came along. But I wasn't going to let them hurt you like they did the other woman.'

'What other woman?'

A shadow passes over his face. 'Forget I said anything.'

'Well, I owe you one,' I say.

He nods. 'Too right.'

The land is sloping down now towards the sea. He starts to run, tripping on some branches that have been laid across it like the edges of a staircase.

'Careful,' I call out.

'What are you waiting for?' he yells back.

'I don't like the sea.'

'Scaredy-cat!'

I tiptoe in. It's shallow and I can feel the grit of sand between my toes.

Tim's splashing his arms and legs. 'Don't you want to get clean?' he calls out. He sounds like a parent rather than a kid. Being on the road makes you old before your time.

'How will we dry our clothes?'

He points up at the sky. 'Sun's out now, innit?'

It's OK for him. He's still got young bones. I daren't risk mine. Then he splashes me playfully. In seconds, he's gone from being a know-it-all to a little boy.

I find myself splashing him back and laughing. The sea is freezing but the kid is right. It does make me feel cleaner. The waves don't seem so fierce in this part of the bay. I sit down in a corner by the rocks and lean my head back in the water.

'Would madam like some shampoo?'

'Ta very much.' I say, holding out my hand. 'Pity I don't have any hair to wash.'

'No problem.'

Tim cups his hand to make a little bowl and chucks some seawater at me. 'Got you!'

I chase him on the sand for a few minutes and then stop. What am I doing? We sit side by side on the rocks.

'Hungry?' he asks.

It's been a few hours since the vicar's biscuits. I nod.

'There's some blackberries up there. Look. I had loads yesterday. Come on. Race you.'

He's there long before me, handing me a clutch of berries. They're sweet and juicy. I gobble them down, leaving dark-maroon stains on my still-damp jumper. 'Nice?' He's back to a kid now, wanting approval.

I nod. Then I do something I haven't done for a long time. I throw back my head and laugh like I'm never going to stop.

'What's so funny?' he asks.

'Nothing really,' I burst out between giggles. I don't like to look weak by saying it's relief. It's not every day you only just escape being stabbed.

Then I grab his hands and twirl him round and round in a circle, as if we're playing a kids' game.

'You're crazy,' he says as we fall in a heap on the ground.

Maybe. But for the first time in ages I feel free.

19

Ellie

My resentment towards my stepmother grew and grew over the following months until it began to burn inside me. Nothing I could do was ever right, whether it was washing up in what she called a 'slovenly fashion' or not making Michael put on his woolly hat when we went out in the garden to play during the chillier months. (The latter was difficult because he never wanted to wear it.)

The other thing that upset me was how Sheila always tried to keep my father to herself. When we were all together in the evenings, watching television, she would sit close up to him on the sofa, holding his hand and whispering into his ear. Sometimes I caught snatches. 'I can't wait for us to be alone tonight' was a frequent one.

One day, something happened that still makes my pulse race when I think about it.

Sheila had left out her bottle of 'anti-anxiety' capsules, as Grandma Greenway used to call them. Instead of being high up in the cupboard, it was on the kitchen counter, next to the large black teapot, in which some tea was brewing. My stepmother always waited five minutes before pouring. She was using that time right now to dress my little brother upstairs. All I had to do was cut open three capsules – maybe four for good measure – whip off the blue-and-white-striped knitted tea cosy and stir them into the tea.

I don't quite know what I intended to happen. I certainly didn't want to *hurt* her. It was like my hand just took over. And I suppose I let it. Sometimes you do things you can't explain afterwards.

When Sheila came back downstairs with Michael, I watched with a mixture of horror and anticipation as she placed the teapot on a pretty crocheted mat in front of her at the table and then sat down between me and my brother.

'I want some,' he whined.

My heart stopped.

But my stepmother seemed amused by Michael's demand. 'You're a bit young for tea, but why not. Let's get a spoon, shall we?'

As she turned to the counter, I pretended to fall, knocking the teapot over. It didn't break but the contents spilled over the table, dripping down onto the floor.

'You clumsy girl!' yelled my stepmother. 'You could have burned us.'

Poisoned, more like. But the guilt about having endangered my beloved brother's life made me apologize profusely.

Naturally Sheila made me confess my 'carelessness' to my father when he got back that evening. 'It was an accident,' I told him. 'I'm sorry.' To my relief, he seemed to accept that.

Sometimes I wondered what he even saw in her. She was always on at him about something she wanted.

'Why can't we have a new car?' she would say. Or: 'Everyone else has holidays abroad. When you married me, you said you'd look after me. You've changed.'

Later I wondered if it was because she felt guilty for getting rid of her mother. When you do wrong, you try to blame others. I know all about that.

One evening there was a particularly loud argument. Michael and I were in his bedroom. I was trying to do my homework while babysitting my brother as instructed so my 'parents' could have dinner in peace. But my father had got back later than usual and the meal was, according to Sheila, 'completely ruined'.

Their raised voices floated up from downstairs. 'Of course I was working. Where else would I have been?'

'I don't know. You tell me. With your fancy woman, perhaps?'

'Sheila, I don't have a fancy woman, as you put it. Just because your father –'

'STOP! I don't want to talk about that. How dare you bring it up. No wonder I . . .'

On and on it went. Michael began to whimper. 'It's all right,' I said, cuddling him. Even though part of me felt jealous that he had such a happy life, I didn't want him upset. 'Would you like to turn the key on my music box all on your own?'

I'd never let him do such a special job before. Carefully I helped his chubby little fingers. But after a while he got bored and we played with his train set instead.

Eventually the voices died down but I used the opportunity to get my father on my side. 'Sheila's so unkind to accuse you of seeing someone else,' I said. 'I know you'd never do anything like that.'

He seemed shocked that I'd even raised the subject. 'Of course not.'

'It's just, well . . .' I said quietly. 'I didn't know whether to say anything, but now I think you should know . . .'

'What, Ellie?'

'I heard Sheila talking on the phone to someone the other day. She kept telling him how much she needed him.'

This was only partly true. Her words had actually been 'how much I value your opinion'. But a little exaggeration never did any harm. Did it?

My father frowned. 'Really?'

To my delight, this led to another big bust-up that night. It woke up Michael. In the morning, my father came down in his blue paisley-print dressing gown, humming and looking much happier than he'd seemed for a long time. I knew it! He'd decided to leave her at last.

'You know that conversation you overheard with Sheila,' he said quietly.

I nodded excitedly.

'She was talking to the doctor about changing her medication. The poor darling told me more things about her childhood last night, which explains why she gets so upset sometimes. We both need to make allowances for her.' He patted my shoulder. 'I know you'll do that for me, won't you?'

I nodded and tried to look kind.

'And, Ellie.' He looked at me seriously. 'Don't ever make up things like that again. I know you find things hard sometimes, but I can't have you lying. Sheila is my wife.'

I expected Sheila to be even more horrible to me after that. After all, I'd been caught out. But instead, she seemed calmer, and actually started being a bit nicer to me, which made me feel even more embarrassed. Maybe it was something to do with these new tablets. The problem was they also made her drowsy and forgetful. Once she left Michael in the bath unsupervised. Luckily I heard him crying and got him out. She made me swear not to tell my father. I agreed to keep the peace because I knew that, if I didn't, she'd find a way of being horrid to me again. Later, I wished I hadn't.

Still, at least I was old enough to be able to get out of the house now.

'I'll be late tonight,' I announced one morning before leaving for school. 'It's craft club.'

My stepmother frowned. She didn't like it when I wasn't around to help out with Michael's dinner.

In fact, I wasn't going to craft club at all. I was visiting Grandma Greenway. The home they had sent her to was near my new school, which was handy. At first she seemed to like me popping in but recently her speech had become rather rambling and her words often merged into sentences that didn't make sense.

'I'm afraid we're a bit confused today,' said one of the care workers as she led me through the lounge where elderly people were dozing in chairs, heads down, watching *Game for a Laugh* on television.

Mrs Greenway was doing neither. She was sitting in a chair with her eyes staring straight ahead at a blank wall as though she could see something that the rest of us couldn't. When I approached, she looked up at me, her face suddenly lighting up.

'You've come to visit me, love! Thank you. I knew you wouldn't forget me.'

It was so good to see her again!

'Do me a favour, Ellie.' She reached down for her handbag. 'My mitts are too stiff to put my make-up on any more. Dab a bit of rouge on my cheeks, would you?'

It was just like the days when I'd help her with her perm rollers. Gently I took the brush, encrusted with powder, and drew a stripe across each cheekbone. 'Very professional!' she said, admiring her reflection in the little black hand mirror she carried everywhere.

'I learned how to do it in *Jackie* magazine,' I said proudly.

'Did you now?' She patted my arm. 'You're becoming quite a young lady, aren't you?' Then her voice dropped. 'I'm very proud of you. You've handled yourself well in a difficult situation. But just remember: don't let that daughter of mine get you down. It won't be long until you're grown up and can live your own life.'

Her words brought a lump to my throat. I gave her a quick hug. I almost confided in her then about the pills I'd put in the teapot – I still felt bad about that – but then the nurse came round saying it was dinnertime. So early! It was only 5 p.m.

'Come again, won't you?' Grandma Greenway grabbed my wrist with her bony fingers. It hurt but I didn't like to say anything. 'Sheila makes out that I'm going soft in the head but I'm not. She just wants me out of the way.'

Then she began to cry. I watched, horrified, not knowing how to comfort her. I tried putting my arms around her but she cried even more.

'Maybe you'd better go, dear,' said the nurse after a bit.

I felt awful, leaving her. There'd been genuine desperation in my old friend's voice. It didn't seem right she should be there. How could Sheila just get rid of her own mother like that?

I was deep in thought as I walked home – I still took care to avoid the pavement cracks – when I heard a voice calling out. 'Ellie?'

It was Peter Gordon. We were still in the same class at school and he sat next to me in history, although we didn't say much to each other. Even though we used to play together in the juniors, I felt too embarrassed to chat in a familiar fashion now we were older. It was that stage when boys and girls feel awkward about talking to the opposite sex while at the same time feeling a certain attraction. He was a tall, thin boy with a mop of dark, glossy hair. Everyone admired him for being in all the sports teams, including tennis and athletics, which were hard to get into.

'I didn't see you at crafts club, did I?' he now asked me.

'No.' I hesitated. 'But don't tell anyone. I don't want my stepmother to know where I went instead.'

He raised his eyebrows. 'I won't.' Then he flushed. 'Were you, er, with someone?'

Surely he didn't think I had a boyfriend? One or two of the girls in my class had started 'dating', as they called it, but no one had ever shown any interest in going out with me. In fact, I didn't know what I'd do if they did.

'No,' I said quickly. 'I was visiting someone who wasn't well. But I knew Sheila wouldn't approve. That's why I need you to keep quiet.'

He smiled. 'You've got my word on that.'

We walked on in silence, but it wasn't an awkward one. It felt rather nice to have confided in him.

'See you tomorrow at school, then,' he said when we reached my house. His house was on a road near ours.

'Yes,' I said. Then, because I didn't know what else to say, I repeated his words. 'See you.'

When I got in, my father was there. He was usually home much later.

'What's wrong?' I asked, my heart sinking.

Sheila was crying.

'Did you leave this out on the kitchen table?' he demanded.

I stared at the bottle of tablets he was holding. The same one that Sheila took out of the cupboard every morning.

'No. Of course not.'

My father looked relieved. 'See, Sheila? I told you she wouldn't. Ellie's much too sensible for that.'

My father's wife had stopped weeping now – I knew they were crocodile tears. Instead, her eyes were blazing. 'It wasn't me. So who else could it be?'

My little brother was playing on the ground with his train set, as if nothing was wrong.

'What happened?' I asked.

My father shook his head. 'I came back home early to find Michael holding the bottle of tablets. If he'd managed to open it, he could have taken some.'

'And you think it was me?'

'You know it was,' hissed Sheila.

I almost told my father then about her forgetting that Michael had been in the bath. But what was the point? She'd only deny it. There was no way I would have left those tablets out.

In that moment, I truly hated her. I looked at my father. 'Who do you believe?' I asked.

I'd put him in an impossible position and I knew it.

'I don't know,' he said slowly.

Sheila burst into another flood of tears. 'You've no idea how difficult my life is, Nigel. I can't cope with her. I've tried my best but she doesn't love me. Look how she won't even call me "Mum". I've had enough.'

'We'll discuss this later,' said my father firmly.

That was usually his way of putting something off. Hopefully by then Sheila would have got over it.

But later, when I'd had my bath and came down to get a glass of water to take to bed, I heard them arguing through the sitting-room door.

'Come on, Nigel. You're not blind. Ellie's been nothing but trouble since Michael was born. Something needs to be done about it. Or goodness knows what might happen.'

'I think you're exaggerating, dear.'

'Don't you dare accuse me of that. Your daughter is a liar – just look what she said about me being on the phone, and then the tablets. Surely you don't believe I'd have left the bottle out? She's a danger to our son. I can't live under the same roof as her any more.'

'No, Sheila . . .' My father's voice was cracked with anguish. 'Please don't leave.'

Yes! I felt like punching the air in victory. Of course I'd miss Michael, but at least I'd have Daddy to myself again.

'Well, that depends on you.'

My stepmother's words made me shiver.

'I have a solution that I think will be better for all of us,' continued Sheila. 'Ellie too.'

'What do you mean?'

My father's voice was so low that I had to strain to hear him.

'I think we should send Ellie to boarding school.'

What? I didn't know anyone around here who went to one of those places. How could they even think of packing me off to live with strangers?

'Surely you can't be serious. Ellie's already lost her mother. I can't let her lose me too.'

'You won't. There are holidays.'

'But I've told you enough times about how I went away to school myself and I was desperately homesick. I can't do that to her.'

'It gave you a good education, didn't it? She'd get a chance that *I* never got in life.'

'That's not everything, Sheila. And I love you just the way you are.'

'Then back me up on this one, will you?'

I could sense my father floundering. 'We need every penny from the sale of your house for your mother's care home. And no one can touch Ellie's trust fund from her grandfather.'

What was a 'trust fund', I wondered.

'We just can't afford it, Sheila.'

My heart soared with relief.

Then I heard her again. 'Actually, that's not true . . .'

My stepmother sounded silky smooth. 'I've been looking into it. The council funds places for children with behavioural issues. I've found a boarding school that takes a certain number of children like her a year.'

'But there's nothing wrong with her!'

'Then you must be blind. I know she's your child,

Nigel, but you have to face the truth. There's something that's not right about her. The doctor thinks so from what I've told him about the knife incident, and her jealousy of Michael. He's happy to give a reference. It's up to you, Nigel. Don't you want to help your daughter? Because if you don't, I wash my hands of you both, to be honest. Either Ellie goes to boarding school and gets the professional guidance she needs, or else I go. And I will take Michael with me.'

20

Jo

'Better get a move on,' says Tim, picking himself up from the sand and making his way up the cliff path. I have to rush to keep up with him.

'The tide will be in soon. It can be dangerous, you know.' A dark look crosses his face. 'Like those people the other month. Got drowned, they did, sitting on the beach and taking pictures with their mobiles.'

I drop my arm, thinking back to the story I'd heard the waitress tell. Could that have been the same couple?

All of a sudden, my happiness disappears like it's got a puncture.

'Did you see them?' I whisper.

He nods. 'Cool phones they were. Got quite a bit for them.'

'You stole them?'

He shrugs. His voice is flat now. The way it is when someone's done something wrong but won't admit it – not even to themselves.

'They got swept back in after.' He shrugs. 'Don't look at me like that. Wasn't like they could use them any more, was it?'

I remember the London lootings in 2011. But this is worse. It's no better than robbing a grave.

I've got this kid wrong. I'd thought he was good. Hadn't he rescued me from being stabbed? But he's an animal.

Just like me.

We walk on in silence.

'C'mon,' he says when the sky begins to darken. 'We've got to find somewhere to sleep. Find a bed to lay your head or else you're dead. Get it? It rhymes.'

'Not bad.'

He shrugs as if it's nothing but he looks pleased. 'I like making up poems.'

How can someone be a poet and pinch phones from a dead couple? I don't really want to be with this kid any more but I have to be practical. He knows this part of the world and I don't.

'Look,' he says, pointing ahead.

There's a weird shape on a hill like a really high tower and no other buildings around it.

'What is it?'

'An old tin mine.'

I've heard stories about those. Makes me shiver, thinking of the poor souls who had to go down there.

He breaks into a run. 'Got to get there before anyone else – then we can say it's ours.'

The thing ahead looks like a ruined, tall, narrow brick building, black with age, with only half the side of a chimney remaining, pointing up to the sky like a warning finger. As we get nearer, I can see it's surrounded by tufts of grass and gorse and broken flint.

Goosebumps begin to break out over my body. I have a bad feeling about this. 'Is it haunted?' I ask.

'Don't be bloody daft. It's only an engine house.'

'What's that when it's at home?'

'They used to put the engines there – the ones that pumped water from the mines. Not much left now but it's better than sleeping outdoors. Look, it's raining.'

It's true. The weather has turned again. It can't make up its mind – a bit like me. 'I don't know,' I say, tripping over a pile of wooden planks and iron bars that are lying on the ground.

The kid makes a face. 'Suit yourself. I'm going in.'

Then he's gone. Just like that.

'Where are you?' I call. 'Come back.'

But there's no answer.

Foxglove (*Digitalis purpurea*)
The markings on the petals are said to show where
elves and fairies have placed their fingers. Leaves used
to be placed in children's shoes to ward off scarlet fever.
But contact with bare skin can cause rashes, headaches
and nausea.

21

Ellie

'You see,' said Grandma Greenway when I visited her in the summer holidays that first year. 'I knew they'd get rid of you. Just like they did to me.'

This was one of her more lucid moments. We were sitting in a large room with bright windows overlooking fields. Around us elderly women, and a man wearing a yellow-spotted cravat, were either dozing in their chairs, heads down, or staring at a blank television as if they were hoping it would magically spring into life.

When I'd first got here, my old friend had been doing the same, but within a few minutes of my arrival she'd perked up considerably. Her neck, which reminded me of a turkey with all those folds of loose skin, rippled as she spoke. 'What's school like, then? Give us all your news!'

I thought of the red-bricked building overlooking the sea in a coastal town not far from Exeter. The other girls had all been there for a whole term before I'd joined after Christmas so they'd already formed their friendship groups. None seemed keen to admit a newcomer – especially one who was as awkward and gauche as I was. They all seemed so much older and more confident than my friends back home. They also appeared to come from wealthy families: many had ponies of their own and spoke of 'second homes' in France or Italy or Greece. Only a handful, like me, had full grants. We were known as the 'free place' girls and were ignored or teased.

'It's all right,' I said, in reply to Grandma Greenway's question. Already boarding school had taught me to hide my emotions. But at night, in the dorm, I would weep quietly into my pillow, wondering what life would have been like if my mother had lived.

How I missed the noisy, warm familiarity of my old school. No one had had airs or graces there. People made a space for you at the lunch table instead of telling you with a stony face that it was 'full'. Still, there was one advantage at the new one. There were more sporting opportunities, even for people like me who weren't naturals.

'I'm in the hockey team,' I added. 'And netball too. It's only the C team, but it's something.'

Her eyes went dreamy. 'Wish my legs could run again.' She looked down at her wheelchair. 'I don't really need this but I'm so slow now that they say it's easier for the staff to get me around.'

That's when an idea came to me. 'Would you like me to take you for a walk round the grounds?'

She looked as if I had just given her a present. 'You're a good girl. Haven't been outside since autumn.'

That was awful! 'Doesn't Sheila visit?'

There was an indignant snort. 'Too busy with the child to bother with her old mother.'

I wasn't sure that was true. Since I'd come back for the holidays, I noticed that my stepmother seemed to spend a lot of time 'resting' and telling me to look after my little brother, who was four now. But I didn't like to say anything to the old lady. It couldn't be easy to be neglected by your own daughter.

Gently, I put a blanket round her shoulders and pushed her out of the French windows onto the top lawn. Luckily there was gravel rather than pavement with cracks.

'Any boyfriends, then?' she asked eagerly as we turned a corner past some bright-red roses.

The question was so unexpected – and unrelated to our previous conversation – that I took a few seconds to reply.

'Come on. Don't be shy. I had a beau at your age.' She sniffed. 'Much good that did me, mind.'

'Tell me about him,' I said, hoping to distract my old friend from her original question. But I'd forgotten how sharp she was.

'So you have got a boyfriend, then! Don't deny it! Tell us who it is. Lives near your new school, does he?'

I felt myself flushing. 'No. He's from here. Actually, he's just a friend. I've known him since I was small. His mum was a friend of my mother's'.

Grandma Greenway's eyes were glittering with excitement. 'Go on. What's his name?'

I was burning red now. 'Peter.'

Just saying it out loud made me feel like a bit of a fraud. Peter was just someone I'd always known.

'Does he write to you?'

'Yes,' I said, flushing madly. I'd been really surprised when I'd received a letter from him soon after I'd started my new school. *Just thought I'd see how you were getting on*, he'd put. Perhaps his mother had made him send it. So I wrote back telling him that it wasn't that bad. Then he'd written again, describing football matches he'd been in and the school's new Debating Society, which he'd joined. He'd sign off with only his name. There was no 'love' or anything like that. But I looked forward to getting something in the post along with my father's weekly letters.

'Bet the other girls are impressed by that.'

'I don't tell them.'

'Then you must.' Grandma Greenway thumped the arm of the chair, scaring a little brown bird that had perched on a twig beside us. 'You'll get more friends then. Girls are like that. They'll see you as one of the crowd.'

Really? I couldn't imagine that happening. When I'd mentioned that my mother was dead, they'd kept their distance even more. Being different wasn't good.

'I expect you'll be seeing your Peter now you're home, will you?'

I flushed again. He wasn't 'my' Peter but it felt nice to hear it. 'We're meeting up to read some poetry, actually.'

'Ha!' Her turkey neck was bobbing with laughter. 'Still use that excuse, do they? Sheila's father got me that way. Then look what happened.'

I remembered what I'd been told about Mr Greenway being killed in action during the war. 'I'm sorry. It must have been awful for you when he died.'

'Died?' Her eyes suddenly went hard. She thumped the side of her chair and her voice turned heavy with bitterness. 'Michael didn't die. He just buggered off after the war broke out in case he got called up.'

At any other time, I'd have been shocked by the swearing. But I was more taken aback by something else. 'Michael?' I repeated. 'But that's what my brother's called.'

Grandma Greenway snorted. 'Named after his grand-father. Ridiculous sentimentalism. The bastard – excuse my language – left me pregnant. It's all right nowadays. Single mothers can get away with it. But back then, no one would talk to me. The kids at school bullied Sheila too. Why else do you think my girl has got such a chip on her shoulder? "Illegitimate" was a dirty word. No one wanted to be born on the wrong side of the blanket in those days. Then, like I said before, she got sent to a foster home 'cos I was struggling to put a roof over our heads until I fought to get her back.'

Did my father know all this?

'Don't you tell anyone, mind,' added the old lady, as if reading my mind. 'I should have kept my mouth shut. Sheila would kill me if she knew I'd blabbed. But I warn you. It's made my daughter all prim and proper so she can get as far away as possible from her past. If she does some-thing she shouldn't – even a small thing – that girl will always deny responsibility. Like that time with the tablets you told me about.'

I was still really smarting about that.

'Well, now you know why she is as she is.' Mrs Greenway let out a deep sigh. 'It was all my fault she didn't have a dad, wasn't it? She didn't ask to be illegitimate and get turned away by society. Messed up her head, it did. So we have to make allowances.'

Did we? I could hardly take it all in. It seemed like she couldn't stop talking.

'When Sheila met your dad, she thought all her prayers had been answered. Been trying to get the right man for years, she had. She was always jealous of your mum. Used to say that she wished she could be like her, with a handsome husband and a little girl.'

I have a sudden memory of Sheila coming round one weekend, asking if my father could help with a leaky drainpipe. My mother hadn't been very pleased because it was right in the middle of our Sunday lunch. I also remember how, after the marriage, Sheila had given away my mother's old clothes my father had kept – he'd been quite upset about that – and changed all their bedroom furniture.

'But I knew things would go wrong. It's her childhood, you see.' Her voice trails away. 'There are some things you never get over.'

She stopped. Her dry, old hand reached over for mine. 'Just be careful, Ellie. That's all.'

Then her head dropped. 'I feel tired now. Can you take me back? There's a good girl.'

When Liam's born, Barry weeps like a baby. 'You've given me a son,' he sobs, holding me to him.

'Careful,' I say. 'You'll squash him.'

He moves away. His eyes are wet. 'I'm going to do my best by you both. Honest.'

He does and all. Least, that's what it seems at the time. Barry gets another job on a building site. I have to keep the baby quiet at night 'cos he has to get up early in the morning. He's always back in time to help me get Liam to bed apart from Fridays. That's when he returns late, stinking of booze. Usually he's got a wodge of money on him, which we need for the rent and food. But one night, I can't find it in his jeans pocket. 'Where's your pay packet?' I ask.

'That's my bloody business,' he says.

Barry only swears when he's had too much booze.

Then he grabs me, shoving his hands down my knickers. 'It's not safe,' I tell him. 'It's the wrong time of the month.'

But the drink doesn't let him listen. The kid's screaming from the cot as he throws me onto our bed.

The next month I'm pregnant again.

'You should have been more careful,' he tells me.

'It was your idea!' I shout back. 'How are we going to manage with another mouth to feed?'

'I've got a job, haven't I?'

'It's not enough,' I snap. 'We can hardly pay the rent, let alone the food bills.'

His face is close to mine. I try to move away but he holds me. 'Not good enough for you, am I?'

His other arm is raised. I begin to shake. Barry's never actually hit me before.

'Of course you are,' I say, stepping away. 'We'll manage somehow.'

But the next month, he rocks up at lunchtime on Friday. Drunk as a lord. 'You're early,' I say.

He laughs. It's not a nice laugh. He sounds bitter. 'Let us all go, didn't they? The bastards cancelled the next building project.'

A coldness passes through me. 'What are we going to do?'

'Go on the dole again until I get another job.' He takes a swig out of the vodka bottle he's got in his hands. Then he puts it down and starts snoring. I move it quickly out of Liam's reach. He's beginning to toddle now and is into everything.

But when I finally get him down to sleep, I find the bottle staring at me. Before I know it, it's empty.

22

Jo

I put my hands out to feel the walls. I can't see anything. I stumble and let out a scream. It echoes round me.

'Tim?' I cry.

'Tim? Tim?' repeats my voice.

I feel steps beneath me. One, two, three. There's a very faint light ahead. My breath catches in my throat. I turn a corner . . .

'Found me, then.'

I jump. 'You scared me!'

The kid is sitting cross-legged on the ground, grinning. He's getting a fire burning. 'Look what I found here! A box of matches. Dry 'n' all. Look – there are all these bits of wood too.'

Anger makes me sharp. 'Why did you go off and leave me?'

'Thought you'd follow. And you did, didn't you?' He pats the space beside him. 'Make yourself at home.'

I'm not sure. 'Is it safe?'

'Seems OK. They filled in these mines years ago. It won't give way.'

How does he know?

Then I feel something hard on the ground next to me.

'Look,' I say excitedly, forgetting my annoyance. 'It's a two-pound coin!'

He shrugs. 'That won't go far.'

'What do you mean?' I'm clutching it safely in my hand. 'We can get a loaf of bread with this and maybe something else too.'

'Or we could nick food for free.'

'And get done?'

He shrugs. 'Hasn't happened to me yet. What about you?'

I can still hear the slamming doors. See the angry faces. 'Don't want to talk about it.'

'Suit yourself. Want something to eat?' He reaches into his pocket and pulls out some mushrooms. 'Picked these on the way.'

'Are they OK?'

He rolls his eyes. 'I can tell you're a townie. So where do you come from?'

'All over the place.'

'Like that, is it?'

'What do you mean?'

'Well, I told you about my mum and her old man. How long have you been on the road?'

I shrug. It's hard to keep up with time. 'A few years.'

'Me, I've been doing it since I was eleven.' He says it like it's a competition.

'Why didn't they put you in care?'

He looks pleased with himself. 'Kept my head down, didn't I? Made sure I didn't get caught. Don't look so shocked. There are loads of kids out there like me. You think they care about us?'

'How old are you now?'

I'd asked him before and he'd told me it was none of my business. But now he seems comfortable enough to tell me.

'Fourteen.'

He ought to be at school, living with his mum. She should have left that boyfriend of hers. But if there's one thing I've learned, it's that nothing happens in the way you think it should.

'Didn't you have any other family you could go to?'

'Don't know where they are. My mum had me when she was a kid herself and her parents threw us out.'

The rain is dribbling now into the shaft through a crack above. My clothes are still damp from the sea and I shiver. 'How did you manage before you fell in with that gang?'

He wipes his nose on his sleeve. 'Slept wherever I could. Sometimes it was an empty building or one of those crisis places. Trouble with them is that you can't stay long 'cos they start asking questions. If they knew how old I was they'd hand me in. I can't get a job 'cos I'm too young. The only thing to do is move on.'

He puts his hands out towards the fire to warm himself and I do the same. 'What happened to you after you got out of prison?' he asks.

'How did you . . . ?' I turn away, thinking of the man in my nightmares, and breathe out loudly as though to get rid of him.

'How did I know?' he says, finishing my sentence. 'You get to spot the signs when you've been on the road as long as me. Touched a nerve, have I?' He reaches into his pocket. 'Want some of this? Might calm you down.'

Is that a joint?

'Thought it might have got damp but it's not too bad.'

I turn away. 'No, thanks.'

He wipes his nose on the back of his hand. 'Well, I like to keep the shit out of my head and this helps.'

He strikes another match, lights up and inhales deeply. It's a sweet smell. I can't help breathing some in myself. 'Go on, then,' I say. He hands it over for a draw.

We sit for a bit with our thoughts and then he talks again.

'When I'm on the road, I'm free,' he says suddenly. 'I'm just me. It's the way I like to be.'

'You're talking in rhyme again.'

He grins. 'I like poetry. Haven't got anything to write it down on so I keep it in my head. Want to hear more?'

He starts before I can even say yes.

'I used to live in a house. My best friend was a mouse.'

He turns to me. 'It's true. My mum had to have the pest catcher in.' His eyes look soft for a second. 'I still miss Squeak. It's what I called him.'

'That's sad.'

'No – it was all right!' The kid's eyes gleam. 'I caught Squeak before they found him and let him go. I wrote a poem about it. But I left it at home.'

I take another puff. 'How do you make up this stuff?' I ask. I don't have the heart to tell him that, in my view, they're rather childish.

He shrugs like it's no big deal. 'I think of something that makes me happy or angry. Then I find a word that goes with it. After that, I go through the alphabet to match the sound. So if I think of "bat", I go "cat", "dat", "fat" and so on until I find something that works.'

I giggle. The spliff is making me feel light-headed. 'Like the fat bat was chased by the cat?'

'Kind of, but that sounds like rubbish, if you don't mind me saying.'

'Piss off.'

We both giggle.

'How about we play a game?' I suggest. 'What rhymes with "run"?'

'Sun,' he says.

'Great. Now you.'

'What runs with "chase"?' he says.

'Face,' I say. Then I get a flash of an angry, furious face, close to mine. Arms raised to hit me. Purple veins bursting on his forehead.

'What's wrong?' asks Tim.

'Nothing,' I say, staring at the fire. 'We need to go to sleep. You go first. I'll stay up and keep watch.'

'What for?' he asks. 'That lot won't come after us. They don't like the countryside.'

'But what if they do?'

As I speak, there's a crack of wood as if someone's trodden on a stick nearby. I hold my breath.

'Just the wind,' says Tim. He looks at me curiously. 'You're really on edge. Is someone after you?'

'That's my business,' I snap back. 'Like I said just now. Go to sleep.'

Greater Stitchwort (*Stellaria holostea*)
Also known as Dead Man's Bones and Old Nick's
Ribs. According to folklore, these delicate flowers can
bring on trouble if you pick them. Beware!

23

Ellie

On the last day before I left to go back to school after the summer break, I had a visitor.

'Someone's here for you!' shouted Sheila. There was a peculiar tone to her voice that made me run down the stairs.

Peter! Despite what I'd told Mrs Greenway about him being 'just a friend', my heart thumped with excitement and apprehension. But if I'd known then what I know now, I'd have slammed the door in his face. Then the accident might not have happened.

Peter was taller and more grown-up than the last time I'd seen him. His voice was a bit deeper than last time. It was very different to stand in front of him, instead of writing to him. It had been quite easy to tell him in my looped inky handwriting (with the odd blotch) how much I loathed biology and that the food at my new school was stodgy. But now I felt horribly tongue-tied and embarrassed.

'Would you like to go for a walk?' he eventually asked. A deep red spread across his cheeks as he spoke.

'I want to go to the swings!' Michael had appeared, and was tugging at my hand. 'Please, Ellie. Please!'

'Take him to the park, can you?' said my stepmother.

'I'm exhausted and we're having a dinner party tonight. Eight people we've got coming round. Goodness knows how I'm going to get ready in time.'

This was the first I'd heard of it. I'd hoped to spend my last evening at home with my father. If only we had more time together to read poetry like we used to. I can still quote by heart my favourite poem by John Masefield that Daddy had taught me about going down to the sea. I had been too young at the time to understand the full meaning but had loved the sound of the words.

'Do you like poetry?' I asked Peter as we pushed Michael on the swing.

His face lit up. 'Absolutely. My favourite is Keats. Are you familiar with his "Ode to Autumn"?'

'No,' I said shyly.

'I could lend you my copy if you like,' he said.

I felt a warm feeling glowing inside me. 'That would be lovely.'

'Get me down from the swings,' commanded Michael. 'I want to go on the slide now.'

'Please,' I reminded him.

'Please,' he repeated, but I know he was just saying it like a parrot. He didn't mean it.

I started to lift my little brother out and Peter reached to help me. Our hands brushed against each other. He looked at me with a smile. Had he meant to do that? A thrill shot right through me.

'Can we take Michael home early?' whispered Peter. 'I'd like to talk to you some more.'

I nodded. My heart was thumping so fast I was surprised he couldn't hear it.

'We've got to leave the park now,' I told my brother.

'No. Don't want to.'

'We've got to,' I said crossly.

'Why?'

'Just because,' I snapped, as Michael started wailing.

'It doesn't matter,' said Peter, looking disappointed as I tried to quieten my brother. 'Another time.'

For the rest of the day I was furious with Michael. He'd made me angry in front of Peter. Now what would he think of me?

Later, when Peter had gone, I went upstairs to pack. I could hear my father's raised voice from the kitchen downstairs. He always used to be a soft-spoken man, but ever since he'd married Shelia there had been lots of raised voices. I crept down the stairs and sat on the bottom step.

'Why didn't you tell me?'

'I did, Nigel. You just didn't listen, as usual. We owe dinner to two of these people. They had us round last month, as you know quite well, and if we don't do the same, they'll think badly of us.'

This was a phrase I often heard from Sheila's lips. Being thought of badly was the worst thing that could happen.

'But it's Ellie's last night,' continued my father. 'I wanted some time with her.'

'What about our own son? Don't you want to spend time with him too?'

'Of course I do. But he's always here. It was your idea that Ellie should go to boarding school –'

'Yes.' Sheila's voice was sharp with dislike. 'It's good

for her. And I was right. She's much politer and more grown-up now. In fact, she's just taken Michael to the playground with – ah, there you are.'

They both spun round to look at me.

'Ellie!' My father gave me a big warm hug. 'Did you have a good time?' he asked.

Michael ran into the kitchen excitedly. 'We went on the slide. Ellie held my hand tightly up the steps and then caught me at the bottom.'

'Peter helped me,' I added. 'We saw his mother on the way back and she said to give you her regards.'

Sheila's thin lips tightened. Any mention at all of someone who knew my mother never went down well.

'By the way, I visited Grandma Greenway the other day,' I added, aware that I was being provocative.

Her eyes narrowed. 'I didn't know that. Why?'

'I wanted to see her in the home,' I retorted, feeling emboldened by her reaction. 'We spent ages talking about her life during the war.'

I couldn't help feeling a sense of pleasure at the unease now crawling over her face.

'What else did my mother talk about?' she asked tightly in the kind of voice that people use when they pretend they don't really care about the answer.

'Oh, you know,' I answered airily. 'This and that.'

Sheila wasn't at all happy now. I had to admit that this made me feel pleasantly superior. Part of me wanted to tell her that I knew she was illegitimate. That would soon put an end to all her airs and graces.

But right now, she was in command again. 'Take Michael upstairs and get him ready for bed, can you? And,

Nigel, go and change. Our guests will be here soon. I want everything to be perfect.'

My little brother was already scampering up the stairs to his room. My stepmother had had someone in to decorate it. One wall was deep blue with pictures of ships and pirates and lighthouses. Sometimes, instead of reading Michael a bedtime story, I would make up my own tales. This was what he wanted tonight.

'Tell me about the crocodile again, Ellie. PLEASE!'

I sat him on my knee and snuggled up to him, wishing now that I hadn't been angry with him earlier on. It wasn't his fault. He was too young to understand. And besides, I was flattered that he cared for me. I was also, to be truthful, pleased that this annoyed Sheila. Sometimes I liked to imagine that Michael was mine. One day I'd love to have children of my own. How wonderful it would be to have someone who loved me as much as I had loved my mother.

'Once upon a time,' I said, 'there was a sailor called Big John. He only had one eye.'

Michael wriggled on my lap with excitement. 'Get to the bit where he loses it!'

'I'm just coming to that,' I said, tickling him so my brother squealed with laughter. 'One day, when Big John was sailing the Seven Seas, he saw a huge crocodile.'

'Go on. Go on!'

'Big John was eating a ham sandwich at the time –'

'Last time it was cheese,' Michael reminded me.

'Sorry. You're right.' My little brother was a stickler for detail. 'The crocodile saw this and came right up to the side of the boat. Now Big John was actually a very nice man so he leaned over the side to say hello and . . .'

We both paused. This was the dramatic moment! I snapped my fingers in the shape of a crocodile mouth. 'And the crocodile jumped up to take the sandwich. But unfortunately, it also got his eye . . .'

Michael clapped his hands. 'But he could still see!'

He remembered all the details from last time. 'Yes! But –'

'Ellie!' We both jumped at the sound from the doorway. 'What on earth do you think you're doing, telling my son stories like that? You'll give him nightmares.'

'He likes it,' I protested.

'That's not the point. It's totally unsuitable. Get out of his room now. I'll put him to bed myself.'

Michael was jumping up and down as I left. 'I want Ellie to finish my story,' I heard him say.

'Well, she can't. She's a very naughty girl.'

After our guests had gone, my father came up to my room with my stepmother. I was still awake, reading my book. Dad had a serious look on his face.

'I've heard what happened earlier,' he said, glancing at his wife. 'I've explained that you just let your imagination get away with you. You're sorry, aren't you?'

Please, said his face. *Apologize, Ellie. It will be easier for all of us.*

I could make a stand. But although I was upset by my father not sticking up for me, I also felt sorry for him. So I gritted my teeth. 'Sorry,' I said.

Sheila nodded curtly. 'Very well. But don't let it happen again.'

As I went to sleep, I vowed that was the last time I'd say sorry to that woman.

24

Jo

When I wake, Tim isn't there. Seagulls are perched on the ruins above, screaming at me. Now it's light, I can see a big square opening next to me that's been partly boarded up with wood. Some of the planks are missing and you can look down, a bit like a deep well. We were lucky. One of us could have fallen into that.

Outside, a heavy mist sits over the wild scrubland.

Where's the kid gone? Has he left me? I stand there, uncertain. What do I do now? You could get lost for ever in a place like this.

Suddenly a shape looms out from my right. My breath catches in my throat. I stumble back against the wall.

Then I see that it's a small figure with floppy hair. Tim arrives, panting, his eyes shining.

'I've been exploring,' he gasps. 'You'll never guess what I've found.' The excitement on his face reminds me of someone I used to know. But I can't quite place him. Or maybe it was a her.

He grabs my hand. 'Come on!'

I follow him across a field and over a padlocked gate. I scrape my arm and it starts to bleed.

'You OK?'

'Fine.' I shrug it off, though it's sore.

'We're there now!' He gives a flourish, as if introducing me to someone. 'Perfect, isn't it? And the best bit is that there's no one else here.'

I stare at the faded blue sign in front of me. MIRAMAR CARAVAN PARK. PRIVATE.

There's a small office like a bungalow with a notice on the front door. 'Closed until 17 March'.

We go for the caravan that's furthest away from the road, near a wood. The sea glistens through the trees. 'They'll give us cover if we have to run for it,' says Tim as he takes off his T-shirt, wraps up a rock in it and uses it to smash one of the windows. 'Go on. Give me a leg-up.'

He tumbles in, head-first, and then opens the door from inside.

'Welcome!' His eyes are bright.

'Wow,' I say, looking around. It's not half bad. There's a proper table with a bench to sit on and a bed too. I don't bother looking in the mirror on the wall. Who cares what you look like? There are more important things to worry about, like where you're going to sleep or find food. The thought sets my stomach off and it makes a gurgling noise.

'We need something to eat,' says Tim.

'Where from?' I ask. 'The Co-Op? I didn't know they were giving food away to the likes of us.'

I would laugh at my own joke if I wasn't feeling so knackered. Yesterday's events have taken it out of me.

Tim is beside himself. 'Didn't you see those shelves through the window of the office? They've got loads of tins on them. I reckon they flog stuff to the caravan people. All we need to do is break another window.

There's a cooker here. Maybe there's still some gas left in the cylinder.'

He turns a dial and it hisses. Looks like he's right. But there's no water from the taps.

I sit down heavily on the edge of the bed.

'Sure you're OK?' The kid's voice is surprisingly tender. 'You're rubbing your hands together more than usual.'

Was I? 'Stop your bloody fussing. I'm just a bit thirsty, that's all.'

He's rummaging through a cupboard. 'Look! Drink this.' It's a dusty, half-empty bottle of lemonade.

I do as I'm told, even though the stuff is flat.

'Now sit there. Don't move. I'll be back as soon as I can.'

While he's gone, I doze off. I'm hammering my fists desperately against a glass door. But instead of trying to get out, I'm trying to get in . . .

I wake with a jolt as the caravan door opens. I can hear barking. What if it's a guard dog? Before I know what I'm doing, my hand has seized a knife from the kitchen drawer.

'Bloody hell. It's only me!' shouts Tim, coming in with arms full of tins and a little white terrier at his side, its coat plastered with mud. 'Put that thing down, will you? Makes me nervous.'

The animal starts nipping my ankles and almost makes me drop the knife. 'What the hell is that?' I say.

'A dog.'

'I'm not blind. But what's it doing here?'

'Just followed me.' Tim was down on all fours, stroking it. The dog started licking its bottom.

'Ugh, stop that!'

'Poor little thing. Reckon he's lost. Maybe someone left him behind. Look. He doesn't have a collar.'

Now it's pulling at my laces. I take a step backwards. 'We can't afford to feed another mouth.'

'Yes we can. Look at this lot.' Tim lays the tins out on the table. 'Got some dog meat too. Doesn't taste so bad actually.'

I feel sick. 'You've eaten it?'

Tim shrugs. 'Once or twice. You've got to take what you can sometimes.'

In all my time on the road, I've not fallen that low.

He tips out his pockets. Stuff falls onto the table. 'Got you some plasters and antiseptic cream 'n' all for that arm of yours.'

I hesitate. Theft is serious business. 'What if someone finds out we've broken in?'

'This place is shut up for the winter.'

'Yes, but suppose they come back to do a check?'

'Stop worrying, old woman.' He says this in a nice way. 'I've got something else for you too. Just wait there. Close your eyes and you'll have a surprise. See? It rhymes.'

'Great,' I say weakly.

'Give me a few minutes and then look through the window. I discovered something round the back.'

After a second, I hear a strange squeaking sound.

I don't believe it. The kid's found a bike! It looks pretty rusty but he's cycling along with his hands held high in the air like he's some clown at a circus, doing tricks. The little white dog is running round, chasing him, yapping with excitement.

Suddenly I can't help bursting into laughter. It's such a relief after all the shit I've had to deal with.

I sit on the step and watch him. Bloody hell! He's gone over the handlebars. But right away he picks himself up, brushes himself down and comes running back to the caravan with that flipping dog racing behind him.

'High five!' he grins, slamming his palm into mine. 'Sorry. Did that hurt? Reckon we've fallen on our feet, don't you?'

Then he picks up the dog, who immediately starts slobbering all over his face. 'We're going to call you Lucky,' he says softly. 'You were lucky to find us and we're lucky to have you for company.'

Maybe he's right. I think back to that spiky-haired woman in Bristol and others that I've met on the street with a dog. People always stop to give them something. This one might help us get back on our feet.

A warm, hopeful feeling creeps into my heart that hasn't been there before. Maybe, finally, my luck's on the way up.

25

Ellie

If I had known that, at the age of fourteen, my life was going to change for ever, I might have made the most of my happiness with Peter. I was becoming more used to my new school. I couldn't say I liked it but Grandma Greenway had been right. Peter's weekly letters – describing what he'd been doing along with some amusing little pencil sketches of his teachers – earned me respect from the other girls when I casually left them around in dorm. Some might say I was too young to fall in love but, looking back, I can see I was desperate for affection, given my home life.

Still, school helped. One of the 'cool' groups invited me to sit with them in the dining room. Even better, I was now chosen when our sports prefect was allowed to pick girls for the top netball team instead of the bottom. My favourite position was shooter. I was, according to my school reports, 'a good all-rounder', coming top at Latin and English. I also joined the Current Affairs Society and genned up on matters like politics. We all admired our prime minister, Margaret Thatcher. How amazing, we agreed, that a woman was leading the country.

Although I'd been a naturally skinny child, I'd now put on weight thanks to the stodgy puddings. I finally began to get periods – one of the last in my class to do so – along with quite large breasts, which I felt both embarrassed about and proud of in equal measure. 'You must ask your mother to get you fitted,' Matron had said.

'She's actually my stepmother,' I corrected her. 'No blood relation.'

The older I got, the more important it was to point out to strangers that Sheila wasn't my mother.

The other girls all had calendars hanging next to their beds in the dorm. They would tick off every day. The date for the end of term was usually circled with a big red ring and a halo of exclamation marks. 'Don't you have one?' asked the girl whose bed was next to mine.

'No,' I said shortly. For me, the holidays had a bitter-sweet feel. Yes, they meant I could go home. But I would also have to put up with Sheila.

That summer, when it was time to pack our trunks, the dorm was buzzing with talk about where everyone was going for 'the hols'. My father had already written to say that we were 'booked for the Dordogne' in France for the third week of August. Even though Sheila had to come too, I was excited. I'd even looked it up in my big geography atlas and devoured as many facts as possible from the *Encyclopaedia Britannica*.

Then I received another letter from my father. The wording was stiff – not like his usual self: *Your mother and I feel you would benefit from going on a summer camping trip run by a church youth organization in Wales. You will go there straight from school and join us in August shortly before we go to France for a week. We will arrange for your trunk to be sent on to us so you don't need to take it with you.*

I burst into tears. How could he do this to me? But I also knew that she was behind it. I could almost imagine her standing there, dictating the words.

How I hated that trip! It rained every day and I got cold and wet. I was too shy to make friends but the others interpreted this the wrong way. 'That girl's really snooty,' I heard one of the boys say. The only interesting part was doing brass rubbings in a local church and collecting shells from the beach. I kept the best ones for Michael. He'd love them. Although, when we were together, I sometimes felt resentful because my parents so clearly favoured him above me, I missed him desperately when we were apart.

Eventually, camp ended. Everyone else's parents collected them by car. I had hoped my father would do the same, but he was at work. Instead, I was instructed to catch the train, and he'd meet me at the station. But as I came out, struggling with my haversack, trying to avoid the pavement cracks, I saw Sheila waiting in the car. She didn't bother getting out to help. Instead, she flipped down the vanity mirror and began applying pink lipstick very slowly and deliberately, as if my arrival was of no consequence to her. Then the back door opened and Michael flew towards me, his arms outstretched. 'Ellie,' he said, clasping his arms around my neck as I knelt down so our faces were close. 'I've missed you.'

I breathed in his smell and held him tight.

'Come back, Michael!' Sheila shouted. 'That's dangerous. Ellie – stop standing in the road like that. Get him into the car safely.'

I was in trouble before I'd even said hello.

Michael held my hand tightly, insisting I sat in the back with him. When we eventually got home – Sheila was a nervous driver and never exceeded 25 mph – he followed me up to my bedroom, watching as I unpacked my clothes, most of which I'd almost outgrown.

'Are you coming with us to France?' he asked.

His speech had come on so fast during my absence. To think he was five now!

'Yes,' I said, picking him up and twirling him round in the air before gently putting him down. 'We'll be able to visit some castles. 'Won't that be fun?'

He frowned. 'Will there be dragons inside? I saw one on television and it scared me.'

'No.' I sat him on my knee, remembering how I'd got told off about my crocodile story. 'Dragons are just pretend.'

He wriggled off. 'Can we go to the park?'

Sheila gave us permission, providing I was 'careful'. We had a great time on the swings. 'I do admire you young mums,' said an elderly woman who was pushing her grandson. 'You have so much energy.'

I flushed. One of the girls at school had taught me how to use mascara so I looked more sophisticated than I used to. 'I'm not his mother,' I said. 'He's my little brother.'

'You don't say!'

I rather liked the idea that a stranger thought Michael was mine. It made me feel special. And I also knew it would annoy Sheila if she knew.

When we got home, Michael still wasn't tired so we played football on the lawn. 'More, more!' he kept yelling. 'Get this one, Ellie!'

'Someone's back, then,' called out my father from the patio doors.

'Daddy!' yelled Michael, hurtling towards him.

I felt a pang even though I knew my father's words had been for me. Michael had his company every day. This was my turn. I couldn't help running up to him like a child myself.

'Good to see you,' he said, giving me one of his lovely warm hugs.

Behind him, I saw Sheila glowering.

'Everything all right?'

'Of course it is,' she said, despite the fact that he hadn't been asking her. 'Why wouldn't it be?'

'Looking forward to the holiday, Ellie?' It was as if my father was ignoring her. I could sense tension. Maybe they'd had an argument. Good!

'Yes.'

'Sorry I couldn't meet you at the station but I had to pick something up for your mother.'

Instantly I felt hurt. 'I thought you were at work.'

'I was.' He looked sheepish. 'But, like I said, I was asked to do chores on the way back.'

Now I got it. My stepmother hadn't wanted him to meet me. She knew I'd be disappointed if he wasn't there, and I had been.

'We've just got an invitation from the Daniels to their lunch party, Nigel,' said Sheila in a brighter voice.

My heart leapt. The Daniels were a local family who lived in a big house and entertained a lot. They were regular customers at my father's stationery shop and my own mother had been friends with Mrs Daniels through church.

Even though Sheila usually didn't like mixing with any-one who was connected with my mother, it was clear she was happy, for snobbish reasons, to make an exception. The Gordons knew them too, and Peter had actually mentioned their party in his last letter to me. He would go with his parents, he said, in the hope that I would be there as well. I promised I'd do my best.

My father groaned. 'Do we have to go? It's a Friday after all. Surely people will be at work. It means I've got to take a day off myself.'

Sheila rolled her eyes. 'It's the Daniels' twenty-fifth and they're holding it on the actual day. Most of the guests are the kind who *can* take a day off work. Frankly, it's an honour to be invited even though it is so late. We're probably filling in numbers as so many people have already left for their summer holidays.' Her lips tightened. 'The children have been asked too. Goodness knows why. Anyway, I accepted. You're always saying you want to do family things together.'

'That's good,' he said with more enthusiasm. 'Now come inside, Ellie. I want to hear all about school.'

'Careful when you go into the kitchen,' called out my stepmother. 'I dropped something just now and haven't had time to sweep it up.'

Blue-and-yellow china fragments were all over the floor. 'No!' I fell to my knees. 'Mummy's cup.' I picked up a small piece, the flowery pattern taking me back years in an instant.

I leapt up and grabbed my father's arm. 'She broke it. She did it on purpose.'

'Come, come, Ellie,' admonished my father. 'I'm sure that's not true.'

Of course it was! Why wouldn't he stick up for me? But all he wanted was to please that stupid woman.

It wasn't fair. I ran upstairs, sobbing, holding the broken china carefully in my hands. 'What shall I do, Mummy?' I wept, lying on my bed. 'I can't take any more.'

26

Jo

Tim makes me have the bed. 'You need it,' he says awkwardly. Someone once taught that kid some manners.

So he and Lucky take the narrow bench by the table instead.

We start getting into a routine. We sleep in late because it's warmer that way. Later, we take it in turns to go foraging for sweet chestnuts. Then we go together to the shop to get more tins. I stand guard while Tim crawls through the broken window at the back. In the afternoon, we listen to the radio – there's an old transistor on the side and we found new batteries in the shop. I like the Steve Wright show. He sounds really nice. We also go for walks with the dog. In the evening, we play snakes and ladders or draughts or one of the other games we found in a cupboard.

For the first time I can remember, I start to relax. We've got everything we need. There's a kettle and even a little red teapot to make tea. We might not have any water inside but there's an outside tap and a bucket. There's also a pile of matching blue-and-white towels which the owners have left in one of the cupboards.

It's almost like being on holiday – not that I remember when I last had one. In a drawer, along with knives and forks, I find a pack of cards. Tim teaches me to play a game called 'cheat'. I don't let on that I already know it.

At night, he talks in his sleep. 'Mum,' he moans over and over again. His cries sometimes wake Lucky, curled up in his arms as if he's always belonged there. Then the dog licks Tim on his face and they both go back to sleep again.

One evening, Tim leaves the dog with me and goes out. 'Got something to do,' he says.

I get all twitchy when it becomes dark and he's still not back. I'm also cross with myself for starting to rely on him. Isn't this why I usually travel on my own? It gets complicated when you're with someone else.

'Where were you?' I demand when he finally returns. I haven't got a watch but the clock on the caravan wall says it's nearly 2.30 in the morning.

'What's it to you? You're not my mother.' Something seems different about him tonight.

'You're right,' I say. 'But it's a scary world out there. I'm just trying to protect you.'

He rolls his eyes. 'I'm the one who saved you, remember?'

True.

'I went for a walk, OK? I wanted some time on my own. Sometimes I feel strange and I need to get out. I'm going to bed.'

I let it go.

This time Lucky chooses to curl up in bed with me. It's like he knows Tim needs to be on his own. I bury my nose in his fur and fall instantly asleep, his warm heart beating against my chest.

When I wake, Tim is peering over me anxiously. 'You OK?'

I sit halfway up on my elbows. 'Why?'

'You were having a bad dream.'

Not again. 'What did I say?'

'You kept calling out, "You killed him."' His eyes narrow. 'Is someone after you? Or is it you that's looking for someone?'

I lie back down on my pillow. 'I've told you, it's none of your business,' I say. 'You have bad dreams too and I don't ask you questions. Want to tell me why you keeping calling for your mum?'

'Piss off.'

'Exactly. Now go to bed.'

After a week, I'm going a bit stir-crazy.

'I'm off for a walk,' I say.

Tim mutters and turns over in his sleep. Outside, the air feels clean and fresh after the stuffy caravan. The dog comes with me. We don't have a lead but Lucky just follows me around. He starts digging in the leaves. 'Any rabbits?' I ask.

His ears are cocked like he knows what I'm saying.

I'm wearing black leggings and a thick navy-blue fleecy sweatshirt that Tim nicked from the caravan shop. I start whistling as we head down a hill and then up another. I don't mean to go far, but somehow I end up in a small village. The signpost has a weird name that I can't get my tongue round. But it's pretty. I find myself wondering if I might be able to find a job here, where they don't ask too many questions. Maybe we could stay all winter.

There's a pub ahead. I wouldn't mind a swig of something strong but I don't have any cash.

And that's when I see the newspaper poster outside a small village shop. It's wet with rain. But the photograph is clear enough. And the words are still readable.

HAS OXFORDSHIRE MURDERER DONE IT BEFORE?

'Get a lot of runaways in these parts, we do,' says a voice.

A large man in a pair of dirty old jeans and a fisherman's jacket is standing next to me, shaking his head. 'Plenty of places to hide down here. Sometimes it works out for them. They stay on and settle. That's if the wind and sea don't get them first. Not to mention the police.'

I turn away, not wanting to talk about it. I didn't like the look of that woman in the photo. She seemed the kind of person you'd want to stay well clear of. I shiver. Part of me thinks I might have seen her before. But where?

By the time Kieran's born, Barry has started to come back later and later. Not just on Friday nights either. Sometimes I've been so busy with the kids that I haven't got his supper ready. He doesn't like that.

'What have you been doing all day, woman?' he'll shout.

'Looking after your bleeding children!' I'll yell back. 'I'm on my knees like you would be if you did anything to help round here.'

'I'm earning the bread, aren't I?'

Then the neighbours thump on the walls to tell us to shut up. If we're not careful, we'll get evicted. There've been complaints before. We're behind with the council rent too 'cos Barry keeps drinking.

Liam is whining 'cos he's hungry. I've had nothing to give him but packet noodles for the last three days 'cos they're cheap. My milk has dried up 'cos I'm not eating properly myself.

Then one Friday he comes back without any cash at all. 'You've spent it all on booze, haven't you?' I yell.

'What if I have? I work for it, don't I?'

'I can't feed us on fresh air.'

'Shut up, woman. You're making my head hurt.'

That's when I see it. An ugly blue bruise on the side of his neck.

'You've been with someone else, haven't you?' I yell.

'So? It's not like you want me any more.'

'That's 'cos I'm bloody knackered with this lot.' I get right in his face. 'Who is she?'

'No one you know.'

Furiously, I batter my fists on his chest. Liam starts to cry. The baby yells.

'Get off me, you stupid woman.'

He pushes me hard. I spin and my face slams against the wall. My nose starts to bleed, just like it did with Dad.

Liam's in the room. 'Daddy, stop it.'

'Go to bed, love,' I say, trying to get him out of here.

Barry comes towards me, his eyes blazing. I won't let it happen. I pick up the nearest thing to hand – the china bowl Barry bought me with his first pay packet – and slam it into the side of his head.

He slumps to the ground. Blood trickles down his face. His eyes are closed. I can't see him breathing.

There's more knocking on the wall from the neighbours. I go hot and cold. 'Think,' I tell myself. 'Think.'

Quickly, I chuck some stuff for the kids in a bag and gather them up in my arms.

Then I run.

PART TWO

After the Accident

Lady's bedstraw (*Galium verum*)
A delicate, yellow flower that smells of new-mown
hay when dried. Brings to mind young lovers lying in fields.

27

Ellie

I've always seen my life in two parts. The days before the party. And the days after. But those twenty-four hours in the middle didn't exist. I couldn't let them.

'It might help you to talk,' Cornelius had told me soon after we met. 'It's a bit like clearing out the kitchen cupboards and then putting the new stuff back.'

He was the chief psychiatrist at Highbridge, who had been put in charge of me. There was no question of me going back to school or having any kind of normal life after what happened.

At first sight, Highbridge didn't seem like a 'secure unit'. It looked more like a smallish stately Victorian home with its warm, red-brick, ivy-clad exterior and courtyard with a clock tower. There was a chime every hour. A deep resonating sound that made me jump the first time I heard it and continued to do so.

Lots of things made me jump then. I got piercing headaches too. They would start in the side of my head in what the nurse called my 'temples'. Especially when Cornelius kept suggesting that I should talk.

'No,' I would always reply.

My vocabulary had become minimal. There seemed no point in saying any more than I had to.

I also found myself bursting into giggles at the wrong time. Cornelius said that sometimes the brain could make you laugh when you really wanted to cry. That didn't make sense to me, but then again, nor did anything that was happening.

I stopped eating. My clothes began to hang loosely and my facial features sharpened. Often my stomach rolled to suggest it was empty but I couldn't bring myself to swallow anything.

'You need food to live,' said one of the kitchen servers kindly when I put three peas on my plate and nothing else.

But what right did I have? Not after what I'd done. So they force-fed me instead, with one of the staff holding me and another pouring soup down my throat from a spoon. It wouldn't happen now, but back then it wasn't uncommon in those places.

Cornelius was a large man with piercing bright-blue eyes who always wore checked shirts without a tie. He reminded me of my old art teacher at school and I felt a bit embarrassed when he invited me to address him by his first name and not his surname. Surely that was disrespectful. In those days, he seemed like a cross between a father and grandfather in terms of age. Later I found out he was only fifteen years older than me.

'If you don't want to talk,' Cornelius said during one of our early sessions, 'would you like to write something instead?'

'I'm not a kid,' I wanted to say. I shook my head.

'Sure?' He opened the drawer of the desk between us and brought out a pen and a notebook. There was no top on the pen and no metal spiral binding on the notebook. Both were considered 'safety risks' in Highbridge. They even took away my music box, which my father had packed in the small case I was allowed to bring with me. 'She might swallow the key,' one of the nurses had said over my head. When you don't talk, people forget you can still listen.

Cornelius was toying with the pen. How many times had we gone through this ritual since I'd arrived? Didn't he realize I had no intention of committing my thoughts to paper? I barely knew what they were myself.

Instead, I looked out of the window. It had white bars across it. I wondered how secure they were. The girl in the bed next to mine told me that, last year, someone from the boys' wing had managed to remove them with a makeshift screwdriver made from a filed-down toothbrush. 'Then he jumped,' she said, matter-of-factly. It was four floors up.

Sometimes I felt like doing that.

'Do you enjoy reading?' Cornelius asked.

I used to. But what was the point? Nothing mattered any more.

He got up and ran his finger along the spine of the many books that lined the walls. Then he stopped and picked one out. 'Take a look at this,' he said encouragingly. I glanced away, but not before I'd taken in the title. *Palgrave's Golden Treasury*. My father and I used to read it together, our heads bowed as one, in the days before Sheila had ruined our lives.

'I don't want to look at it,' I say gruffly.

'Fair enough,' he said brightly, as though I'd said the

right thing. 'Poetry can help us express our emotions but you don't need to read it right now. These things take time.'

These things? A surge of anger welled up inside me. Standing up, I kicked my chair onto the ground. Cornelius frowned. 'That's not really going to help, is it, Ellie?'

How can he tell? What did this man know about me? Picking up the poetry book lying between us, I threw it at him. It grazed the side of his head. A red mark appeared. A trickle of blood ran down. 'I wish you hadn't done that,' said Cornelius sadly. He pressed the green button on the wall behind him. Instantly the door opened and two men in white came rushing in. They held my arms behind my back.

I knew what would follow because this had happened on our very first session too. I would be taken to Solitary until I behaved myself again. Then I would go back to the room I shared with the girl who had told me about the boy who'd jumped. I'd still have the nightmares that haunted me night after night, paralysing me so that I'd wake in a pool of sweat, unable to move with terror. And Cornelius would continue to encourage me to talk.

But I had to resist. Because if I didn't, I might tell them the truth about what really happened that day.

12.05 p.m., 17 August 1984

It's the day of the Daniels' lunch party. My stepmother has been in a state of excitement over the last few days, even buying two different outfits 'in case the weather changes', despite my father warning her that we 'have to be careful about money'.

'Stop trying to ruin my fun, Nigel,' she retorts. 'It's not as though I get much of that.'

I like it when they argue.

'Will everyone hurry up and get in the car?' she snaps. 'We're going to be late.'

I'm trying, but Michael thinks it's better fun to play hide-and-seek round the house. Eventually I catch a flash of his red T-shirt as he crouches behind my bedroom door. I scoop him up, tickling him affectionately. He roars with laughter.

'This is no time for games,' scolds my stepmother, addressing me as if I am the one to blame. When she turns her back, I stick my tongue out at her. Michael promptly does the same.

'Don't,' I whisper, both horrified and amused. 'You'll get us both into trouble.'

Sheila might even ban me from going to the lunch party. That would upset me more than anything. I can't wait to see

Peter, even though I'm really nervous at the same time. What if he doesn't like me any more?

'Nigel,' says my stepmother coldly when we get in the car. 'Why are you wearing that shirt? I thought we'd decided on the maroon.'

My mother had given Daddy the shirt he had on. I remember clearly. It was for his last birthday before she'd died.

'I think he looks nice as he is,' I hear myself saying from the back.

Sheila turns round and glowers. 'What business is this of yours?'

Then she casts her eye over my outfit. I am wearing a pink strappy sundress which I had made myself in domestic science. Actually, I'm rather proud of it — the teacher had told me I had a 'flair' for sewing.

'That neckline is too revealing,' declares my stepmother. 'Don't you think, Nigel?'

My father makes an 'I'm sorry' face in the driver's mirror. Both he and I know there is no point in arguing.

'Go and change,' she commands. 'Both of you.'

I've shot up in height since last summer. The only other dress I possess is navy blue with a Peter Pan collar, which makes me look much too young. My stepmother had promised my father to take me shopping for more summer clothes but it hadn't happened.

Yet what choice do I have? So I get out and stomp upstairs and put the wretched dress on to keep the peace.

My father comes down in maroon. It was my mother's least favourite colour.

Eventually, nearly half an hour late, we set off.

28

Jo

When I get back to the caravan site, my mind is so full of noise it takes me a second to register that something's wrong. There's a big car by the entrance. One of those huge things that take up the space on both sides of a lane. I can hear shouting. Then I see Tim coming towards me.

For a minute he appears younger. More vulnerable. Then he looks up and I can see his eyes harden with determination. He catches me by the arm. 'Come on. We've got to get out of here. The bloody caravan-site owner came back to do a check. Told me that he was going to call the police. Quick.'

Lucky and I race along after him down a narrow dirt track. 'How do you know where we're going?' I puff.

'I don't.'

We keep on, barely jogging now as my breath comes in short bursts. The track is sloping downwards. The sea lies below. Every now and then there is a rough step where someone has put a plank of wood across to make it easier for walking. It's muddy after the rain. I slip. Tim steadies me. He slips. I steady him.

'Now what?' I ask. We're on the beach. Lucky is racing on, burying his nose in the sand every now and then and trying to dig out a rock to play with.

I look back at the way we've come. No one seems to be following.

'Move it, Lucky,' says Tim sharply. 'There's no time to mess about.'

We follow the coast path for three days, sleeping under bushes and foraging for food. My legs are aching, my feet have got blisters and my toenails have grown so much that they're pushing against the ends of my trainers. We see signs to Penzance, but I don't fancy going back there. Then we see another signpost. MOUSEHOLE.

I like the name. A mousehole is somewhere you can hide.

Together we walk in silence. Even Lucky stops running ahead and instead falls into line with us. The stones on the beach hurt my feet. Part of the sole is now coming off one of my trainers. Shoes are the most difficult things to replace when you're on the road. Who knows where I'll find another pair.

To think I'd thought we'd be OK. That we might even be able to stay for the whole winter. But people like me can never really get on in life. I should've known that.

'Nearly there.' Tim scrambles over a huge rock covered with seaweed and shells, holding out his hand to help me follow. 'Looks like a harbour.'

All I can see are some old boats, sitting in mud. *Hope 2*, says a sign in white letters on the side of one. I can't help wondering what happened to *Hope 1*. A fisherman is sitting next to it, mending a net. He glances up at us and then down at his work again.

'Look!' Tim grabs my arm in excitement. There's a packet of chips on the pavement, right in front of us. I suddenly realize how hungry I am. Tim dives forward. At the same time, there's a scream and a flash of white. A seagull has got to them first.

'Fucking thieves.' There are actually tears in Tim's eyes.

'It's all right,' I say, biting back my disappointment. It's just like that time in Bristol when that woman beat me to the chips. But now I've got to be strong for the kid. 'We'll get something else to eat.'

That's when I see the blood. Tim has a gash on his cheek, not far from the scar. 'Bastard scratched me.'

'We need to wash that,' I say. 'It could get infected.'

'Got your bloody first-aid kit with you, have you?'

'Very funny.' I point to a pub sign a bit further along the road. 'Find the toilet there. Put some soap on it.'

We step inside hesitantly, trying to look like we belong. There's a fire blazing in the corner. My muddy feet leave stains on the nice carpet. Will I get told off? Tim heads through a doorway marked 'Toilets.'

A man carrying a tray of glasses comes up to me. I wait for him to throw us out. It's what usually happens. Instead, he bends down and pats Lucky. 'There's a special area for dog owners in that part of the bar. Want a biscuit, do you?'

'Yes, please,' I say.

He laughs as though I've said something funny. Then he puts his hand in his pocket and takes out a bone-shaped treat. Lucky wolfs it back in one. I'd do that if someone gave me a biscuit too.

The smell of food is making my stomach turn over. I try to block it out while Tim is gone by looking at the photographs on the walls of boats and fishermen staring out at me. One shows this massive fish that some bloke 'landed' back in 1871.

'Really cool, aren't they?' says a woman in a voice that sounds like an American I once met inside.

I nod, not wanting to get into conversation.

'You in the queue for food?'

I shake my head.

'I don't want to interfere but my husband and I saw you outside just now when that bird got the fries. I've read about seagull bites. They can be real dangerous. Is your kid OK?'

Just then, Tim comes back. The cut is still bleeding. Lucky begins to whine like he knows something's wrong.

'Cute dog,' coos the woman. Then she looks at Tim's cheek. 'Think I've got something for that.' She opens a really fancy beige handbag with a gold clasp. 'Here they are! Antiseptic wipes. I carry them everywhere when we're on vacation.'

'Thanks.' Tim's eyes are watery again. I'm beginning to learn he can turn them on and off. 'It's my birthday 'n' all.'

Tim hadn't mentioned any birthday.

'Mum and me are on the road and we haven't eaten for ages.'

Then I realize that his 'birthday' is all part of the act. He's trying it on. This boy is smart!

'Oh you poor things. Listen, why don't you let us buy you a meal as a birthday present?'

'Wow! That would be great, wouldn't it, Mum?'

I nod enthusiastically. I'd give my right arm for something to eat.

'Good.' The woman looks as though we've done her a favour instead of the other way round. 'You know, I've been shocked by how many people need help in Britain. We just didn't expect it. Now here's a menu. Order whatever you want. Get a sausage for that cute dog of yours too. What's he called?'

'Lucky,' I say. 'But we don't need any charity, thanks.'

I try to pull Tim away but he pushes me off. 'Mum, please.'

The woman touches my arm. I jump as though she's burned me. She sees my reaction and steps back. 'I'm sorry if I've offended you,' she says. 'My own kids are so far away and I miss them. Let me help you and your boy. Call it a gift from one mother to another.'

Should I trust her?

My head says no. I've trusted people in the past and look what happened. But my stomach is on empty. Tim is hungry too.

Maybe we'll take a chance.

Primrose (*Primula vulgaris*)
A symbol of safety and protection. In ancient times, a bunch was placed on the doorstep to encourage the fairy folk to bless the house and its inhabitants.

12.50 p.m., 17 August 1984

'Ellie! Ellie! Can we play I spy?'

'No,' I say shortly. The traffic has been slow and I am getting worried, which in turn makes me irritable. We're already late. What if Peter thinks I'm not coming and decides to go home?

'Don't be difficult, Ellie,' hisses my stepmother from the front. 'Play nicely with your brother.'

'Don't want to.'

Michael looks upset. Instantly, I reproach myself. 'I'm sorry,' I say, stretching out my hand to him. He gives me a sulky look.

'I spy with my little eye,' I begin, 'something beginning with "C".'

We play for a little while, spying clouds and a car. It reminds me of the games I used to play with my father before Sheila came along. 'Dad,' I say. 'Why don't you have a go?'

I lean forward, patting his back.

'Don't touch your father when he's driving,' Sheila snaps. 'He might crash.'

'Fine,' I snap back. 'We won't play any more.'

29

Ellie

After a while, I lost track of how long I'd been at Highbridge for. But it must have been some time since I'd thrown that book at Cornelius because there wasn't a mark on the side of his head any more.

Cuts take time to heal. But sometimes they stay in your brain. One thing was certain. There was something wrong with me. I heard everyone saying so.

I was back in my old room now, although I had a different roommate. No one said what happened to the first. It was like that there. People came and went. I could ask but I still didn't want to talk – at least, not to others. Occasionally I practised out loud at night when the other girl was asleep. I wanted to check I could still do it. But my tongue stuck to the roof of my mouth. It reminded me of a piece of ice my mother had shown me in a book before she was ill. 'It's called a "stalactite",' she'd explained. 'You can remember it because it has to hold on "tight" to the roof.' The memory made me feel sick.

Months passed. Things happened that I don't want to remember. So I have shut them out of my head. But one day at Highbridge in particular still stands out.

'Morning, Ellie,' said Cornelius brightly when it was my turn to see him after breakfast, which, as usual, I had hardly touched. His room was cold. Outside there was frost on the ground.

Ignoring him, my eye fastened on a spider's web hanging from a beam. I couldn't see the occupant so maybe he'd managed to escape. Perhaps it was a 'she'. I wished I could run away too, but if I did, where would I go?

'Ceilings are interesting, aren't they?'

Why couldn't he just stop talking? Immediately I looked down at the ground.

'So are floors. Did you know that the Romans invented underfloor heating?' He pushed a picture across the desk towards me. It was a house, just like the Roman villa my father had taken me to years ago. Before Michael.

'Does this look familiar to you?'

Instantly I knew this was a trick. He wanted me to tell him my feelings about those days before it happened.

I picked up the picture. It was on glossy paper as though it had come from a magazine. Very carefully, I folded it into two. Then I tore it along the crease. Cornelius said nothing. I took one of the smaller bits and folded that one in half. It was very important to make sure that the two sections were exactly the same size. Then nothing could go wrong. I tore those bits in half too.

I was aware of Cornelius watching me. I was also aware of the green emergency button behind him. I wouldn't mind going back to Solitary. My new roommate was so irritating with her snuffling.

'You went there with your father, didn't you, Ellie? Were you happy then?'

I took the remaining large bit and scrunched it up into

a ball. I threw it in the air. Then I caught it. Up and down. Up and down.

The rhythm was soothing.

'How would you change things if you could go back to that day with your father, Ellie?'

I watched the piece of paper fall down into my hands. Purposely, I let it drop onto the ground. It was so light that you couldn't hear it fall. I wished it was a brick so it would make a big, loud sound. Anything to drown the agonizing noise in my head.

'What do you think you'd say to him?'

I ran towards the window with the bars. *Bang Bang Bang* went my head on the metal.

'Stop!' Cornelius's voice rang behind me. 'You'll hurt yourself.'

Good.

He must have pressed the green button again because more arms were around me then, pulling me away. I could feel blood trickling down my face. There was, I'd discovered, nothing that could really describe the taste.

'Get her to the San,' ordered Cornelius.

A nurse patched me up. She told me I was lucky not to need stitches. And then they took me to Solitary. Peace at last. I lay down on the mattress, which was on the floor for safety. They gave me something to help me sleep. I swallowed the tablets greedily, desperate for the blackness that would soon overtake me.

30

Jo

The American woman ('Call me Mary-Lou, dear') tries to buy me a glass of cider while we wait. 'We love this stuff, don't we, Doug?' she says to her husband, who doesn't say much. If you ask me, he's not too keen that his wife has taken on some waifs and strays. You get that with couples. There's usually one who wants to do good and the other has you down as a murderer.

'I don't drink much,' I say.

'Is that so?'

I see her looking at me, thinking that all people like us must be alkies. 'What will your son drink?'

I could tell her he's not my son but then I'd have to explain too much.

'I'll have a beer,' he says.

'No you won't,' I cut in quickly. 'You're not old enough.'

He scowls but Mary-Lou and her husband nod approvingly. 'We have to watch our boys too. How about a lemonade, honey?'

Tim swigs it back – and another – before the food arrives. We've ordered steak and chips. He eats it, head down as if he's swimming in his plate, occasionally coming up for air. Despite my rolling stomach, I have to stop after a few mouthfuls. The meat feels heavy. It's been so long since I had decent stuff like this that my teeth – more used to cold baked beans – can't work their way through.

'You've had enough?' says Mary-Lou like I've let her down.

'Sorry,' I say. 'But I'm stuffed already.'

Tim leans over in my direction and grabs the rest of my steak without so much as a 'please'. He wolfs it down as if I might try to snatch it back.

Something's loose inside my mouth. I pull it out. It's a tooth that's been giving me some gyp for a while. It bleeds a bit but it doesn't hurt. It's not the first I've lost and it won't be the last.

'That's unlucky. Is there a dentist near here?'

I laugh out loud.

'What's so funny?' says the woman's husband.

'We haven't been to a dentist for years,' says Tim, his mouth half full.

'That's shocking.' The man gives me a look as if to say that I'm a bad mother.

'You need a fixed address for that, don't you?' continues Tim. I shoot him a 'shut up' look but the food seems to have loosened his tongue. I start to hum with embarrassment.

'Don't mind Mum,' says Tim. 'She does that when she's worried about stuff.'

Mary-Lou lowers her voice and speaks in a hushed tone. 'Honey, forgive me for asking, but do you and your kid have anywhere to sleep tonight?'

'Course we do –' I start to say but Tim cuts in.

'We're running away from my dad. He used to hit us, so Mum said we needed to leave. Been living in a caravan for a bit but then the owner chucked us out.'

That kid can spin a good yarn. The trick is to mix truth with lies. Always sounds better.

'How awful.' Her husband's face starts to look a bit kinder. 'What will you do?'

'Dunno. Maybe sleep in a field somewhere.'

They're talking now, this Mary-Lou and her husband, up at the bar. Looks to me like she's arguing with him. I pretend I need the toilet so I can eavesdrop. As I walk past, I catch some of her words. 'It could happen to any-one. Just think. What if it was one of our boys? Wouldn't you want someone to help them?'

Maybe she's going to give us some money. That would be good!

When I come back, they're at the table again. 'Listen up!' says Mary-Lou. Her face is shining with pleasure. 'We're staying at a hotel near here and we'd like to pay for you to stay there too.'

Tim jumps up. 'We're not fucking like that.'

'Like what, dear?' Mary-Lou looks alarmed.

'It's OK,' I say, pulling Tim down to the table again. He shakes off my arm.

'He's just scared you're coming on to him,' I explain.

Mary-Lou and her husband seem shocked, like some-one has threatened to smash their faces in.

'Some people pretend to be kind but they're after some-thing else,' mumbles Tim. He has a distant look about him. I shiver. Once more, I wonder what he's been through.

'We meant we'd get you a separate room from us,' says Mary-Lou quietly. 'Somewhere warm and dry for a night. Would you like that? The hotel takes dogs. I saw one there this morning. Think of it as another birthday present.'

'OK,' says Tim slowly. But now I'm beginning to panic. Supposing these do-gooders begin interfering. What if they decide to say something to the police? Yet the temptation of having a proper bed is just too much . . . And perhaps if they feel really sorry for us there might be something else we can get out of them.

'OK,' I say.

It's a risk but we've got to take it.

1.10 p.m., 17 August 1984

We carry on driving. The car is hot and stuffy even though the windows are open. It's the kind of heat which makes your skin sweat and your head muzzy. The sort that makes you want to take it out on someone.

Michael begins wriggling around in the back of the car. He seems to think it's funny to kick me. Not hard but enough to leave scuff marks on my dress.

'Don't,' I say, edging away as far as my seatbelt will let me. Normally I wouldn't have minded too much but I want to look my best for Peter.

Ever since I found out through our weekly letters that he is coming to the party too, I've been counting the days until I see him. The other girls at school will expect me to tell them what happened when I get back. I'll have to come up with something or else they might start ignoring me again.

'Stop arguing in the back,' grumbles my stepmother.

'It's not my fault,' I retort. 'Michael was kicking me.'

'No I wasn't,' he pipes up. 'I was just playing.'

'But –' I begin.

'I knew it was a bad idea to have you back for the rest of the holidays,' spits Sheila. 'Maybe we shouldn't take you to France next week with us after all.'

'Please, Ellie,' says my father, glancing at me in the mirror, his eyes pleading. 'Let's just leave it at that, shall we?'

It's not fair. I wish she'd just disappear. Get out of our lives. For ever. And right now, part of me wishes Michael would go with her too.

31

Ellie

The days at Highbridge blurred into the nights, or was it that the nights blurred into the days? It was hard to tell. But when I went out for what they called my 'morning constitutional' with one of the staff, I noticed that the frost had gone and that there were primroses in the woods where they took us for walks. They had been another of my mother's favourite wildflowers, along with forget-me-nots.

I liked it there because there weren't any pavement cracks.

Sometimes we had 'open days' when families could visit. I always stood by the door of my room, hoping to be called. But my father never came for me. Was it any wonder? (We have open family days here in prison too. And just like at Highbridge, none of my 'loved ones' ever turns up.)

Angie, the girl who shared my room, always had visitors. One night, she leaned across to me. 'My brother sneaked something in,' she whispered. 'He said it would help.'

She pressed a small tablet into my hand. 'Go on. I've got more for myself. They're happy pills.'

I didn't deserve to be happy but I found myself taking one anyway. 'Thanks,' I said. I still couldn't say much more than one word at a time.

At first I lay there in the dark, not feeling anything, but

then our room filled with reds and blues and yellows and greens. I felt light-headed and found myself dancing around. Nothing mattered now. Not even . . .

'What's going on?'

I was only vaguely aware of a voice. I wanted to tell it to go away and let me carry on having fun. I hadn't felt as light and carefree as this since I was a small child with my mother next to me, gathering flowers in the hedgerows. Then I sensed some hands helping me into bed. When I woke up, Cornelius told me that it wasn't my fault. Angie had gone now. 'But you must never take tablets again unless we give them to you,' he said. 'Otherwise it will make you ill again. Do you understand?'

Not really. But I pretended to. It seemed easier.

One morning when the bell-tower clock had struck eight and sunlight was streaming in through my window, Cornelius came into my room along with a woman I hadn't seen before. 'This is Julia,' he said. 'She's our new crafts instructor.'

I'd never seen anyone with such lovely long red hair before. I touched my own hair, which I'd chopped off myself with Sheila's kitchen scissors after it happened. It was getting a bit longer now. But it shouldn't be. I didn't deserve it.

'Hi, Ellie,' she said brightly. 'Nice to meet you. Do you like cooking?'

I thought back to the butterfly cakes Sheila had made after my real mother died, before she became my step-mother. She'd fooled me into thinking she was kind. She was vile. But she still didn't deserve what I'd done to her.

'No,' I said.

242

'How about knitting or sewing?'

I had a mental flash of my mother, when I was little, knitting every evening. Those were the days before she got ill. After she died, I found rows and rows of little matinee jackets in her bedroom. They had been intended, my father had told me, for the brothers and sisters that never came.

'No,' I said.

Julia was beaming as if I'd said the right answer. 'Then maybe arts and crafts? I know you like Roman villas.'

Why did these people keep telling me they knew what I did and didn't like?

'I thought we might make a mosaic.'

'No,' I was about to say. But then I stopped, recalling the mosaic wall my father had shown me all those years ago. 'How do they do it, Daddy?' I'd asked.

'It's a real skill,' he'd told me. 'You need to put all those tiny pieces together in a very careful way.'

'Shall we have a go?' said Julia.

I still wanted to say 'No' but my father's memory placed a finger on my lips.

'Yes,' said my mouth. 'Please.'

I found myself fascinated by the small bits of brightly coloured shapes Julia gave me to stick on a patterned piece of paper.

'Brilliant.' She leaned closer. 'Is there anything you'd like to tell me about a garden, Ellie?'

Green. Trees. Sunlight casting shadows on the lawn. Orange and pink roses. Glasses with sparkling bubbles. A warm hand. Michael.

'No,' I moaned.

Then I tore up the flower picture just as I had destroyed

the Roman villa and all the other things that Cornelius had given me.

But this time, fragments kept coming back. Lunch party. *Do we have to go?* So I walked across to the wall and smashed my head against it to get my father's voice out of my head.

The alarm screamed. Three men in white coats burst through my door.

Then I heard someone yell three words. No – three letters. I'd heard them before but didn't know what they meant.

E. C. T.

32

Jo

I must have died and gone to heaven! There's this huge bed with a soft blue cover on it and loads of fancy cushions as well as pillows. I can't help leaping on top and bouncing up and down like a kid. My stomach isn't sore any more. I feel like a different woman.

On the other side by the window is a smaller bed. ('Sure you don't mind sharing a room?' Mary-Lou had asked. 'The hotel only has a family suite left but you can have the dog in it too.')

'It's got its own bathroom,' said Tim, jumping in and out of the shower with his shoes still on. 'Look! It's big enough to live in!'

I walk round the room, running my fingers along each piece of posh furniture from the sofa to the DVD player. There's even a bowl of fruit. 'I feel like royalty,' I say, peeling an orange.

The kid gives me a high five. 'Not bad, is it?'

Lucky jumps up at us, barking with excitement.

There's a knock on the door. It's Mary-Lou. 'Thought you might like this.' She's holding out a couple of carrier bags.

'Thanks.' I grab them eagerly. Bags are really useful for loads of things on the streets.

But there's something in them. I shake out two pairs of black tracksuit bottoms and a turquoise fleece. They've got a label inside with the words 'Relaxed Leisure Wear.' They're really stylish but, most importantly, warm. There are socks too, along with a thermal vest and black tights and plain white pants.

'I had to guess your sizes,' says Mary-Lou. Her face is shining once more. I remember one of my old friends saying that there are some folk that get a real kick out of giving. 'There's a beret at the bottom too. Might keep your head warm out there.'

My hair had started to grow in short spiky tufts since I'd last shaved it. But it was still no protection from the weather and I'd lost my old beanie somewhere when running away from Tim's gang.

Then she presses an envelope into my hand. 'I want you to take this now just in case we're gone when you wake. We have to leave early to get a connection, but sleep in if you like. Check-out isn't until ten.'

I'm so gobsmacked that by the time I remember to say thank you, she's gone.

'Look at these!' I say to Tim.

But he's sitting on the sofa, dirty trainers up on the fancy blue pattern, playing with the remote controls. A cartoon roars into life. 'I used to watch this when I was a kid,' he says dreamily.

I realize that somewhere out there is a woman who can't sleep or eat for not knowing where her son is.

'Ever thought of getting in touch with your mum to let her know you're all right?' I ask.

'And get beaten up by her bloke again?'

'Maybe she's kicked him out by now.'

'Bet she hasn't.'

'How about trying to find your dad?'

Tim spits with disgust on the nice carpet. 'Walked out on us before my mum even had me.'

'That must have been hard.'

'I can deal with it.'

Why is it that, even if our families are crap, we still need to belong somewhere?

I go into the bathroom, taking my clothes in with me. In the caravan, we'd never had clean stuff to change into so we just slept in what we wore. It feels like there's an awkwardness between us now in this posh hotel room that hadn't been there before.

Still, I think, *this is pretty amazing, isn't it?* I lie back in the bath, wriggling my toes under the hot water. Then, just to see what happens, I fiddle with a lever thing near the taps. Suddenly a gush of water comes out from this great big shower above me. It's freezing.

I let out a scream.

'You OK?' asks Tim from the other side of the door.

By now I've found the bit that gives you hot water.

'Great,' I yell back. The water goes into my mouth and I find myself laughing because it's all so bloody funny. Who'd have guessed that we'd end up in a palace like this? There's even a hairdryer on the wall – not that I need one – and a whacking great mirror.

There's a tube of toothpaste on the side in a packet with a new toothbrush. It's been so long since I cleaned my teeth that I've got used to my doggy breath – though I noticed the American woman took a step back when she got a bit close earlier. The paste is fresh and minty. Nice!

'Your turn,' I say when I come out.

Tim's still lying on the sofa, watching cartoons with Lucky snuggled up in his arms. 'I'm all right as I am.'

So he's still pissed off with me.

'Don't you want to wash?'

'What's the point? We're only going to get dirty again.'

I glance at my now-clean fingernails. 'It makes you feel good.'

'Getting used to this kind of high life, are you?'

'Maybe. Why don't you put on your new clothes anyway?'

''Cos the stuff she bought me is too small. It's trainers I need.'

We both do. My feet are still rough and raw from where the soles have come away. I find a 'room service menu' card and cut out two shapes with some tiny scissors from a little sewing kit on the side. Then I stuff them inside my shoes as a makeshift. Not brilliant but they'll do for a bit.

I go to bed, leaving Tim to watch the television. He's glued to the screen like he's in another world. I'm in another world too. The mattress is so soft that I am sinking into it. I can't remember the last time I slept on a pillow. I'm out before I know it.

I wake with a start. It's dark apart from the light of the telly, which is still on. But there's another noise too.

It's Tim.

'Mum, Mum.' He's talking again in his sleep and crying at the same time.

Lucky is making little whimpering noises and licking Tim's face.

I get out and kneel down next to him. 'It's all right,' I say, stroking his arm.

It seems to soothe him. His cries turn into quiet sobs. Then into steady breathing. In the end he settles. I watch his face, which looks even younger now he's having a kip, and gently pull a strand of hair away from his eyes. It's like I really am his mum. Makes me happy and sad at the same time.

Then I tiptoe back to my bed. But I can't sleep. I sit upright in the end, thoughts running through my head. Half of them don't even make sense.

I get up. I fancy another shower – I'll probably never be in a bathroom like this again – but I don't want to risk waking the kid. I finger the soft white towels, stroking them. They're too big to take with me in my plastic bags but I can nick some of those lovely soaps. Then I get dressed in my new clothes and leave the old ones in a pile in the corner.

There's some fancy hotel paper in the chest of drawers below the mirror. I write two notes in big capital letters.

I take a last look at Tim curled up in bed, calm now, with Lucky in the crook of his arm. I leave the first note on the floor next to him so he'll see it when he gets up. I find myself blowing them a kiss. Must be getting soft in my old age.

Quietly, I shut our bedroom door. Then I tiptoe down the corridor to where the Americans are sleeping and shove the second note under their door.

Feeling like shit, I go downstairs. There's a desk – all shiny like someone has been polishing it every day of its life – and a young girl with a swishy brown ponytail.

Maybe 'cos I look clean now in my new clothes, she doesn't shoot me that 'you don't belong here' stare that the bloke on the desk had given us when we arrived yesterday.

I go outside. The wind has picked up. Shivering, I make my way to a public phone box I saw yesterday on the way to the hotel.

My fingers shaking with cold and nerves, I dial 999.

'Police, please,' I say in a made-up voice. 'I'm ringing about a missing boy. He calls himself Tim but I don't think that's his real name. I know where he is.'

1.23 p.m., 17 August 1984

We're almost there.

My stepmother is giving me last-minute instructions.

'Don't think you're one of the guests,' she snorts dismissively. 'You're only coming to babysit Michael. When we arrive, take him outside and keep an eye on him while your father and I talk to friends.'

Usually I wouldn't mind. I love looking after my brother. But being away at school has given me a different perspective on how I'm treated by my stepmother. Not only is she rude to me but she also uses me as an unpaid servant. And Michael's behaviour in the back of the car has upset me.

Everything was all right when it was just Daddy and me.

33

Ellie

From my prison-cell window, I see a large white van arrive. It pulls into the courtyard below. Uniformed armed guards are bringing out a woman. She is young and is wearing beige trousers and a smart jacket, which suggests our latest 'resident' might have come straight from court.

She looks bewildered, just as I did when I arrived at this place. Like she's being led to the gallows. It was a bit like that at Highbridge.

ECT is frowned upon now, and even back then many professionals had stopped using it. But this was a private institution, and the people who ran it were a law unto themselves.

We were in a different part of the San. This part looked like an operating theatre, just like the one in *Angels*, which I used to watch on television with Grandma Greenway long before Michael changed everything. The walls around me didn't have any pictures. There was a light blaring down on me. I was lying on a raised bed. A man in a white coat who said he was an anaesthetist was there, and also Cornelius.

One of the nurses was holding my left hand. Another, my right. There were straps across my chest to restrain me. I could feel something on my head too, rather like a helmet. There was no way I could make a dash for it.

'Start counting backwards,' said Cornelius. 'Ten, nine, eight . . .'

When I opened my eyes, I thought for a minute that I was back in my old bedroom with its pretty blue-and-pink-flowered curtains and the bed that my brother Michael liked to jump on.

'Ellie? Can you hear me?'

My father! He'd come to get me out of bed for school. Afterwards, we might go to the park. Michael would want a swing. *Push me, Ellie. Push! Higher! Higher!*

'Ellie?'

This didn't sound like my father's voice, I realized. It was much deeper. And he couldn't be getting me out of bed for school because I was at boarding school, wasn't I? Maybe there'd be a letter from Peter in my pigeonhole and a drawing from Michael with a big red crayon cross for a kiss at the bottom.

'How do you feel, Ellie?'

A man was looking down at me. His piercing blue eyes seemed familiar but I couldn't quite place him.

'What's my name, Ellie?'

I tried very hard but I just couldn't remember. Saliva was drooling down my mouth. It felt wet and nasty.

'Do you know where you are?'

I started at the white walls and the lights. It didn't look like boarding school after all.

Suddenly I felt sick. I retched violently into a bowl that someone was holding out for me. And then I fell asleep again.

*

The experience was repeated several times. It must have gone on for months because when we began, there were leaves on the trees outside. When it finally finished, the branches were bare. But it's hard to be specific, because the 'treatment', as they called it, affected my short-term memory. I was also very tired. No longer did I struggle when they said it was time for 'another session'. I allowed them to strap me to the bed. I just didn't have the energy to fight back.

I even began eating again, opening my mouth obediently when one of the nurses spoon-fed me porridge. 'Good girl,' they'd say when I started to do it myself. Before long, my waistbands got tight and my cheeks grew puffy.

I stopped trying to hurt myself too. In fact, I couldn't remember why I'd begun to do it in the first place. When it was family visiting day, I no longer hit my head on the wall simply because no one had come to see me. Instead, I helped to hand round little sponge cakes with a fixed smile. 'How very kind,' gushed one of the mothers.

It made me feel good.

Then I heard her whisper something. 'I've read about her, I think. Isn't she the girl who . . .'

I didn't hear the rest. But it didn't matter. I was happy here.

One of the other good things about the ECT was that they stopped asking me what had happened that day. In fact, I couldn't really remember it myself any more. It became like a black hole in my mind. Erased like the drawings I screwed up in art class even though the teacher told me they were good.

It was spring when I began to start proper lessons.

There weren't many of us. Not everyone was 'able' to reach this stage.

'You've done very well,' Cornelius told me.

My desk was near a boy of about my age who kept passing me notes. They always had the same five words.

I want to fuck you.

I felt sick. Hot. Then cold. What if he came into my room at night? Our doors were locked but supposing he got through the window?

So I took the note to Cornelius and the boy no longer attended my classes.

'He's been moved somewhere else,' I was told.

Good. The last thing I wanted was to get pregnant and be responsible for a child. What if I hurt it by mistake? Mind you, I hadn't had periods since the accident, and the one thing I did remember from reproduction at school was that you needed them to have a baby.

The days came and went. It was hard to keep track of time. But I was – or so I was told – making good progress. I no longer needed ECT. Instead, I was on a cocktail of different-coloured pills and attended daily therapy sessions. I was also doing well in my lessons and won a silver fountain pen as a prize for being the 'most promising' student.

When I'd first come here, I might have used it to cut myself. But now I couldn't wait to write my next essay with it. The teacher said I showed 'exceptional talent', especially in English. There were, apparently, special circumstances in which universities would accept 'people like me'. I just had to work very, very hard.

Cornelius said we would have to 'wait and see' how I got on. But Julia was more encouraging.

'You can do this,' she said. 'It's your opportunity for a new start.'

Her confidence gave me an excited thrill. When the others were glued to the television in the lounge, I stayed in my room, studying. Sometimes I'd feel a small fragment from the day of the incident floating into my head while I was working. But then I would let it float right out again, just as they'd told me to.

I did so well that they moved me to a different part of the building. There weren't any bars on the window any more. I could have just opened them and run away. But I didn't want to. We also had what were called 'group sessions', when we talked about how we felt.

'Happy,' I always said when it was my turn.

'Do you want to hurt yourself?'

I frowned. 'Why would I?'

On my eighteenth birthday I was allowed to have a mirror in my room. Glass was no longer considered a safety risk for me. I looked more like my old self. Was that good or bad? I wasn't sure.

I joined in the singing sessions, although sometimes I had to mime the words – any line that included 'mother', 'father' or 'brother' made me sick inside, even though I took care not to get upset in case they made me have the ECT treatment again. When I was allowed into town I tried to disguise from my carer the fact that I avoided the pavement cracks. I concentrated really hard on my studies and passed three A levels. I was the first one at Highbridge ever to do that.

Soon I was packing my bags. I was going to university to do a degree in English Literature.

And to meet a man who would change the course of my life.

34

Jo

It's still black outside. I heard someone in the pub last night saying it wouldn't be long until the clocks changed. A seagull screams overhead. Makes me jump. There's one now, fighting with a pizza packet on the pavement. A crust is hanging out of its mouth and the creature eyes me triumphantly. 'This is mine,' the look says.

Just as well I'm not hungry. After last night's dinner, my stomach is still fit to burst. My plastic bags – one in each hand – are heavier too, thanks to the two rolls of posh bog paper I took with me from the hotel room.

I walk along the harbour, watching a fisherman getting his boat ready. He nods at me and then goes back to wiping down the sides. I remember the fun Tim and I had in the sea. I get a twinge of guilt.

'Don't get soft,' I tell myself. 'Get a move on.' I glance behind me. No one. I realize that when Tim was with me, I wasn't so scared, constantly on the lookout for danger. But all my old fears are crowding back.

I'm walking down a narrow cobbled street now. The tall, thin houses are painted in blues and pinks. What I'd give to live in one of them. The curtains are closed. Some have shutters, firmly secured to keep the likes of me away. I pass a shop selling paintings. There's one in the window of kids running along a beach, laughing like everything is happy in the world.

I stare at the price. Two thousand quid. Bloody hell! This world is crazy.

I'm at the end of the village, and there's a big road ahead with no proper pavement. A car goes past, scarily fast. The bastard almost hits me. I could still be in that warm safe hotel room if I'd stayed put. When was the last time I'd fallen on my feet like that? Had I been a bloody idiot to leave it behind?

That reminds me. The envelope. I take it out and count again.

Ten, twenty, thirty, forty . . . fifty quid. There's a message I hadn't noticed before, with pretty writing. *Hope this will help for a bit.*

My eyes feel wet. *What the hell are you doing crying?* I think to myself. *This is your lucky day.* I stifle the feeling of guilt.

Behind me there's the sound of an engine. It's not a car this time. It's a bus. I put out my hand, expecting it to go past because I'm not at a proper stop. But it pulls up.

'Get on, love,' says the driver. He has a friendly burr to this voice. 'Where are you off to?'

'Tintagel.'

For some reason, the name jumps out of my mouth. I'd seen it on a leaflet in the pub last night when the American couple were talking about places they wanted to visit. There had been this picture of a steep path leading up to some old ruins and another of caves.

'Going a long way, aren't you?' says the driver. 'You'll need to change a few times to get there. But I can put you right when we get to the depot. Single or return?'

Lives like mine are a one-way ticket. 'Single.' I hand him one of the tenners.

'Got a fiver instead?'

If I was still in my old stuff with grime on my face, I bet he'd have been less friendly. But it's amazing what a set of new clothes and a clean body can do. I try to make my voice sound a bit posher too to go with it.

'Sorry,' I shrug. 'Just been to the cashpoint. They didn't do anything smaller.'

He makes an 'I know what you mean' expression and then gives me the change. I go to the back of the bus and count it carefully. I mustn't trust anyone.

Especially not myself.

1.30 p.m., 17 August 1984

The Daniels live in an enormous house with wisteria climbing up the front and a massive gravel drive where other cars are also parked. It looks like we're not the only ones to be delayed by the traffic, as others are still arriving. 'You go in while I find a space,' says my father to us all.

I spot Peter immediately as we go inside. We both flush. He's taller than I remembered and is wearing fashionable skinny jeans. I feel horribly self-conscious about my too-tight dress. Peter, I notice, has also grown a proper moustache since I'd last seen him. It's a bit wispy but it makes him look like a man. I begin to feel even more nervous.

His mother gives me a warm hug. It reminds me of the days when she and my mother would take Peter and me out on picnics in the summer before she became ill. 'Lovely to see you again, dear. How is boarding school? I know Peter's missed you. He only came along today because you were going to be here.'

Peter goes a deep red and shuffles from one foot to the other, throwing me a 'Sorry my mother is so embarrassing' glance. It makes me feel a lot better. I'm not the only one with nerves.

Meanwhile, Sheila has taken one look at Peter's mother and, recognizing her as one of my mother's old friends, walks *on, her head held high. How rude. It makes me hate her even more.*

'I can't wait to spend some time with you,' whispers Peter. I can't believe it. Perhaps he really does like me!

But Sheila has already ruined it. 'I've got to look after my brother,' I say, glancing down at Michael, who's clinging to my dress.

He looks disappointed. 'OK. You'd better bring him along too, then.'

35

Ellie

His name was Roger. He was thirty four. Young enough to be mistaken sometimes for a student but old enough to be my tutor.

I'd chosen Reading University. It was what was known as a 'red-brick university'. It wasn't ancient like Durham but it didn't have the stark modern architectural features of, say, York. I had visited them all but chose Reading because it felt safe with its pretty green campus. I liked walking. Highbridge had had beautiful grounds. In the last two years, I'd been allowed to wander round them on my own. They helped me feel I was free.

I'd fallen in love with a particular hall of residence which I'd spotted in the university prospectus. It looked just like an Oxford college with its beautiful leaded windows and entrance arch – and, as it turned out, the building had indeed once been owned by that prestigious university.

The only drawback was that I had to share my large Victorian bedroom with another girl. I'd hoped for a room of my own for privacy's sake. She was from Newcastle and I found it hard to understand her accent. When she said 'bath', she pronounced the 'a' like 'a' in 'apple'. But at the same time, the place was warm and chummy. My roommate played lots of songs by a band called The Pet Shop Boys – she was amazed I hadn't heard of them before but I could hardly tell her about High-bridge, where popular music wasn't big on the agenda. She was very friendly. Too much so. I often had to deflect her questions about my home life or lie, and then hoped I would remember exactly what I'd said. Instead of going out with her crowd I threw myself into my studies again.

Victorian literature was my favourite subject. The lecturer was called Roger. He didn't know about my past. Cornelius and Julia, who had helped me fill in my admissions form, had explained that certain staff at the university needed to be aware of my 'background'. But they also promised that this was confidential. It would be a clean start.

'Forgive me,' Roger said in one of our private tutorials when we were halfway through the first term. 'But I can't help feeling that you would have been a perfect extra Brontë sister.'

I wasn't sure how to take his words. Was he commenting on my writing?

'Well, I'm certainly not Branwell,' I said quickly. I wasn't trying to be smart. I just wasn't sure what to say and that was the first thing that came out.

But Roger seemed impressed with my reply. 'That's very true.'

Then he inhaled his pipe and leaned back in his chair before blowing out the smoke in small puffs. I liked the smell. And I enjoyed the fact that he looked quite comfortable in my presence. I wasn't used to that. At Highbridge, the staff had pretended we were 'normal' but I knew they didn't think so underneath. It was as though they were always on the lookout for one of us freaking out again or doing something crazy.

'Ah, Branwell,' Roger repeated, bringing me back to the present. 'Now there's a character. He couldn't have been easy to live with. How do you think he affected Emily's writing?'

'Perhaps she wrote to shut him out of her head,' I shot back. The craft sessions at Highbridge had helped me do that. Concentrating on small things helped you forget the big ones. Thinking about it made me edgy, hence my sharp reply. But Roger didn't seem perturbed.

'Do you think so?' He frowned but not in a disapproving manner; more as if he was interested in my point.

'Perhaps.' Swiftly I changed the subject. 'Have you been here long?'

He turned to face me. Instantly, I wondered if I'd been too familiar. But I wanted to stop him from prying into my own circumstances like my roommate was always doing.

'No.' He blew out another curl of smoke. 'I'm new. Like you.'

Then he looked as though he was going to say something but stopped. 'For your next essay, I'd like you to discuss whether Mary Ann Evans would have been equally famous if she had written under her real name.'

Goosebumps broke out all over me. I'd insisted on legally changing my surname when applying for university. I was scared someone might recognize it from the newspapers. Cornelius had advised against my decision, declaring that part of my recovery process was to 'own' what had happened. But I'd turned eighteen by then and was entitled to do what I wanted. Mary Ann Evans had been thirty-seven when she adopted the nom-de-plume George Eliot.

'Fine,' I said, gathering my books.

Normally I would go straight to the library after a tutorial, but our conversation had unsettled me so I caught the bus into Reading instead. It was still a novelty to be able to do this. In the last year at Highbridge, those of us who were preparing to leave had been allowed to visit the local town on our own. But it was much smaller than Reading and, as I now made my way to the shopping centre, I started to feel closed in. Squashed. Threatened. One woman glared at me for treading on her toes. Her angry eyes reminded me of Sheila's. Her hand raised to my face on that final day . . .

Shaking, I headed for a small coffee shop, where I concentrated on my breathing – a technique that Julia had taught me. 'Inhale from the bottom of your solar plexus. Hold for a count of seven. Breathe out for two. Hold for a count of five. Breathe out fully.'

I was doing fine until my eyes fell on a copy of the *Daily Mail* that the previous occupant of my table must have left behind.

The headlines leapt out at me. FAMILY WIPED OUT IN HORROR CRASH BY TEENAGE DRUNK DRIVER.

The bitter taste of bile rose into my mouth. I pushed the paper away. But the photographs of the victims still grinned out at me in my head. I stood up to go – luckily I hadn't ordered – but as I did so, I spotted a familiar figure coming in. I put my head down, hoping Roger hadn't seen me, but it was too late.

'Ellie,' he said warmly. 'Twice in one day. What a pleasure.'

I presumed he was just being polite. I knew nothing of flirting in those days.

'You're not going, are you? I could do with some company.' He touched my shoulder briefly. The physical gesture took me by surprise and I stepped back. 'Won't you have a coffee with me?'

'Sorry,' I said, my mind going back to the newspaper. 'I need some air.'

'You look a bit peaky. Are you OK? Come on, let's get you out of here.'

He suggested a short walk along the river. I kept my eyes straight ahead along the towpath, not knowing what to say.

I expected Roger to talk about work. Maybe he wanted to go over the George Eliot essay. But instead, he wished to know whether I liked Reading and whether I'd made lots of friends in halls.

These personal questions made me feel awkward. Was such familiarity allowed? But this was university, I reminded myself. The real world, where I was considered an adult. Even so, when our hands brushed accidentally, I drew further apart from him, just as I had done earlier. If he took offence, he didn't show it.

We talked about Oxford, where he'd been an under-graduate, and then stayed on to do his Masters and PhD. 'It was a privileged existence,' he said. 'I don't come from the kind of background where you dine in an ancient hall and have scouts — that's their word for cleaners — to tidy your room every day.'

I thought of Highbridge with its Gothic towers and the staff who cleaned up after us. He glanced across at me. 'What about you?'

I spun him the same sanitized version of the truth I'd given to my roommate. 'My mother died young and I was sent to boarding school.'

'Really?' Roger raised his eyebrows. They were thick and black. Manly. A bit like my father's. 'Did you like it?'

'I learned to be independent,' I said truthfully.

'Did your father marry again?'

My fingers clenched themselves into little balls. 'He's not around any more,' I said.

It wasn't what he'd asked but it seemed to do the trick. 'I'm sorry.'

'Don't be,' I retorted briskly. 'There's no need.'

He tried to make more small talk but I answered only 'yes' or 'no', rather as I had with Cornelius when I'd first met him. I'd made a mistake in agreeing to go for this walk, I told myself. The sooner I got back, the better.

'Please.' He placed a hand on my shoulder. I took a step back. He bit his lip. For a minute, he looked like a small child. 'I didn't mean to pry just then. I only asked because my own mother died when I was eleven and my father married again. My stepmother was jealous of his past and I left home as soon as I could.'

I'd misjudged him. Didn't I hate it when people did the same to me? Instantly, I felt terrible. 'I'm sorry,' I said.

He shrugged. 'It's life. Messed me up for a bit, though. Made me take some wrong decisions.'

Considering we barely knew each other, his frankness took me back. I didn't know whether to be flattered or shocked. After all, he was staff and I was a mere first-year. By then we'd stopped by a yellow sports car with an open roof. 'Would you like a lift back?'

'No, thanks.'

'Right.' I could tell he was offended. I wanted to explain that I hadn't meant it, but then I'd look like an idiot. 'Well, I'll see you at the next seminar, then.'

I still felt shaken when I got home. Part of this was down to the newspaper headline about that poor family. But my fear – or was it excitement? – also came from having been with Roger. I couldn't work out if I liked his company or not. It made me feel uncomfortable.

After the bus had dropped me off at the campus, I made my way to the English department and left a note in Roger's pigeonhole to say that I wished to change my options. The Victorian period wasn't for me after all. I'd decided to do the early twentieth century instead, which was being taught by one of his colleagues.

When I got back to hall, my roommate was making a cup of tea in the corridor kitchenette. 'You're a dark horse,' she exclaimed.

My heart started to thump. She'd found out what I had done. Somehow it had leaked out. I'd have to leave. So much for the new start Cornelius and Julia had promised.

'The girl opposite saw you in town with that dishy English lecturer, Roger Halls. Are you going out with him?'

I was filled with relief, even though it took time for my pulse rate to calm down.

'No, I'm not,' I said firmly. 'We just happened to bump into each other in a coffee shop.'

'So you're definitely not dating him, then?'

'Why are you so interested?'

'Only trying to look out for you, that's all. I heard he was married.'

I pretended to act casual. 'He's my tutor. I don't fancy him.'

'OK.' She didn't sound like she believed me. 'But word has it that he's got a bit of a roving eye. Just be careful.'

Roger had a wife? Part of me felt disappointed for reasons I couldn't explain to myself. But that didn't mean he was a cheat. Perhaps he'd merely been trying to be friendly towards me in town. His company had been, despite my initial doubts, a welcome change from my usual solitude. I began to regret my decision about dropping out of his classes. Besides, if my roommate was correct, it was all right. There was no way I would have a romantic relationship with a married man, only a platonic one.

'Going out again?' asked my roommate.

Pulling on my duffle coat, I slammed the door behind me without answering. If I ran fast enough, I might get there before Roger checked his post.

The note was still there. Tucking it into my pocket, I turned and bumped straight into him. His blue jumper under the tweed jacket felt warm to the touch. It smelled of tobacco.

'I'm sorry,' he said.

'It was my fault,' I stuttered.

'Did you want something? The department is about to close.'

'I was . . . well, I was hoping to see you actually.'

I found my face reddening.

'You were?'

'Yes. I . . . I'm struggling a bit with the Victorian view of female emancipation. I wanted to include it in the George Eliot essay. I meant to mention it this afternoon but . . . well, I forgot. I couldn't get hold of the books you recommended – they've all been borrowed from the library.'

He took out a key from his pocket. 'I could lend you some of my personal copies if you like. Come on in.'

'He's got a bit of a roving eye. Just be careful.'

'It's all right,' I said, staying outside. 'I've got to be quick. My boyfriend is cooking supper.'

'I didn't realize you had one. You didn't mention him earlier.'

Why do lies always catch me out? Besides, it wasn't any of his business.

'Well, he's a sort of boyfriend.'

He laughed. 'Ah, that old one.' He pressed the books into my hand. 'Here they are.' His voice sounded artificially bright. 'You can return them at the next seminar.'

I kicked my way back to hall through the crisp autumn leaves, feeling even more confused than I had before. Only a few minutes earlier, I'd told myself I wouldn't have anything to do with a married man. Yet seeing him face to face just now had shaken me. Why did Roger Halls have such an effect on me? Was it just because it sounded as if he'd had his problems too? Or was it because he was the first person in years who seemed genuinely interested in me?

36

Jo

The driver was right. It takes bloody ages to get to Tintagel. When I get off, there are loads of coaches around and plenty of people too. In one way it's good because I can hide in the crowd. Once more, I look over my shoulder. No one's following me. At least, not as far as I can see.

It will be evening soon. My stomach, which had been so full earlier on, is now rumbling and my muscles are stiff after sitting for so long. I walk past a bakery. The smell makes my mouth water. I buy a cheese and onion pasty, taking care not to flash the rest of the money in the envelope.

It's getting colder. I don't want to spend my precious cash on a bed and breakfast but it's better than huddling up against a damp hedgerow. That's when I realize. I left my carrier bags on the last bus along with the bog paper and the fancy soap. I kick the wall with anger. A man walking past gives me a scared look. 'I'm not dangerous,' I yell out.

I want to cry, but instead I wander up and down the main street and others leading off it. All the bed and breakfasts have 'No Vacancies' signs outside.

Looks like I'm going to have to sleep rough again. Perhaps I can find a barn or something. I follow a sign pointing to Tintagel Castle and wander down a steep path. Then I catch my breath. Below me is this massive drop with cliffs and the sea below.

I know this place. Or am I imagining it? I hold on to the wall in front. The stone cuts into my hands. My head is dizzy. My skin starts to sweat. I'm going to fall.

'Get a grip,' I say to myself fiercely, turning away from the sea.

Then I see it. A small yellow flower growing out of the rough grass at the side of the path. I kneel down on the mud and stroke it. The tiny petal is like velvet.

That's better. I'm breathing more regularly now. I make myself walk, checking over my shoulder again and again, though I'm not sure why.

The path goes on and on with the sea still on my right. I follow a footpath sign and then another. I go up and up. I don't look down in case I get another dizzy panic spell.

The sky has gone pink and red, like a film sunset.

I'm going up some steps now. I'm panting 'cos they're so steep. I take a quick look at the sea. It's even further down than before. I make myself look away and keep going. Getting easier now. The ground is flatter. Then my skin prickles. Ahead, I can see a man crouching down. He's got something in his hand . . .

There's no one else around. *Run*, I tell myself. But he looks up and sees me.

'Hi.' His voice isn't exactly posh but it's not rough either. His face is unshaven and his skin is brown, like he's been outside a lot. 'Beautiful evening, isn't it?'

If I make a dash for it, will he be able to catch me?

'Don't mind me,' he says. 'You just enjoy the view.'

That's when I realize that the thing in his hand is a stick of red chalk. Slowly I move nearer. He's crouching down over the most beautiful picture I have ever seen. It's of the sea below of us, the bridge and the steep path leading up the cliff. The colours are really cool. Blues, pink, yellows. Blimmin' heck! He's drawing on some paving slabs.

'What do you think?' he asks.

'It's amazing.' Unable to help myself, I crouch down next to him. 'What happens if it rains?'

He shrugs. 'It'll get washed away.'

'What a waste!'

'No worries. I can do another. Saves buying a canvas every time. And people are really generous about donations, so I can get fresh chalk.'

There's a plastic box next to him with coins in it. So that's why he's being so nice. He wants money from me. I scramble up to my feet, thinking of the envelope the American woman gave me. There's no way this bloke is getting his mitts on that.

'Sorry,' I say. 'I've got nothing to give you.'

'Doesn't matter. I'm just glad you like my work.'

'I've always wanted to draw,' I find myself saying suddenly. Sounds daft for someone like me to say that, I know. But it's true.

He hands me the yellow stick and makes a mock flourish. 'Be my guest.'

Feeling like a complete fool, I press the chalk down hard on the stone. It snaps in two.

'A bit softer,' he says. 'Like this.'

His hand takes mine. Normally I'd hate this, but for some reason, the touch of his bare skin against mine sends a pleasant heat up my arm.

'That's right. Now you try.'

This time I manage not to break the chalk. He looks approvingly. 'Nice flower.'

'It's the one in the hedgerows,' I say sharply.

'Ah yes. The gorse. A survivor, that one. Lasts whatever the weather chucks at it.'

Then he stands up, dusting himself down. He towers over me. This bloke is tall! 'On the road, are you?'

His question pisses me off. How does he know? I've got clean clothes on and I washed my hair back in the hotel. OK, so my toes are sticking out of my trainers and those cardboard replacement soles aren't much use.

'What makes you think that?' I ask.

'I know the look,' he says. 'I'm moving around too.'

'I'm getting a place of my own soon,' I say quickly.

If I repeat it enough times, I might believe it myself.

'Sure. Just takes time, doesn't it?' He puts his chalks carefully into a box like each one is something precious, and then slings his rucksack on his shoulders. 'Come on, then.'

1.35 p.m., 17 August 1984

Michael jumps up and down, tugging my hand. 'Can we go in the garden? I've brought a tennis ball with me. Look!'

He's hidden it in his pocket. It's one of mine. He must have stolen it from my room.

It's not fair. I just want to be on my own with Peter and tell him all about my awful stepmother.

'Great idea.' Peter takes Michael's other hand.

What's he talking about? I thought he was as irritated at babysitting Michael as I am.

'I'm in the cricket team at school,' continues Peter. 'Is that all right, sir?'

That last question — so polite! — is directed at my father, who has just come into the house after parking the car. He seems distracted, as if searching for Sheila through the crowd of well-dressed, brightly chattering, glass-clinking guests. There she is! Standing with some man on the other side of the room and making that fake laugh of hers. My father sees her too.

'Yes,' he says, over his shoulder. 'Of course. Just make sure you stay in the back and away from any cars that are still arriving, won't you?'

'Come on,' whispers Peter. 'If we go outside with your brother, we might be able to find some privacy.'

37

Ellie

Even though I'd decided to stay in Roger's tutorial group, I kept my distance. Nevertheless, part of me felt this pull towards him, which scared me. It was as though I was two people: the one who felt really special when he praised me for my 'insightful essays', and the one who wanted to push him away because of the rumours that he was married. Though I had noticed he didn't wear a wedding ring.

I spent most of my first year working. My roommate despaired of me. 'Why don't you come to the student union ball?' she asked. 'You might find a boyfriend,' she added, clearly hoping to do so herself.

'I don't like that kind of thing,' I mumbled.

'You've never been – so you won't know until you try. Come on. It'll be fun. At least let me show you how to put on eyeliner. It would make a real difference to your face.'

It did. But as a new grown-up me appeared in the mirror, I had a glimpse of my stepmother, who had always worn heavy make-up herself. 'What right do you have,' I could almost hear her saying, 'to doll yourself up after what you did to me?'

'How can I take it off?' I said, panic rising.

'Calm down. You wipe your eyes with this.' My roommate shook her head. 'You're weird, Ellie.'

Didn't I know that already?

Yet that evening, I couldn't resist standing outside the union hall, listening to the music with the floor shaking as everyone danced around inside. If things were different I could have been one of them. Free and happy and having fun.

I stayed in Reading after the summer term ended. What choice did I have? I'd been discharged from Highbridge without formal support. I had no family to turn to. There were a certain number of rooms set aside for foreign students who didn't go home. I was the only English person there. Everyone else had returned to their families. At least money wasn't a problem. Since my eighteenth birthday I'd been receiving an allowance every month from the trust fund my grandfather had set up for me – far more than I needed.

Before long, I grew to like being at uni when hardly anyone else was around. The hall was peaceful without the public schoolboys chucking bread rolls and names at each other. The gardens were beautiful and I would sit there on a bench by a lovely magnolia tree, reading. That summer I was working my way through H. E. Bates. I preferred his books about the Larkin family to his more serious novels, because they were a family that loved each other.

One day in August, when it was particularly warm, I braved a sundress. Usually I liked to cover up my arms because of the scars. But it was too hot to wear sleeves.

'You're still here?' asked a voice.

I didn't need to look up to see who it was.

'Yes,' I said.

I waited for Roger to ask why I hadn't gone home but he didn't. It was as though he respected my need for privacy. I liked that.

'I'm staying too.'

Then I did look up. He was holding a brown envelope. 'My decree absolute,' he said, stroking it as though it was precious. 'It's been a long wait, but it's here now.'

'What's a decree absolute?' I asked.

He seemed surprised I didn't know. 'It's a legal document to say that my marriage has finally ended.'

It was a sign of the times that I'd never met anyone who was divorced before. I was both shocked and excited. So that meant he was free, then . . .

'Are you sad?' I asked.

My years at Highbridge taught me that sometimes the straightest questions were the best – even though it wasn't always wise to give straight answers back.

'Yes. And no. We were too young when we met, but perhaps we could both have tried harder. It's strange to think of facing life alone.' It was as though he was talking to himself.

'It's not so bad,' I said spontaneously.

'Really?' He stared down at me. 'You know, the thing I like about you, Ellie, is that you're different.'

'Is that a compliment or not?' I asked, thinking of my roommate's comment before the ball, which still rankled.

'Of course it is.'

My heart swelled with gratitude. We'd all known we were different at Highbridge. It was our biggest fear. Each of us had been there for a terrible reason. How were we ever going to lead normal lives? I was the only one who

283

had gone on to uni. But already I was beginning to wonder what I was going to do afterwards. Supposing a prospective employer looked me up in the newspaper archives and found out what I had done, despite the fact that I'd changed my name?

'I was going to cycle down to Sonning this afternoon,' Roger said, interrupting my thoughts. 'Would you like to come? It's a really pretty place on the river with a lovely pub.'

A lot of students rode bikes, but not me. The responsibility was too great – it was why I'd vowed never to drive. What if I injured someone? 'I haven't cycled for years,' I said.

'That's all right. You never forget.' Then he glanced at the scars on my arms but didn't say anything.

Embarrassment made me rude. 'Don't you have anyone else you can ask?'

'Yes – but it's you I want to go with. You'd be doing me a favour.' He looked at the envelope in his hand. 'I need to clear my head from this failure.'

'It's not a failure,' I said quickly. 'Just see it as a new start.'

'You know what? You're right.'

Was I? If only he knew. For years, I'd dreamed of leaving Highbridge with all its rules and regulations so I could be free. But now I was alone in this new world, able to do whatever I wanted, and I was terrified of making another awful mistake. What if this was one more? And I wasn't only talking bikes . . .

But Roger was right. It was easier to get on a bicycle again than I'd thought. I was so busy concentrating on balancing and looking ahead that I forgot to worry about hurting anyone. Even so, it was a relief when we arrived at Sonning in one piece.

'Aren't the views beautiful?' he said, pointing out the river snaking by as we sat in the back garden of a pub. He had a pint of real ale. I, as usual, had lemonade.

'Yes,' I said, forcing myself to look at the water. So unpredictable. Just like roads. And planes. You didn't know when disaster was going to strike.

Later, when we walked back to our bikes, I almost stood on a pavement crack. To avoid it, I swayed. He put out his hand to steady me. 'Thanks,' I said, blushing furiously. I bent down to undo my padlock. When I stood up, his face was close to mine. In that instant, I knew he was going to kiss me.

'No,' I said, taking a quick step back and nearly falling over my feet as I did so. 'Sorry.'

His forehead crinkled as if he was confused. 'Do you mean "No" as in you're not ready now or "No" as in you don't want this ever?'

'I don't know.' My face was red. Hot. Shamed. How could I tell him the truth?

'I can give you time,' he said, reaching out to catch my arm.

I nodded. 'OK. Thank you.' Then I got on my bike. 'May I follow you?' I said. 'I'm still a bit nervous.'

'Ellie,' said Roger gently. 'You never have to be nervous when I'm around. I'm here for you.'

A burst of gratitude flooded through me. The only other person who had ever said anything similar was my father in the old days, before Sheila.

Yet what did Roger see in me? It was only later that I realized my reluctance had spurred him on. Roger had been used to women falling at his feet.

I was his first challenge. When he'd said he didn't want to lose me, he really meant that he didn't want to fail.

38

Jo

His name is Steve. At least, that's what he tells me. He's a street artist, which means he draws on pavements or any-where else on the ground that 'takes' his pastels. He wears these funky open-toed sandals – apparently he's been on the road for so long that he doesn't feel the cold any more – and he's got long light-brown hair that curls on his shoulders. The length suits him, though it might look weird on any other middle-aged man. (I reckon he's a bit younger than me but not much.)

He used to be an accountant. He tells me this as he leads me across the bridge I'd seen earlier. Is he telling the truth?

'How come you're on the streets if you were an accountant?'

'I like it better,' he replies simply. Then he jumps over a step and holds out his hand. 'Want some help here?'

His touch feels warm. Natural. Then I shake myself. Don't be so bloody daft.

'This way.' He scrambles down the last slope. It's so dark now that I can barely see. Sand rubs between my toes.

'Don't worry. The place I am taking you to is above the

tidal level.' His voice rises with excitement. 'I can't wait to show you. Up here.'

We're at the mouth of a cave. It stretches out before us like a dark tunnel. What? 'I'm not going in there.'

'Just follow me. Please.'

I don't know why but I can't disobey. Years ago I saw this thing on telly about a hypnotist who put a girl in a trance. I feel like that now. The walls of the cave are closing in on me. My head scrapes against something hanging down from the top. I scream. 'What's that?'

'It's OK,' says Steve. 'They're just stalactites. You can remember the name because they have to hang on "tight" to stay put. Stalagmites are the ones that grow upwards from the ground.'

I've never met anyone like this bloke before.

He stops. 'Close your eyes,' he says, putting his hand over them. Now I know he's going to kill me. It's my own bloody fault for coming here. What the hell was I thinking of?

'Open,' he commands, like he's some magician.

I can barely see a thing. My throat tightens with fear. 'Hang on,' says Steve's voice. 'I've got a torch in a bag somewhere.' I hear him fumbling. 'Ah. Here it is. Now you can get a better view.'

There are rock shelves round the sides. On one, there's a sleeping bag. There's a blanket too and a Primus stove. Over there is a stack of tins and bottles of water.

'How long are you going to keep me here for?' I whimper.

'Keep you here?' His voice is soft. 'You're not my prisoner, Jo.'

Earlier, when he'd told me his name, I'd told him mine. Now I wish I hadn't.

'Well, it seems that way to me.'

'If you'd rather, I'll take you back to the town,' he says. He sounds hurt. 'You could try and find somewhere to sleep. But I warn you. It's not easy. There's no crisis centre here, and even if you've got money, the B&B people don't care for us. They think we'll leave fleas in their beds.'

I hesitate. He sees it. 'Or,' he continues, 'you can stay here with me and I'll cook a bean curry on that stove over there. Do you eat chillies?'

Does it bloody matter? Supposing he comes onto me like Paul had in Bristol?

'You can have my sleeping bag,' says Steve, as if he's reading my thoughts. 'I've got a blanket. Separate ends of the cave, if that's what you're worried about.' Then he touches my arm. 'Honestly, Jo. You've got nothing to worry about. I'm not that kind of person.'

'So who are you and why did you really stop being an accountant?' I blurt out. 'Did you break the law?'

He strikes a match to light the stove as he speaks. 'Course not!' He looks thoughtful. 'It's a bit of a long story. I'd wanted to be an artist at school but my parents thought I should get a proper job. So I trained as an accountant. Did it for years. Worked in the City.'

'Didn't you have a family? A wife, I mean. Children?'

'I'd have liked to. I was actually engaged to someone. But she changed her mind at the last minute. Said I was boring.'

His voice sounds as if someone's punched him in the gut. Poor bloke.

'Then one day, during my lunch break, I saw this man on his knees outside the National Gallery. He was drawing on the pavement, using chalks. I stood, amazed by the picture of the London skyline. He said he was homeless. I gave him a few coins. Every day after that I stopped to talk to him and buy him a hot drink and a sandwich. One day he handed me a yellow stick. "Why don't you have a go?" he said. "Put in the sunshine."

'So I got down on my hands and knees too, in my pin-striped suit, and did just that. I felt a sense of freedom I'd never had before. I went straight to my office and handed in my notice. When I told my parents, they thought I'd cracked up. But at least no one could accuse me now of being boring.'

He makes one of those dry laughs that doesn't sound funny. 'At first, I told myself I was taking a sabbatical to walk the South West Coast Path. But when I finished, I didn't want to go home. So I just turned round and went back into Cornwall. It's been fifteen years now. I'll be fifty soon.'

'How do you pay for food?' I ask, watching him empty a couple of cans into a saucepan and begin stirring.

His reply has a 'who cares' sound to it. 'I do OK with my street art. My parents are always offering to help out but I want to do this alone. I chose to go. It's my responsibility. I keep in touch every now and then; they're almost eighty now. Sometimes, I go back to Cambridge to visit them. My father – he was also an accountant – told me he wished he'd had the balls to do what I'm doing. My mother frets because I've never married or had children.'

I squat on the ground, where Steve's put down a

blanket. 'Didn't you find it tough on the road after being in a fancy office?'

'Sure. Once this bloke in a doorway tried to slash my throat because I'd taken his spot accidentally but I talked him out of it.'

'What did you say?'

'I told him it wasn't worth ending up in prison for the rest of his life. I've found that if you talk to people, they're less frightening than you think. And the street art helps. Folk always stop to chat about the pictures and why I do it. I have one rule. Always tell the truth.'

Is he crazy? It's dog eat dog on the road. Everyone knows that.

Steve gives the dish a final stir and then spoons some beans into a bowl. 'Here. Try this.'

I start to eat with my fingers. This stuff is good!

'Sorry. I forgot to give you this.'

He hands me a plastic spoon and then takes a mouthful himself. He asks, 'What about you? How did you end up here?'

I try to remember my manners and finish my own mouthful like him before speaking.

'I made wrong choices with men and drink,' I say shortly. I feel bad for leaving things out but he doesn't need to know everything.

'Actually I'm sober now,' I say quickly. 'I'm just trying to find somewhere safe. Get a place, get a job.'

He looks at me thoughtfully and for a second he reminds me of someone else from a better time. Or maybe it's just my imagination.

1.37 p.m., 17 August 1984

On our way out to the garden, one of the waitresses offers us a glass of champagne. I've never had alcohol before. 'Try it,' urges Peter.

My father had always told me I had to wait until I was sixteen before my first drink but I want to look grown up in front of Peter. Besides, my father and Sheila are lost in the party crowd now.

It tastes cool. Sparkly. One of the popular girls at school had been expelled for smuggling a bottle of gin into another dorm. Apparently it had 'gone to her head', whatever that meant. I wait for this to happen to me but I feel just the same.

'Can I have one?' demands Michael.

'No way,' I say. 'Do you want to get me into even more trouble with your mother?'

Peter gives me a sharp look. I'd told him a bit about Sheila in our letters. 'Still like that, is it?'

I nod, not wanting to say any more in front of my brother in case he reported it back. 'Ellie says you're a pain in the arse,' he'd told Sheila during the last holidays. This then went back to my father and I lost half a week's pocket money. The irony was that I didn't usually use dorm language like that — it had slipped out of my mouth in one frustrated moment with my brother but he'd remembered it!

Now Michael, cross that I hadn't let him have a drink, has run on ahead, through the big French windows and out to the lawn. Peter and I walk side by side down through the enormous garden to find him. His left arm brushes mine. It sends the most delicious thrill through me. Did he do that on purpose? Slowly, daringly, I let mine brush his back.

39

Ellie

Students like me who had shared accommodation in the first year were given beautiful large individual rooms in our second. I loved my privacy. My roommate had become too curious. Once she had asked if she could borrow a tampon. I told her I never used them. She'd rolled her eyes. 'A sanitary towel, then?'

'Sorry,' I'd said briskly. 'I don't have periods any more.'

'*What?*'

I should have kept my mouth shut. But the truth was that they'd stopped after Michael and never come back.

I shrugged. 'Just one of those things.'

'But . . . well, how are you going to have kids one day?'

'I don't want any.'

'Why not?'

'They're too much of a responsibility.'

My roommate had given me a strange look. 'You really are different, aren't you?'

Maybe she was right. I didn't fit in with any of the other students. They were so happy. So carefree. They all seemed to be on the pill and having one-night stands. They did stupid things without realizing the possible consequences. One of my roommate's friends abseiled down the hall tower for a dare. Everyone else thought he was amazing. 'Idiot,' I told him to his face. 'You could have killed yourself or fallen on someone.'

My roommate stopped saving a place for me at dinner. I didn't like the way she and the others whispered about me. Maybe that's why I accepted Roger's next invitation to a bike ride. And the next. Before long, it became a regular event at weekends.

I loved the freedom of cycling through the beautiful Berkshire countryside with its woods and bridleways, past beech trees and silver-birch branches hanging overhead. Sometimes we'd have lunch in a pub and have earnest discussions about novels we were reading. I was going through a J. P. Donleavy stage and was obsessed by *The Ginger Man*. At first, I deflected questions about my family. When he pressed me, I gave him a sanitized version (without mentioning Michael or Highbridge), ending with the truth that there was no one in the world I could turn to.

'I'm so sorry,' he said. 'Well, you're not alone now.'

For a minute I thought he was going to give me a hug. But he didn't. I was both relieved and disappointed.

Roger didn't want to talk much about his previous life either, although I got the impression that money had been tight when he was growing up. He also mentioned that he was the first person in his family to go to university.

In the winter, we went for walks. Once when I slipped on an icy slope, he caught my hand. This time, it felt warm and safe. 'You can keep it there if you want,' I said.

'You're sure?'

I nodded. He didn't go any further. I was grateful for that.

Roger also introduced me to Leonard Cohen. I preferred

his soulful music to the Carpenters. I would sit on the floor of his flat, my head against his legs. But whenever he tried to touch me again, I moved away. 'I'm sorry,' I said. A flash of Peter in the Daniels' garden came into my head. 'I'm not ready yet.'

He seemed more amused than irritated. In gratitude, I tried to do things that I thought would please him. I bought myself a Marguerite Patten cookery book and made my first steak and kidney pie. Unfortunately, I'd missed out the stage where you had to cook the meat before adding the pastry. But he ate it anyway and didn't die.

The months were going by. Finals were looming. By my third year, I was beginning to panic. I knew my work. I'd revised enough. Suppose I looked at the exam paper and couldn't answer anything? 'That won't happen,' Roger assured me.

Yet my fear just kept growing. Cornelius had warned me about this. 'Your actions before the incident with Michael made you feel a failure, amongst other things. We've worked hard to help you realize that isn't the case but you may find these emotions returning when faced with a big challenge in life,' he'd told me just before I'd left Highbridge.

He was right. I could barely walk into the examination room. When I looked at the downturned paper before me, I could actually see it dissolving into little tiny bits. Melting. Shrivelling. I broke out into a cold sweat.

'No.' I staggered to my feet. My hands gripped the edge of the desk as I tried not to fall. The invigilators shot me an alarmed look. 'I can't do this,' I cried.

Every face in the room turned to look at me. 'It's that weirdo,' whispered a boy from my hall. Someone led me out. Roger was in the corridor. (Later, I found he'd just adjudicated another exam.)

'I can't do it!' I repeated hysterically.

'Yes, you can.'

He put his arm round me and shepherded me out of the building.

He drove me to the medical centre. There were 'special facilities' there for those who didn't want to take the exam in a hall, Roger told me. I recognized a few faces, including a seemingly arrogant and highly intelligent boy from my seminar group.

I was put in a room of my own. Without the pressure of an exam situation, I could breathe. I wrote, my hand not stopping.

Afterwards I felt so stupid. But Roger reassured me. 'Exam fear is a horrible thing. But it happens to a lot of people.'

'I'm scared of everything,' I told him.

'I can see that,' he said, stroking the palm of my hand. 'But you're all right now.'

We were in his rooms by then, I was so worked up that I couldn't even remember getting there after the exam. There was a modern white leather sofa in the middle. We were sitting on it. Close. 'You need something to calm you down,' he said, lighting a cigarette. (What had happened to the pipe?) 'Try this.'

I didn't smoke. But I took a suck. He was right. After a second it melted the edge of my fear away.

'You're beautiful,' he murmured.

No one had ever called me that before. I was flattered that a man like Roger would want me. I still didn't really like him touching me. But it was nice to be looked after and admired. And besides, I would never have sat my finals if he hadn't rescued me. I owed him.

Two months later, I began to retch in the morning. 'You're pregnant!' exclaimed Roger when he found me bent over the lavatory.

'How do you know?'

Tenderly, he wiped the vomit from my mouth with a piece of loo paper.

'I recognize the signs.' His face was beaming. 'I thought your breasts had got bigger.' Then he frowned. 'But you told me you couldn't have children.'

'I can't,' I wailed.

As I hadn't had periods for so long, I'd presumed I couldn't conceive. That was fine by me. The responsibility of having a child's life in my hands was too much. But now my worst nightmare – or one of them – had come true. How could this have happened?

'You must have got pregnant just as your body decided to start to menstruating again,' said the doctor. I could tell from his disapproving face that he'd read my medical notes. He knew! Roger had insisted on coming along with me. What if the doctor let something slip? My skin began to crawl with terror.

'What are you going to do now?' The doctor's face was stern.

I felt as though I had done something terrible again.

'Get married, of course,' said Roger firmly. 'Aren't we, Ellie?'

40

Jo

When I open my eyes the next morning, I don't know where I am for a bit. Then it hits me. Steve. The cave.

I'm warm, thanks to the silver thermal blanket Steve insisted I wrapped around me. 'One of my customers bought me two, so I've got a spare,' he told me.

By customers, he meant the folk that dropped him coins because they liked his pictures.

I ease my legs over the cave ledge, desperate for a pee. 'You're awake,' says a chirpy voice. Steve is crouching over the Primus stove, boiling some water. 'I expect you'd like to use the facilities.'

'The what?'

'The loo.' He waves an arm towards the opening of the cave. 'The council's still kept the public conveniences going out of season, which is nice of them. It's up the steps. Want me to show you?'

'No, thanks. I'll find them.'

The sky is streaked with pink and grey. Cold air fills my lungs and I grab the rail, pulling myself up the steep steps towards the LADIES sign.

Stripping off, I wash my private bits with soap. At least there's some left in the bottle on the wall – it's not always the case in public toilets. I dry myself with rough green paper tissues. I wash my scalp too.

That's better. I feel almost happy. 'You old fool,' I tell myself, frowning. 'Just because you've met a decent man for a change, you're acting like some bloody teenager again.'

I make my way back to the cave.

'How do you take your tea?' asks Steve. 'I'll put in milk and one sugar for energy, shall I?'

He hands me a blue tin mug. I cup my hands round it to keep them warm. He notices. 'Here.' He wraps that silver thermal blanket round my shoulders again. 'I don't have much for breakfast, I'm afraid. But there's an egg roll that someone gave me yesterday.'

Nice. It's still wrapped up like it's brand new. I'm used to half-eaten stuff that someone has thrown away.

'What about you?' I ask.

'Thanks, but I'm not hungry.'

'Don't be silly.' Then I break the roll in half and shove one bit in his direction. We both wolf down our share.

'So,' he says, getting to his feet and gathering his stuff. 'Better get going, then.'

I feel disappointment weighing down on my chest like a stone. Of course he's going his own way now. What else did I expect?

'Want to come with me?' he asks. 'You could help take the money.'

For a minute I think he means I could help him steal. Then I realize he's referring to the coins folk give him for his pictures. 'They just drop them into your bowl, don't they?'

'Yes. But you have to keep an eye on it – which I can't always do when I'm drawing. Besides, it would be nice to have the company.'

There's got to be a catch. 'Why are you being so nice to me? What do you want in return?'

'Nothing, Jo.' He shakes his head. 'I just think the world needs to be kinder, and if I can do a bit, it all helps to add up.'

This bloke is too good to be true.

1.40 p.m., 17 August 1984

My head feels like it's whirring, and everything seems really funny. That's not normally like me. Maybe it's the champagne kicking in. But Peter seems to think it's funny too. In fact, he appears amused by everything I am saying.

'I can't see Michael,' I tell him, trying to be serious.

'Don't worry,' he laughs. 'He can't go far.'

Then he takes my hand. Holds it properly, fingers interlaced between mine. His thumb strokes my skin. I can barely breathe from happiness yet I am also worried about my little brother.

'I love your letters,' Peter says. He holds my hand to his lips. This time there can be no mistake. 'I think of you a lot, you know.'

'Really?' I say. But I can't concentrate. Where is Michael?

Then I spot him. A flash of red in a hammock strung between two trees. Rocking gently from side to side.

I relax. That will keep him busy for a bit.

'I think a lot about you too,' I say shyly.

'Let's go somewhere quieter,' says Peter.

41

Ellie

It wasn't until we'd been married for a year or so that I found out why Roger had been so keen to marry me. It wasn't the baby. It wasn't even the money – although he'd clearly been taken aback when I told him about the trust fund soon after he'd proposed. No. It was because he thought he could mould me into the woman he wanted me to be.

For all his charm and good looks, Roger was actually a very insecure man. He'd already told me that his parents' marriage had broken up because his father had had several affairs. A psychologist might say this accounted for my husband's inability to stay faithful. But I'm getting ahead of myself here.

I had my own reasons for marrying him – aside from the fact that I was pregnant, of course. It's hard for girls nowadays to understand how different it was back then. It was only just becoming more common for couples to live together without being married. If you had a baby 'out of wedlock', you were looked down on in certain circles. And, as Roger said, it wouldn't look good for his academic career if he was an unmarried father, especially as the mother had been one of his students.

That was if I chose to have the baby.

'We could have an abortion,' I'd blurted out.

'What on earth do you mean?' He looked shocked. It wasn't as easy then to terminate a pregnancy as it is today.

I couldn't tell him the truth. 'I don't feel ready to have a child,' I muttered.

'But we'll do this together,' he said. 'Don't you want to marry me?'

Marriage? I thought that would never happen to me. It wasn't just that I was small and mousy and not nearly as pretty as all the other girls around me. It was because of Michael. Who would want to marry me after that? But maybe I could continue keeping it a secret from Roger. I couldn't imagine being without him. Looking back, I realize that he had begun to represent the safety I had grown to feel at Highbridge. Although I hadn't wanted to go there at first, the institution had – along with Cornelius – grown to be my substitute family.

At university, the same pattern repeated itself. I didn't want to be at university in the first year. I was uncertain about having a relationship with Roger when I first met him. Yet both grew on me until I was scared of leaving either of them.

And so I found myself accepting Roger's proposal. Perhaps, at last, I could have a normal life.

'Are you happy with a register office ceremony?' he'd asked me.

The less fuss the better as far as I was concerned. 'Yes,' I told him.

'And you're sure there aren't any relatives you want to ask?' he probed gently.

'None at all,' I said.

I'd have liked to have asked Cornelius but it was too risky. Roger must never know where I had spent my formative teenage years – or why.

Instead, I invited my old roommate and a couple of other girls on my course, who seemed surprised to be included. But I had to bring a few people or it would look odd. Besides, I also wanted to prove to them that I wasn't as 'weird' as they'd thought after all. Roger's guests comprised some fellow tutors and their wives, plus his father, whom I'd never met before. His stepmother was 'busy'. The truth was that they were having a trial separation.

My new father-in-law was a small, bowed man, so different from his son both in looks and demeanour that I almost wondered if they were related at all. 'Buying a place of your own, are you?' he said, making no attempt to hide the envy and curiosity in his voice. 'Very nice, I must say.'

We were in a small hotel after the ceremony, having lunch. It didn't feel as though I'd just got married. As a young girl, before the accident, I'd dreamed of the usual fairytale wedding with a beautiful Cinderella ball dress. Instead, I'd deliberately chosen a loose cream corduroy shift in a pinafore style, in order to hide my small bump. Over it, I wore an embroidered shaggy Afghan coat, although it looked out of place in the warm weather – another attempt at disguising my figure. I also had my hair permed as a last-minute, spur-of-the-moment decision. Afterwards, when I looked in the mirror, I could see it didn't suit me, which made me feel even more self-conscious.

'When's the baby due, then?' Roger's father asked as we tucked into avocados stuffed with prawns.

I looked up aghast. 'Shhh,' I said.

Roger's father had laughed, wiping the back of his mouth with pink sauce. 'They all know, love,' he whispered loudly, gesticulating to the rest of the table. Then he put his sweaty hand on mine and squeezed it tightly. 'But don't you worry! A shotgun marriage can work out just fine providing there's enough of the readies.' He gave me a wink. 'And it seems there's plenty of those.'

Then he looked serious. 'Just be careful that . . .'

He stopped.

'Careful about what?' I asked.

'Nothing, duck.' He shook his head. But I had a feeling that he was going to warn me about Roger. An uneasy premonition ran through me.

I didn't know my new husband had applied for a post at Oxford until he received the letter saying he'd got it. 'Why didn't you tell me?' I asked. We'd been on the verge of buying a rambling Victorian semi in Reading that I'd set my heart on.

He'd shrugged. 'I suppose I wanted to make sure I was successful first.'

I was beginning to learn that my new husband feared rejection more than anything else. My heart went out to him. 'Well, you were,' I said, giving him a hug. 'And you deserve it.'

He beamed. I'd said the right thing.

This was, I learned during those early months, very important if I wanted to keep Roger happy. On the rare occasions when I didn't say the right thing, he sulked and often stayed out late without warning me.

When I asked why he hadn't rung, he would say that he'd been in a work meeting and hadn't been able to interrupt it. Or he would claim that he had called and I hadn't heard. 'If you worked, you'd understand,' he'd say. Yet he was the one who had told me that I shouldn't seek paid work because a 'woman's job is to bring up the children'. A stronger woman might have stood up to him. But I wanted to keep the peace.

Even so, I still questioned some of his decisions. 'Are you sure we should buy our own home even though they've offered us accommodation in college?' I asked just before we signed the contract for a pretty thatched cottage in a village north of Oxford. It wasn't as spacious as the Victorian semi in Berkshire that I'd fallen in love with but it had a long garden that Roger said would be perfect for children.

His voice became patronizing, as though he was the lecturer and I was the fresher again. 'Quite sure. I don't want our privacy invaded by students all the time. Besides, it's a foot on the property ladder.' Then his eyes darkened, as if remembering it was my money that was paying for it. 'Why? Don't you want my name on the deeds?'

The thought had never occurred to me. 'Of course I do,' I said quickly. 'It's just that I'm going to feel lonely in a village with a baby. I won't know anyone.'

He put his arms around me. This was becoming increasingly difficult, as my stomach was growing. 'We don't need anyone else apart from ourselves,' he said. I felt him hardening against me. Gently I pushed him away. I never knew where I was with Roger. Sometimes he was loving and sometimes he was distant.

'Not now,' I pleaded. 'You might bruise the baby.'

'Rubbish!' He laughed, but I could hear the frustration. 'The books say it's perfectly all right to have sex during pregnancy.'

'But I'm scared,' I burst out. 'What if something happens to it?'

To my horror, I felt myself become almost as hysterical as I had at Highbridge. 'Most women have a mother to talk them through these things,' I sobbed. 'I don't have anyone.'

'Shhh, shhh.' He stroked my hair. 'You're a grown woman. Besides, you have me. It will be all right. I promise.'

But I was terrified. I wasn't capable of looking after a child. Michael had proved that. What if it got ill or I lost it or . . . The possibilities were so vast that I felt physically sick with worry.

I had another fear too. Supposing it was a boy? A constant reminder of my wickedness? How would I cope then?

The fear grew and grew until it became impossible to ignore. I found myself reaching for a pen and paper to write a letter to the only person I'd ever truly loved. Someone whom I hoped might, after all this time, forgive me.

Naturally, I did it when Roger was out or he would have asked who I was writing to. But when I finished and read it through, I ripped it into tiny pieces. Who was I kidding? I was beyond redemption.

42

Jo

Steve and I make our way to 'this great spot' near the coach station. We sit on a bench. Steve opens his rucksack and takes out an old biscuit tin that says 'Cookies From Cornwall' on the lid. Inside are chalks of every colour I could ever think of. Red, blue, green, yellow . . .

Then I watch as he crouches down on the pavement and starts to draw. As if by magic, a castle appears with a little tower. Then cliffs and the sea. There's the bakery (in purple) over the road from us here. And a pub in pink.

'Wow,' says a woman walking past with a big black Alsatian that comes up almost to her knees. I shrink back; something about that dog fills me with fear. But I try not to show it as she fumbles in her pocket and drops a coin into the bowl.

'Thank you so much,' says Steve. 'I really appreciate it.'

He says it like he genuinely means it, as he does every time someone gives him something. And you know what? I reckon he does. But he also knows his stuff. As the morning goes on, the bowl fills up. 'You need enough there to show that others have given because that makes people feel they ought to as well,' Steve tells me. 'But you don't want too much because then they think you don't need it.'

Nice thinking. 'I've never seen another beggar get all this money,' I tell him admiringly.

'That's because I'm not a beggar,' says Steve, looking away. Too late, I see I've offended him. 'I'm an artist. I'm giving people pleasure. And I'm also teaching them things.'

It's true. Every few minutes, someone stops to ask Steve how long he's been doing this for, whether he'd always drawn and how he actually makes those lifelike shapes. Each time, he patiently tells them his story about how he used to be an accountant and jacked it all in. Sometimes I see a flash of envy on their faces. They listen to him for ages, like they don't want to leave. He's got the kind of friendly, deep voice that keeps you there. Me included.

'I wish I could draw like you,' I say.

'Want to have another go?'

His hand closes over mine, guiding a stick of yellow over a pavement square. I'd tell another man to piss off but Steve's different from any other man I've known. 'It's the sun, shining down on the castle. See?'

It's like a child's picture. Makes me feel happy and also sad at the same time.

'Now if you make an oblong here with a triangle on top and then sweep the chalk round to the left like this, you've got a tower. That's it! I reckon you have a knack for this.'

'Come off it,' I snort. 'You're having me on.'

'I wouldn't say something unless it was true, Jo.'

He's too nice. My instinct says I should leave him and go it alone. But I can't. It's like some invisible cord has tied me to him.

Halfway through the day, we stop for a 'breather'. Steve makes me take some of the money in the pot. 'Buy a decent pair of trainers,' he insists. 'Go on. You've earned it.'

I feel guilty because I could use the Americans' money. But for some reason I don't want to tell him I have it. Perhaps I'm embarrassed because he'd probably think I shouldn't have taken it.

I buy some trainers. They're pink with purple laces. They make me feel different. Younger. More adventurous.

Before I know it, the sun's going down and the woman from the bakery brings over a couple of warm pies. 'Leftovers,' she says, talking just to Steve.

Then she eyes me like I'm scum.

'Saw you the other day, didn't I? You bought a pasty off me. Together now, are you?'

'None of your bloody business,' I want to say.

'She's learning the craft,' says Steve. 'Jo's doing very nicely.'

It's not often I get praised.

'How are you getting on in that cave of yours?' she asks. 'We're OK.'

We. The word gives me an excited shiver as I tuck into my pie. Cheese and onion. I don't think I've ever tasted anything this good.

The bakery woman shoots me another filthy look.

'It's getting colder,' she says, still ignoring me. 'You don't want to stay in that cave for too long. And like I've said before, you need to be careful. The sea could cut you off.' She shakes her head. 'We lost a man that way last year. Local, he was. Thought he knew what he was doing.'

I think back to that couple who died and Tim nicking

313

their phones. Even Steve is looking less certain now. Maybe he's not as streetwise as he makes out.

'I've got a spare room if you want it,' continues the woman. 'My son has just gone off to uni and, well, you're welcome to it for a bit.'

Again, she's speaking to him. Not me.

'That's very kind of you,' says Steve. He finishes his mouthful first before speaking again – so polite. 'But I can't leave my friend in the lurch here.'

'Don't be daft,' I want to say. 'We've only just met.' But I keep quiet. What the hell is happening to me? The last thing I need is another man to mess up my life.

'I suppose she can come too.'

Steve looks at me. 'Want to?'

'OK,' says my big gob.

We climb the narrow winding stairs at the back of the shop. I wouldn't even mind sleeping on one of the steps.

The woman throws open a door. There's a double bed with a chest of drawers and a proper wardrobe. On the wall is this poster of some kids playing the guitar with a pretty girl yelling down a mike. The name Honey Joy is at the bottom. Must belong to her son.

'There's a shower through there,' she says, pointing to a doorway at the back of the room. 'It's a bit tight, but it will do.'

Steve throws his arms out in a 'thank you' gesture. 'What can I do to pay you back?'

'Are you stupid?' I want to yell. 'She wants *you*, that's what.'

'Maybe you could do a bit of decorating for me,' she says. 'Since my husband went, it's been a bit difficult.'

I bet it has.

'It would be a pleasure,' he says.

'I'll leave you to get some sleep, then.' She shoots me daggers. 'Try not to hum too loud, will you? The sound-proofing isn't great.'

She shuts the door. 'That woman fancies you,' I say.

He laughs like I've said something funny. 'No, she doesn't.'

'Does!'

'She's just being kind. I told you before, Jo. If you give pleasure to people and are kind to them, they are good to you back. By the way, don't pay any attention to her comment about your humming. I rather like it.'

Half the time I don't even know I'm doing it so I say nothing in case it makes me seem more stupid.

Then he looks at the bed. 'You have that. I'll sleep on the floor.'

'That's not fair. I'll go on the floor.'

'We could,' he says slowly, 'sleep with pillows between us.'

I shrug, trying to look like I don't care. 'OK.'

That night, I toss and turn, conscious of Steve's breathing. Once more, I remember the last time I slept with a man. I try to push it out of my head but it keeps coming back.

I wake to the sound of screaming. Then I realize it's me.

'Shhh.' Steve's bending over me in the dark. 'It's all right. You had a nightmare.'

'What did I say?'

'You kept calling for help.'

I freeze with fear. What else might I have come out with? But I keep quiet, and just allow him to remove the pillows and rock me to and fro like a baby. 'Go back to sleep,' he whispers. 'You're all right now.'

In the morning, he is still next to me. I look down on his face as the sun streams in through the window. You can judge someone better when they're sleeping. His eyelashes are long. He looks as though he doesn't have a care in the world.

Something inside me goes soft. *Who are you kidding?* I ask myself.

No man in his right mind is ever going to want me.

1.45 p.m., 17 August 1984

We are in a little side part of the garden where there are
masses and masses of orange and pink roses. 'So beautiful,'
I say, thinking how my mother had cared for hers so much.
    'Not as lovely as you.'
    No one has ever called me that before.
    Peter pulls me to him. My heart begins to pound. His arms
are around me. He smells nice — like soap. His face is close to
mine. Could he? Yes. He's going to kiss me!
    'Ellie?' says a voice behind me. 'Peter? What are you doing?'
I break away just in time.
    Michael is beside us, his face screwed up in horror and
consternation.
    'I was helping your sister get a fly out of her eye,' says Peter,
cool as a cucumber.
    Part of me is shocked by his lie but another part is
impressed. I try not to giggle.
    'You're meant to be playing with me,' says Michael.
    'We were,' says Peter, 'but you ran off.'
    'I climbed into that hammock but then I fell out.' Michael's
eyes fill with tears. 'I got a bruise. Look!'
    There is indeed a big blue mark but it's not bleeding.
'You'll be all right,' I say.

317

Peter nods. 'I get bruises like that all the time when I play sport. It's part of being a man.'

Michael stares at him, awestruck.

'Can you throw that ball for me?' asks my little brother, handing it over.

'Sure.' Then Peter raises his arm and throws it high into the air. It soars out of the rose garden and onto the Daniels' huge lawn. 'Quick,' he says. 'Go and find it.'

Then Michael runs out of the rose garden. And out of sight.

43

Ellie

The labour pains came a month early. It was the phone call that did it. When Roger had been safely out of the house, I had rung Cornelius at Highbridge to tell him the news of my marriage and pregnancy. I think I'd wanted to prove that I'd got 'better'. But it had been a mistake.

'Have you told your husband about your history?' he'd responded. 'If not, I strongly suggest you do so. Marriages should have no secrets.'

I could feel his disapproving tone as if he was standing right by me, saying it to my face. Swiftly, I'd ended the conversation.

But it was too late. Cornelius's questions had gone right to the heart of all my fears. The midwife was going to have my medical notes. What if she said something in front of Roger?

A trickle of water ran down my leg. Seconds later I felt a twinge, like my stomach had cramp. Then another one.

I stumbled to the phone. 'Sorry,' said the secretary in Roger's department. 'He was meant to have been running a tutorial today but he cancelled it. I'm not sure where he is.'

The pains were coming faster. This couldn't be right! They should be slow at the beginning, according to the lady at the Tuesday-evening antenatal group Roger and I had been attending. Maybe something was wrong. I needed to get hold of someone.

Staggering to the front door, I saw my elderly neighbour, Jean, weeding her garden. At least, I considered her elderly in those days but she was probably no more than early sixties. We were on 'How are you?' terms but no more. Roger liked us to 'keep to ourselves'.

But now wasn't the time for qualms. 'I think I'm having the baby!' I cried. 'I'm a month early.' Instantly, she threw down her trowel and was at my side.

'Let's get you to hospital,' she said. 'No point hanging around for an ambulance.'

Jean drove me in her little blue Ford Fiesta, weaving her way in from the Forest Hill direction towards the Radcliffe. 'Do you have a mother I can ring?' she asked.

I shook my head. If only.

'Anyone else?'

'Just my husband. I've already left him a message.' Then I let out a cry as another pain seized my body in an agonizing vice.

'I'm sure he'll get here soon.'

I can barely remember arriving at the hospital or the exact order of events. But I do recall lying on my back on a bed with Jean holding my hand and the midwife telling me not to push.

'But I have to!' I screamed. It was as though my body was in charge and I had no control over the things it was doing.

The antenatal teacher had stressed the importance of a 'drug-free birth'. Instead, we should breathe our way through it and 'distract the mind' by mentally recalling all the baby items we had bought. I'd refused to go shopping for carrycots or prams, telling Roger that there was still plenty of time. The truth was that it felt unlucky to do so in case it jinxed everything.

'Give me something for the pain,' I somehow managed to gasp.

'It's too late for an epidural, dear, but we can get you some gas and air.'

A mask was being placed over my mouth. For a minute, I felt as if I was being suffocated. Then I began to relax. I started to half-dream things, just like you do before falling asleep. A beach. Sand. A child running along the water's edge. He was going in. The waves were over his head. I couldn't see him any more.

'NO!' I screamed. 'Come back!'

'You can push now,' said the midwife. 'Well done. Good girl.'

'Save him!' I screamed. 'He's going to drown.'

'It's all right, Ellie.' The nurse's voice was calm and confident but I knew it was just an act. 'The gas and air is making you hallucinate.'

The boy was coming out of the sea now. But his face was white. I knew he was dead. He was staring at me with a 'How could you?' look on his face.

'I'm sorry, I'm sorry,' I wept.

Then I felt Roger's hand on my brow. 'I'm the one who should be sorry, darling. I only just got your message. But it's all right. I'm here.'

My husband had arrived?

'Where's Jean?' I gasp.

'She's gone now.'

'Has something happened to her too?'

'Of course not. Just concentrate on our baby. One more push . . .'

'If you don't mind, Mr Halls, I'd rather you left the instructions to me. One big push, Ellie, and then . . .'

I could feel something sliding out of me with a whoosh. It was all so fast that I wasn't even aware of it hurting – not like the previous bit.

'It's a girl!' called out Roger. 'We've got a daughter.'

Thank God it wasn't a boy. But the room was silent. 'Nurse?' said my husband in a strange voice I'd never heard before. 'Why isn't she crying?'

But I knew why. It's because people like me deserve to be punished.

44

Jo

Steve wakes. I pretend that I haven't been watching him
but I can tell he isn't fooled. 'You had a nightmare,' he
says, shifting quickly towards his own side of the bed. 'I
don't want you to think I'm taking advantage, but you
were so upset . . .'

'I know. I remember.'

His face is all worried. 'Do you often have them?'

I think back to how I used to wake Tim, and Paul's
crowd, with my rantings and ravings. 'No,' I say, crossing
my fingers to stop him asking more questions.

'I have dreams,' says Steve thoughtfully. 'They usually
involve changing trains, which, according to this book I
read once, is a sign that something is going to happen.
Occasionally there's a baby in it. That means I'm going to
embark on some new project.'

He laughs. 'It's funny really, especially as I've never had
a child. What about you?'

I shake my head firmly. 'No children in my dreams.'

'But have you ever wanted one – a child, I mean?'

My breath feels like it's trapped in my chest.

'It's hard enough looking after myself.' I try to laugh
it off.

'You're right. Mind you, I do sometimes wonder if I've missed out on something.'

Steve turns abruptly and gets out of bed. He's wearing a pair of tracksuit bottoms that he'd put on last night in the shower room. His chest has got brown curly hairs on it. It should feel weird, sharing a room with a bloke I don't really know. But it doesn't.

He flings back the curtains and opens the window. It's cold but nice. Outside, the trees are gold and yellow and brown. Little flecks of sunlight dance on the walls. I hear a seagull screaming.

'Beautiful, isn't it?' he says softly.

I get out of bed. Something makes me walk towards him. We stand side by side, looking out. It's like he's burning me even though we're not actually touching.

'Better get going,' he says, moving away to pick up his rucksack. 'We need to get to work.'

I feel all cold again. 'Isn't it too soon?'

When you don't have a watch, you learn to tell the time without one. I reckon it's about 6 a.m. or maybe 6.30.

'No. It's perfect. Tourists rise early to cram it all in. And the locals are up and about, getting their morning milk and bread.'

'Aren't they too busy to stop and watch?'

'Wait and see!' He grabs my arm. Suddenly his face is covered with a huge grin. 'Come on.'

I follow him down the stairs but the bakery woman is coming up. 'Thought you'd like to take this,' she says, pressing a white paper bag into his hand. 'It's a croissant. Still warm.'

I can smell it from here.

'Sorry,' she says coolly to me. 'I need the rest for my regular customers.'

Cow.

Steve insists on sharing it with me as we walk down the high street. There's a pitch, he tells me, which he wants to get to first before anyone else.

'So there are other street artists?'

'One or two. But none are like me.'

He doesn't say this boastfully. It's more of a fact.

'There's a *Big Issue* chap too,' he adds. 'Nice fellow.'

I almost tell him then that I used to be a seller myself but I manage to stop just in time. The less he knows about me, the better.

The day might be bright but hell it's nippy. 'The trick is to keep your hands moving,' Steve tells me, crouching down. He hands me a pink piece of chalk. 'Shade in that corner of the paving slab, can you?'

'All on my own?'

'You'll be fine.'

Steve's picture starts out like a few lines that don't mean anything. Then they grow into a row of cottages with little pointed windows in the roof. A church spire and then a pub.

'Cool, mate,' says a voice above us. 'How do you do it?'

It's a young man with a guitar slung over his shoulder. I give Steve a 'Don't bother with him – he looks skint' look. But Steve spends ages answering the youth's questions and telling him how he started. Then the kid begins talking about his life too and how he's in a band touring from the States. When he goes, he places a twenty-pound note on the ground.

'Bloody brilliant,' I say.

'I know.' Steve's eyes are shining. 'Amazing to meet him, wasn't it? He comes all the way from a place called Chattanooga in the Deep South. I'd love to go there one day.'

I don't like to tell him that my 'bloody brilliant' remark was aimed at the twenty.

Then a mother gets her toddler to drop in a pound coin. 'Clever boy!' She claps like he's done something really neat. Someone else buys us a cup of coffee each. One fat old bloke stands and gases about the 'painting' for ages but doesn't give anything. 'It's not fair,' I complain.

'I don't mind.' Steve sits back on his heels, surveying the proportions of a new row of cottages in blue and yellow. 'It gives my hands a break.' He passes me a piece of violet chalk. 'How about doing the sea now?'

I make a squiggle. The stick snaps in half. Now what have I done? Automatically, I say 'Sorry! Sorry!' and flinch, shielding my face with my arm.

'Are you OK?' Steve's voice is shocked. 'Has someone hurt you in the past, Jo?'

I don't know what to tell him, so I just look down at the broken chalk in my hands.

'Do you want to talk about it?'

I shake my head.

'I'm sorry. Life can be very cruel.' He hands me one half of the broken chalk stick. 'You're all right now.'

1.47 p.m., 17 August 1984

'Come here,' says Peter, taking my hand. His voice is thick. 'I saw a woodshed when we arrived. Let's go.'

But before we can move, Michael comes racing back into the rose garden.

'You throw really well,' he says.

'Thanks,' Peter says grimly. He catches the ball which Michael clumsily chucks at him. 'See if you can do one like this.'

Once more, he hurls it into the sky.

Again, Michael goes running after it. 'See you in the woodshed,' I call out.

'Why did you tell him where we were going?' snaps Peter.

'I thought it might put him off,' I say. 'We could really go somewhere else.'

'Good idea,' says Peter, looking around.

I feel a twinge of guilt and then push it away. I'm always looking after Michael. I deserve some time off.

45

Ellie

'Why isn't our baby breathing?' shouted my husband again.

Someone answered but I didn't hear the reply. I lay on the bed, rigid with shock, conscious of people scuttling around me. There was a quiet, taut air of emergency.

And then it happened.

A thin reed of a cry, so high-pitched that I look around for the bird that must somehow have flown into the room. Then another, slightly lustier. And again. 'Is our baby all right?' shouted my husband. 'Will someone please tell us what's going on.'

'We've cleared some mucus,' said the midwife reassuringly. 'She's fine now.' Then she placed a small slithery body into my arms. A wrinkled, bald face stared up at me, its mouth open, clearly furious at having been ripped from my womb to face this uncertain, unreliable world outside. *I didn't ask for you, either,* I thought. But then, as I looked down into my daughter's eyes, I felt an unexpected tugging from inside, coupled with a flash of recognition.

'She looks just like you,' breathed Roger, stroking her tiny cheek with his thick, stubby index finger. He's calmer now. Completely different.

'No,' I wanted to say. 'She looks a bit like . . .'

But I couldn't even bear to say the name in my head.

Taking a deep breath, I tried to steady myself. 'Like you,' I say. 'She has your nose.'

Gently he put his arm around me and pulled me towards him, the baby still in my arms. 'I love you so much, my darling. We're a proper family now.'

When I look back, I don't know how we managed, especially in a rural area like ours. Today there is so much more help for young mothers. They have baby groups to go to; nurseries where they can drop off their children and go back to work; there are WhatsApp and Facebook groups to seek advice from.

Amy was a chesty baby, always prone to coughs and colds. She also got croup, which terrified me with that harsh dog-like sound. I was constantly on alert. Every noise she made reverberated around my head and set my heart leaping.

'Just fill the kettle and sit in the kitchen with the steam,' the health visitor advised. But it didn't always work. Even when she was well, the responsibility was overwhelming. 'I'm not fit to look after you,' I would whisper to Amy when we were on our own. Her blue eyes would fix on me – she was focusing now – as if she agreed.

Roger, on the other hand, had far more confidence, even though he had had no experience of babies either. 'You just need to read about it,' he informed me, handing over the latest of the childcare books he kept buying. He tapped the cover, showing a beaming mother, father and child. 'It's all in here. Rather like a car manual. You simply have to look it up.'

As if on cue, Amy began to yell in my arms.

'Give her to me,' said Roger, his voice softening. Gladly, I handed her over. He cradled her against his chest. Instantly, she stopped crying. 'See?' he said triumphantly. 'Babies like to feel secure. They can pick up on your worries. Just relax, Ellie.'

But I couldn't. Nor could I tell him why.

Roger seemed to take pride in the fact that he was better at calming Amy than I was. It made me feel even less confident and, when he was at work, I honestly felt I couldn't cope. One day, when he was at the university, Amy was so sick that the vomit flew out almost to the other side of the room. In a panic, I ran to my neighbour.

'Babies are often sick, especially when they've had enough,' Jean said reassuringly, taking Amy from me and holding her against her shoulder, gently patting her back. 'But she seems perfectly happy now. Leave it a couple of hours and then try another. She'll soon let you know when she's hungry.'

'How?'

'By crying.'

'But she does that anyway!'

Jean gave me a quick hug. 'It's very hard when you're a new mum but you'll soon learn. We all make mistakes.'

Hadn't I already made enough of those?

It was a great comfort to me when Jean started to come over regularly after that, especially as Roger was always at work. He needed to continue teaching during the Easter and summer vacations, often helping overseas students or those who had theses to finish. I knew it wasn't just my imagination that he was starting to spend more and more time away from home. But after a while, I found I didn't care. When he was back, all he seemed interested in was our daughter, with whom he was almost besotted. I got the feeling that he relished having the upper hand when it came to bringing her up. And he didn't like it when I said Jean was good at calming Amy too.

'Has that woman been round again?' he'd ask if he returned to find two coffee mugs in the sink.

'I'm grateful for her company,' I'd tell him.

'Just don't let her get too close. I don't want some nosy neighbour knowing all our business.'

My husband carried on with his constant disapproval of my new friend, almost as if he was jealous of her. One weekend, when Amy was about three months old, I got the courage to answer back. 'She's not nosy, and besides, I don't have anyone else to talk to. There aren't any other women in the village with children of Amy's age. I don't drive and the buses are irregular. Anyway, you're never here.'

'That's because I'm trying to support my family.' His voice raised in anger and woke Amy, who'd been dozing in her carrycot.

'Now look what you've done.'

Even as I yelled back, I was aware that we were both tetchy from lack of sleep and – on my part – fear. What if I did something wrong? Supposing I dropped her by accident? What if she stopped breathing?

'I'm just scared,' I said, bursting into tears. 'Having a baby is such a responsibility. I'm sorry.'

Instantly his arms were around me, stroking my back. 'I know,' he soothed. 'I understand.'

His mouth was on mine. His hands were now feeling

my breasts, swollen with milk. Then they went lower. Gently I pushed him away. 'Not now, Roger. It's only the afternoon.'

'What does that matter?' he murmured, pulling me down onto the sofa.

'Amy . . .'

'She's gone back to sleep.'

Panic was beginning to mount inside. When I'd been pregnant, I'd managed – with a few exceptions – to keep Roger at bay by telling him that sex might cause a miscarriage or that it was too uncomfortable. But now I'd just had my three-month check, and the doctor had informed me, with a broad grin on his face, that it was 'perfectly acceptable to resume marital relations now'.

The truth was that I didn't want to. I was too exhausted looking after Amy.

But Roger wasn't giving up. 'I need you.' His voice was thick. Husky. He was pulling off my pants. 'No, please,' I said. 'I'm not ready.'

'Come on, Ellie. It's been too long.'

Later, as I lay there, I consoled myself by saying that a man like Roger needed to fulfil his needs. I owed him after everything he had done.

For some weeks after that, Roger's behaviour towards me was much kinder. He even told Jean that she didn't need to 'rush off' when he came home early and found us having a cup of tea together with Amy bouncing on her knee. His arrival had taken me aback. I'd been so busy that I hadn't had time to hide another letter I'd started to write that morning, which was still out on the table. Luckily I managed to pick it up surreptitiously while Roger was making small talk with Jean and throw it on the coal fire in the sitting room next door. (I'd wanted to use some of my money to install central heating but Roger said it was better to invest it.)

I watched as the page curled up and then wilted as the flames devoured it.

46

Jo

Days and then weeks go by. It's hard to keep up when you're on the road. But according to Steve, it's November already. For the first time I can remember, I feel safe. Content.

How stupid of me.

'We're lucky with the weather,' says Steve one morning, looking up at the clear sky from his usual crouching position on the pavement.

'It must be crap when the rain washes your work away,' I reply, pulling my now-grubby turquoise fleece around me. It might be dry but it's bloody cold.

'Or,' he says, as he draws the apricot outline of a sunset, 'you can see it as an opportunity to start again when it's dry.' He sits back on his haunches, surveying his new picture. 'The great thing about street art is that you don't have to pay for a fresh canvas every time. There's always a pavement. And if the cops come along, well, I just move on without any hassle. Sometimes, though, they want to talk about my work. Never judge a book by its cover. That's my motto.'

This man is amazing. He's not just talented. He sees life differently. He's nice to everyone but he's no wet blanket. And something draws me to him that I can't explain.

Not long after that, Cassie (as the bakery woman told Steve to call her) knocks on our door. She has a problem, she says, with the waste pipe under her kitchen sink. Would he mind coming to look at it?

When he's gone, I wash out my knickers and put them on the radiator to dry. Steve has bought me some fleecy pyjamas from the market ('Like I said before, you've earned it'), so I pull them on and go straight to bed on my side. I've got used to our arrangement now. Sometimes, though, our legs brush in the night. The touch makes me ache with a longing that I haven't had for donkeys' years.

I drift off but the next thing I hear is shouting down below followed by Steve's footsteps pounding up the stairs.

'What's going on?' I murmur sleepily.

'You were right.'

Steve is sitting next to me. He's put the light on and I can see shock on his face. 'Cassie made a pass at me.'

I rub my eyes. 'Of course she bloody did. I told you before. It's obvious she's got the hots for you.'

He looks upset. 'I suppose I thought . . . that is . . . well, after my fiancée walked out on me, I decided I didn't want anything to do with love again. But now, well . . .'

'So you *do* fancy Cassie?' I burst out.

'No.' He takes my hands. 'Don't you get it, Jo? It's you I want.'

I go hot and cold like my body is burning. 'I'm too old for this.'

He is lacing his fingers with mine. 'Age doesn't matter, although I don't think there's much of a difference between us.'

If he thinks I'm giving him my date of birth, he's mistaken. I can't help thinking that the fewer facts I give him, the safer I will be.

'The point is that I can feel this connection between us.' He is looking straight at me. 'And I think you can feel it too.'

Why can't I lie like I usually do? Instead, I say nothing.

His hands are stroking my back. Every bone in my body is on fire. I keep looking into his eyes as he slowly takes off my top. I want this.

When we finish, I lie in the crook of his arm. 'You're beautiful, Jo,' he says dreamily.

I snort. 'Don't be daft.'

He strokes my shaved head. 'I mean it. I love the fact you don't try to be anything else but yourself.'

'I used to have hair down to my waist,' I mumble. 'But it was easier this way.'

'Suits you.' He's running a finger along my cheekbone now. 'It brings out the structure of your face.'

Embarrassed, I change the subject. 'Cassie won't like this,' I say.

'She already knows.'

I lean on one shoulder. Now it's my turn to trace his jawline. The stubble feels rough. I like it. I have a flash of a smooth-shaven cheek and push it away.

'What do you mean?'

'It's why we had an argument. I said I wasn't interested in anyone else apart from you.'

My whole body feels alive with joy.

'Then she said we had to leave, first thing in the morning.'

I jump out of bed. 'Let's do it now. We can go before the morning.'

'I was thinking we should move on to Boscastle anyway.'

'Where's that?'

'A few miles further up the coast.' Steve is laughing. He makes me feel like we're runaway lovers.

I'm out of bed, getting my stuff together. 'Then what are we waiting for?'

We catch a bus. He pays. It makes me feel guilty after everything else he's forked out for. We've slept together now. It's different. So, as we sit, arm in arm like a pair of teenagers, on the back seat, I tell Steve about the money I've still got from the Americans.

'I probably should have told you before,' I say. 'But . . .'

I stop, not wanting to admit that I'd saved it for emergencies rather than go halves on the food he'd been buying from his street art.

'But what?' he says.

'Nothing.'

'OK.' He shrugs like it's no big deal. Other blokes would have pushed it.

'Where are we going to sleep tonight?' I ask, wanting to change the subject.

'Something will come up.' He begins to whistle cheerfully while staring out of the window at the fields and the odd small village with a shop.

'How can you be so certain?'

'It's the way life goes. If you give to people, you get back. Goodness creates goodness.'

That unease crawls through me again. I turn away and focus on the fields rushing by.

Boscastle is a pretty village with loads of tea shops and a bridge. We set up on a pavement away from the river bank. Steve starts to draw a map with the bridge and the church and all the other stuff. People stop to stare and ask questions like they always do. We make twenty quid in the first hour. Then this bloke hangs around for a bit. He's got beads in his hair and his jeans have those fancy slashes across the knee. He makes me feel nervous. But then I see it's Steve he's interested in.

'I run a small craft studio near here. Can you do this kind of work on paper? I might be able to sell it.'

'Thanks, mate. We only use the pavement because we're travelling at the moment. But we're flattered all the same. Isn't that right, Jo?' He gives my shoulders a quick squeeze as if I am a real artist like him.

We find a bus shelter to sleep in that night. It's warmer when there are two of you to cuddle up. When we wake, there's a couple of bananas on the ground and two bottles of water. People sometimes do this. Like Steve says, there really are some good ones out there.

I speak too soon. There's a cop coming up. 'I'll have to move you on,' she says, all full of herself in her uniform.

'Why?' I sit up angrily. 'We're not doing any harm . . .'

Steve puts a hand on my arm. 'Of course, officer,' he says. 'We understand.'

We pick up our stuff – Steve wanted to buy me a rucksack instead of my plastic bags but I wouldn't let him – and get moving. 'I liked it here,' I said.

'Me too. But we'll find somewhere else. Might as well get the first bus and see where it goes.'

Then the bloke with the ripped jeans comes past, walking a dog. 'Off already?' he asks.

Steve shrugs. 'We were told to move on.'

'Find your breakfast all right?'

'So *you* left us those bananas?' Steve shakes his hand. 'Thanks, mate. Really good of you.'

The bloke seems to think for a minute. 'How would you like to mind my studio? I've got to go away for a month and I don't want to leave it empty. You could work there and sell your own stuff. I've got materials you can use.'

He glances at me. 'There's a small bedroom at the back that you and your girlfriend can sleep in, if you're happy to manage the shop.'

I get a warm thrill passing through me at the 'girlfriend' bit.

'But you don't know us,' says Steve.

'I can tell an honest face. Anyway, I like to help artists out and – well, I've got a brother who lives your kind of life.' A shadow of sadness crosses his face. 'You'll be doing me a favour, because it means I won't be losing business.'

'If you put it that way,' says Steve, 'we'd be happy to help out. Wouldn't we, Jo?'

It seems too good to be true.

Soon it's December. There are lights all over the town and a buzz of excitement. People are buying loads of Steve's sketches for presents. We've decorated the shop with tinsel. I pretend it's ours. I dare to feel happy.

340

'Take some time off,' Steve tells me early one morning. 'Explore the village a bit.'

I've been wanting to go into the Boscastle witchcraft museum for ages. It sort of pulls me to it.

So I pay my entrance, using the coins Steve has given me. But from the minute I go in, I feel uneasy. *Times have changed*, I keep telling myself, as I read about all the women who were pushed under water until they drowned just because they cured folk with herbs.

When I come out, I sit on a bench to have a bit of a think before going back to the studio. Someone has left a newspaper there. It flutters in the breeze. A page flips over. And that's when I see it. *The search is still on for . . .*

Below is a photograph of a woman and a man. Not old but not young either. He has his arm wrapped round her shoulders, tight, as if he wants to hold her there for ever. She's got this stiff smile on her face like she's pretending for the camera.

I try to read the words but they're dancing in front of my eyes. I go cold all over.

Quickly, I walk back, my chest thudding. Steve is sketching in charcoal. 'Makes a change from chalk,' he says.

He glances up and gives me a warm smile. I can't look at that kind face any more. Instead, I run upstairs, get my stuff and shove it all into my plastic bags.

'Where are you going?' he says when I come down.

I make my voice sound hard. 'I'm leaving.'

'Why?' He drops his charcoal.

I can't tell him the truth – that I've got this black sinking feeling that says I've got to leave him, though I don't know why. Then I think back to how Steve had told me about his fiancée telling him he was boring and how hurt he'd been.

I bite my lip. 'I'm sorry, Steve. But I don't think we're right for each other after all. You're . . . well, you're boring. I need more thrills.'

He looks like I've just ripped his heart out.

'But I thought we were good together.'

'Well, we weren't,' I say, pushing past. 'And by the way, that street-art stuff of yours is crap.'

I've shown my true colours now. I want to cry. But then I grit my teeth and move on.

1.50 p.m., 17 August 1984

Michael is back with the ball before we can find somewhere else to go.

'More, more,' he pleads.

I can tell that Peter is getting as fed up as I am. 'Can't we take him back to your father and stepmother?' he asks after sending a ball down to the other end of the garden yet again.

This is getting worse and worse. 'Sheila has told me I've got to look after him.'

'That's not fair. She treats you as though you're some kind of Cinderella servant girl.'

'I know. But what can I do about it?'

Michael is running back to us, as keen as ever. 'Again,' he demands. Peter raises his arm. Catches the ball. His short-sleeved shirt shows his arm muscles rippling. I feel a thrill of excitement that someone as handsome as him is actually interested in small, mousy me.

'He's got to get fed up with this soon,' says Peter.

I shake my head. 'Michael would do this for ever if he could.'

He groans. 'Well, I'll throw a few more balls and then we'll take him back to the house and say he's getting tired. Your father and stepmother will have to accept that. After that, we can come out into the garden again for some privacy.'

His hand reaches for mine. 'I've been dreaming of kissing you for ages.'

'Me too,' I whisper.

He smiles. 'Not long now.'

47

Ellie

A couple of weeks later I start feeling sick. Could it have been the fish I cooked last night? Yet Roger, who'd eaten exactly the same, was fine. Then I was sick again the following day. My mouth tasted as if it had swallowed something metallic. It all felt very familiar.

'You need to see the doctor,' Roger told me, but I knew what the verdict would be. This time, I saw a young GP who had recently joined the practice. If he'd read my notes, he didn't seem to show any disapproval. Perhaps he hadn't had time.

'I didn't think I could get pregnant if I was breastfeeding,' I said.

'Old wives' tale, I'm afraid. Never mind. It's good to have two children in quick succession. My wife did the same. You can get it all over with.' Then he grinned. 'That is, unless you go on to have a third.'

The thought was terrifying. I could barely cope with the responsibility of one, let alone two. It was almost impossible to push a pram along a street without touching a pavement crack. I was a bundle of nerves. Waiting. Watching. Something would go wrong again soon. It always did.

As the months passed, the brief truce between Roger

and me had come to an end. I was getting bigger and told Roger I was sorry but that I was too tired when he tried to touch me at bedtime. To make it worse, Amy was a poor sleeper and her high-pitched persistent cries made Roger snappy. 'I need rest if I'm going to work the next day.' So sometimes he stayed over at college in tutor accommodation. When I pointed out that this left me without any help in getting our daughter up in the morning and that it would be nice if he was around, he was angry and defensive. 'What else do you expect me to do?'

Once, I was sitting on the village bench when I must have dozed off. I woke with a start. For a minute I couldn't see Amy. Panic shot through me like an electric shock. Then I realized I'd put the pushchair to one side of me instead of it being in front as usual. Still, anyone could have taken her while I was sleeping. How could I have been so negligent?

After that, I wouldn't let our daughter out of my sight. I didn't even like Jean holding her any more. I made Roger wash his hands before he picked her up. My own were red raw from doing the same. I spent hours cooking baby food and then throwing it away in case it wasn't clean enough. I bought jars instead but then fretted. What if they had been infected during the manufacturing process? I realized to my horror that I was acting just like Sheila had done when Michael was small. Perhaps I should have been more sympathetic.

'You've got to relax a bit,' Roger told me.

But I couldn't. Everything was a potential danger. As for this baby growing inside me, I was convinced that my luck had ended. I had one healthy child. How could I possibly be entitled to another?

Then, one day, there was a knock on the door just as I was taking the washing out of the twin tub. Amy was screaming because she wanted my attention. I scooped her up to answer, her little fists pummelling my chest with fury.

It was Jean.

Amy's howls of protest got louder. 'Sorry, this isn't a good time. Can we talk later?'

'Is anyone else around?' she asked, glancing behind me into the house.

'No. Why?'

She ignored my last question. 'Then I think you need to take time to listen to something,' she said quietly.

My chest began to race with terror. Somehow she must have found out about my past. Now she'd tell Roger. He might take Amy away from me . . .

'I've thought long and hard about this,' she began. 'I didn't know if I ought to tell you but I've decided that I will.'

She shuffled uneasily from one foot to the other. 'I went on a day trip with my women's group the other week to Chipping Norton. I saw Roger there. I don't think he spotted me. But the thing is, Ellie . . .'

Her voice faltered.

'Go on,' I said. This wasn't the revelation I'd expected.

'He was in a car just outside a pub. Kissing a young woman.'

Roger didn't get home until 9 p.m. that night. He was 'teaching late' again. I'd spent the last few hours since Jean's bombshell on autopilot. No, I'd told her rather abruptly,

347

as though she was responsible. I didn't need her to stay with me. I'd sort this out for myself.

'You know,' Jean said, 'some people manage to ignore this sort of thing. Our generation often turned a blind eye.'

Then why had she told me? I'd rather not have known. Ignorance is bliss. At least, it would have been for me.

By the time I heard Roger's key turn in the lock, I had paced the ground floor of our cottage, again and again, going over the possibilities in my head. I'd almost decided that Jean's 'turn a blind eye' suggestion might be best – but then I saw Roger's face. He didn't even look at me. Instead, he walked straight past and into the kitchen. 'No dinner again, I see.'

Normally, I'd have apologized profusely. Since Amy had become more mobile, I'd got really behind with evening meals because I was always running after her. This second pregnancy was also more tiring than the first – the baby had started to kick fiercely – and I could feel the energy constantly draining out of me.

But today my husband's tone unleashed something inside.

'Jean saw you,' I blurted out. 'In Chipping Norton. You were with a woman.'

He stopped dead. 'What on earth are you talking about?'

Relief shot through me. So Jean had got it wrong.

I went hot and red. 'She said you and this woman were kissing in a car.'

'And when would I have time for that?' His face was close to mine. It was furious. 'I'm working every hour that God gives me to look after my family and keep this place going.'

I resist the temptation to point out that it was my money that had bought the cottage.

'Please, Roger.' Despite myself, I sounded penitent now rather than accusing. 'I'd rather you just told me. Are you having an affair?'

'No, I'm not. Although if I was, no one would blame me. It's not as though my wife is interested in sex, is she? I'm expected to live like a bloody monk.'

I tried to put my arms around him but he shrugged me off. 'I don't feel comfortable being close to a woman who doesn't believe me. As for our nosy neighbour, who clearly needs her eyesight checking, I don't want you seeing her again.'

It seems strange now to think that a husband could actually forbid his wife from doing something. But some men like Roger still remembered their own fathers' and grandfathers' attitudes.

I could have argued back but I didn't want to upset him. Perhaps a small part of me preferred to live in ignorance. It was easier than dealing with a broken marriage.

So I did what my husband commanded like a dutiful wife. I told Jean that I was busy when she called round. After a few occasions, her disappointed face showed she'd got the message. As for Roger, he began coming home earlier. His evening classes had 'stopped'. I forced myself to have sex even though it was uncomfortable and – on my part – something to be endured rather than enjoyed.

A month later our son, Luke, was born. On time. No complications. 'One of each,' said the nurses when Roger and a shiny-eyed, excited Amy visited. 'How lucky is that?'

Lucky? Were they joking? Luke's little pert nose and

piercing blue eyes made my stomach churn. The resemblance to Michael was shocking. Every time I looked at him, I saw the accusation in his face. 'You're a bad mother,' this baby seemed to say as it bit into my cracked nipples hungrily, making me wince with pain.

'Here,' said the midwife. 'Use this cream. It will help.'

But nothing could salve my conscience. Any good that had come from my therapy at Highbridge was now dissolving. 'Breast is best,' declared Roger when I said I wasn't going to feed him myself any more. 'You said you'd try harder after Amy.'

It wasn't a question of 'trying harder', I wanted to say. But I knew he wouldn't understand. Instead, I lied and told him that the health visitor said Luke wasn't gaining enough weight and would be better off on baby milk. But the truth was that I didn't think my own milk was good enough for him. How could it be, after what I had done? Then I spent ages sterilizing and re-sterilizing the bottles in case I was infecting him with hidden germs. 'Surely you don't need to do that,' said Roger, clearly irritated.

Oh, but I did. My guilt and anxiety also made me write another letter. But this time, instead of tearing it up or burning it as I'd done before, I ran down the lane and put it in the post box. It made a thud as it joined the other letters inside.

Only later did I discover I'd opened Pandora's box.

48

Jo

I can't get Steve's face out of my mind. So I do the only thing I can. I walk and walk. With each step, I talk myself out of him. I tell myself that it would never have worked. That I am doing the right thing. That I don't deserve him. Never did.

I reach the end of the town, and start walking through a big tourist car park. I need to find a bus stop – or maybe hitch a lift – and get as far away from here as I can. There's no way I want to bump into Steve again. Once more, I look over my shoulder to check I'm not being followed.

'Come on, ladies,' says a voice. It's a young man shepherding a group of women into a blue-and-silver coach with a sign on the front. PLYMOUTH CHRISTMAS SHOPPING TRIP.

I try to push my way past but a hand touches my arm. 'Joyce, it's this way. Come on, love. You're late.'

The man has clearly mistaken me for someone else, yet I find myself being swept up the steps. 'You've got it wrong –,' I start to say but the coach is already moving. The other women are busy nattering to each other. No one takes any notice as I plonk my bottom on the only empty seat at the back. Any minute now, I'll be caught out. But the longer I can stay on, the further I can get away from

Steve. I close my eyes and pretend to be asleep. I allow a couple of tears to creep silently down my face, keeping them hidden as I turn towards the window. I try not to think about him. After a while I feel tiredness overtaking me.

I wake up to someone shaking me. 'Who are you?'

It's a woman with a sharp face. The bus has stopped, I realize. We're in a big car park. Outside I can see a sign with the words JAMAICA INN.

'Who are you?' she repeats. 'You're not one of us.'

I sit up, stretching my aching back.

'It's not my fault,' I say. My mouth is throbbing with a dull toothache that seems to have come from nowhere. 'That man over there told me to get on the coach.'

Her eyes roll. 'He's hopeless. I'm going to report him when we're back.'

'But where's Joyce?' whines another woman.

They stare at me as if I've done something to her. I begin to feel afraid.

'I've just said, haven't I? I only did what I was told.'

Voices are being raised now. Folk at the front are turning round to look at me. The young man is making his way down the coach. 'What's going on?' he says.

'This woman says you told her to get on. But she's not part of our group.'

'Great. That's all I need.' He glowers at me. 'Why didn't you say?'

'I tried to, but –'

'So where is Joyce?' someone interrupts.

'I'll ring her,' says a shrill voice.

'What about this one?' says the woman who woke me

352

up. She jabs a shiny red nail at me. 'You'll have to throw her off the coach. It isn't fair. She hasn't paid like the rest of us.'

'That's plain daft,' I snap. 'The man told me to get on. You can't charge me for something I didn't ask for.'

'I've got hold of Joyce!' calls out the shrill voice. 'She says she was only ten minutes late but we didn't wait for her.'

There are a couple of mutterings about 'serve her right for not being on time' and 'teach her a lesson'.

'I'm hungry,' says a small woman with pale-yellow hair who'd been sitting in front of me. 'Can't we sort this out over some food? "Includes a visit to Jamaica Inn for lunch", it said on the leaflet.'

'But what about her?' hisses another face.

The young man is speaking urgently into his mobile. It's clear he's getting a telling-off because he keeps apologizing. 'He'll get sacked for this,' says someone. 'Quite right too.'

I almost feel sorry for him.

'You're to stay on until we get to Plymouth,' he says to me.

'I hope you're going to make her pay for her meal,' says someone else.

'Oh, for goodness' sake,' says the woman with yellow hair. 'You can see she's got no money. She can have Joyce's lunch, can't she?'

No one talks to me at the big table that's been reserved for us. That's fine by me. I pull my beret down further over my eyes — even though we're inside — and concentrate on the pile on my plate from the buffet. God, it's good, even though my tooth is beginning to hurt more.

Then I go to the toilet. Always a treat to sit on a proper seat. Nice loo paper too. It's the soft kind. I stuff some into one of my carrier bags. But then I think of Steve and put it back.

I return with the others to the car park. The biting wind cuts right through me. We pass a silver Volvo. A couple appear to be having a bit of a row in the front. In the back, a young boy has his snub nose pressed against the window, staring at me.

I look away. The sooner I get on the coach the better.

Shrinking back into my seat, I pretend I'm not here. It's what I do best. The country roads stop and we go over a big bridge. There are streets and houses now and then a sign that says WELCOME TO PLYMOUTH. There's a marina and a big shopping centre. If I can hide away from the security guards before closing, I might be able to doss in there.

The coach continues a couple of minutes longer and then pulls into a car park. The doors open. 'Wait, please, ladies,' says the young man. 'I need to give you instructions about meeting up at the end of the day.'

'Where will you go?' asks the woman with yellow hair.

I shrug. 'Somewhere warm and dry, with any luck.'

She looks at me curiously. 'Are you all right?'

Her sudden kindness makes my tongue loose. 'Not really. I don't know where I'm sleeping tonight.'

Even though I have the American money, something tells me I ought to hang on to it for real emergencies. If I play my cards right, I might get something for free here.

She looks shocked. 'That's awful. Look, I only use my credit card nowadays – but take this.'

She fiddles with the clasp on her watch and hands it over to me. 'This cost over two hundred pounds when it was new. You could sell it and get some money.'

You could knock me down with a feather. 'Why are you doing this?' I ask.

She shrugs. 'Believe it or not, I know what it's like to be down on your luck in life. I was as poor as a church mouse until I married my second husband.' She glances at the watch. 'He gave me that.'

'Don't you want to keep it, then?'

She shakes her head. 'I divorced him – to be honest, you'll be doing me a favour by taking it off my hands. I was going to give it away anyway to get rid of the memories. Now off you go. And good luck.'

I don't need telling twice.

2 p.m., 17 August 1984

'You must be hungry,' says Peter when Michael comes running back to us like an enthusiastic puppy. 'Why don't we take you back to the house and find your parents so they can give you something to eat?'

But Michael isn't having any of it. 'No. I want to stay here with you.'

Peter is starting to look really annoyed. Any minute now, I tell myself, he'll go back into the house on his own. Supposing he starts talking to my old friend Christine, who has also come with her parents? He might start to like her instead of me. I can feel all my excitement slipping away. What will I tell the others at school if Peter goes off me? That's when I get the idea.

'Wait,' I say quickly. 'Supposing we play hide-and-seek?'

Michael's eyes light up. 'I love that game.' He points at Peter. 'You hide first.'

'OK.' Peter winks at me. 'But we've got to make sure that we all take turns.'

'We'll count to fifty, won't we, Ellie?'

'There's only one rule,' I add. 'No one can go into the copse. There are too many trees there and someone might get lost.'

I glance at Peter. He seems to be reading my mind. The copse would be an ideal place for us to hide out in as long as

356

Michael doesn't go into it. He nods approvingly at me. A thrill runs down my spine.

'OK,' agrees Michael happily. 'Come on, Ellie. We've got to count so Peter can get away.' He reaches for my hand, his skin warm against mine. 'One, two . . .'

49

Ellie

From my cell, I can see a small slide and a couple of swings for children who visit so they can keep contact with parents, grandparents, family and friends. I watch them with a terrible pain in my heart, remembering the times I used to take my two to the local playground. I'd made friends with a new mother who had moved to the village. Her children were almost the same age as Amy and Luke. She used to go with me and we'd watch as they all played on the rusty swings and slide. But after a while she asked too many questions and I stopped seeing her.

I didn't bond with any of the other mums in the village either. This was a small rural community, where families tended to know everything about each other. My new acquaintances all had mothers willing to babysit and give advice. They seemed so much more confident than me.

In an effort to fit in, I joined the Women's Institute but I only got to one meeting, because they were held in the evenings and Roger liked me to be home when he was. When I was invited on the annual outing to Woodstock, my husband was most put out. 'What about the children?' he'd asked. I didn't like to point out that I was always with them every day and that he often came home late.

I spent most of my days trying to find things that the

children enjoyed. I attempted to get them interested in wildflowers, as my mother had done with me, but when I caught Amy trying to eat the dandelion I was helping her to press, I panicked. They could be poisonous, according to the little notes my mother had written in her gardener's handbook in that distinctive loopy writing of hers. So that was the end of that. Instead, we went for long walks whenever it was dry enough, or to the mobile library, which pulled up outside the village hall twice a month.

Sometimes we caught the bus into Oxford to look round the Ashmolean Museum. I loved it but the children got restless after a bit.

Occasionally I nodded across the fence at Jean, and we exchanged pleasantries, but that was it. I missed my neighbour's company, but I couldn't afford to upset Roger.

All I had to do was steel myself at night when his hands began to explore my body. Afterwards, he was nice to me unless he'd had too much to drink. Then he was sarcastic and cruel. 'You don't really like sex, do you, Ellie? What's wrong with you?'

'Nothing,' I stuttered, but he just laughed nastily.

'I knew you were naive when I met you but you didn't let on that you were frigid.'

I winced with pain. Maybe if I'd explained, he might have understood. But I was too scared to come clean. So we limped on.

Then my husband announced he'd signed up for the squash club in college. One evening, he returned with his shirt inside out. 'I had a shower afterwards,' he explained. 'Must have put it back on the wrong way.'

It seemed plausible enough and yet . . .

On another occasion, when we were sitting on the sofa watching a film while the children were (miraculously) both asleep, the phone rang. When I picked it up, it went silent.

'That's happened a few times recently,' I said.

'Really?' That irritated look, which I knew all too well, flitted across Roger's face. 'We need to do something about cold calls. They're an invasion of privacy.'

Then, one morning after Roger had left for a full day of teaching, came a package addressed to me. This was unusual. For a minute, my heart skipped, hoping it was finally in response to the one I'd sent all that time ago. But the postmark was local. I examined the bulky brown envelope with its typed capital letters.

I tore it open, unable to wait any longer to see what it contained. Out fell my husband's college scarf; the tutors often wore them in solidarity with the students. Why would someone have posted it to me? Instinctively, I held it up to my face.

The perfume wasn't mine.

All day, I told myself that it couldn't be true. But Jean's words kept haunting me even after all this time. In a car. Kissing a woman.

Turning a blind eye no longer seemed an option. I had to know the truth.

'Oh yes,' said Roger, when I showed it to him that night. 'It's just a silly prank. Some of my colleagues have never grown up.'

My heart soared with relief. He didn't seem at all bothered. So it must be all right.

'But why would they do that?'

'Universities are full of politics. You ought to read David Lodge's novels.'

Read? Hah! I didn't have time for such a luxury. I was too busy and exhausted from looking after the children. I'd lost track of current affairs. In fact, I couldn't remember when I'd last read a newspaper.

The day after, a similar brown envelope was pushed through the door. This time it contained two cinema stubs for the Odeon in Oxford for last Tuesday, which Roger told me was his squash night. Unease washed through me. 'I didn't see any film,' said my husband when I told him. 'And I wasn't in the city centre either. If this happens again, maybe we should report it to the police. It's harassment.'

'Isn't that a bit dramatic?' I asked.

Roger shrugged. 'You clearly don't trust me. And if that's what it will take for you to drop this, we should file an official complaint.'

'Of course I trust you.' I shivered. 'It's just that I'm scared. I don't like the idea of some anonymous prankster sending me things like this.'

'Nor do I, but the best thing to do is ignore it. Then whoever it is will get bored after a bit. Let's leave it at that, shall we?'

So I didn't bother reporting anything. For some weeks, nothing else happened. Then one day there was a knock at the door. A young woman stood there. Her cool green eyes studied mine as though she had a confidence far beyond her years. She seemed angry. 'I sent you the scarf and the cinema tickets,' she said in an Irish accent. 'Since that seemed to have no effect, I thought I'd turn up in person in case you didn't believe me. Here's a little present for you.'

She handed me another brown envelope, walking away before I could shove it back at her. I opened it to find a photograph of her with Roger, their arms around each other. Both smiling at me. I felt sick. My mind went into a whirl. No. Please no. It didn't prove anything, I told myself. It might just have been a college event. She was a student with a crush on him. But when I casually told Roger over supper that night, he went silent. My heart chilled.

'OK,' he said finally. 'I admit it.'

'What?'

I felt as though I was on a film set. This was happening to someone else. Not me.

'She's called Melanie and she wants us to be together.'

This can't be true. 'Do you . . . do you love her?'

He hesitated. 'It's serious,' he said.

'No!' I heard myself sobbing. 'What about the children? You can't just walk out on us like this.'

'She doesn't want the house,' Roger continued as if he hadn't heard me. 'She just wants me.' He seemed flattered. 'Unlike you. No. Don't pretend. I can always tell when you're faking it – that's when you can be bothered to have sex at all.'

There was a sound from the children's bedroom. 'Daddee. Daddee. Story-eee.'

'See,' I said. 'How can we manage without you?'

Amy had scrambled out of bed now and was running up to the table. She leapt into Roger's arms. Luke began yelling. I gathered him up from his cot and brought him in.

Suddenly I had a flash of my father, telling me about Sheila. *'Please can't you call her "Mum"?'*

'We're a family,' I wept. 'Please don't do this. Stay with us.'

He closed his eyes for a minute as if he was too tired to listen. 'I'll decide in the morning,' he said.

That night, I didn't sleep a wink. When I looked across at him as the early-morning light began to dawn, I found Roger staring up at the ceiling too. 'What are you going to do?' I whispered.

'I'll give her up,' he said flatly. 'I've got no choice.'

'Thank you,' I wept. 'Thank you.'

'There's just one thing.' His voice was icy cold. 'You are never to mention this to anyone. I don't want the department hearing about this.'

And that's when I realized. Roger hadn't made his decision to stay for the sake of us, his family. He had done it for his career. Last year, when I'd gone to a Christmas drinks do with my husband, someone had mentioned that a senior tutor had got a student pregnant and had been made to leave. He was, apparently, still looking for a job. 'Quite right too,' said the woman who had told me. 'It's absolutely disgusting.'

My husband clearly feared a similar fate. But whatever his reasons, at least he was staying with us. 'We'll make this work,' I told myself fiercely. 'We have to, for the sake of the children.'

After Roger had left for work, there was a knock on my door. 'Forgive me,' said Jean. 'But I heard arguing last night through the walls. Are you all right?'

It was her kindness that broke me. I began to cry,

telling her everything, despite Roger's warnings to stay silent. It was such a relief to unburden myself. Then I panicked. 'You mustn't tell anyone,' I pleaded. 'Roger would kill me.'

Her mouth tightened. 'I knew it was him I'd seen in Chipping Norton that day.'

'Do you think it's the same woman?' I asked.

'Doesn't matter. It just shows he's capable of it.' Jean bit her lip. 'Clever of him to suggest you went to the police. He was banking on you not doing that.'

'Have I got this wrong,' I asked slowly, 'or have you had a similar experience?'

My neighbour nodded, her mouth a straight line. 'I took the hard way out. I insisted on a divorce. Now, in my older years, I find myself wondering if I made too much of a fuss. Maybe I shouldn't have said anything to you.' Then she shook herself. 'Listen. Why don't you leave the kids with me today and go out for a couple of hours on your own? I'll look after them in your house so they've got all their things.'

Roger wouldn't be pleased. But he wasn't going to be back until later. I had to admit that the thought of being able to think clearly without the demands of two small children was tempting.

So I took the bus into town and wandered round the colleges. I hung about outside Roger's and watched the young women coming in and out. None looked like the confident one with the Irish accent who had turned up on my doorstep. I couldn't think of her by name. It would have made her too real.

One day, I promised myself, when the children were at

school, I'd train as a teacher and find work. Maybe that's what I needed. But then I thought of my medical records. Would anyone employ me?

When I got back, Jean met me at the door. Instantly, I could tell something had happened. 'The children are all right,' she said swiftly. 'But you had a visitor.'

'That girl again?'

She looked at me. 'No. It was a man. He said he was your father.'

I didn't know what to say. I'd told Jean, as I had everyone, that I didn't have a family any more.

'I'm not going to ask questions,' she said. 'He left you this.'

It wasn't a long note. There was no address at the top. Or date.

Ellie [no 'dear'],

   Thank you for your letter, which Cornelius kindly forwarded, telling me about Luke and Amy. The older I get, the more I find myself thinking of the past. I was in your area and called in on the chance you might be there. At least I got to see my grandchildren. The resemblance is extraordinary. Luke, in particular, is so like Michael, isn't he?

   Dad.

There was a small package with it. Inside was my music box.

'It belonged to my mother,' I whispered, stroking the carved wooden top. 'After she died, it made me feel she was still with me.'

Jean gave me a brief hug. 'Are you all right?' she asked.

I nodded. This was all my fault. I knew I'd made a mistake in digging up the past as soon as I'd posted that letter to my father via Cornelius. I should have ripped it up or burned it like the others.

'We all have our secrets,' she said quietly.

Roger certainly had his. But in comparison with mine, they were nothing.

50

Jo

Plymouth has got loads of people in it; so many more than Mousehole and Boscastle. I wonder for a minute if Tim and Lucky are back with his mum. Then I think of Steve squatting down on another pavement. Fiercely, I push them out of my head, remembering what a friend had once told me: 'If you want to survive, you've got to put number one first.'

A man bumps into me and I start. 'Sorry,' he mumbles. My heart continues to beat fast, long after he's gone.

I gaze up at the shiny glass building I'd spotted from the coach. I take a look inside but there are security staff everywhere. When I come out, giddy from the noise, I see a sign for a Pop-up Christmas Market. Maybe I'll try my luck there. In my experience, stallholders don't ask as many questions as shopkeepers. It's not very big – more toys and tinsel than anything else – but there's a man over there with an 'Antiques and Bric-a-Brac' sign.

'How much will you give me for this?' I ask, showing him the blonde lady's watch.

He holds it up to his ear. 'Works, does it?'

I pretend to be offended. 'Would I bring it to you if it didn't?'

'You'd be surprised what people do.'

He makes a play of examining it. 'Twenty quid,' he says.

'Come on,' I snort. 'We both know it's worth more than that.'

He eyeballs me. 'Then why don't you take it to one of the fancy jewellers round here?'

I shrug. 'So you don't want it, then?'

'Yours to sell, is it?' he asks.

I think of the silver bracelet I'd flogged back in Bristol. 'Of course it is.' I make myself sound as posh as possible.

'Thirty-five quid, then, and not a penny more.'

'Forty.'

He hands it back to me and turns away.

'All right,' I say grudgingly. 'I'll take thirty-five, but it's daylight bloody robbery.'

He must have known I'd accept because he's already got three tenners and a fiver in his hands.

'Times are tough,' he says, shrugging.

I pocket the notes. With any luck, this and the American money will see me through for a bit.

'Know of any hostels round here?' I ask.

'I do, but they're more than likely to be filled up by this time of day.' Then his face softens. 'There's this community café that does hot meals and even has a shower room, mind. It's about twenty minutes' walk from here. If you leg it, you might get there before they shut. Go out of here and take the second left and then a right. Past the traffic lights and then left again.'

'Thanks,' I say.

Then he looks at me. 'Don't I know you from somewhere?'

I pull my beret down. 'I've just got one of those faces,' I say. Then I hurry off.

The café is packed with all kinds of people. Babies are yelling, toddlers are running around, young kids are boogieing and a couple side by side in wheelchairs are holding hands. Everyone else is sitting at groups of tables with balloons and paper hats, stuffing their faces.

'Welcome,' says a woman with pearls round her neck. 'Come on in. Strictly speaking, we're full for our Christmas tea but I'm sure we can find you a place. What's your name?'

'Jo,' I say, keeping my beret on and staring around.

'Nice to meet you, Jo.' She's actually shaking my hand. 'Why don't you come and sit here, next to Diane? She's one of our volunteers. We're on our puddings now but I'm sure we can find you some roast chicken and veg.'

I wolf it down and then have a double helping of Christmas pudding. 'You look as though you needed that,' says Diane.

She's got kind eyes. I like her.

'Are you travelling?' she says.

I'd hoped that my turquoise fleece might be smart enough for people to think I was one of them. Then again, it needs a good wash now.

'Sort of.'

'Got anywhere to stay tonight?'

'No.'

For one crazy moment, I hope she'll offer to put me up at her place. But she doesn't.

'We've got some hot showers here if you fancy a wash,'

she says. 'There's a washing machine too. We could give you some other clothes while yours dry.'

'Why?' I demand.

'What do you mean?'

'Why do you want to help me?'

She touches my arm gently. 'See all these people?' she says softly. 'Most of them don't have homes to go to or else they live in what we call "challenging situations". We're a charity, so we just try to do what we can.'

A lump comes into my throat. For all the bad people in my life, it seems there's always a good person who comes up every now and then. Once more, I try not to think about Steve.

'Now, why don't we get you sorted and then you can join in the party games.'

'That sort of thing isn't for me,' I say.

Diane laughs. 'You might change your mind.'

She's right. When I come out from the shower – in a pair of black trousers and a pink jumper, which I chose from a box labelled 'Women's Medium Size' – the others are playing pass the parcel. Someone shifts up for me and I take a place. The parcel stops in my lap.

'Open it!' everyone yells out.

There's a sparkly pink hairbrush inside. 'But she's got no hair,' says one of the older kids. There's a silence. Then I laugh and everyone else does too.

After that this tall lanky bloke – who reminds me of a grown-up Tim – starts playing a guitar and we sing along. Every now and then he makes a wrong note on purpose and we all laugh.

It's dark outside now. People are beginning to leave.

Every time the door is opened, there's a blast of cold air. I wish I was back in the bakery. The hotel seems like it never happened.

Maybe I'll use my precious money to fork out on a bed and breakfast after all. 'How much do you think it will be?' I ask one of the volunteers.

'The cheapest is going to be forty pounds at the least. That's if you can get one so late in the day. Leave it with me. I'll ring round.'

When she comes back, I'm almost the last one left. 'Sorry. They're all full up. So are the hostels.'

'I'll sleep in a bus shelter, then,' I say.

She shakes her head. 'The police will just move you on. We might have a tent to spare. Let's have a look. Might be able to get you a thermal sleeping bag too and a rucksack instead of those plastic bags of yours. There's a public space outside town where they let you pitch. I can give you directions.'

I still don't want to leave this warm place. 'Can I come back tomorrow?'

She shakes her head. 'We're only open three days a week, and because of the Christmas break you won't find anyone here until after New Year. Sorry.'

Carrying the tent under my arm, I head back out into the streets. Snow is beginning to fall. It's not thick. More like fluffy wet drops of rain. They mix with the tears running down my cheeks. I wish I hadn't gone to that centre now. The warmth and kindness there make all this harder to bear.

I walk and walk. It's further than the woman had said, but eventually I find a field where there are some other tents. Some of the occupants have got torches shining and I can see people moving around inside. I've never put up a tent before but the volunteer was right. It's not that difficult.

Then I crawl into my sleeping bag, wearing all the clothes I've got for warmth. I can't sleep. There are noises outside. I'm sure I can hear something chewing at the canvas. I turn on the torch that the volunteer gave me but I can't see anything. What if it's a rat? There'd been a few mice in the caravan and I'd freaked out until Tim had gently gathered them up and released them into the wild.

'I once had a mouse who lived in a house, along with a louse.'

I miss the kid with his rhymes. And I miss Steve.

But there's no going back now.

2.07 p.m., 17 August 1984

My head is still feeling light from the drink. My stomach is empty with hunger. No one's bothered to come out with food for us. And my brother won't let us take him back inside. If we do, he'll shout and scream and then Sheila will be angry with me.

'Come on, Ellie,' sings Michael, tugging my hand. 'Let's go and find Peter!'

We search the garden. It's much bigger than ours. There are, as we've already discovered, lots of little parts which are sectioned off from the others with hedges.

'Where are you?' calls out Michael.

There's a scuffling noise from behind the woodshed.

'Got you!'

'Clever boy!' Peter ruffles Michael's hair, grinning at me. He must have made that sound on purpose so he would be discovered. 'Now it's your turn.'

I feel my heart thudding. He'll kiss me soon! What will it be like? I've heard some of the other girls talking about it. The idea of touching tongues seemed a bit yucky but apparently you soon get used to it.

'No.' Michael is tugging my hand again. 'I want Ellie to have her turn.'

375

'But it's always the person who finds someone who has to go,' says Peter sharply.

'I don't care. I want to look for her with you. Pleeease, Ellie.' Michael's voice starts to sound all whiny.

'All right, fine. I'll hide. Close your eyes, then.' I wink at Peter.

Michael has his eyes closed and has begun to count. One. Two. Three . . .

I lean over to Peter and whisper: 'I'll be in that bit of the garden with all those wildflowers.'

51

Ellie

The pattern was always the same. Every few years or so, Roger would come home late. There might be a stray hair on his shirt or a strange smell to it. The phone would ring and there'd be no one at the other end.

When I questioned him, he took great offence and always had an answer for everything. Of course, he had to be late sometimes. There were staff meetings. Evening tutorials. A department drinks party that apparently I'd been invited to but had turned down because of the children. ('What do you mean, you don't remember?')

As for the blonde hair on his shirt, that was ridiculous! Anyone can get something on their clothes. ('Unlike you, Ellie, I'm in a working environment.') The phone? Cold calls were a scourge of the time. Then he would sulk as though all this was my fault for not trusting him.

So I just let it pass, telling myself that I was the bigger transgressor out of the two of us, even though he did not know it. Besides, if I was more attractive and tried a bit harder in bed, Roger might not feel the need to stray. But the most important factor was the children. I had to keep the family together. I knew all too well how dangerous a broken family could be.

By now Roger had written several academic papers – his special subject was 'Victorian Women in Fiction' – and was beginning to make a name for himself. He went to a couple of international conferences, one in Florence and another in New York.

'Be safe,' I said, hugging him tightly before he left. What I really meant was, 'Don't stray,' but I was too scared of saying anything in case it rocked the boat.

But when Luke and Amy became teenagers, they weren't afraid to ask questions. 'Why does Dad always have to go away so much?' asked Luke before another trip – this time to Poland.

'Because he's a very important man.'

Roger preened as I spoke. I hated myself for flattering him and yet I kept finding myself doing it.

'Why don't you work, Mum?'

'Because your mother likes to look after us,' chipped in my husband. This is what he always said, as though I had no other purpose in life.

The only thing I allowed myself to do for fun was my mosaics. My rediscovery of my old hobby had started soon after Jean had sold her cottage. In some ways this was a relief, as she was the only one outside Highbridge who knew my father was alive. But in another way I missed our clandestine meetings hugely. Meanwhile an artist had moved in. She built a studio in her back garden and invited me to look inside.

'I used to do mosaics at school,' I said carefully.

Her eyes lit up. 'I'm running a course on that next month. Why don't you come along? Bring some old china with you that you don't mind breaking up.'

The children were at school. So I did.

We hadn't been allowed to actually smash pieces for mosaics at Highbridge in case we self-harmed. But I found it very therapeutic to do this now. When I brought down the hammer on an old mug, wearing protective glasses to shield my eyes, it felt good. So too was the act of gluing the back of each piece and sticking it on the surface of a vase or a simple piece of plywood. One woman was making mosaic tables. 'I'd like to do that,' I said.

So I went on a couple more courses and then began making my own at home. When I clinched my first sale at a craft fair, I felt really good about myself. That didn't happen very often. I bought myself a black lacy push-up bra because I thought I might be more attractive to Roger. 'What on earth are you wearing?' he laughed when he saw me in it. 'You look like some stripper.'

I felt cheap. Dirty. I couldn't even take it back because I'd cut off the label and worn it.

So I pushed it to the back of the drawer, where it stayed as a reminder of my folly.

Of course, the family were my main focus. I was still a nervous mother – I rang Luke's school on the eve of a canoe trip to say he had a temperature and couldn't go. He was furious with me. The truth was that I feared he might have an accident. But the mosaics helped to distract me.

Occasionally, there were family holidays when things almost seemed all right. Once we went to Devon, where we had a glorious beach holiday in a pretty seaside town, staying at an old hotel that Queen Victoria had gone to as a child. One day, at the owners' suggestion, we visited the nearby ruins of a castle with the unusual name of Berry Pomeroy.

'What an adventure,' said Roger as he drove us down a narrow lane where the bushes pressed against the window while squeals of excitement came from the children in the back. He took his left hand off the driving wheel to reach over as he spoke. I squeezed it back gratefully.

'But it's just a ruin,' said Amy disappointedly when the tall, imposing castle loomed up before us.

Luke was more impressed as we picked our way through the stone courtyard and stared up at the empty windows. 'Cool! Do you reckon people were murdered here?'

I shivered inside. Any reference to blood, death or accidents still unnerved me.

Roger was reading the guide book. 'They say that it's the most haunted castle in Britain. There's one ghost – the Blue Lady – who can be seen at night. She killed her own baby. Apparently its father was her father too.'

'That's gross, Dad.'

I turned away.

'Where are you going, Mum?'

'Back to the car. It's too cold for me.'

Even though it was a warm sunny day, my bones felt frozen.

'That was different, wasn't it?' said Roger when they joined me back at the car. 'How about an ice cream?'

'Great,' I chipped in. Anything to pretend we were an ordinary family again. Without the ghosts of the past or the infidelities of the present.

The years rolled on. 'Make the most of your children,' people would tell me. 'They grow up so fast.'

But that wasn't true, as I knew all too well. Look what had happened to Michael.

Just before Amy was about to go to university, we had a big row about how many clothes she needed to take. I couldn't admit to myself that I was scared her departure would alter the carefully constructed family I had fought to keep together. Later on, Luke came into the kitchen where I was making coffee and sat down heavily at the table with a long face.

'I know you're going to miss your sister,' I said. 'We all are.'

'It's not that,' he mumbled.

I pulled up a chair, putting my arm around him. Even though Luke was taller than me now, I still wanted to cuddle him as I had done when he was a small boy. 'Then what is it?'

He looked down. 'I can't tell you.'

'It might help to get it off your chest.'

'I don't want to upset you.'

I got that nasty cold feeling again. 'Just tell me.'

He spoke, looking down at the floor. 'I heard Dad on the phone this morning. He was telling someone that he missed them.'

My mouth went dry.

'Maybe he was talking to Granddad.'

Roger's father was in a care home now with dementia. His lucid periods were few and far between.

Luke's voice was quiet. 'When he saw me, he put the phone down fast.'

'I'm sure there's an explanation,' I said quietly. 'Why don't you go and help your sister finish her packing?'

At first I decided not to say anything. I didn't want Amy to go to uni on a bad note. But shortly after she left, the phone bill arrived in the post. Usually I left this for Roger. But this time I opened it. The same number came up again and again. Now my son suspected, things were different. I wasn't going to keep quiet.

'You might have had the decency to ring your girl-friend from another place!' I shouted at Roger after Luke had gone out to see some friends.

'What on earth are you talking about, Ellie?'

I waved the phone bill in front of him with the calls that I'd circled in red. 'Tell you what. Why don't you call this number right now?'

He looked sullen. 'I don't want to.'

'Because I'll find out you're having an affair?'

I waited for him to come up with some kind of explanation. But instead, he shrugged as though he'd given up caring.

'Look. I'm sorry. It didn't mean anything. It won't happen again.'

But, of course, it did.

Try as I might to keep it away from them, the children weren't stupid. Nor were they so forgiving. 'As soon as I can, I'm getting out of here,' Luke told me. 'Maybe Australia. I might do a degree there instead. You can come and live there with me if you want, Mum.'

Sometimes Amy directed her anger at me. When I wouldn't let her drive to Newquay for a summer holiday with uni friends in case they had a crash, she flew at me. 'You're *so* unreasonable! No wonder Dad doesn't love you any more.'

Her accusation punched me in the stomach. Yet I knew it wasn't true. Roger did love me in his own way. He simply couldn't resist other women because he needed that assurance. Just as I had needed him so I could pretend to the world that I was a good wife and mother.

There's a lot of pretence here in prison too. We say we miss our families. But the truth is that many of us are inside because of them. And I am no exception.

52

Jo

It's Christmas Day tomorrow. Doesn't make any difference to me. Every day is the same on the road. I roll up my sleeping bag and pack up my tent, shivering. Every one of my bones feels like it's cracking with the cold.

I need to eat. To get warm. I walk into town until I find a pizza shop and look in the big refuse container at the back. There's two packets on the top. Four whole slices of pizza. I gobble them down fast before someone can snatch them from me.

If I don't find somewhere to shelter quickly, I'm going to freeze to death. It happens. Earlier this week I saw an ambulance picking up a body from a park bench. I watched his straight, rigid legs with a fascinated horror.

I walk through the streets as quickly as my aching legs will let me. A young couple are standing in front of a jeweller's window, looking at rings. 'I love that one,' she coos. I feel a touch of envy. A woman goes by with a little dog in a red-and-white woollen coat with 'Happy Christmas' on it. I wonder what Lucky is doing? Supposing Tim hasn't been allowed to keep him? My tooth, which had gone quiet for a bit, now starts to throb again.

I think for a moment of the bedroom above the bakery and the hotel room. Neither seems real.

There's the sound of clanging ahead. A group of men and women are taking apart metal poles and pulling down awnings. I must have come back to the market. There's a banana lying on the pavement, its skin half open. Swiftly I pick it up, stuffing it into my mouth.

'Hungry, are you?' asks a man. It's the bloke I saw yesterday who told me about the café.

I nod, embarrassed.

'You're the one that sold me the watch, aren't you?'

I nod again. It's hard to talk now because my tooth hurts so much.

'Nice piece. Got any more?'

I shake my head.

He eyes my rucksack and sleeping bag. 'Looks to me like you might need somewhere to stay the night.'

What, and wake up to find he's taken my money?

'Hiya,' says a woman coming up in tight jeans and a leather jacket. She slings an arm round the bloke like she's saying 'This one's mine.'

'Just being friendly, Madge.'

'When aren't you? Talk the bloody hind legs off a donkey, you would.'

She slaps his bottom affectionately and he plants a kiss on her cheek. I feel a stab of pain, remembering the warmth of Steve's body.

'Why don't you come back to our place?' he says. 'It's not much. But there's some hot food and it's warmer than here.'

'What do you want in return?' I ask suspiciously.

'Nothing. Let's just say we've been in your position

before. It's Christmas. You don't want to be on your own, do you?'

It's not being on my own that bothers me. It's the cold. If it was just the man, I wouldn't risk it. But the woman makes it feel safe. So I find myself getting up and following them.

2.09 p.m., 17 August 1984

Cow parsley. Speedwell. Wild roses . . .

Seeing them takes my mind back to those lovely times when my mother was alive and we would press them into a book. My eyes begin to smart. Usually I try not to cry about her because it hurts too much. But today I feel stranger than usual. Like everything is too near the surface.

Then I hear Michael's and Peter's voices. 'Coming to get you!' I wait and wait.

Where are they? I'd told Peter where to go. I can hear them exploring other places. The greenhouse. The woodshed again. Doesn't he want to find me? If I don't make sure we have time on our own soon, I'll lose him for ever.

'Got you!'

I jump as Michael touches my back. 'Peter said you might be here but I wouldn't believe him.'

'Just goes to show you can be wrong,' says Peter tightly. 'Come on. Now it's your turn.'

'OK,' beams Michael. 'But shut your eyes. No cheating!'

Peter winks at me. 'Cross my heart and hope to die.'

We close our eyes and listen to Michael's receding footsteps.

'One, two, three . . .' intones Peter.

'Quick,' I hiss. 'Run to the copse.'

53

Ellie

I know people might think that I was stupid and pathetic to have forgiven Roger for so many years, but I saw it differently. It was worth putting up with his moods and infidelity because I'd managed to keep our children safe. Emotional damage from broken relationships can be just as painful – if not more so – than a physical attack. Of all people, I knew about that.

So I was heartbroken when Luke finally fulfilled his threat and emigrated to Australia. 'I'm sorry, Mum,' he'd said one evening, when he'd overheard Roger and me rowing again. 'I don't want to be near that man any more. You might be able to turn a blind eye but I can't. I'll never forget that phone call I overheard. He makes me sick. I've told him so.'

Roger, of course, told all our friends how proud he was of our son taking such an 'adventurous step'. But I could hardly bear to look at my husband. 'This is your fault,' I hissed in bed that night.

'I don't know what you're talking about. I can't help it if a silly young man gets ideas in his head.'

After Luke went, the silent phone calls stopped. Roger also started coming home from work earlier than he used to. At first, I wasn't sure how we'd cope without the children to bind us together. But over the next few months and then years, Roger and I settled into a fairly comfortable routine. By now he'd retired: a move which surprised me, as I thought he'd carry on for longer. But he was 'tired' of teaching and wanted time to write that novel he'd been banging on about for years.

I forced myself to overcome the fear of making new friends and joined the tennis club. I also threw myself into voluntary work, particularly with a local prison and also a homeless charity, as I'd always been saddened by the number of people living on the streets around us. Roger and I even went to Toronto and Vancouver. It was our first holiday on our own! Apart from the sex, which I had to force myself into, it was amazing. Perhaps we'd weathered the worst. I began to take more care with my appearance and even booked myself in for a make-up consultation. Why hadn't I worn foundation before? It suited me.

'Do you want to come and visit me in Australia?' Luke suggested during one of our mother-and-son phone calls.

'We'd love to,' I told him.

'Not him.' Our son's voice was tight. 'Just you.'

'Maybe,' I said doubtfully. 'If he lets me.'

'It's your life, Mum.'

But it wasn't. I just wish I'd been able to keep Roger's cheating from the children.

Amy had surprised us all when she'd announced she was getting married. 'You're so young,' I couldn't help saying when she rang to tell us. 'And you haven't even graduated yet.'

'Don't worry, Mum. We'll manage.'

When she brought her fiancé back to meet us, Roger and I were pleasantly relieved. I could tell that Charles was a good man – not the kind to mess around. Or so he seemed.

The following month, Amy coyly announced that she had a 'surprise'.

My heart sank. I knew it. 'Are you . . .' I started to say.

'Yes, Mum.' Her face glowed. 'I am! We've already had a scan but we decided not to ask about the sex. We don't want to know.'

'That's . . . amazing.'

'Mum? Are you all right?'

I ran into the downstairs cloakroom just in time. Everything I'd just eaten for lunch came pouring out. It was nerves. Shock. What if history repeated itself? Sheila's screams flashed into my head. Supposing something went horribly wrong? My daughter wasn't ready for a child. How would she keep it safe?

'Sorry,' I said when I got back. 'It must have been something I ate.'

'Or perhaps you've got sympathetic morning sickness,' chipped in Roger, looking pleased at his own joke. 'Now let's get on with planning the wedding, shall we?'

For a man who had been so careless with his own wedding vows, Roger was determined that his grandchild wasn't going to be born out of wedlock. As he walked our daughter down the aisle, with that all-too-visible bump, his face beamed with pride. For my part, I was a bag of nerves.

During Amy's pregnancy, I continued to be terrified about my grandchild's imminent birth, imagining all kinds of horrendous scenarios. I also hoped with all my heart that it would be a girl.

Then we got the call from our son-in-law, to say Amy had gone into labour. Together, Roger and I paced the floors of a London hospital. 'It will be all right,' he said, squeezing my arm. Ironically, I felt closer to him than ever before.

At last a midwife came out, beaming. 'You can come through now!'

I ran. Nothing could stop me. In my daughter's arms was a small, pink, wrinkled scrap.

'You have a grandson, Mum!'

A flash of Michael's blond curls came into my head. I began to cry.

'Sorry,' I gulp. 'I'm just so emotional. He's really tiny.'

'He's nearly nine pounds, Mum!'

Roger seemed stunned. 'Am I really a grandfather? I feel too young.'

Trust my husband to bring the attention back to himself, I thought.

'Do you want to hold him, Mum?'

What if I dropped him? My old fears came flooding back. But all eyes were on me. I couldn't say no. It would look too odd.

Gingerly I cradled this little bundle in my arms. My grandson's eyes stared up at me trustingly. *If only you knew*, I thought, looking down at him. *You wouldn't love me then. No one would.*

Then my daughter began to cry. 'I'm scared, Mum. I don't know what to do with a baby. Supposing I get it wrong?'

My son-in-law looked nervous too.

They needed me, I realized. I had to be strong for my daughter and her family. Somehow, I had to try to put the past behind me for their sake. 'Don't worry,' I said, more confidently than I felt. 'We're here for you. Aren't we, Roger?'

I glanced up at him. He nodded. 'Yes.'

Josh's birth changed everything. He brought Roger and me together in a way we had never been when our own children were little. Amy and Charles had set up home in London and we spent nearly every weekend driving there and back so we could be with him. When Amy got a job as a PR executive, we would often go up to look after him for days at a time.

I had resolved that I would stay strong for my daughter, and I was as good as my word. I refused to allow myself to panic even when Josh, who had recently started to toddle, banged his head on the corner of the table. 'Are you sure he's all right?' asked Roger.

'He's fine, aren't you, Josh?' I said. Within seconds he'd stopped crying.

'You seem far more relaxed with him than you were with my children,' commented my husband. He often used the word 'my' as if to reinforce possession.

'But it's not the same this time,' I replied, 'because you can give them back at the end of the day when you're a grandparent.' I didn't explain I was determined not to pass on my fears.

'You look different,' commented one of my friends on the homeless charity soup-kitchen team. 'There's a real glow about you.'

When I looked in the mirror I could see she was right. Nothing had prepared me for that intense, fierce love in my chest for Josh. His birth even made me even more sensitive to the injustices of the world. I found myself crying over a documentary about families in Britain who could barely afford to feed their kids. I didn't like the idea of my grandson growing up in a world where you could have immense wealth and also people sleeping rough on the street. So I offered my help at the food bank, upped my hours in the soup kitchen and always bought a sandwich and coffee for the lady with the shaved head selling the *Big Issue* outside Boots. 'There but for the grace of God go any of us,' I told myself.

Josh was speaking now, although he couldn't get his tongue round 'Granny' so I became 'Ganny'. Every time we arrived at their place, he would fly into my arms, hugging me and plastering me with kisses.

I would die for him, I knew. I would do anything in the world to keep him safe. I just wished I could see him more often.

Not long after Josh's first birthday, my daughter called. 'How would you feel if we moved down to Oxfordshire, near you?' sang Amy's excited voice.

By then we had moved from our original village cottage. Roger had cleverly invested some of my trust fund in shares and they had done well enough for us to buy a pretty cream-and-yellow Queen Anne house on the outskirts of a bustling market town not far from Oxford.

'Charles has been offered a transfer. The money is brilliant and because of the difference in house prices, I can afford to work part-time – as long as you don't mind helping out.'

'I'd love to!' I exclaimed.

My happiness was complete. Roger and I were better than ever before, and I had my precious grandson. I allowed myself to think that I had finally emerged from the darkness. This was my new start.

Then, one day, I had a visitor. I had just come back from a 'raising money for duvets' committee meeting, I found a taxi waiting outside. Roger met me at the doorway. His face was set. My first thought was Josh. 'What's happened?'

'There's someone to see you,' he said. 'She's in the sitting room.'

'Who?' I asked, trembling. Please don't let it be another of Roger's liaisons. Hadn't he promised to put that behind him?

My husband looked at me steadily. 'She says she's your stepmother.'

At that moment, I knew it was over. I'd been waiting all my life for this.

My mouth went dry. 'I can explain . . .'

'Later,' he said. 'I think you'd better go in and see her first.'

I barely recognized the woman perched stiffly on the edge of my sofa. Gone was the heavy eye make-up. Her face was creased now like a tortoise's skin. She was grasping a walking stick. But her eyes were as accusing as they had been on the last terrible occasion I'd seen her. 'I've come to tell you in person about your father,' she said.

I sat down heavily.

'As I've already told your husband, he died last week.'

I couldn't take it in. My daddy, who had comforted me when my mother had died. I had ruined his life and now I'd never be able to make it up to him. Yet my throat was closing up with grief, regret and anger – not just towards him but towards myself as well. 'How?' I asked.

'They said it was pneumonia.' She staggered to her feet and advanced towards me, beating her stick on the ground. 'But I know it was a broken heart. You caused his death, Ellie. Just as you killed my son.'

54

Jo

We go along a big noisy road past these old stone walls and gaping arches without windows that are just standing in the middle of the traffic on a roundabout. 'Used to be a church that got bombed during the war,' the market guy says, noticing me looking at it.

'Why haven't they built it again?' I ask, shouting over the traffic.

'Maybe it's to make us remember the past.'

I shiver. Better forgotten, in my book.

It's getting dark and cold. My tooth is throbbing so much that I can't think straight. My feet drag.

'Not long now,' he says as we turn down a side street. 'My name's Nick, by the way, and this is Madge. What's yours?'

'Jo.' No one asks for your surname on the street.

'Where've you been travelling, then, Jo?'

'All over.'

I speak shortly because my mouth hurts. But I'm also nervous. Never give too much away. Someone gave me that bit of advice years ago. I've already broken it more times than I should.

We go left and then right. Finally, we get to a small terraced house with a boarded-up window in front. There's a dustbin on the path with the lid off. A cat is sniffing round an empty tin on the cracked paving stones. Nick takes a key out of his pocket with a long string attached to it. It takes a bit of time to open the door but then it eases.

'Come on in.'

I breathe in the smell of fags and weed. Booze too. There's heavy metal playing. 'Turn that bloody rubbish down!' yells a bloke sitting cross-legged in front of me. Then he closes his eyes like he's sleeping upright.

'That one's into meditation,' says Nick.

A stack of bikes is leaning against a wall. No carpet. Just floorboards. There's some flowery, faded blue-and-pink wallpaper that's peeling off like it's damp. Trainers are all over the floor along with hoodies and empty crisp packets and beer tins.

Madge notices me looking. 'There are quite a few of us here,' she says. 'But we all fit in.' Her eyes narrow. 'Why are you holding your jaw like that?'

'Toothache,' I groan.

'You've come to the right place, then.' Nick slings his arm around his girlfriend. 'My Madge used to be a dental nurse.'

'Want me to take a look?' Her voice is kind. Gentle. Not jealous, like it was before. Maybe now she's had a chance to look at me properly, she can see I'm no competition.

I nod.

'Come into the kitchen.'

It's so tiny that I can barely get in. There are five or six people, sitting or leaning against the sink, smoking roll-ups. Empty takeaway cartons are everywhere and there's a stench of Chinese food. The sink is piled high with dirty mugs. The floor is sticky to walk on.

'Make a space for the lady, can you?'

Madge gets me to sit down at a kitchen table that wobbles when I touch it. Then she opens a drawer and takes out a tin box. 'Just got to put my tools in boiling water for a minute.'

'Can't resist a mouth, can you, love?' says a man with a stomach the size of a football.

'Piss off. The lady needs help. Open up.'

The pain has muddled my head so much that it takes me a second to realize she's talking to me.

'Bloody hell. I see. Looks like it needs to come out. Here, take these.'

She presses two pills into my hand.

'What are they?'

'Just swallow them. They'll dull the pain.'

'Give us some of them, can you?' asks someone else.

'Shut up and let me concentrate.'

After a bit, I begin to feel spaced out. Then I see Madge holding a pair of pliers. 'No,' I say, trying to push her away.

'It's OK, love. It'll all be over in a minute.'

The pain! It's like my mouth's being dragged out of my head. 'Stop!' I want to yell. But I can't talk because she's pulling away like there's no tomorrow.

'Shit, Madge,' says someone. 'She's bleeding like a stuck pig.'

'Spit into this,' says Madge. 'Better come and lie down for a bit.'

I don't remember much more.

2.10 p.m., 17 August 1984

We race through the garden, taking care to duck and dive under trees to avoid Michael, who would be hiding himself. At last we reach the copse. 'He won't be here,' I gasp, standing against a silver birch, ignoring the possibility of bark stains on my dress. 'We told him it was out of bounds. Remember?'

Peter laughs. 'That was pretty clever.' Then he moves towards me. 'At last,' he whispers.

I can hardly breathe as his mouth comes down on mine. His tongue probes as though it's looking for something. The girls had been right. It does feel yucky. Or maybe I'm doing it wrong.

But then he takes my head in his hands and softens his tongue a bit, and suddenly it all seems wonderfully natural. He gives a little groan, almost as if he's in pain.

'You're beautiful,' he says. We kiss some more, and I forget about everything.

Then his hands begin to touch the outline of my breasts. 'No,' I say, breaking off.

He frowns. 'Why not?'

I don't want to tell him that I'm scared. One of the girls at school has a sister who got pregnant from 'going too far'. Apparently that meant she'd allowed a boy to touch her in parts that weren't allowed until you were married.

The trouble was that I didn't know which parts.

'I don't want to take any risks,' I say, repeating a word the other girls had used a few times when discussing sex. I'm not even sure what this means. But Peter appears to understand.

'We won't,' he says softly. 'But nothing can happen if I touch you above the waist.'

'Are you sure?' I ask.

His voice is thick. 'Absolutely.'

His hand begins to stroke my chest over my top. My body starts doing strange things, pressing up against him. Then somehow we are on the earth, and I can feel Peter's hand on my bare thigh.

'I can't find you,' calls out Michael's voice faintly.

Peter's mouth is bending down to kiss me again. His hands are exploring further. I should say no.

But I am lost.

55

Ellie

Sheila looked up at Roger, who was standing, clearly shocked, a few feet away from me. 'I don't know how you can live with a killer.'

That's when I realized. My stepmother had banked on the fact that I hadn't confided in my husband. Her final act of revenge was to destroy the life I had built up for myself. And she'd succeeded.

'I didn't . . .' I started.

'Don't make excuses!' she thundered. 'You and I know the truth. And just in case you try to make up even more lies, I have told your husband everything.' Then she turned to Roger. 'Perhaps you would escort me outside now to my taxi.'

I sank, stunned, in my chair by the French windows overlooking the garden. When my husband came back, he took my stepmother's place on the sofa at the other end of the room as if he wanted to be as far away from me as possible.

'Why didn't you tell me about Michael?' he said coldly.

'Because you wouldn't have married me,' I cried out. 'Would you?'

His silence was enough.

'Please don't tell the children,' I begged. 'Amy would never let me look after Josh again.'

'Are you fit to do so?'

'Yes,' I wept.

'I always thought there was something odd about you.' He was speaking as if to himself. 'You were in a loony bin for four years.'

'Don't call it that.'

He ignored me. 'And you're still crazy now.'

'I'm not!'

'Yes, you are. Look how you're always accusing me of having affairs.'

'But you *have*!'

He makes a dismissive hand gesture. 'Just the odd dalliance. But it's nothing, Ellie, compared with what you've done. Is it?'

After that, we lost whatever small happiness I'd tricked myself into thinking we'd found. Roger was no longer penitent. In fact, he relished having the upper hand. Every time I asked if he was going to be home late, he threw me the kind of look that said, 'I have every right to be.'

Once, when Amy and Charles came round for lunch, they started talking about a terrible case in the news in which an exhausted young mother had fallen asleep while looking after her toddler. The child had then caught his neck in the cord of the sitting-room blinds and strangled himself. 'She deserves to be locked up for ever,' said my daughter. 'How can she live with herself?'

Roger stared straight at me. I held his gaze for as long as I could and then I looked away.

Then he started to accuse me of little things I had or hadn't done. 'Did you move my watch from the bedside table?' he asked one day.

I promised him I hadn't – Roger hated me touching his possessions. But it 'turned up' on my side of the bed a day later. 'I don't know how that happened,' I said.

He gave me a strange look. 'Are you sure?'

The accusations continued to the point where I didn't know if they were true or not. 'Out of sugar again?' Roger asked. We couldn't be. I'd bought a packet only the other day to make cakes with Josh. But he was right. There was barely a teaspoon left. Luke was back from Australia for a brief visit at the time. He looked as though he was going to defend me but then stopped. Maybe he thought I was going crazy too. Perhaps I was.

In the couple of years before my stepmother's visit, I had begun to feel more confident about looking after little Josh, but now I worried about him all the time. 'It's OK, Mum,' said my daughter when I panicked about him going up a high slide in the park. 'He can do it. You seem a bit edgy recently. Dad's being all right with you, isn't he?'

'Yes,' I said quickly. At least it seemed Roger had stuck to his promise not to tell the children about my history. But I was reasonably certain that he'd started to see someone again. His smell was different. By now I knew the signs.

I went to the doctor for something to help with the anxiety. My GP was new. I managed to get a prescription for tranquillizers, but when she handed the piece of paper over, she added the words, 'I gather you had these before.' She didn't need to mention Highbridge.

'Yes,' I said.

'Some traumas can last for years,' she said slowly. 'I know you had help at the time but would you like any more therapy now?'

'No, thank you.' What would be the point?

Then one of my friends from the tennis club took me to one side.

'I don't want to speak out of turn, Ellie, but there's something I think I should tell you.'

I knew the tone. It was Roger again.

The woman this time, according to my friend, had just joined the club. Her name was Carole. She was a former model. Beautiful. Confident. Twice-divorced. Wealthy. She and Roger had been seen checking into The Randolph at lunchtime last week.

Instantly I went through the old routine of riffling through his pockets. Nothing. Then I got up in the night to check his mobile, taking it with me into the kitchen, terrified in case he'd wake up and find me. Again, nothing.

Only then did I think of the laundry pile. Roger had taken to doing his own washing since retirement. 'It will give me something to do,' he had said. I'd thought he was being helpful. But there it was in the pile before me. Barely noticeable, but enough. A smudge of coral-orange lipstick on the collar. I always wore pale pink.

The scene that followed is imprinted on my memory. It runs frequently, as if stuck on a track it cannot break out of.

Those same words. *This is the real thing. We've put down a deposit on a place in Clapham. The thing is, I love her.*

I was back at Highbridge again. Hysterical. Uncontrollable. Violent. I grabbed the nearest thing to hand. A pair of kitchen scissors. I plunged them into my wrist.

'You were lucky not to have sliced your artery,' said the young doctor after we 'explained' I'd cut myself while taking the string off a joint of meat. 'You must take more care.'

I expected Roger to tell me that I was mad to have cut myself. But he was much cleverer than that. He pretended to be kind instead. Or was he being genuine? By then, I hardly knew myself.

'I'm sorry about Carole,' he said with a subdued air when we got home. He proceeded to help me out of the car. 'You're right. It is too late to break up our family. I'll end it with her just as long as you promise not to hurt yourself or anyone else again.' He sighed. 'And if you really want, I'll have marriage counselling too.'

I was so overwhelmed with relief that I believed him. More fool me.

56

Jo

When I wake, I'm in a room with loads of other people. The air stinks of sweat. I've got small scratchy lumps all over my wrists and ankles. I scratch till I bleed. Then I get up and stumble to the window. It's all misted up. When I wipe it with my sleeve, I see a big crack with little lines going out like a spider's web. Outside, it's still pitch-black.

Bloody hell, it's cold. I hug my arms round myself. Still, it's not as freezing as a park bench or that tent.

My mouth doesn't hurt any more, I realize. My tongue explores the soft, fleshy hole left behind. It tastes of dried blood. God, I need a pee. But where's the toilet? Ouch. I trip over an empty beer bottle. There are cigarette stubs on the frayed carpet. A cat shoots past me. 'Wants feeding,' says a voice.

It's Nick, the man from the market. He's only wearing a pair of shorts. I want to look away but, to my embarrassment, I can't. There's black hair sprouting out from his chest. He stretches up in front of me as though he's only just got out of bed. 'Happy Christmas!'

'What's so bloody happy about it?' I want to say. But then he might ask questions about family and stuff.

'Is your tooth any better now it's gone?' he asks. 'My Madge is good at taking them out. Reckon she enjoys it.'

Then he sees I'm holding myself. 'The bog's through there.'

Cold air is streaming through a broken window. There's no toilet roll. Just a pile of newspaper by the side.

Next to the toilet is a bath with more empties inside and a lump of yellow soap. The washbasin has a whacking big hole in it like someone's dropped something heavy and broken it. I run the tap before realizing and the water pours through onto the floor. There's a toothbrush with a curled, stained head. I haven't cleaned my teeth since the bakery. Not that I'm going to use this thing. I might be down and out but I've got my standards. This looks like everyone else might have used it.

I go into the kitchen. Nick has got the kettle on.

'Coffee?'

He hands me a mug. It's got a chip on one side with 'I ♥ Plymouth' on the other. I gulp down the coffee to get warm.

'Toast?'

He hands me a cold slice.

'No butter, I'm afraid. We're out until we can get our hands on more cash.' He pats my hand. 'Here's the thing, Jo. We've looked after you, right? My girlfriend sorted out your tooth and we've given you somewhere to kip for the night. Breakfast too. So we need you to do something in return for us, OK?'

I've been expecting this. It's how it usually works on the road. You do something for someone and then they have to do something back.

'I can help out in the market,' I offer.

He laughs and wipes his mouth with the back of his

hand. 'I'm talking about a different kind of work.' His eyes narrow. 'I don't normally trust someone I've just met but you're in a bit of trouble yourself, aren't you, Jo?'

My skin goes hot. 'What do you mean?'

He folds his arms, looking pleased with himself. 'You see, Jo, I used to be a cop till things stopped going my way. But I've still got that feeling that tells me when someone has something to hide. Course, I could just ring one of my old mates in the force to check up on you but . . .'

I begin to quiver.

'Thought you'd see it my way.' He leans forward, speaking quietly. 'I need you to pick up a package for me. Then bring it back straight away. Got it?'

My heart sinks. No way. I'm not stupid. Sounds like he's talking about drugs. But maybe, if I agree, I can get out of here and find somewhere safe to hide. Then I remember that it's Christmas Day. Nothing will be open.

'When do I go?'

'Now.'

He reaches into his pocket and brings out a bit of paper. 'Here's the address. I've done you a little map. Take a gander. It's not far from here. Twenty minutes there and back, max. I'd do it myself but let's just say that the bloke at this place doesn't want to see my face again.'

Fear prickles my skin. 'Is he violent?'

'Nah. Not if you do what you're told. Now get moving. And if you're not back straight away, I'll make that call. Wouldn't want that, would you?'

The clock on the church tower says 6.23 a.m. The streets are still empty. I pass an elderly man sleeping on a street

411

corner huddled up in an old blanket with his grey hair spouting out. Poor bloke. I tuck a fiver into his jacket pocket from my precious American and watch money, which I keep stuffed down my bra. Hope no one nicks it from him before he wakes.

I follow the directions on the paper. It's a newsagent. 'Closed' says the sign on the door, but there's a bell at the side. I press but no one comes. My fingers are bloody freezing so I press it again.

'Hang on, hang on,' comes a posh voice. 'I heard you the first time.'

A large man with a big belly and a white beard opens up. His face creases with suspicion. 'You're new. Who sent you?'

'Nick.'

He spits on the ground. 'Don't mention that man's name.' He thrusts a bag at me. 'Here it is, then.'

I peep inside. It's the *Daily Mail*, rolled up in a tube.

'It's all there,' growls the man. 'And don't ask what it is.'

'I wasn't born yesterday,' I snort.

He looks up and down the street as if someone might be watching. Then he turns back and gives me a hard glare. 'Don't I recognize you from somewhere?'

'They say we've all got a double,' I reply, shrugging casually, though my heart is pounding.

He gives me another glare. 'Clear off, then, before anyone sees you.'

I walk back quickly, checking over my shoulder every few minutes. As soon as I've handed this over, I'll go. How daft I'd been to think that the market man was going

412

to help me. Everyone wants something in this world. A memory of Steve flashes into my mind and I push it back.

Do I turn right here or left? I can't remember. Then I see the ruined arches in the middle of the roundabout. I know where I am now, and finally find the road Nick had taken me to last night. There's the house. My heart thuds with relief. The door's locked. I bang on it. Someone looks out of the window. 'It's her,' I hear a voice say.

The door swings open. Nick snatches the bag off me.

Madge is there too, her arms folded. 'You had no bloody right to do that.'

I thought she was talking to me at first but she was yelling at Nick.

'I had to. Who else could I have sent? You were out like a light.'

'But we don't fucking know her –'

'It's all right,' I say, interrupting. 'I won't talk. You can trust me.'

Madge is staring at me like she's trying to make up her mind. Then she stops suddenly and looks over my shoulder towards the road. 'What the fuck . . .' she starts.

At first, I think she's having a go at me. Then my blood freezes. Police sirens. The sound of running feet. 'You bloody bitch!' screams Madge.

I can't move with shock.

Madge is out the door, belting up the street. I watch as one of the policemen catches her. I stand, stuck to the spot, as the other pins my arms behind my back. 'This is her, Sarge,' he calls. 'Not the other one.'

In the car, I see the large man with the beard who gave me the newspaper just now.

I see a flash of blond hair. The cord in my hands.

'Elinor Halls,' come the words. 'I am arresting you for the murder of your husband, Roger Halls.'

PART THREE
The Trial

Meadowsweet (*Filipendula ulmaria*)
Also known as Bridewort because it was laid on the ground for the bride to walk on. Associated with death, as the scent of its flowers was said to induce a sleep that was deep and fatal.

57

I'm standing in Plymouth Crown Court in front of the judge. The place is almost empty. According to my lawyer, this is my bail hearing. A door opens. A woman comes in. She is slim and pretty with sad eyes. Something stirs inside as though I ought to know her name. But I don't.

'How could you have done it, Mum?' she calls out.

Mum? What does she mean?

I hear the court clerk's voice. 'To the charge of murder, do you plead guilty or not guilty?'

I am 'refused bail' and sent to a remand centre until my trial. This could take months, I'm told, as there are loads of others like me, waiting to see whether they'll be freed.

My cell has a narrow bed down one side with a shelf to put my stuff on. There's a bed on the other side for my cellmate – a thin, suspicious-looking girl – and a toilet in the corner, which we have to share.

I'm given a job in the kitchen, washing potatoes. I'm not allowed near the knives.

Most people here do nothing but moan. 'This place is shit,' they're always saying. But we've got a roof over our heads, haven't we? There's running hot water. Regular meals. A bed. A telly in the communal lounge. It's no hotel, but it's OK.

Hotel. I have a dim memory of a room. A boy. But then it goes.

My mind is confused. I feel tired. It's like a heavy fog is sitting on my shoulders all the time. The psychologist I've been seeing said she was going to come back, but she hasn't.

Instead, I am told I've got a visitor. Who would want to see me? When they give me the name, it sounds vaguely familiar but I don't know why.

My heart starts to pound as I wait with the others. We have to line up and then we're led into the visitors' hall. I look at all the tables where relatives and friends are sitting. And then I see him.

Michael. The name pops into my head. But he's all grown up. I run up to him and try to put my arms around his shoulders but he's too tall.

'No touching,' says an officer firmly.

'Michael,' I say out loud. I don't know how I know him but I do know that I love him.

The grown-up boy's smile looks sad now. 'I'm not Michael, Mum. I'm Luke. Your son. Don't you remember?'

I hesitate. I don't recall the name. But there's something else.

'Australia,' I blurt out.

'That's right. I've been in Australia but now I'm back to help you.' His voice breaks. 'You're so thin and frail.'

He makes to take my hands but the officer stops him. 'Amy's still upset,' says this Luke. 'But she'll come round in the end.'

Amy. Amy . . . That sounds familiar too.

His voice goes quiet. 'Do you remember Josh?'

I rack my brains, but can't be sure.

'He used to call you Ganny.'

I have a sudden sharp memory of another blond child flying through the front door towards me, arms outspread. I start to cry but I don't know why.

The tall blond man places something in my hands. I stare down wonderingly. It's a carved wooden box. There is an edelweiss on the top. Instinctively I know there is a key underneath. I turn it and then lift the lid. A song fills the air. It sings of my mother dancing with me round a room when I was a child. It sings of a small blond boy called Michael whose very name cuts into my heart like a knife. And it sings of another blond child. One who died because of me.

'It's all right, Mum. Please don't get upset. It wasn't your fault.'

'But it was,' I wept. It's beginning to come back to me now like random jigsaw pieces. Some of them fit together but others don't. 'Josh isn't here any more.'

'Yes,' says the man who says he is my son, putting his arms around me, rocking me back and forth like a baby. 'He is.'

I stare at him. 'What do you mean?'

He speaks softly. 'What exactly do you remember?'

'The red T-shirt,' I gasp. 'Floating on the water.'

He is stroking my hands now. The officer isn't looking. Round and round, as if to comfort me. 'Yes, but Josh wasn't inside it. He was safe at the side of the pond.'

Tears gush down my face. How? Why? I have so many questions that they can't get out of my mouth. 'Thank God,' I gasp. 'My baby. My precious baby . . .'

Then the stroking stops. He lets me go and looks at me with fear in his eyes. 'But do you remember what happened to Dad?'

The officer announces I have another visitor. Apparently I signed something to give permission. But I don't remember. Nothing seems real at the moment and my head feels woozy. I am still coming to terms with what Luke has told me. Part of me is so relieved that I am almost floating. The rest is shocked beyond belief. I am led into the visits room. It reminds me of a school gym, with bars on the windows instead of walls. Officers patrol, eyes vigilant as they stride past chairs and tables. One side is for us. The other for them. Sitting, waiting, is the woman from the bail hearing. Can this really be the daughter they've told me about?

Amy's beautiful dark hair curls softly on her shoulders. She's wearing a cream jacket. The sight triggers a memory of a shopping trip. Hadn't we bought it together? Before Carole had come into our lives and ruined everything?

'How could you, Mum?' she starts.

'I'm sorry,' I choke. 'Forgive me.'

My daughter bursts into tears. Her grief is like a knife in my chest. I move forward to hug her but she pushes me away. Every mother wants to comfort her child, no matter how old. But I have lost the right to do so.

I glance around. This isn't a private place. We're not the only ones who are having an emotional meeting.

'I miss Dad so much,' weeps my daughter.

'So do I –'

'Don't you dare say that!' Amy hammers on the table

between us with her fist. 'You killed him. Josh could have died too, from your neglect. And it was all your fault.'

Don't I know that already? Haven't I been telling myself that every second of every minute of every hour since Luke told me the truth. Ever since my old music box triggered all those buried memories.

'You've no idea what it's been like for us!' yells Amy. 'How could you just have taken off and left us for four and a half months?'

The tears have stopped now. In their place is naked anger on my daughter's face. 'We didn't know if you were alive or dead – and to be honest, there were times when I wished you had vanished for good. Don't you feel at all guilty?'

'Yes. Of course I do.' I put my head in my hands.

'We had to tell Josh that his grandfather was dead.'

A bolt of fear shoots through me. 'Did you say that . . .'

I can't bring myself to finish my sentence but she knows what I mean.

Amy looks at me with distaste in her eyes. 'No. I didn't reveal that his grandmother was a murderer.'

'Thank you,' I weep.

'Don't. I did it for him. Not you.'

She stands up. 'I made a mistake coming here. Just seeing your face makes me sick. You don't deserve to be a mother. I'm going.'

Frankly, I don't blame her. I wish I could leave me too. Just as they say I did before.

2.15 p.m., 17 August 1984

Michael's voice rings out not far from us. 'Ellie? Where are you? I give up.'

Peter draws away from me. 'Perhaps you had better go and find him.'

'No,' I say, frantically, pulling him towards me. 'He'll be all right.'

'Ellie!' I vaguely hear my brother's voice again. 'I'm scared now.'

But I can't stop.

I don't know how long we carry on for. When we eventually draw apart, my mouth is deliciously sore and bruised. My head is spinning with happiness.

'I love you, Ellie,' Peter says.

My heart leaps. I hadn't been expecting this! But it seems only polite to say the same thing back. 'I love you too,' I gasp.

He bends down and picks a forget-me-not that's growing in the copse. Then he gives it to me. I clutch it to my chest, remembering how it had been another of my mother's favourite wildflowers.

'I'll keep this for ever,' I murmur. 'Thank you.'

And then I remember. Michael.

'Coming to find you!' I call out.

Silence.

'He was looking for us earlier on,' I say, beginning to panic. 'He'd given up hiding because we were so long.'

'Maybe he's gone back to it,' Peter says. 'How about the woodshed? I suggested that as a good spot early on.'

But he isn't there.

He's not in the vegetable garden either. Or the rose garden. Or behind any of the trees.

A cold feeling clutches my chest. 'Michael!' I scream out. 'This isn't funny. Where are you?'

58

It's amazing what our brains can do, when pushed to the limit. My psychologist says she thinks I have 'Complex Post-Traumatic Stress Disorder with Dissociative Fugue and Anxiety'. Triggered, she thinks, by the sight of my grandson's red T-shirt in the pond. But the way I think about it is that my brain was so scared that it had to hide from itself.

All I can say is that I can't pinpoint any particular time when I stopped being Ellie and became Jo. Now I don't even remember my Jo days at all. But CCTV clearly shows me getting on a coach in Oxford and getting off at Bristol. Other cameras in different places show me walking through an area of the city known as Stokes Croft. I have a shaved head and wear scruffy clothes. I am well and truly in another woman's skin.

They say I failed to recognize my own children after my arrest. How awful is that?

It was seeing Luke that helped to bring it back. Luke, with his strong resemblance to Michael. Luke, who had given me back the music box with all its meanings over the years. Sound, they explain, is a strong memory trigger. I suppose my brain was finally ready to face what I'd done.

'Are you one of those schizos?' my cellmate keeps asking.

I try to tell her it's not as simple as that but she doesn't get it. Once the women in prison found out who I was, they began calling me the 'posh killer'. I don't want to think about the 'killer' bit. I still can't believe it. But the DNA evidence leaves no room for doubt, according to Barbara, the barrister Luke has hired to handle my case. Equally damning is the evidence from the security cameras Roger had had installed in the house after a spate of burglaries. At my insistence, ironically. The tape clearly shows me strangling my husband with a phone cable. I refused to believe it until they allowed me to watch. I sat, my hands over my mouth, shocked beyond words. Was that really me? How could I have done something so wicked?

But the camera doesn't lie. The date for the trial keeps moving. Apparently there's a backlog to get through. I am told to prepare for what might be a 'long wait'.

'The important thing, Ellie,' Barbara tells me, 'is that you tell the truth. The jury can usually tell when someone's genuine.' But what is the truth, if I can't remember it?

The structure of my days in prison provides a certain comfort through all this. In a way, it reminds me of Highbridge. We have 'Education' in the morning, but this is mainly aimed at 'residents' (as we're known) who haven't had much in the way of schooling for one reason or another. I find myself becoming more popular when one of the women in my wing discovers I have a degree. 'Can you help me with my English homework?' she asks during free time after tea.

Another woman requests advice on her Open University essay. I am happy to lend a hand. It makes me feel useful and it also means some of the women are nicer to me. Others give me a wide berth, scuttling past as if I might hurt them too. Some are openly aggressive. 'I don't talk to murderers,' spits one when she passes me in the corridor. Then there are my silent enemies. The other day, after our weekly gym session, I went to change and found faeces in my shoe. The officer in charge told me to 'clean it out and put it back on'.

At night, I toss and turn in my narrow bed, trying to get comfortable on my brick-hard pillow. I often hear women shouting and banging their doors, with officers warning them to 'pipe down'. Sometimes I hear sobbing through the walls. Once, an alarm went off when a woman cut her wrists with a knife she'd stolen from the kitchen. I'm not sure what happened to her. No one tells you much in prison. Outside it's summer. Then autumn.

I have been in prison, all told, for nine months now. Finally, the day of my hearing arrives. I am taken to the court in a van. The handcuffs rub against my wrists and weigh them down along with my fluttering heart. Two guards take me through the back entrance and into a court cell, where Barbara is waiting.

'Just remember everything we've talked about,' she tells me. She seems different. It's not just her gown and wig. It's that nervous edge to her voice.

To be honest, I'm not sure if I care one way or another. Winning the trial won't bring my family back. The stark reality is that I am no longer Jo. I am Ellie Halls, the woman who murdered her husband.

The guards take me up a steep flight of steps into the

court. I emerge into the middle like a matador in a bull ring except that I am the bull. I am in the dock. Only then do I allow myself to look around.

The court is packed. I can't see my children. Then I remember what Barbara told me. Witnesses aren't allowed to hear what goes on in court until they are called. But I can spot familiar faces in the public gallery above. There are friends from the tennis club, the book club and the homeless committee I once belonged to in Oxfordshire.

My fingers bite into my palm as I search for Carole with her long, glossy brunette hair and designer shades. I'd like to pin all the blame on her but, in truth, she was merely the final straw. Either way, she's not here. I fancy I see Jo for a minute but perhaps that's just my imagination. She'll be long gone.

Now the judge has come in. The case is starting. The courtroom is rippling.

Barbara has explained that the prosecution will start by outlining its case against me.

I close my eyes, trying to shut out the details as accusing words ring through the court in an educated, pompous accent. 'Elinor Halls – also known as Ellie – killed her husband in cold blood, as shown by her DNA on the cable wiring and tape from security cameras in her own home. Her family was devastated. Instead of staying to face justice, she went on the run for over four months, disguising herself as a homeless woman, until she was finally apprehended by Devon and Cornwall police . . .'

I close my eyes and try to blank out the rest. I'm vaguely aware of witnesses being called to testify against me and then Barbara cross-examining them. There is a policeman who declares that, despite a nationwide hunt for a homeless woman known as Jo, whom I'd claimed would corroborate my evidence, no one has been found. He says it in a way as if I have made it up. As though Jo doesn't exist.

Then a voice announces something that chills me to the bone: 'Call Carole Kent.'

I stiffen. So that's why my husband's mistress wasn't in the public gallery. I want to be sick as she strides boldly to the witness box. Her long, slim legs in that beautifully cut lemon suit are not lost on the court. All eyes are on her.

After a few preliminary questions, the prosecution barrister gets down to it. 'Did you have an affair with Roger Halls?'

You can almost feel the tension emanating from the jury and the gallery. My husband's lover is looking right at me. My heart thuds so hard in my chest that I feel I am going to pass out.

'I wouldn't call it just an affair,' Carole's irritating little-girl voice sings out. 'We were in love.'

I wince.

'What did Mr Halls tell you about his wife?'

She gives a cold laugh. 'Where do you want me to start? He said she was a liar and that she could twist words to make it look as if she was always in the right.'

'It's you who's lying!' I want to yell out. 'It's what *he* had done – not me.'

'He also said that she was mentally unstable.'

'In what way?'

Carole's eyes now fill with tears. 'He told me that when she was younger, a child had died in her care.'

The court gasped.

'It gave her a nervous breakdown. Roger said that her behaviour could be totally unpredictable.' She's weeping loudly now. 'And he was right. She killed him, didn't she? If you ask me, that woman should be locked up for good. Otherwise she will kill someone else.'

The judge instructs Carole to be silent. Only facts are allowed. Not suppositions or emotional outbursts. Barbara told me this beforehand. But I can see from the jury's faces that the damage has already been done. There are more witnesses but Carole's evidence is surely enough to send me down.

At last it is time for Barbara to put my story forward. My barrister's voice carries an air of quiet authority. Very different from the angry indignation of the prosecution. 'Roger Halls is dead,' she says. 'No one can argue with that. But I intend to show that my client suffered from diminished responsibility at the time. I will now call the defendant, Ellie Halls, to give evidence.'

Blood thunders in my head as I am led to the witness stand. For a few moments I can't hear or see what is around me. My palms sweat. My mouth is dry. I don't know if I can do this.

Barbara and I have got to know each other pretty well during her visits to the remand centre. But how can any-one else understand me when I barely understand myself?

'Ellie,' she says in that soft voice of hers which can, as I know all too well, get tough when she chooses, 'I'd like you to take the court back to the day of your husband's death on 17 August 2019. Can you describe what hap-pened in the events leading up to it?'

'I was looking after my four-year-old grandson, Josh.'

My voice begins to shake again. 'We were playing in the garden. It looked like my husband was talking to someone on the phone in his study. He seemed upset. I . . . I thought it might be Carole, because I'd bumped into her that morning in town and she'd claimed they were still seeing each other. She even knew about a playhouse which my husband had bought our grandson. Roger and I had an argument. Then I realized that I'd taken my eye off Josh.'

My knees begin to judder. 'I ran round the garden look-ing for him. That's when I saw that part of the fence between us and our neighbour had been broken. I squeezed through the gap and saw . . .'

I clutch the rail in front of me.

'. . . I saw a pond. They'd just put it in. My grandson's red T-shirt was floating on the water.' I feel my voice rising in hysteria. 'I thought he'd died . . . It took me back to . . .'

'To what, Mrs Halls?'

My voice cries out. 'Please, I can't.'

'Very well. I respect the fact that you are still in a fragile state. We will return to this later. Can you tell the court what you did next?'

I've been through this already with both Barbara and the therapist in prison. But now I baulk, aware that all eyes are on me. I don't want to speak. If I do, it will become real.

'Mrs Halls. Please answer the question. The court needs to know the truth.' Barbara is sounding tough on purpose. She warned me of this in advance. She has to pre-empt the scepticism of the prosecution.

I try to compose myself. 'I . . . I raced to the house to

tell Roger. Then I saw he was still on the phone. He was walking up and down, arguing with someone. Pleading.'

I can barely breathe.

'My gut instinct told me he was still talking to Carole, though I couldn't hear the actual words. He hadn't even come out to look for Josh. He . . .'

I take a deep breath. Barbara gives me a gentle nod as though to give me strength.

'I pulled open the doors and screamed at him – that he'd killed our grandson by making me take my eyes off him.'

I stop. My throat is sore. I can't breathe.

'And then what happened?'

'He pushed me away as if the person he was speaking to was far more important. I fell against a table and broke a tooth. It caused me problems later on and had to be taken out.'

I stop for a minute, running my tongue round the gap, which is still there.

'I can only remember some bits after that. I remember his – Roger's – face all red and angry-looking.'

I don't tell them that the face I really saw was my father's after the accident.

'I don't remember running away. Or talking to Jo, like the witnesses said I did, or her giving me her clothes.'

'How did you pay for your bus ticket?'

'I don't know. I don't remember any of it.' My voice rises into the air with anguish. 'I wish I did.'

Then I crumple onto the ground. Am I going mad? It wouldn't be the first time . . .

*

A recess is called so I can 'compose' myself. I sip some water. Barbara tells me I am 'doing well'. Then it is time for me to be cross-examined. The barrister on the other side clearly doesn't believe a word of what I've been saying. 'Forgive me, but this complex medical diagnosis does seem rather convenient.'

She declares this in a way that makes it sound like she is pointing out an obvious fact. 'Wouldn't we all like to be someone else if we have done something we shouldn't have?'

Someone in the jury snorts, as if in amusement.

'Especially,' she continues, 'if that "mistake" is a crime.' She pauses. Her face grim. 'The crime of murder.'

Another jury member, a man with long sideburns, nods.

'What evidence do you have to prove that you genuinely believed you were Jo, a homeless *Big Issue* seller, instead of trying to convince us that you suffer from various psychological conditions?'

Why is she asking me this when I've already explained? 'As I said earlier, I don't even remember being Jo.' My hands twist themselves in nervousness. 'But it's true. You have my word.'

'Your word,' repeats the prosecutor. She faces the jury. 'Mrs Halls – who has already admitted to killing her husband – wants us to take her word.'

There's a nervous titter.

'You also want us to take your word that you didn't know Josh was still alive.'

'Of course I didn't!' I cry out. 'I genuinely thought he had drowned.'

The barrister glances at her notes. 'Is it right that you

were on the streets from August until the end of December last year?'

'I don't remember.'

'I see. You were arrested in Plymouth. How well do you know the city?'

'I don't. Not really. I mean, I do recall going on a family holiday to the south-west as a child, before my mother died.'

My eyes close briefly. CCTV cameras had apparently shown me arriving there on a coach. Was it possible that, deep down, I had held some kind of positive association with the place?

'Despite what you've just said, the jury might find it hard to understand how you "became" Jo. Why her, in particular? Why not, say, a celebrity such as the Duchess of Sussex or Marilyn Monroe?'

There's that titter from the jury again. Yet, she has a point.

Where do I begin? It's complicated. But my psychologist has helped me to understand this and I have to try. 'I'm not sure. Maybe it's because I don't know any celebrities. But I did get to know Jo before . . . before Roger died. From the minute I met her, part of me actually envied her. I liked the fact that she was free to go where she wanted. I wrongly thought at the time that she wasn't burdened by responsibilities. Now I can see my attitude was embarrassingly patronizing. How can anyone understand another's life unless they live it?'

But I deliberately don't say that I thought she'd have no time for anxieties such as treading on pavement cracks and that I had admired the way she swore like a trooper.

There are some things, I decide, which are better left unspoken in court.

The jury are listening, as if rapt. It feels as if I am having a private conversation with them. 'I knew a lot about her life. She told me she had been in and out of prison and what it was like. She told me about her life in children's homes, where she hadn't been able to settle and frequently ran away from school. Her children were taken into care and she lost touch with them. I had nightmares when she told me about a friend of hers on the road who'd had her throat cut by a tramp high on meths. I was struck by her fear that you were never safe on the road. I suppose it was all there in my head.'

'And how do you explain your suspicious behaviour? You changed your appearance to look like her.'

'I don't remember shaving my head — maybe it was because I caught lice and it was itching.'

Barbara sits down. There's a short silence before the prosecution breaks it. 'Very nicely told, Mrs Halls. Tell me, is it also true that you once tried to find accommodation for Jo in town?'

Barbara is looking worried. The prosecution might, she'd told me, appear to be nice. Then they'd use what you say to stab you in your most vulnerable place. But I can only tell the truth.

My voice is cracked and dry. 'In my role on the homeless committee, we were having discussions with the council. In the meantime, I wanted to put her up in our summer-house, but my husband wouldn't let me. He said it was "dangerous", and that, for all I knew, she might murder us in our beds.'

There's a hush. The irony of this isn't lost on anyone.

'Were you aware that the police had questioned her about a recent spate of burglaries?'

'No.'

I begin to feel nervous. 'If I had, I wouldn't have asked her into our house.'

'You actually invited her into your home, didn't you?'

The prosecution's voice takes a sharper edge.

'Well, yes. It was pouring with rain and she was drenched to the skin. So I gave her some dry clothes.'

'And what did your husband have to say about that?'

'He was out.'

'Did you tell him later?'

'No.'

'Would you say you were naive? Impressionable, perhaps?'

'No. I was just trying to be a decent person.'

'Would you say you were a liar?'

'NO.'

'Did her plight strike a chord with you?'

'Yes. But that wasn't why –'

'Is that because you lost your own home as a young girl when you were sectioned and sent to an asylum?'

I wondered how long it would take for this to come up.

'"Asylum" is an old-fashioned word,' I retort. 'It was a private institution.'

'As you will. You were treated for a breakdown there, I believe.'

'Yes.'

'I see. Later, you became involved with prison work too. Can you tell us more about that?'

Why does she want to know? 'A friend from my book group asked if I'd be interested. She encouraged me to apply to be on the local Independent Monitoring Board – a voluntary team who go into prisons to check that everything is being run as it should be.'

Once more, I hadn't realized that I was going to be in the same situation myself before long.

'Some of us – including me – also helped with reading for prisoners who weren't so literate. I gave it up when Josh was born to have more time with him.'

'Why did you volunteer to work in a prison in the first place?'

'I thought I had a duty to give something back to the community – and because I was lucky enough to have a home and children myself.'

'Isn't it true that all these experiences helped you to deliberately concoct an elaborate false identity over many years? Those people in there were your research.'

So this is where she's leading to.

'No.' How can I make her understand? 'They might have seeped into my psyche but I wasn't aware of it.'

'Psyche.' The barrister repeats the word as if she doesn't believe in it. 'I see. Tell me, Ellie, how important is family to you?'

The lump in my throat is almost too big for me to speak. 'Very,' I manage.

I have a flash of my mother. Her soft skin smelling of roses. I can still see her gathering wildflowers with me, telling me the story of the forget-me-not.

2.20 p.m., 17 August 1984

'Michael!' I call again, this time louder.

Peter is behind me. 'Don't worry,' he says. 'He's probably gone back into the house.'

Of course. I begin to run. 'Wait,' says Peter, catching up. 'We need to work out what to say to them.'

It doesn't matter. I just need to find my brother.

I run faster. 'Michael!' I yell as we race down the lawn and across the patio, where there is a crowd of adults having drinks and giving us disapproving looks as though we're misbehaving.

It takes me a while to find my father and stepmother. Eventually, I see them in one of the large sitting rooms. Sheila is chatting animatedly to another woman about how she is going to join the local golf club because 'the social life is meant to be rather good'. My father is standing next to her, clutching a wine glass, staring into the distance.

'Have you got Michael?' I gasp, running up to them.

'Ellie, I've told you before. Don't interrupt . . .'

Then her face changes as she registers my words. 'What do you mean? I thought you were with him.'

I hear Peter's voice behind me. 'We were playing hide-and-seek with him but he just ran off.'

As he speaks, I catch Sheila looking me up and down. I'm

440

all too aware that my dress is crumpled and there is green lichen down one side from where Peter had pressed me against the tree to kiss me.

My stepmother clutches my arm, her long red nails biting into my bare skin. 'Show me where you last saw him.' Her voice rises shrilly. 'Where? Ellie! WHERE?'

59

It's the fourth day of my trial. I drift in and out but every now and then I am struck by certain figures, like this pretty woman in a floral dress. Then I realize it's Hilary, my prison psychologist.

'PTSD has three main characteristics,' she says. She speaks in a calm, clear voice of authority and I sense that the jury is listening keenly. 'They are avoidance, intrusive thoughts and hypervigilance. One of the symptoms of avoidance is dissociation. This is definitely not done out of choice, so one cannot argue that it is a convenient "excuse" for murder. Dissociation can happen when a person is triggered by a disturbing or distressing experience which relates to a past trauma.

'It's important to understand that there is a spectrum of dissociation or dissociative states. They start with the most common, like when we day-dream through a talk or fail to remember how we got to a destination – even if we were driving.'

Many of the jury members' heads nod in agreement at this.

'The spectrum,' she continues, 'goes onto more serious dissociation, where the person appears to be distant for a short while or even longer. There is also a fugue state, which is what I believe Ellie to have been in. This can include confusion or loss of memory about identity, and possibly the assumption of a new identity to compensate.

The sufferer then leaves his or her familiar area, appearing to be travelling purposefully.

'In my opinion, the sight of Ellie's grandson's T-shirt floating on the pond triggered the same intense feelings she experienced when her brother, Michael, died.'

There's a snort from the jury member with long sideburns that suggests he doesn't believe a word of it.

'Moreover, Josh – Ellie's grandson – was the same age as her brother, Michael. It can be classic behaviour for someone who has suffered a childhood trauma at a certain age to behave erratically and be overemotional when their own child – or, indeed, grandchild in this case – reaches the same age.'

One of the other jurors rolls her eyes as if she doesn't buy any of it. This isn't going well. If I was one of them, I might feel the same. But, undaunted, Hilary continues. 'It's also been shown through documented case histories, such as soldiers returning from Afghanistan, that certain smells, colours, noises and other sensory reminders can take someone with PTSD straight back to the horror of the event which caused it in the first place.'

The man with sideburns is sitting forward now, listening more intently. 'In Ellie's case, it is likely this was water as well as blond hair and the colour red. But there was something else too: the loss of her mother all those years ago and a wretched life with her stepmother. On the morning of 17th August last year, she had just bumped into her husband's mistress, Carole Kent. This brought back her old fear that this woman might break up her family just as her own had been broken, all those years ago.'

The psychologist is looking directly at the jury. 'Anyone who has experienced divorce or death will surely understand this.'

There's a slight ripple, with some uncomfortable-looking faces.

Barbara glances at her notes. 'Can you tell us more about how PTSD is linked to identity confusion?'

'I can. It's unlikely that Ellie would have been diagnosed with PTSD in 1984. Indeed, the condition was only added to the *Diagnostic and Statistical Manual* in 1980, and was still relatively unknown ground for some practitioners. Instead, she was considered to have depression, which was one reason why she had ECT – electroconvulsive therapy. If we were to diagnose her now, it is likely that it would be PTSD and a complicated grief reaction. Typical signs include avoidance and taking on a new identity. This could be a younger self or a made-up person or maybe a celebrity. I have one client who is convinced she is Michelle Obama.'

A ripple runs through the court.

'Occasionally,' she continues, 'it is a person who is known to the patient. I believe this is why Ellie thought she was Jo. However, I must stress that these labels can be misleading since individuals behave in different ways. For instance, some critics might think Ellie has a dissociative identity disorder. In fact, this is usually when the patient adopts two or more personae. The main point I wish to get across is that, whatever you call her condition, Ellie genuinely believed she was Jo even though she now no longer has any recollection of this.'

'But why, as the prosecution asked earlier, would Ellie

become this particular woman?' asks Barbara. 'Why not, say, someone in more fortunate circumstances?'

Hilary's tone is firm. 'First, it is not a matter of deliberate choice. Ellie's own explanation seems perfectly plausible to me. Jo represented freedom. She lived a life on the road, close to nature, not answering to anyone – as flawed as that perception might be. Or perhaps it was simply because Jo was just so different to Ellie. A way for her to completely leave her trauma behind.'

As she speaks, it's as though Hilary is describing another person. Did I really do this? Yet it's true that I had felt a strange affinity for the homeless woman I'd befriended. I'd sometimes thought that but for the grace of God, many of us could be in the same position.

'Is that so?' The prosecution barrister is cross-examining, now. She has her hand on her hip and is making her scepticism very clear.

'Is it possible that there is another diagnosis?'

'There is the potential it could be a personality disorder or adjustment disorder, but that wouldn't account for all of her symptoms. The only diagnosis I can find, bearing in mind Mrs Halls's symptoms, is complex PTSD with dissociation.'

'Is there anything else you can tell us about Ellie's *condition*?'

'Plenty.' Hilary's lips tighten. I sense she has been challenged on this before. 'It is common to blame yourself for the original trauma, just as Ellie was blamed for Michael's death. Her parents had left much of the responsibility of parenting to Ellie. This guilt later left her susceptible to finding a controlling partner who continued that punishment.

PTSD can also leave the person in a hypervigilant state. In Ellie's case, this was the constant fear that something awful might happen to those around her. Such as her grandson.'

Another psychologist is called to the witness box. It's one of the staff who treated me alongside Cornelius. I don't like what I hear. So I block it out.

I only tune in again when I hear the phrases 'memory loss' and 'shutting out the truth'. 'Ellie did exactly this in Highbridge,' the same psychologist is saying. 'It was her way of coping. Then she repeated the same pattern after Roger's death – further proof that it was all in her psyche rather than a deliberate attempt to deceive.'

Other people speak. Again, I lose track.

But then I see Amy giving evidence. My daughter. I hold out my hands towards her – even though she's too far away for me to reach – but she stares at me coldly. My heart chills with fear.

'Dad wasn't perfect, but I loved him.'

Her eyes flash. It reminds me of the time when she was a teenager and overheard Roger and me rowing about a student of his. Soon after that, I'd had to tell her off about some homework she hadn't done. 'Stop nagging,' she'd spat. 'No wonder Dad doesn't want you any more.' That really hurt, even though I knew she was taking her anger against him out on me instead. Now she was doing the same.

'We had to tell our son that his granddad was dead.'

Even though I already knew this, I feel sick to the core. My daughter's voice is angry now as it rings round the courtroom. 'He kept asking for his grandmother so we had to tell him she'd gone on holiday. Each day he still wakes up and asks if Ganny is back.'

A cry escapes my lips.

All that pain I've tried so hard to bury has risen again. I want to know how Josh is doing at his new school. Who is taking him there now I'm no longer around? Who are his best friends? Does he still love cricket? I ache for his warm little arms around me. His soft hair against my cheek.

I'd wanted Amy to bring my precious grandson to visit me in prison. There were plenty of 'family facilities', including a special room for children to play with relatives. But when I suggested it, she'd accused me of being 'mad' and said that it would 'disturb him even more when he had to leave'. She was right, of course. On both counts.

'I hated Mum at first when the police thought she'd killed Dad,' continues my daughter. 'And I was furious with her for taking her eye off Josh. He could have drowned. We nearly went out of our minds when she was missing. But I've been doing a lot of thinking since she was arrested. My brother, Luke, and I have found out stuff about her that we didn't know.'

For a minute she pauses. My breath catches in my throat.

Amy continues.

'She'd never told us much about her childhood. It doesn't excuse her from killing Dad. But she was a good mother. And a wonderful grandmother. My son, Josh . . . he misses her. He talks about her all the time.'

'I miss him too,' I call out.

Again the judge intervenes. 'Please don't interrupt. I've already had to warn you. It doesn't help your case.'

My daughter's eyes meet mine. I think – I hope – I see a glimpse of forgiveness behind the coldness. But then she's gone.

My son is in the witness box now. Luke tells the court that his father was a 'manipulative bully'. 'Dad made out that Mum imagined his affairs,' he said. 'It was enough to make anyone flip. He also pretended that she'd done things when she hadn't. Once, when I was back home visiting, I found him emptying a bag of sugar into the bin and then later he accused her of lying when she said she had only just bought it. It sounds like a little thing, but when there are lots of them, they add up. I was going to tell Mum about the sugar, but Dad said that if I did, he'd tell her that I was doing drugs. At the time I was going through a bad patch but I'm clean now.' He holds his hands over his face. 'I shouldn't have let him get away with it.'

Drugs? Is that what we'd driven him to? I want to hug him. Hold him. My son. The child I don't deserve. Not after what I did.

2.25 p.m., 17 August 1984

As the four of us run back into the garden, Peter is babbling, trying to justify what had happened. 'Just shut up!' I want to scream. The only thing that matters is finding my brother. I don't care how much trouble I get into as long as he is all right.

'Michael was having a great time with us,' Peter blusters. 'We were playing hide-and-seek. He's probably still hiding, waiting for us to find him. It wasn't our fault he went missing.'

But it WAS. We'd deliberately hidden from him in the copse where we'd told him not to go. And then I'd ignored his little voice, calling for me. Telling me he was scared because he couldn't find us. I want to be sick. None of this feels real.

Sheila is running crazily in all directions round the garden, shouting his name. 'Michael! MICHAEL!'

'Show us exactly where you were when you last saw him,' says my father urgently, grabbing me by the elbow.

I shake as I try to get my words out but they are stuck with fear. 'Like I said, we were playing hide-and-seek. We counted to fifty and then —'

My father cuts in. 'I said WHERE?'

My mouth is dry. 'Over there,' I say quietly, pointing.

'In the copse?' shrieks Sheila. 'So that's why you've got

450

green marks on your dress. You two were at it while my son just went off unsupervised.'

'It wasn't like that,' says Peter desperately.

'Yes it was.' I hear my voice crying out. 'I'm sorry. I wasn't thinking . . .'

'Whose idea was it to play hide-and-seek in a big garden like this?' screams my stepmother.

'Mine,' I whimper.

Sheila seizes me by the collar of my dress. My throat hurts. 'You little slut! If anything's happened to my son, I swear to God that I will personally make you pay for it for the rest of your life.'

'Sheila.' My father's voice is sharp. Scared. 'Let's just concentrate on finding Michael, shall we? He has to be here somewhere.'

60

It's the second week of the trial. Or maybe the third. Who knows? A woman is called to the witness box. Her surname is White. Even though my barrister had told me that she had come forward because I had apparently 'helped' her son, I can't remember any of it.

'My son, Alastair, ran away from home when he was eleven,' she tells the court. 'I didn't know then but it turned out that my now ex-partner had been abusing him.' Her voice comes out in choking sobs. 'My boy was missing for three long years. He went by the name of Tim.

'Then the police got an anonymous call from a woman who said he was in this hotel room in Cornwall. They found him and brought him home. We've worked things out. I'll always be grateful to her.'

She wipes her face with a tissue. 'When we read about the trial in the papers, my son saw her picture and recognized her. So I told the police and that's why I'm here.'

Either she's lying or I've lost my mind. I don't recall travelling with a young boy or ringing the police about him.

She looks straight at me. 'I want her to know that Lucky's settled in real well and that my Alastair still writes his poetry.'

Poetry. Why does that ring a bell? I swallow the big lump in my throat.

Then Barbara gets permission to recall Carole to the stand. I feel sick just looking at her.

'Was Roger speaking to you on the phone when his wife, by her own admission, attacked him?'

'Yes.'

'And can you tell us the details of your conversation?'

'A few months earlier, Roger had broken up with me, saying that his wife had cut herself because she couldn't cope with him leaving. So he decided to "put his family first".' She says the last bit in an ironic tone. 'Bit late for that, like I told him.'

I can see some of the jurors frowning at this.

'But that morning, I'd seen his wife in town. She looked happy and I . . . well, I felt jealous. She didn't deserve Roger. It was me he really loved. Not her. He was just staying out of duty.'

'Did you talk to Mrs Halls?'

Carole shrugs. 'I might have.'

'Can you tell the court what you "might have" said?'

She isn't looking at me now. 'I said Roger and I were still seeing each other.'

'Was that true?'

She's staring at the ground. 'No. I was about to move back to London. I should have left earlier but the purchase of my new place was delayed.'

'Did you tell any other lies?'

She looks slightly ashamed now. 'I insinuated I was there when Roger had chosen his grandson's playhouse. Actually, I happened to be at the garden centre on my own when I saw him buy it. He was with the little boy so he pretended not to notice me. But I know he did.'

My mind returns to Roger's words when I'd accused him of buying it with Carole. 'It wasn't like that . . .' he'd said.

'What happened after you told her that?'

'She called me a liar.' Her face is black. 'It was on the high street. Anyone could have heard. I was livid. So when I got home, I rang Roger.'

'What did he say?'

'That he wanted to stay with his wife. But then I heard her voice. It was clear she'd caught him on the phone.'

'What time was that?'

She gives an elegant shrug. 'I don't know precisely. Some time after lunch.'

'Then what happened?'

Her face turned sour. 'Roger rang off and said he didn't want to talk to me any more. He insisted it was over and that I must never contact him again. Then I . . .'

She stops.

'Please continue, Mrs Kent.'

'I threatened to kill myself if he didn't commit to me. I didn't mean it. I just wanted him to leave that stupid woman and be with me . . .'

Her voice breaks. She is in tears. I recall Roger's pleading voice on the phone. He would have been trying to talk her out of it . . .

The rest of the proceedings go back to being a blur in my head, yet I am aware of various witnesses, all testifying to my 'good behaviour', including friends from the homeless committee, the Independent Monitoring Board and the food bank. A rough-looking man who claims he slept in a Plymouth squat alongside me says that another man, Nick, often picked up homeless women to use as mules for carrying drugs. Again, I have no memory of this. It makes me feel strange and uncertain. And guilty. How is it possible that I have lived another life without knowing?

Our neighbour also appears, corroborating what I said. 'The little lad got through a hole in the fence – I hadn't noticed that the contractors had damaged the panel when they were putting in the pond – and went straight into the water. I was gardening at the time and ran over. The weeds had got tangled round the neck of his T-shirt – the poor lad was almost being dragged down – so I had to get it off him before pulling him out. I was wrapping him in a towel up near the house when his grandmother burst through. I tried to call out to her but it was like she was transfixed. She just stood there, staring at the pond.

'I started running towards her but then she disappeared back through the fence. I thought she was going to come round via the front, so I just took Josh inside and waited. Then we went round to the Halls' house but no one answered.'

A vicar from Cornwall with a boyish, gangly frame is called. Barbara had told me about this witness too. Again, I don't recall him, although those orange trainers stir something inside. 'I came forward when I read about the case in the papers,' he says. 'I recognized the picture as being a woman I tried to help when I found her in my church. I think she ran away because she thought I'd blame her for the broken collection box. But I'd already suspected it was a gang from Falmouth who'd given us trouble before.' He looks sad. 'She ran off before I could tell her.'

I did?

'I couldn't help noticing that she'd hung something on the prayer tree,' he adds.

My barrister nods. 'The jury members have been given a photograph of this piece of evidence but would you like to give more details to the court, please?'

'Glad to do so. We have a small model tree at the back of the church with paper on the side for people to write prayer messages to God and then hang them on a branch.' The vicar puts his hand in his pocket. 'In fact, I brought it with me.'

'Would you read it out?'

'Certainly. It's the words to Brahms' Lullaby. "Go to sleep, go to sleep . . ."'

The song I used to sing to Michael when I put him to bed at night! The same one which my mother had sung to me, though I had no idea it had a name. Tears begin to roll down my cheek.

'Call Peter Gordon,' says the clerk.

Peter? I stiffen. Surely it can't be 'my' Peter?

I stare at the rather dull-looking grey-haired man who walks across the court towards the witness stand. How is it possible that this is the boy I once knew who changed my life all those years ago? Who had put me off sex because I'd felt so guilty after our fumblings in the Daniels' garden that had led to Michael's death. I could easily walk past him in the street without recognizing him. He gives me a quick glance and then looks away. 'Is it true that you were with Mrs Halls on the day of the tragic events involving her brother, Michael?'

'Yes.'

He speaks in a quiet voice that is barely audible.

'Louder if you don't mind, Mr Gordon.'

'Yes,' he repeats with an agonized look. Then he turns to the jury as if he himself is on trial. 'I have lived with the guilt for the rest of my life. I blame myself – it wasn't just Ellie. We tried to shake Michael off so we could have some time to ourselves.' Then he covers his face with his hands.

Something makes me glance up at the public gallery. There is a woman looking down at him with pity. Instinctively I know it's his wife.

The jury's faces are a mixture of sympathy and disgust.

'How would you describe Ellie's home life?' asks Barbara quickly.

'Miserable. My mother used to say that her stepmother treated her disgracefully and that her father was too weak to stand up to his new wife. They often cut her out of family holidays and used her as a free babysitter without allowing her a life of her own. My mother also knew Mrs Greenway, Sheila's own mother, who has now passed on.'

I feel a pang in my heart. Although common sense told me that my old ally could surely no longer be alive, the news grieves me. 'After the accident,' continues Peter, 'Mrs Greenway asked my mother to visit her in the home Sheila had put her in. The old lady was extremely upset and very emotional. Apparently she told my mother that neither Ellie nor I should hold ourselves responsible and that Sheila should have taken more care of her child herself. She also said that her daughter had had two sides to her. She could be charming when it suited her and also highly manipulative. The pills for her depression apparently affected her behaviour. Her father left before she was born and she always had mixed feelings towards her children – both Ellie and Michael. She could, according to the old lady, be quite selfish, and at times this led to neglect.'

'Could you tell us any more?'

My palms sweat as I wait to hear what Peter will say next. 'Only that Ellie never stood a chance with a childhood like hers.' He throws a beseeching look at the jury. 'She deserves our pity.'

There are no further questions. He leaves the stand without looking at me. There is no need. We are irrevocably tethered by the binds of the past. 'Thank you,' I mouth to him. But is it enough?

I am being called back to the witness box to clarify 'certain issues which have arisen'. I clench my fists so that the nails dig into my flesh, preparing myself for the inevitable next question.

'Can you tell the court exactly what happened in the garden on that day, Ellie?'

I can't get away from it any more. I have to speak. Barbara has told me this. I owe it, she says, to Michael. When she puts it that way, it's easier.

The judge has allowed my barrister to read the jury a summary of my memories – the ones I told her about during our sessions. But when she finishes, I have to fill in the final moments. I close my eyes. It allows me to pretend I am talking out loud to myself. I am more able to express my true feelings that way. The court is silent.

2.32 p.m., 17 August 1984

My chest feels sick with chilled fear. I can hardly breathe. The garden is empty apart from four people playing croquet. Why aren't they doing something to help?

My father is going into what my mother used to call his 'official' manner. 'You search this part of the garden, both of you, and we'll take the other side. We need to let everyone else know too.'

Then he cups his hands around his mouth and raises his voice. 'My son has gone missing! Can everyone please help us look?'

The croquet couples join us. So too do Christine and her parents. 'Don't worry, dear,' whispers her mother to me. 'I'm sure it will be all right. I remember you and Christine going off together in the park when you were little. Your mother and I were so worried but we found you by the swings, safe and sound.'

Yet they hadn't been neglecting us as I had Michael . . .

I glance at Peter. This can't be happening. It just can't be. I should never have suggested hide-and-seek. I shouldn't have hidden in the copse. I shouldn't have ignored my little brother when he had called out to me in distress . . .

'He's got to be here somewhere,' says Peter boldly as Christine runs along beside him. 'Bet he's in the woodshed.'

460

He isn't.

My stepmother is still crying out his name but in loud sobs now. 'MICHAEL, MICHAEL!'

My father joins in. His tone too is increasingly desperate. 'MICHAEL? WHERE ARE YOU?'

What started as a game has become a nightmare that is too horrifying to contemplate.

We've all reached the bottom of the garden now. He couldn't have gone any further, could he?

Then I see a small iron gate I hadn't noticed before. Where does it lead to?

At that moment, a large bird soars over. It looks down as if it recognizes me. Even though I don't know what has happened, a crazy thought flits through my head that this bird is my brother's spirit.

I race towards the gate. It is open.

And then I hear a terrible sound. It's worse than a scream. It is inhuman. And it's coming from me.

'NO! NOOOO!'

There is a swimming pool. With a small body in a red T-shirt floating on the top. Face down. A tennis ball bobbing on the surface next to it.

61

'Your brother had drowned,' says my barrister quietly when I'd finished. It is a statement rather than a question.

'Yes,' I whisper. Once more, I have a flashback of my stepmother's voice, after they had taken the body away. 'The wrong child died,' she'd wept. 'I wish, to God, it had been your daughter instead.'

'It made the news,' she continues, holding up the *Daily Telegraph*. 'This is dated 18 August 1984. The headline reads CHILD DIES IN "TRAGIC ACCIDENT".'

Even now, it still doesn't seem true. It's too big to take in. The agony on my father's face will haunt me to this day. So too will my stepmother's anguish. 'You as good as drowned him yourself!' she'd screamed, flying at me and scratching me down the sides of my face with her nails. 'You were always jealous of him.'

Yes. I was. He was the favourite. And if Sheila hadn't come along, it would have just been Daddy and me. But I also loved my little brother. I wouldn't have hurt a hair on his head.

But I've learned now that you can sin by *not* doing something as easily as you can by doing something. My mistake had been to take my eyes off my brother. And then I'd made the same mistake with my grandson thirty-five years later.

'After the funeral,' continues Barbara, 'you tried to kill

yourself by slashing your wrists with one of your father's razor blades.'

What else could I have done? I couldn't go on living any more. 'You can't even get *that* right!' my stepmother had screamed at me. I had missed the main artery. 'You don't deserve to be alive.'

I could barely look at my father. His grief – and my role in it – haunted me day and night. It was an impossible situation for us all. I took out my pain and anger by locking myself in my room and hitting my head against the walls. When my father broke down the door to get me, I tried to jump out of the window. When he pulled me back, I pummelled his head with my fists because he'd stopped me from killing myself.

'You had a breakdown and were sectioned at a private institution called Highbridge.'

'Yes.'

I think about Cornelius and my ECT treatments, which numbed some of the pain at the time but failed to quell the anxiety I carried like a sack of coals on my back. My periods stopped; a common side effect of trauma. Horrible news – especially about children being killed – would make me sob uncontrollably.

If I hadn't accepted that sparkly drink from the waitress, my mind might have been sharper and I might have looked after my brother more carefully. So I'd vowed never to drink after Michael's death.

'What was the attitude of your father and stepmother towards you when you were in Highbridge?' asks Barbara, cutting into my thoughts.

'They blamed me for Michael's death.'

'Did they ever visit you there?'

'No,' I say quietly.

'Are you sure?'

I hesitate. 'Apparently my father did try to see me on a few occasions but I refused to let him. I don't remember this – the ECT treatment affected my memory. Cornelius told me later. Yet afterwards, when my children were born, I had a sudden yearning to show him his grandchildren. So I wrote, telling him about their births. I'd hoped this might bring us together again. One day, when I was out, he actually came to our house. He didn't stay to wait for me but he left a note with my neighbour, Jean. It said he was deeply upset by the likeness between Luke and Michael. It was the last contact between us.'

I stop, wincing at the pain these words give me.

'So he didn't forgive you.'

'I like to think he might have done so in his heart,' I say, thinking of my mother's music box he had left with Jean for me. 'When he died, my stepmother came to tell me. My husband was shocked that I'd been in a "loony bin", as he called it. He kept threatening to tell the children. I sensed he enjoyed holding this against me.'

'What effect would you say the tragedy had on you emotionally?'

'I was haunted by the fear that I might hurt my own children by mistake or be negligent, as I had been with Michael,' I continue. 'I was terrified of losing my family, especially when Roger had his affairs.'

I pause for breath. It's all falling out of me now. The truth. The pain inside. 'When I became a grandmother, my determination to keep the family together became even stronger.'

Despite the gravity of the situation, my heart bursts with warmth.

'When I knew my daughter was pregnant, I was initially scared in case something happened to her child too. Bad luck seemed to run in our family. Yet from the minute they put Josh in my arms, I was filled with the most amazing love I had ever known. It was almost as if he was my own. I swore that I'd be strong for him.'

I can see some women in the jury nodding.

'But after my stepmother visited me I became anxious again. I felt terrified the whole time. Supposing I did something wrong? On one occasion, Josh nearly choked when I gave him a small piece of carrot. He coughed it up within seconds but I shook with fear for ages afterwards. I watched him like a hawk when he was with me.' My eyes fill with tears. 'That day . . . with the pond . . . it was the one time when I'd let him out of my sight. It was only a few minutes but . . .' I stop, choking back the sobs. 'I was so angry with Roger. And myself. I didn't mean to . . .' I begin to sob uncontrollably.

The judge calls for a brief recess while I compose myself. There are so many conflicting emotions in my head that I cannot think straight. I lose track at times of who speaks when.

After a break, we continue.

Barbara takes up from where she left off. 'Later that day, you took to the streets?'

'Yes,' I mumble.

I get a sudden flash of something that Carole had said at the tennis-club dinner when she'd first moved down from London. There'd been a collection for our homeless charity, but she'd refused to contribute. 'People on the streets are there because they like it,' Carole had claimed dismissively with a toss of that hair.

'What a ridiculous generalization,' I'd protested.

She'd glared at me and looked away. Was that before or after her affair with Roger had started?

Who knows? At the time I thought she had a heart of stone.

But at least she's not guilty of murder.

After lunch, there are more surprises. The man in the witness box looks familiar, though I can't quite place him.

'Would you tell the court how you know the accused?'

'I was an undercover police officer deployed to keep an eye on the homeless situation in Bristol.'

Again, Barbara has told me about this witness. Once more, I don't remember him. Apparently I lived rough for a few days in Bristol but then took off again. I can't imagine doing such a thing.

'We were investigating a drug ring. I only saw the defendant briefly. She was older than most of the others there. I felt sorry for her. She had bad dreams. At one point I distinctly heard her call out "No", and also screaming the name "Roger".'

I go hot and cold. I still do that, according to my cellmate.

'She also seemed very nervous and was constantly looking over her shoulder as if someone might be following her.'

Jo used to do that. It was habit, she'd told me. Was it possible that subconsciously I'd taken on that mannerism too? Or was there a part of me that knew I was guilty?

I'm still taking this in when Roger's old professor is called to the witness box. 'Is it true that Roger Halls was forced into early retirement because of alleged sexual harassment towards students?'

What? I never knew that.

'It is true.' The professor glances at me apologetically. 'We all felt sorry for his wife, although some thought she chose to turn a blind eye.'

Will this go for me or against with the jury? It's hard to tell.

Then comes someone who I used to know all too well. Cornelius.

'Whilst in your care, did the defendant give any indication of homicidal tendencies?' asks the prosecution's barrister.

Cornelius looks at me. Sadness is written all over his face. 'She expressed extreme emotions when she was under our care. On certain occasions, Ellie said she wished her stepmother was dead.'

Did I? Then again, there are huge chunks of Highbridge that I don't recall, perhaps because of the treatment or because my mind has blocked out the bad bits.

'In your view, was she capable of acting on her emotions and actually killing someone?'

Cornelius glances down as if he wants to avoid my eyes. 'Possibly,' he answers quietly.

'What of her brother's death? In your professional opinion, did she purposely neglect her brother in the hope that harm would come to him?'

He looks up now. His voice is louder. 'No. I think she was simply a young woman who needed affection. She was distracted by her first love.'

'A distraction which cost the life of a child.'

'Yes,' murmured Cornelius.

The barrister interrupts. 'I object, My Lord. This is a comment from counsel – not a question – and is prejudicial.'

The judge agrees, but the point has been made.

'May I add something else?'

What is Cornelius going to say now? Hasn't he ruined my credibility already?

'If it is relevant.'

'I believe it is.' Cornelius is looking straight at me. 'When Ellie went to university, a handful of staff were aware of her background. I was given to understand they were from admin, but apparently I was mistaken. We had a meeting with them beforehand to go over details of her case. Roger appeared particularly interested when it was mentioned that she had family money to pay for her degree. I didn't realize that he was a lecturer and that he would be teaching Ellie.'

I want to be sick. So my husband knew about Michael before we got married – even though he had seemed so shocked by my stepmother's revelation?

'I had reason to believe,' adds Cornelius, 'that Roger Halls sought Ellie out because he knew she was a well-off young woman. One he could manipulate.'

My mind flashes back to the comment my father-in-law had made at the wedding. *A shotgun marriage can work out just fine providing there's enough of the readies.*

'It was obvious to me,' continues Cornelius, 'that it suited Roger Halls to have a wife who would be so grateful to be given a "normal life" that he could treat her however he liked.'

'Did you not warn Ellie of this before the marriage?' The barrister is now asking the questions.

'I didn't know about it until she wrote to me after the event. By then it was too late and I didn't want to interfere. However, I did write back to ask if she'd told her husband about her past. I hoped she'd realize that he already knew, and that either she'd leave him, or they'd be forced to confront things and talk.' Cornelius is still looking at me. 'But as Ellie didn't reply, I suspected that she hadn't.'

He was right. I'd been too scared in case it frightened him away. Marriages should have no secrets. Isn't that what Cornelius's letter had said? But now it looks as though my money had been one of my attractions.

Cornelius is speaking again. 'In my opinion, Roger Halls was a bully. He was waiting to use his "discovery" about Ellie's past to keep her under his thumb.'

I want to deny it but I can recall all too clearly my anguish when my husband 'found out' about Michael from my stepmother.

'Did your husband ever abuse you physically, Mrs Halls?' my barrister asks.

'No. He didn't,' I reply from the dock.

'Emotional abuse?'

'I suppose. But I let him. I didn't feel worthy.'

Then comes Jean, my old neighbour. She sends me a warm, kindly look that makes me want to cry. I am not deserving of it. I close my eyes as parts of her testimony wash over me. 'I sensed Ellie was an anxious mother when she moved in, but as I got to know her better, I could see why. Her husband was a controlling bully.' Her lips tighten. 'He was also unfaithful. I saw him kissing a woman in a car park once and I agonized over whether I should tell Ellie. In the end, I did. Of course, he denied it.' Her tone hardens. 'Men like that are clever.'

A couple of heads in the jury nod.

'Then one day her father turned up out of the blue. There was something about the way he spoke that suggested he had once loved her very much. He couldn't take his eyes off the children. On more than one occasion, he kept calling Luke by the name of Michael.'

I put my hands over my ears. I can't bear to hear any more.

It's time for the speeches. The prosecution has already portrayed me as a needy, neurotic, spoiled woman whose wicked actions destroyed the lives of her little brother and husband. 'This is a woman who will not hesitate to kill if she does not get her own way.'

My barrister, Barbara, is now making her closing address.

'I ask you all, is it any wonder that Ellie Halls lost her mind after seeing what she thought was her drowned grandson? A trauma that was a repeat of her brother's tragic death thirty-five years before. Surely it would be wrong to convict this woman of pure and simple murder. I would also like to point out that, in 2015, coercive control, such as that exercised by Roger Halls, became a criminal offence. Ellie was clearly a victim of this – first at the hands of her stepmother and then her husband. This should be borne in mind when you make your decision.'

The jury looks at me with stony faces. I have no idea what they're thinking.

I am taken down to a court cell while the jury makes its decision. All kinds of thoughts are churning round my head. Barbara has already warned that I might well get life. I deserve it. I should never have killed Roger. But I will pay for it now. By the time I get out, little Josh will be a young man. I will have lost his childhood. And he won't want anything to do with me. I have broken up the family that I fought tooth and nail to preserve.

Then I am brought up to the court again.

'All rise.'

My mouth is dry. I sway on my feet. There's a sudden flash in my head of the little blond boy with the cheeky smile. Michael, my brother, who had looked so much like my own children and my grandson. In a weird way, I feel he is standing right by me now.

The clerk of the court faces me: 'Please stand up.'

She turns to the jury. 'Will the foreman of the jury please also stand. Have you reached a verdict upon which you are all agreed?'

'We have.'

I wait to hear my fate.

62

One year later

'That's right,' I say to Josh as he carefully puts the tin of tomato soup into the cardboard box marked 'Food Bank'. 'Well done. We're nearly finished now.'

His little face frowns. Like his mother, he has Michael's nose. 'Why can't people just buy food from the shops instead?'

'Because some don't have any money.' I kneel down next to him, wrapping my arms around him. Breathing him in. For a while, back in my old life, I thought I'd never have this again.

'But why doesn't everyone have money?'

'For lots of reasons.' How could I ever explain? My life on the road was only for four months, but that was long enough. There are others out there who have been home-less for years and will always be.

Some end up in prison with lengthy sentences. It could so easily have happened to me. Barbara had warned me to expect 'a lengthy stay' inside. So, like many in court, I was amazed when the foreman had given the jury's verdict. My mind briefly goes back to that day.

'On the charge of murder, do you find the defendant guilty or not guilty?'

'Not guilty.'

473

There was a gasp.

'On the alternative charge of manslaughter, and on My Lord's direction, do you find the defendant guilty or not guilty?'

'Guilty.'

Barbara's face was tight. This was what she'd been hoping for. But we still didn't know how long I would get.

'Sentencing will take place in twenty-eight days. Until then the defendant will remain in prison.'

It was a nail-biting wait. But then, in a move that the judge himself acknowledged was 'exceptional, owing to the circumstances', I was given a two-year sentence. He took into account that, by the time of my trial, I had already spent nine months in prison, which was the equivalent of an eighteen-month sentence, as they're frequently halved by parole. I would never have thought this possible. But Barbara explained that the law had changed. 'Emotional abuse is now being taken as seriously as physical abuse. You also clearly made an impact on the judge.'

It helped that the judge was, according to my barrister, a grandparent himself. His sentencing remarks were certainly empathetic. 'You never recovered from a traumatic childhood accident for which you blamed yourself. You then went on to marry a manipulative man who played mind games and was constantly unfaithful. When you realized during an argument that your grandson had gone missing on the anniversary of your brother's death – and then thought he too had died in almost identical circumstances – you snapped. Not only had history appeared to repeat itself but you also thought you had lost your own daughter's child, which prompted a reaction wholly out of character. Although this does not excuse homicide, it is my view that your responsibility for the killing was substantially diminished. Justice requires that you are given a second chance.'

If I break the conditions of my release, I will be sent straight back to prison. But I haven't. I won't. There's no need to.

'Can't we just magic up some money for the poor?'

My heart aches. 'Sometimes, Josh, magic doesn't work.'

His brow crinkles with disappointment. 'But it's got to. The music box is magic, isn't it?'

My grandson may be seven now, but he still believes in such wonders. Long may it last. 'Yes,' I say softly. 'It is.'

One of the first things he and I did together after they'd released me from prison was play with my old music box. I'd been scared my grandson wouldn't remember me – children can forget and I looked different with my hair even though it had started to grow back – but he'd flown straight into my arms. 'Ganny,' he'd called out, burying his face in my waist as I'd leaned down to greet him.

I'd breathed him in, feeling his soft cheek against my rougher one; my chest melting as he put his little arms around my neck.

Part of the conditions laid down by the court was that I had to have permanent approved accommodation and report regularly to my probation officer. I would have liked to live with my daughter and son-in-law. By then they'd moved to a seaside town near Exeter – for a new start – but understandably they were concerned about my mental state. What if I got sick again? Supposing I hurt

Josh? Or them? The very idea cut me to the quick, but I had to see their point of view. I had acted entirely out of character. I needed extensive therapy. I was also terrified in case I flipped back to my 'other self'.

But Luke – bless him – declared he was coming back from Australia for 'however long it needed' to look after me. He rented a bungalow for the two of us near his sister so I could see my precious grandson under supervision.

At first, I wasn't sure about living so close to water. Try as I might, I cannot banish the memory of the swimming pool in which Michael drowned and the pond that I thought had claimed my precious Josh's life.

But my psychologist told me this could be a perfect opportunity to face my fears and get to know my family again. I won't pretend it's been easy. When I went over on my first visit, I was stunned by the sight of my old music box in Josh's bedroom.

'We played it together when you were gone,' said my daughter. 'I thought it would be comforting for him when Josh kept asking for you.'

'I knew you'd come back, Ganny,' he piped up. 'I kept playing the music box so the magic would bring you.'

We all cried then.

'We'll have to take you shopping,' added Amy, in a voice that suggested she was trying to change the subject. 'Your clothes are hanging off you, Mum.'

It was true that I'd lost even more weight in prison. But the important thing was that I was reunited with my family and that I was free.

As for Roger, the only way I can cope is to block him out of my head. Even my daughter rarely mentions him. I sense it's a step too far for her to forgive me completely. Meanwhile, my beloved grandson is at the local school. His class has nature walks on the beach. At first the sea scared me witless with its uncertainty. Calm one minute, raging the next. Rather like life.

But the best bit is that I see Josh every day. I am now allowed to take him to school so my daughter can go to work (although that will change soon when she goes on maternity leave again). We read together. We play games. We hunt for shells. We take our fishing nets down to the rock pools. And we've even hired a beach hut for the summer. We gather wildflowers and press them between the pages of a book, just as I did as a child. And we make blackberry jelly together, using an upturned stool with muslin tied across the top as a sieve for the berry juice. 'This was your great-grandmother's recipe,' I say to him. His little face lights up with wonder at the sight of her loopy writing (just like mine) in faded ink.

'Where is she now?' he asks.

I want to tell him that she's looking down on us but I don't want to scare him. 'She's not here any more,' I say. 'She'd have been very old now.'

Josh gazes up at me worriedly. 'But Mummy says you're getting older. You won't die, will you?'

'Not for a long time,' I say quickly, giving him a warm hug. 'Now let's see how that jelly is doing.'

Death is a subject that frequently comes up during my sessions with the psychologist. She's about my age and a grandmother too.

'Grandchildren feel like your own children, yet they

have an extra hold on your heart,' she tells me. 'There's a bond that you can't really describe until you are one yourself.'

How very true.

'Grandparents often say that the wonderful thing about grandchildren is that you can enjoy them and give them back at the end of the day.'

I used to tell myself the same thing.

'But I didn't give him back,' I burst out, thinking about Josh by the side of the pond. He could have drowned just as my little brother had.

'You've paid your dues,' she says gently. 'That's the other thing about grandchildren. They accept us for what we are.'

I hope she's right. I'm not certain that my daughter will ever really forgive me for taking away her father. And why should she? It was a heinous crime.

So far, Josh, with his smooth skin and constant air of excitement ('Wow, Ganny. Look at that squirrel!') doesn't know what I did. Yet.

I've already agreed with my children that we will tell him when he is a little older. I don't want Josh finding out about his grandfather without being prepared. Discovered secrets can be the most harmful of all. I'm dreading his reaction, to be honest. What if he can't forgive me? I'm also still terrified in case my mind turns against itself again. Supposing I find myself in someone else's skin without knowing? But I'm trying to live one day at a time. The psychologist says it's the best way. 'Nothing in life is certain,' she says to me. 'But that's all right.' She says this with an extra emphasis on the last two words so it sounds like a rhythm. I repeat this over and over in my head as a reassuring mantra. It helps me believe that there was nothing wrong with me as a child after all. What *was* wrong was Sheila's treatment of me, and then being blamed for Michael's death, which led to everything else that happened to me. At least, this is the only way I can deal with it.

'Are we going?' Josh asks now, bringing me back to our mission.

'We sure are.' I've found myself lapsing into the odd American phrase thanks to watching cartoons on television with him. I carry the food box under one arm and hold Josh with my right hand. He tries to pull away.

'I'm old enough to walk on my own, Ganny.'

'I know you are,' I lie, 'but it would be nice if you held my hand to look after me.'

I'm only saying this to persuade him to stay put. Josh is going through an independent stage when he wants to do everything on his own. Readily now, he agrees, and we walk towards the church hall to deliver our contribution to the weekly food bank.

I'm constantly amazed by the different kinds of people who turn up. Some, you can tell from their clothes, are on the road. We try to find them accommodation but many say they're 'not bothered'. Often, as I know all too well, this means they're scared of filling in official forms that might reveal their past.

Then there are the embarrassed-looking parents with children in pushchairs or babes in arms who seem for all the world as though they could belong in a supermarket queue, able to buy their own stuff. But as our coordinator says, poverty comes in all shapes and sizes nowadays.

When I first offered to help out, I was quite open about my own background. I didn't want any whispers. My voluntary job is a reminder of that other side of life that I glimpsed so briefly on the road. Every now and then I will see something, like a woman foraging desperately through bins for discarded sandwiches or pizza crusts, that stirs a faint recollection. But it's still all so unclear. Maybe I'll never know how much of it is real and how much I've created, having heard all the people who testified at my trial. At times, when I try to settle down into my warm bed at night, I feel the walls and roof closing in on me and a strange desire to take to the road again.

'I've been through what you have,' I tell them. They don't believe me until I go into detail. Then something flickers in their eyes. They see that I was one of them once and they allow us to give them the help they need. It might be emergency accommodation or it could be a hot drink and a meal before they go on their way, armed with supplies like a thermal sleeping sheet.

I always keep my eyes peeled for Jo, my alter ego. Sometimes I fancy I see her in the food-bank queue but that would be too much of a coincidence. I hope she is all right. I have nightmares about someone hurting her. I like to think she's been rehoused and is warm and dry. But maybe she doesn't want that. There's a danger in putting your own hopes and expectations on other people. I know all about that.

'When we've been to the food bank, can we go swimming?' asks Josh, running along by my side.

This is something else I've had to steel myself for.

When you live by the sea, it's even more important to learn to swim.

'OK,' I say. 'But you might want to stay in the hall for a bit. There's a bring-and-buy fair and there could be some trains.'

Josh is mad on steam engines. My little bungalow is stuffed with toys for him, including a train set.

'Have you got any of your tables there?' asked Josh.

'Sure have!'

I'd kept up with my mosaics except that, instead of using broken glass and ceramics for the table tops, I now use shells. Josh loves helping me. The proceeds go to the food bank. I find it therapeutic. Meanwhile, Alastair's mother, with whom I keep in touch, tells me that he's going to be self-publishing his poetry on the internet, under his street name of Tim White. I've promised to order a copy when it's out.

The church hall is packed. Josh and I deliver our box to the food-bank corner and then browse the stalls. 'Hold my hand,' I remind him, but he is tugging me towards a stand. 'Look, Ganny!'

In fact it's not so much a stand as a large blackboard lying on the ground. Before us lies an intricate map of Exeter, complete with a picture of the rather beautiful railway station and a train track winding its way through the countryside to the sea.

'Don't touch,' I warn my grandson. 'It's made of chalk. You might rub it off.'

'It's all right,' says a voice. 'I can draw it on again. Besides, I like it when kids join in. Want a go yourself, sonny?'

I know that deep tone. Startled, I look up. I find myself staring at a pair of bright-blue eyes and a tanned, weathered face.

Something moves inside me.

'Jo?' He looks shocked.

'I'm sorry,' I say. 'Do we know each other?'

'Of course,' he murmurs. 'They said in the papers that you'd forgotten who you were.'

A prickle of unease runs through me. 'I don't understand.'

'It's Steve. We were . . . friends, once,' he says. 'I knew you as Jo then,' he adds.

Luckily Josh is picking up a yellow chalk to make a second sun. 'I don't remember that time,' I whisper, drawing him away so we can speak more openly. One of my friends from the homeless committee sees us talking and takes the hint, leaning down to offer some more chalks to Josh.

The stranger is looking at me as if trying to make sure I am speaking the truth. 'You don't recall how we parted, then?'

I'm beginning to feel deeply embarrassed now. 'No.'

'It doesn't matter,' he says turning away.

'But it does,' I burst out. I don't know why I am saying this. As far as I'm concerned, I've never seen this man before in my life. But there's something about him which pulls me to him. And I can't help sensing he feels the same way.

'I need you to tell me . . .' I say. 'How we met, about you, and what . . . what we did.'

'You're sure?' he says.

No. Yes.

'Wait a minute, please,' I say.

I ask the same friend to watch Josh carefully for a short time. Then I go into a corner of the room with Steve, still keeping an eye on my grandson. 'Tell me everything,' I say quietly.

I listen, at times not knowing where to look, especially when he gets to the point where we were, as he puts it, 'intimate'. He is flushing too. 'I want you to know,' he says, 'that I don't do one-night stands. I really loved you, Jo.'

'Ellie,' I correct him gently. 'And I feel something for you here.' I touch my chest. 'I just can't remember you here.' I touch my head.

He nods. 'Who knows what any of us are like, deep down? When I read that stuff in the paper about you killing your husband, I felt that something had to have gone badly wrong. You just didn't seem the type.'

'I didn't think I was either,' I reply slowly.

'There's something else,' he adds.

My heart quickens. It doesn't sound good.

'You broke off with me because you said I was boring.'

'I did?'

I don't know much about Steve but I sense from what he's just told me about having thrown up accountancy for street art that he's anything but boring.

'I think,' he says slowly, 'that you just said that to get rid of me.'

'Why would I do that?'

'Shortly after you left, I saw a big piece about you in the paper. There was a picture of you with your husband,

483

Roger. They were looking for you. I guessed you were worried I might hand you in.'

'Would you have?'

'Yes, I think I would have had to.'

'Good.' I nod. 'That's the right answer.'

He looks relieved. 'You've really been through the mill, haven't you? But I'm so proud of you for coming out the other side.' He glances shyly at me. 'And you look great, if I may say so. When I last saw you, you were bald. You have fabulous cheekbones, mind, so you could get away with it.'

I'm not used to such compliments. I don't know what to do with them. My old mousy straight hair is now a chic elfin style. Amy says it suits me. The hairdresser suggested I dye it a deep chestnut. I'm thinking about it.

'By the way,' he adds. 'I'm no longer on the streets. I've found a job with a charity that promotes art in prison.'

Sounds interesting. I'd like to know more but my friend is coming back to me now with my grandson.

'Ganny, I'm hungry,' says Josh, tugging at my hand.

'Sorry,' I say to Steve, 'we've got to go now.'

'Wait.' He places a hand on my sleeve. I think of Peter and panic. I'm not making that mistake twice. Josh has to come first. I can never neglect him as I did Michael.

'I just wondered if you and your grandson would like to take part in something I'm helping to organize. It's called The Big Draw and it's to encourage people of all ages to explore their artistic side.'

I hesitate. Josh is jumping up and down. 'I love drawing. And Ganny's quite good at it too.'

Steve smiles. 'I know she is.' Then he glances at me.

'It's next Tuesday. We're holding it here in the hall. Hope to see you.'

'Goody,' says Josh jumping up and down. 'Can we go to the beach on the way home, Ganny?'

I can't help glancing back as we leave. Steve is smiling. A warm feeling glows inside me. I give him a brief smile and then turn round, concentrating on Josh, his warm small trusting hand knotted into my fingers.

We have a great time, running up and down the sand, building castles and jumping in and out – barefoot – of the shallow waves lapping on the shore. But on the way home through our seaside town, those pavement cracks seem to loom up at me even more than they used to before.

'Why are you walking funny?' asks Josh.

I stop, recalling that young girl with the sick mother who had clung on to Sheila Greenway's hand on the way home from school. That's when it had started to get out of control.

'Certain people,' I say slowly, 'think that something bad will happen if they tread on a pavement crack.'

My grandson looks scared. 'It won't mean you have to go away again, will it?' His eyes begin to fill with tears. 'I missed you so much. And Mummy cried a lot.'

'Of course not,' I say with a lump in my throat.

'Must I walk funny too because of the cracks?'

I let him catch my fears.

'No,' I say firmly. 'That's just a silly story. It's perfectly safe to walk on them.'

He jumps right on one as I speak.

'Your turn, Ganny!'

Am I ready for this?

'Go on,' he urges, his little face bright and shining.

How can I refuse him? I land on the crack fair and square.

I'd like to say that I feel fine. But these things don't change overnight. They take time. Part of the old me is shaking with fear that something will go wrong now. Yet I also sense Jo at my shoulder, telling me not to be 'so bleeding daft'.

Between the two of us, I tell myself, I have to emerge into someone else. A new me. An Ellie who is stronger, like my *Big Issue* friend. Wiser. More forgiving – not just of other people but also of herself. It's the only way to end the old pattern of guilt and recrimination and unhappiness being repeated down the bloodline, generation after generation. This has to stop at me. Right now. My grandson and his children's children deserve a new start.

'I'm tired, Ganny,' says Josh. So I gather him up into my arms, even though he is getting heavy now. His head rests trustingly on my shoulder.

Together, we make our way home. Our best foot forward.

63

Jo

I bet you don't want to know any more of my sob story. As you've already heard, its the same as all the rest, anyway – dad who hit me; care home to care home; only to find a husband who hit me. Prison. Even though the bastard deserved to die. Lost my kids. Lost my house. Lost everything. Finally freed. More shitty men. More trouble with the police. You know the score.

But there's one good deed I've done. One thing I'm proud of.

One August morning back in 2019 – a real scorcher it was – I came across this lady who'd been helping me out. Ellie, her name was. She gave me some money like she always did but then this other woman turned up. Right tart, she looked. She started bitching about how she and Ellie's husband were having a thing together. I felt really sorry for Ellie. I've been messed around by blokes myself . . .

Then, a few hours later, I saw her again. I nearly didn't recognize her. Ellie's hair was a mess and her eyes were wild. She kept gabbling the same thing over and over again. 'I've killed him.'

'Who?' I asked. 'Who did you kill?'

Then she looked at me with an expression on her face that I'll never forget. 'My husband.'

At first I thought she was having me on. Then I recognized the same fear that I'd felt with Barry, my old man. I didn't need to think twice about it. But we had to be quick or the police could be here. Someone might have spotted her already. So I grabbed her by the arm and dragged her down a side street. I gave her some of my clothes to put over her smart ones and a load of magazines. That way, someone might think she was a *Big Issue* seller. Some money too for a ticket. 'Run to the bus station,' I told her. 'Then get away as fast as you can. You can catch a connection to Oxford and then somewhere else.'

I could ill afford that cash and those mags. But I reckoned she deserved it after everything she'd done for me in the past. Gave me a nice warm feeling in my heart, it did.

The next day, there were journalists all over the place. A bloke had been murdered in cold blood by his wife. I knew in my gut it was Ellie. She'd always seemed such a nice, gentle person so I reckoned he must have deserved it. I decided it would be best to make myself scarce for a bit. I went to London, but it was too big, so I drifted my way down to Bristol where I still am. I like it here. There are a lot of others like me who've found themselves down on their luck. We all help each other.

I kept seeing her picture in the newspaper headlines on and off for a few months. No one knew where she was. I got really worried. Nice women like her aren't safe on the streets. I know that all too well. I had to learn the hard way how to look after myself. On my first week out of prison for Barry's murder, someone tried to rape me. I bashed his head against a wall.

Anyway, back to Ellie. Later that year – around Christmas

it was – I heard they'd got her. Been calling herself Jo, she had. I was quite chuffed by that. Then I read all this stuff that said she really did think she was me. Maybe she'd gone a bit mental. The streets can do that to you. So can men. I thought about going to her trial to say she was a decent woman. But if I did that, they might do me for being an accessory 'cos I'd given her clothes and magazines and money.

Her case was all over the papers. When they let her go free, I did a little dance right there in the street! But when I went back to my hostel that night – the council had got me a place at last – I started thinking about my life. Ellie was going to have to start again now. She had to prove she had changed. Maybe it was time for me to start again too. So I got some help to give up drugs and drink, like Ellie had kept telling me to do before she went on the run herself. Then my social worker helped me track down my kids. They were grown up by now, of course. Liam wanted to meet me but not Kieran. He can't forgive me for what I did to his dad even though I tried to explain. Kieran's got kids of his own now. It's a crying shame that I can't see my own grandkids. Maybe when they're older, they'll get that I'm not so bad after all.

I often think about Ellie Halls. I can't help remembering that expression on her face when she told me she'd killed her old man. She was scared. I knew that all right. And panicky. Yet there was something else in her eyes. If I'm not mistaken, it was relief. Whatever that bloke had done to her, he was no longer around to do it and she was glad of it.

I'd never have put Ellie down as a murderer.

But then, who knows what goes on in other people's minds?

So it's nice to look back at that moment in time, and
Wonder if I've been inspired.
Because it's me that now chants, and sings songs of
Peace – and thanks for that soup when I was tired.

Excerpt from *Poems from a Runaway*,
by Ben Westwood

A Note from Jane

Dear Reader,

I grew up near London and have always been troubled by the issue of homelessness in our cities. When I moved down to Devon nearly ten years ago, there initially seemed very little evidence of it in our seaside town. But a few months later I became aware of a middle-aged man sleeping in the doorway of a church. Like many others, I sometimes put a pasty and a coffee by his side although, to my shame, I didn't stay to talk or ask if he needed help. Then, one cold January morning, when I was walking my dog along the seafront at about 7 a.m., I noticed a pair of legs sticking out from a shelter on the promenade. At the same time, an ambulance silently rolled up. It was the man who'd been sleeping outside the church.

Our town was shocked. This wasn't London, we thought. That sort of thing didn't happen here. Yet clearly it did. Determined to do something, we formed a local committee to help those on the streets, offering food, drink and housing advice among other services. The scheme has been running for nearly four years. The volunteers – whose professional experience ranges from council rehousing to fundraising – have not only helped people find permanent accommodation but have also given crucial support to people on the verge of homelessness.

It's been frightening to see how easily people can become homeless, and many end up on the streets because of mental health issues. When I was researching the problem, I found a study by the Mental Health Foundation (www.mentalhealth.org.uk) showing that a huge 80 per cent of homeless people in England reported that they were sufferers – much more than the 25 per cent of the general population who will have a mental health problem in their lifetime. Many of them suffer from varying forms of post-traumatic stress disorder.

All of this left me with the burning urge to write about someone who, because of past trauma, had fallen through the net.

I've also been interested in post-traumatic stress for personal reasons. When I was five my mother had a terrible accident whilst we were on holiday. I can remember it as clearly as if it had happened yesterday: my father's desperate car race through a remote, unfamiliar part of Cornwall to get her to hospital and then her plea for me to kiss her goodbye on the hospital trolley. I refused because her charred skin made her 'smell funny'. My mother was in hospital for several months and I will never forget the pain of her absence or my continuing shame for not embracing her.

As I got older, and became a mother myself, I became increasingly consumed by guilt about that incident. I didn't want to talk to my mother about it for fear of causing distress, and then, before I could summon up the courage, she died at the age of fifty-six from cancer. Similarly, I didn't want to upset my father, so I tried to push it to the back of my mind. But about ten years ago, I bit the bullet and talked to a professional. I felt rather silly because it had happened so long ago. Now I feel as if a load has been lifted from my shoulders. Ellie's experiences in the book are very different, but I couldn't have written about PTSD without having been forced to confront my own trauma.

During my research for this novel, I met a young man called Ben Westwood. He had left home at the age of eleven in the nineties and been homeless through his teens. However, he managed to turn his life around and has since written a collection of poetry called *Poems from a Runaway* about his time on the streets. I would like to make it clear that Tim, the runaway in my novel, is not based on Ben. Ben was good enough to write me a poem specifically for *I Looked Away*. If you'd like to buy his book, he would be delighted. You can find it on Amazon and on www.benwestwooduk.blogspot.co.uk.

Finally, I'd love to hear your personal experiences of homelessness or post-traumatic stress or both. Even though you may not have gone through either, I hope you will still enjoy *I Looked Away*. As well as tackling contemporary issues, it also shows the joy of family life – something I've discovered in particular since becoming a (youngish) granny. Happy reading!

Love, Jane x

Acknowledgements

A great deal of research went into *I Looked Away*. I would like to thank the following people in particular:

Claire Pooley, traumatologist, EMDR psychotherapist and mental health nurse.

Anne Waddington, barrister-at-law and psychotherapist.

Dr Nuria Gene-Cos, consultant psychiatrist for the Traumatic Stress Service.

The Maudsley Hospital, London.

UKCP: the UK Council for Psychotherapy.

MIND, the mental health charity (www.mind.org.uk). 'We're here to make sure no one has to face a mental health problem alone.' Great support for families of sufferers too.

Open Door in Exmouth (www.opendoorexmouth.org. uk), a wonderful warm charity that provides food and activities for the community, including a café, skill-learning opportunities, child contact space for parents to spend time with children they no longer live with, and a night-shift of volunteers who walk the streets to provide help and a listening ear. The Open Door relies on donations. If you feel you can help, please get in touch with Open Door through its website.

Ben Westwood. Ben used to live on the streets and was kind enough to help me with my research. He has now turned his life around and is a published poet. He would be thrilled if you bought his book *Poems from a Runaway*:

A True Story, which tells the story of his life in verse form. Available from Amazon.

Richard Gibbs, a former judge, who advised me on legal issues. Any mistakes are my own.

Katy Loftus, my super-talented editor with a unique eye.

Rosanna Forte, her rising-star assistant.

Jane Gentle, my super-efficient and resourceful publicist.

Georgia Taylor, whose social media skills are awesome.

The brilliant Rights team at Penguin.

Kate Hordern, my amazing agent who took me on a tour of Bristol.

Trevor Horwood, my copyeditor with an eagle eye (and sense of humour).

Natalie Wall, editorial manager, for her organizational skills.

The Prime Writers; a unique network of supportive authors.

My family and friends for their understanding when I go up to my study for 'half an hour' and come down five hours later.

Many thanks to the fantastic charity CLIC Sargent, who asked if they could auction off a name in my new book. Barbara Enticknap was the winner. I used her first name for one of the barristers (although, as far as I know, this is the only resemblance between the two!). You can find out more about the charity at www.clicsargent.org.uk.

And finally – though absolutely not least – huge thanks to my loyal readers. Your support means so much to me. Do follow me on Twitter @janecorryauthor.

I Looked Away: The Science Behind the Story

As an author who often writes about mental health, and about characters whose experiences may be different from my own, I always speak to several experts in order to make sure my books are factually accurate. As part of my research for *I Looked Away* I interviewed several specialists on complex post-traumatic stress disorder, the condition from which Ellie suffers after the death of Michael and then after Roger's murder. I contacted the British Association of Counselling and Psychotherapy (BACP), who put me in touch with Claire Pooley, a traumatologist, EMDR psychotherapist and mental health nurse.

JC: Claire – can you tell us a bit about complex post-traumatic stress disorder, and what causes it?
CP: Complex PTSD (which is different from PTSD) arises from severe, prolonged, repeated, inescapable trauma that is usually interpersonal in nature and often occurs in early life. Child abuse and domestic violence are common causes, and multiple military deployments often result in the onset of the condition later in life. The consequences of traumas like these are severe. If the abuser was a close and trusted adult, such as a family member, close friend, religious and/or spiritual leader or teacher, it may disrupt healthy attachment styles and bonding.

Complex PTSD can cause difficulties in identity and boundary awareness leading to potentially difficult and abusive relationships, lack of self-protection and an inability to control one's emotions. In turn, this can lead to other difficulties such as indiscriminate sexual behaviour, bingeing and purging, self-harm, aggression, suicidal thoughts, gambling and drug or alcohol abuse – all of which increase the risk of other adverse events.

JC: And could you explain the link between dissociation and complex PTSD – the diagnosis my character Ellie has?
CP: There are two useful ways of describing it. Briere and Scott (2006) describe dissociation as 'A disruption in the normally occurring linkages between subjective awareness, feelings, thoughts, behaviour and memories, consciously or unconsciously invoked to reduce psychological distress.' Kluft (1992) describes it as 'mental flight when physical flight is not possible'. Dissociation, one might say, anaesthetizes physical and psychological pain by taking the mind elsewhere.

However, not all dissociation is like Ellie's – it's often described as being on a continuum. We all dissociate sometimes. Most people can describe a time when they have been travelling and have arrived at their destination without remembering the whole journey, or when they have been watching a TV programme and realize they can't recall what was said. This type of dissociation happens very often and is completely normal.

Further along the continuum people might suffer from memory loss, sometimes finding that they are unable to recall important personal information about themselves, discovering later that they have taken part in events of which they have no recollection, or having large chunks of time for which they are unable to account. People or places familiar to them might seem unreal and they might feel detached from their own body. In extreme dissociation, people may split off aspects of their selves and experiences, developing two or more distinct and separate personality states. The other personality state might be a fictional person or someone they know. It might even be possible for a character with complex PTSD and dissociation to recall past experiences recounted to them by another person and interpret them as their own memories.

JC: Ellie displays a particular symptom of dissociation – a dissociative fugue. Could you tell us a bit more about that?
CP: Dissociative fugue is when a person becomes completely detached from their real identity and assumes a new one entirely. The charity MIND describes it as 'travelling to a different location and taking on a new identity for a short time (without remembering your real identity)'.

JC: Please describe 'triggers' and how they play their part.
CP: We know that the experience of trauma is held in the body and is generally re-triggered through a reminder of the five senses. For example, if it were a trauma with fire, it may be the smell of something burning or the sensation of heat on the skin, a sound of crackling or sizzling, something they saw, perhaps a colour or an expression on a face or perhaps a lingering taste in the mouth. This then

might reignite the feelings experienced during the time of trauma.

JC: What kind of treatment is given to help someone return to his or her original state of mind?
CP: We may use breathing exercises and ways of recognizing those body sensations and exploring differing ways to change the senses, such as holding something textured or smelling citrus essence etc. The World Health Organization (WHO), National Institute for Health and Care Excellence (NICE) and the American Psychological Association (APA) all recommend eye movement desensitization and reprocessing (EMDR) and trauma-focussed cognitive behavioural therapy (TF-CBT) as the recognized effective treatments for PTSD.

For more information, visit www.emdrassociation.org.uk and www.tfcbt.org

References

American Psychiatric Association, *Diagnostic and Statistical Manual of Mental Disorders, Fifth Edition (DSM-5)*, American Psychiatric Publishing, 2013

John N. Briere and Catherine Scott, *Principles of Trauma Therapy: A Guide to Symptoms, Evaluation, and Treatment*, Sage Publications, 2006

R. P. Kluft, 'Discussion: A Specialist's Perspective on Multiple Personality Disorder', *Psychoanalytic Inquiry*, 12 (1992), pp. 139–71

mind.org.uk

Christiane Sanderson, *Counselling Skills for Working with Trauma*, Jessica Kingsley Publishers, 2013